"You prom

him.

"I did, but nov... ...maybe that's not such a good idea."

She frowned. "Why not? Are you a klutz? Two left feet?"

He smirked. "No, I'm a great dancer."

"Sprained your ankle? Pulled a muscle?"

"No."

"Is it me?" She pulled a face. "You don't want to be seen dancing with me in front of your friends? I promise I'll behave from now on with the hors d'oeuvres."

"Stop. None of that. It's just that I'm...your teacher."

"Oh, for God's sake, we're an hour from Angel Falls. No one cares about that."

He shrugged. "I care."

She scanned his face. "Okay, I get it. I respect that." Her hand dropped from his arm.

He was suddenly free to bolt, the safe thing to do. Yet his body refused to comply. In the background, the clinking of silverware against glasses grew louder throughout the room as people called for the groom to kiss the bride.

"I-I'd better go," she said with a small smile.

She started to walk away. He noticed the fire department guys watching her, one in particular. And there was his friend Jack, holding a drink, ready to pounce.

"Gabby," he called after her. Applause and cheers

sounded through the room as the bride and groom acquiesced to the crowd's demand.

She turned and lifted her brows. "Yes?"

"You're right. I'm taking things too seriously. Will you save me a dance?"

She tapped her index finger on her cheek. "Okay, fine, but you seem a little fickle. And my dance card *is* almost full."

He laughed out loud. She was gorgeous, spirited, irresistible. Who could blame him for wanting to spend more time with her?

And it was only a dance, right?

Praise for *Then There Was You*

"Emotional, heartwarming romance you can't put down."

—Lori Wilde, *New York Times* bestselling author

"Liasson will make you laugh and melt your heart in this can't miss read."

—Marina Adair, #1 bestselling author of *Summer in Napa*

"Ably tugs at the heartstrings with this poignant contemporary."

—*Publisher's Weekly*

"A delightful and sexy small-town tale of love lost and found!"

—*Fresh Fiction*

"*Then There Was You* was captivating and unputdownable."

—Underthecoversbookblog.com

"Ms. Liasson has delivered one of the best books!"

—HarlequinJunkie.com

Also by Miranda Liasson

Then There Was You

the way you love me

MIRANDA LIASSON

FOREVER
New York Boston

Cover design by Elizabeth Turner Stokes
Cover illustration by Tom Hallman and Elizabeth Turner Stokes

Forever
Hachette Book Group
1290 Avenue of the Americas, New York, NY 10104
forever-romance.com
twitter.com/foreverromance

First Edition: January 2019

Forever is an imprint of Grand Central Publishing. The Forever name and logo are trademarks of Hachette Book Group, Inc.

ISBN: 978-1-4555-4182-9 (mass market), 978-1-4555-4183-6 (ebook)

Printed in the United States of America

OPM

10 9 8 7 6 5 4 3 2 1

For Ed, always.
And for anyone who's ever wanted
to change careers.

Acknowledgments

Many thanks as always to my agent, Jill Marsal, who is amazing.

Thanks to my editors at Forever, Amy Pierpont and Alex Logan, who helped sort out a story where literally everyone seems to be writing a book. (Well, almost everyone, except for Cade's three-year-old daughter.)

Thanks to the team at Forever Romance, Gabi, Estelle, and Jodi, who work so tirelessly to get the books out there.

To my partners in crime, Sandra Owens and AE Jones, thank you for being there for me and for being my friends.

For my readers—thank you for reading my books, sharing them, and letting me know you enjoyed them. For my friends who come and chat with me often on my Facebook page—thank you for your time, your humor, for cheering me on, and for being a part of my life, which is so much richer with you in it. For the old Irish saying "What's for you will find you," I must thank

Violet C. Thanks, Violet, for your wisdom and sense of humor, and of course for your friendship.

Last but not least, I have to give a thousand hugs and kisses to my husband, Ed. We never knew where life would lead us, and surely the world of romance fiction wouldn't have been among our wildest guesses, but I'm so grateful that I get to make this journey with you.

The quote "There is nothing to writing. All you do is sit down at a typewriter and bleed" looms large in this story. As my copy editor pointed out, it was probably *not* said originally or perhaps at all by Ernest Hemingway, however, I chose to keep the Hemingway attribution for this story. So now I must acknowledge that it was probably said first by either the popular sportswriter Walter Wellesley "Red" Smith or by the novelist and sportswriter Paul Gallico. You can read all about the controversy here: https://www.hemingwaysociety.org/quotation-controversy-writing-and-bleeding. Whoever said it, I can attest to the fact that in my experience it is most certainly true…but perhaps in the best way, if bleeding means putting your heart and soul into something that you love.

the way you love me

Writing is easy. Love is hard.

—Nonna

Chapter 1

♥

At 4:45 on a Monday afternoon, Gabriella Langdon fiddled with the tiny card on her solid mahogany desk, proof that she'd finally achieved the perfect life. The card was rectangular, the shape of a ticket, and made of costly paper stock. It was lined in a gold scroll and embossed with script lettering you could feel with your fingers, like Braille. *Congratulations for making partner!* it said. In the break room sat a tiny, perfect, half-eaten cake, chocolate ganache with beautiful icing flowers, decadent and rich, just like Lockham, Stockholm, and Gleason, the senior partners in her law practice (or, as her brother, Rafe, referred to them, *Lock 'em, Stock 'em, and Fleece 'em*).

"We're so proud of you," Rachel, her stepmom, said from her spot on the forest-green velvet chair in front of her desk. "What an accomplishment."

Funny, but Gabby didn't quite feel it was *her* accomplishment, despite all the hard work she'd put into law school and the ensuing years. Her father had helped her to land this job. In fact, her dad had helped her to get into law school, desperate as he was to give her some direction. So she'd finally made it, finally proved she had direction and a responsible job, but the victory felt... hollow.

Her nonna, who sat next to Rachel, said, "We're always proud, except she looks worn out, doesn't she, Rachel? Look how pale she is. And thin."

Nonna's comment was accompanied by hand gestures and a big sigh, part of her Italian genetic makeup. Gabby reached up to pinch her cheeks. Pale? How could she be pale? She had her grandmother's nice olive coloring. She was *never* pale. "I haven't been out in the sun much this summer, Nonna. But now that I'm partner, I'll get some color." She was lying through her teeth. She might never see the light of day again.

"It's already the end of August," Nonna said. "Summer's almost over."

"I think she looks fine," Rachel said. "Maybe she's tired from packing." She turned to Gabby. "I am a little worried about your hours."

She *was* tired from packing. The downtown Cleveland condo she'd owned with her ex-fiancé had sold, and she'd had to move out ASAP. "I'm just getting established," Gabby said. "I'm sure things will settle down." *Another fib.* The partners worked just as hard as the associates. Maybe harder. That was just the way it was.

"You've lost your sparkle," Nonna said. Nonna might have early dementia, but she always called 'em like she saw 'em. "You know what your grandfather would say."

"What was that, Nonna?" Her grandfather had died long ago, but Nonna still spoke frequently and affectionately about him.

"He'd say, 'You only have to polish the shoe once to get it to shine.'" Nonna demonstrated the quote with emphatic hand motions. "'After that, you start rubbing off the leather.' Too much work is no good."

Her grandfather had been a kind, practical man with no shortage of sayings. Though Gabby and her siblings tended to suspect he may have made most of them up himself.

Gabby's lackluster state could be attributed to the fact that things in her personal life weren't exactly going great. She'd broken up with her fiancé, Malcolm, a year ago. Her only current prospect was Milo Blumenthal, the managing partner in her practice with the soft middle and the pale, pale skin who brought stinky sandwiches to work and had asked her out *twice* the previous week.

Plus she was a few months shy of thirty-one, which wasn't old by any means but made her wonder if everything she wanted in life was going to pass her by—love, children, and something she wanted desperately but couldn't even describe: a sense that she was in the right place, doing the right thing with her life. She felt as if she was performing in the expected fashion, and to everyone looking in, she was doing great! Fantastic! So why didn't she feel that way?

"We'll talk more about what's wrong with you at Sunday dinner," Nonna said.

"Can't wait," Gabby said with a forced smile. Sunday

dinner was Nonna's solution to everything—it had been a tradition in Gabby's family for generations, and everyone knew attendance wasn't optional. Even when her brother, Rafe, had broken his leg a few years ago, they'd relocated it to his hospital room. No kidding.

Through the glass panel of her office she could see Milo pacing in the hall, glancing at his watch. He tapped on it and mouthed, *Time is money*.

Gabby glanced at her own watch, gave him a little wave, and smiled sweetly. Her family was more important than Milo's obsessive timekeeping, plus it was after five o'clock and he could stick it.

Nonna stood, lifted a large shoebox from the floor, and placed it on Gabby's desk. "This is why we're here. I want you to look through these for me."

Gabby took the heavy box and shook it. She could hear papers shifting from side to side. "What's in here, Nonna?"

"My fortune," Nonna pronounced.

Gabby exchanged glances with Rachel before taking off the lid and flipping carefully through the top items in the box. Old bank statements, a CD for $5,000, an old life insurance policy for $100,000.

Gabby tended to have a disproportionate number of elderly clients who wanted to get their wills in order, many of whom saved their important documents in shoeboxes just like this one. She wasn't quite sure why she was a magnet for the good, decent people of her town, who needed their wills drawn up but would never be big moneymakers for the firm, much to Milo's chagrin. But she loved chatting with them, or sometimes just listening when they needed someone to talk to.

Something sparkly from the bottom of the box caught her eye, a gold chain with a pendant. But not just any pendant. A trapezoid-shaped piece of white marble with gray veins. Nonna's family was originally from Tuscany, near Cararra, and the pendant certainly looked like it was carved from a piece of Cararra marble.

"That's for you," Nonna said.

"Oh, what is it?" Gabby asked, holding it up to see.

"It's for finding the love of your life."

Gabby narrowed her eyes. She was known among her siblings as the romantic one in the family, but she could never top Nonna's often fantastical romantic leanings. Such as her staunch belief in their town's legend.

The centerpiece of their little town of Angel Falls, Ohio, was a beautiful bronze statue of two angels whose arms and wings joined together to form a big heart. It was stationed at the head of the bridge that was built over the lovely falls the town was named for. Legend had it that any couple who kissed in front of the angels, tossed a coin into the water, and had their picture taken would have true love forever. Tourists came from all over to spend a day in the quaint town, shop the Main Street shops, dine in the cute restaurants, and, of course, get their picture taken.

She didn't really believe the legend; it was more for the tourists anyway. Once she'd tried to get Malcolm to throw a coin in the water to cement their love for all eternity, but he'd laughed at her and said it was too silly.

Good thing, in retrospect.

But this tale...she'd never heard it before from Nonna. Nor had she ever seen this piece of jewelry. And she would know, because Nonna used to let them play dress-up with all her beads and baubles, as she called them.

Gabby fingered the smooth, white surface hooked by a gold cap to the chain. It felt like a worry stone, like someone had fretted on its smooth surface many times with their fingers. "Were you wearing this when you met Grandpa?"

Nonna went quiet, which was unusual. "Your grandfather didn't give that to me." Then, she said, gesturing, "You need to put it on."

Gabby didn't put much credence in the town legend. Nor did she have any reason to believe in even more romantic folklore, but she slipped it on. "Thanks, Nonna. It's beautiful." To Rachel, she shrugged and said, "At this point, I'll try anything."

"Gabriella, you're young," Rachel said. "You're just in a little dry patch right now."

"She's not that young," Nonna said.

Gabby wasn't that young when she was with Malcolm either, but she had still made mistakes. She'd thought she was in love. He was John Stamos handsome and successful, the kind of guy she'd thought would please her high-achieving family. She'd spent a lot of time giving herself pep talks that yes! yes! she could make this work, because she was thirty and *hurry*, because another guy might not ever come along.

"Gabby just needs a stroke of good luck," Rachel said. "And I've been working on it. Our new minister is handsome, funny, and a great guy. And he's *single*."

Her stepmother literally clapped her hands. "And guess what? I've arranged for you to meet him."

Oh no. "Rach, I appreciate it, but I don't think it's a good idea—"

"You promised to let me have a go at it."

That she had. In a moment of desperation, she'd acquiesced to Rachel's offer to help. Rachel knew so many people as the owner of the high-end antiques store on the main drag, Gabby figured Rachel would have a much better chance of finding someone than she would, holed up in her office night after night.

Thankfully, Nonna interrupted Rachel's matchmaking. "I'm tired, Rachel. Let's go get a cheeseburger before you take me home, what do you say? Gabriella, can you come with us? You can get those awful chicken nuggets you like so much."

"Thanks anyway, Nonna," Gabby said. "I've got some work to finish up."

"Nonna," Rachel said, "I was going to bring you back to our house for dinner tonight. I thought we could throw some chicken on the grill and make a quick pasta salad. Doesn't that sound healthy?"

"Forget the cooking. Let's get a cheeseburger," Nonna said, never one to let healthy food stand in the way of her and a great burger.

Hmmm. Nonna wasn't usually insistent, nor did she often favor fast food over homemade. But hey, cheeseburger cravings—or in Gabby's case, chicken nugget cravings—were real, and who was she to question? Rachel stood and offered a hand to Nonna, who took it and hoisted herself carefully from the chair. A little stab of sadness went through Gabby; she could never seem to accept the invariable signs of aging that seemed to be getting more frequent with Nonna.

Gabby held her breath. Rachel was the most health-conscious person she knew. She rarely ate meat, and she jogged and practiced yoga. A cheeseburger probably hadn't passed her lips in years.

"You know, it *is* a nice evening," Rachel said. "Maybe we should drive through for cheeseburgers and eat them outside on the patio tonight. I'll even open a bottle of wine, what do you say, Rose?"

"That sounds lovely," Nonna said, winking at Gabby. "How about we get French fries too?"

"Sounds perfect," Rachel said seamlessly, her inner horror completely disguised. Another reason Gabby loved Rachel.

"Bye, you two," Gabby said, walking them to her door. "Thanks for coming by."

"Don't forget to charge me for your time," Nonna said. "We can take the money from all my stocks."

Gabby kissed her grandmother on the cheek. At least Nonna had retained her sense of humor through the dementia. "Thanks, Nonnie. I'll send you a bill." No, she wouldn't, but saying that made Nonna happy.

"Want us to pick you up some nuggets for later?" Rachel asked.

"Sorry, can't tonight," Gabby said to Rachel. "But I'll be over to Nonna's later." It was Gabby's turn to keep Nonna company tonight, an arrangement she'd made with her siblings because they were worried about Nonna being alone.

"Okay," Rachel said, kissing her goodbye. "Don't work too hard."

"You sure you can't come?" Nonna asked. "It's dinnertime and you're still working. And you're too skinny."

Gabby knew they were not going to let the dinner thing go. To Nonna, refusing food was a sin of the highest order. "Well, the truth is," Gabby confessed, "I signed up for a creative writing class that's being taught by a big-time author." For courage—in order to learn how to *really* write instead of all the scribbling she did that seemed like it was going nowhere. "Actually, the first class is tonight." She didn't want to be rude and glance at her watch, but she had a lot to do before she left for class. And it was getting late.

"A writing class," Rachel said, a little hesitantly.

"Another class?" Nonna asked. "Aren't you done with all the classes?"

It was true that Gabby had a handful of different majors in college, and she had tended to take a lot of different hobby-type classes for fun after she graduated from law school to help make her job a little more bearable.

"This one is different, Nonna. I want to learn how to write a book. A big, juicy saga with plenty of drama, true love against the odds, and...kissing." Lots of great kissing. And the hope of finding love, because regardless of what had happened to her, she still believed it was possible, and she would never lose hope.

"I like kissing," Nonna said.

"Is your teacher anyone I know?" Rachel said.

"Caden Marshall. I never knew him, and he left Angel Falls years ago. He's a *New York Times* best-selling writer."

Rachel frowned. "Paige's son. You know Paige, who owns the book shop, right?...He's a few years older than you. You sure you don't know him?"

"I only know the rumors that went around," Gabby said. She didn't care whether the rumors were true, as long as the man knew how to teach writing.

"He was a nice boy," Rachel said. "For a time, he walked the dogs after I'd broken my leg skiing. But I don't know if success corrupted him. It happens, you know."

"What happened?" Nonna asked.

"He was brilliant," Rachel said. "His first book was a runaway bestseller. But then his wife went to the tabloids and accused him of stealing her ideas. It blew up into a big scandal and his reputation was ruined. The divorce was quite notorious in the papers."

Gabby had remembered his mother being so proud. Paige had lined the front window of her bookshop with copies of his book and created a massive stacked display right near the front door.

"Rumor has it he hasn't written anything since," Rachel said. "And Paige says the ex hardly sees their little daughter."

Paige had quietly defended her son, refusing to take her son's books out of her shop window even though kids had egged her windows and the Ladies Historical Preservation Society had snubbed her.

"Oh, I remember now. His book was very depressing," Nonna said. "I read it in my book club. But he is very good-looking. Dark, handsome, and tortured. Like Heathcliff."

"We don't want Gabby to fall for her professor," Rachel said, sounding a little panicked. "He's riddled with scandal, divorced, and has a child. We want Gabby to make a smart, uncomplicated choice, don't we?" She smiled hopefully.

"Gabby is like me," Nonna said. "Her passions rule her sense sometimes."

"Nonna, you're the most sensible woman I know," Rachel said. "And Gabby learned a lot from her broken engagement. I know she's going to make a wise choice next time."

Ugh. Gabby loved her family but it was time for them to go. She put her hands up. "Look, I'm not going to fall for my scandalized professor, okay? And I don't care about his past, as long as he can teach me writing."

"Well," Rachel said. "Good luck with the class. It sounds exciting."

"You can tell us all about it on Sunday," Nonna said.

Gabby saw them out, then shut down her computer and tidied up her desk. She fingered the beautiful necklace one more time. Maybe it should upset her that her family was campaigning to find her true love, since clearly they didn't believe she was capable of finding him on her own, but frankly, Gabby didn't mind the help. Her oldest sister, Evie, was married with two adorable kids, and her sister Sara had just married the police chief, Colton Walker, last Christmas and was now blissfully happy. And Rafe... well, Rafe was Rafe, and at twenty-eight, he still wasn't showing any signs of settling down.

When Gabby thought of happiness, of the life of her dreams, other things besides money came to mind. Like sitting on a big, old front porch on a hot summer evening, sipping iced tea and holding hands with someone. Kissing while lying on a blanket and making love under the stars, the piney scent of the woods fresh and clean. Having a love like her grandparents had known, which had endured for decades.

She'd never had an experience like that, a soul mate who made her feel that she was exactly where she should be in her life, with the person she was meant to be with. Where she could slow down enough to enjoy a good book and a cup of tea or knit a friend a baby gift or go for a long, cleansing bike ride through the parks just outside of town.

No, life had gotten too fast. Too busy. Too out of control.

That dream seemed about as far away as New Zealand. Or tucked away in one of the romance novels she sneaked a few pages of every night before she collapsed into bed. Alone.

She turned off her office light and locked the door behind her. On to writing class. And sensible decisions.

Chapter 2

♥

Milo had asked Gabby to do one last thing on her way out, and now she was running late to her first class. Great. Just great. She drove around the John Herschel Glenn College campus, circling the parking lot over and over with the acuity of a vulture eyeballing prey, along with six other cars doing the very same thing. Rain clouds were hovering, another reason to park and get into class. Suddenly, right smack in the middle of her present row, a spot opened up.

She accelerated, flicked on her blinker, and was just about to nose her Honda Civic into it when a shiny black F150 truck coming from the opposite direction pulled directly in front of her and scooped up the spot. She hit the brake fast to avoid smacking into the rear bumper of the truck and came to a screeching halt. Her body flew forward toward the windshield and then snapped back, thanks to her shoulder belt.

A few choice words bubbled to her lips, and a

certain finger might have begun to twitch of its own accord.

Gabby laid on the horn—one long, satisfying push on the wheel. For about three seconds, she felt all the stress and tension from her day melt into that blaring bleat of sound. Until the driver's door of the pickup opened. She didn't know much about trucks, but judging from the chrome rims, mud flaps, and LED light bar, it was likely driven by some guy who could potentially start a confrontation. One of those I-own-a-big-truck-so-therefore-I-own-the-world types. The sensible thing to do would be to just move on, because now she was going to be late for sure.

The guy exited the truck, leaving the motor idling, and walked with a long-legged stride toward her car. To her surprise, he didn't look like a crazed truck owner at all. Nor was he a college kid but a man, tall and lean, saved from being rangy by good, hard muscle evident in the way his legs filled out his faded, well-worn jeans and in the way his button-down chambray shirt fit over his broad chest. He looked dangerous, all right—dangerously hot.

She made out a dark head of thickly layered hair, worn a little longish over his collar. He looked pissed off, his well-defined brows knit down into a deep V. From the set of his five-o'clock-shadow-lined jaw, she could tell that he was not going to give up without a fight.

His good looks threw her, but not as much as the cartoon character stickers and smattering of tiny fingerprints on the back window behind the driver's seat.

Something about the stickers—or maybe it was the

fingerprints—deflated her anger. And her fear. How scary could a man be who probably had a car seat in the back seat of his truck?

Suddenly he was next to her, signaling her with a roll-down-the-window sign.

She hit the automatic lock button, just in case. Maybe he was a maniac. Did he look like a maniac?

Oh no. He looked like *sin*.

She cracked open the window, but she braced her hands on the wheel, ready to peel out backward or close the window on his fingers if he tried to reach in and strangle her. She'd read about that once.

He seemed to note the fact that her car had stopped inches from his, then assessed her with hazel eyes that were an intriguing mix of green, brown, and blue, surrounded by little crinkly lines that placed him solidly in his early thirties. "I'm sorry for taking your spot," he said, "but I'm late for my first day of class." Then he flashed an overly bright smile just imperfect enough to be human. "Surely a nice woman like you would give a guy a break?" He met her gaze head-on with those beautiful eyes.

She frowned and tapped her fingers on the wheel. Clearly this was a guy who was trying to charm his way out of conflict. And judging by his looks, it had probably worked for him many times before. He probably had a reputation for stealing hearts as well as parking spaces. "I'm late for class too."

"I really need it—probably more than you do." He smiled again—an utterly false smile that did not reach those fascinating eyes of his. *Uh-oh.* Not only was he flirting with her, he was also being arrogant. Strikes One and Two.

She rolled her eyes. "Pu-lease. Don't think you can stun me with your good looks." Except she did feel stunned. He was *gorgeous*.

He glanced around nervously. "Look, ma'am," he said, "I'm *not* flirting with you. I just really need this space right now."

"*Ma'am?* Exactly how old do you think I am?" *Ma'am*, everyone knew, meant at least forty. She wasn't forty! She wasn't even thirty-one yet.

"I apologize again for taking the spot, but I really have to go." Before she could say *Hey, hold up a second, buddy*, he was walking away, raising his hand in a backward wave as he jogged to his truck.

She couldn't help watching him walk to his vehicle. His stride—graceful, purposeful—was hard to take her eyes off of. Not to mention he had the kind of narrow man butt that filled out those comfy old Levis just right.

Oh, what was wrong with her? She was doing womankind a disservice, noticing the smoking-hot body of this man who was clearly an asshat.

For no apparent reason, he glanced back and caught her staring at him. His frown resonated across the parking lot, as deep and foreboding as the impending night.

Caught ass watching! As if that weren't bad enough, he got in his truck, threw it in gear, and plowed the rest of the way into the spot, without a glance backward.

While she sat there drooling at his behind.

And as if Mother Nature were having a laugh at her expense, the skies opened and it began to pour.

Gabby barely noticed in light of the rudeness. The *gall*. And shame on her for drooling over his butt. Shaking her head, she threw her own car into drive and moved on through the full-to-the-brim lot.

Maybe what everyone said was true, that she really did have terrible judgment in men. And jobs. And everything else. And how had she allowed herself to get sidetracked from her goal of getting to class on time by a great butt? Well, no matter. She'd never see him—or *it*, for that matter—again.

* * *

Caden Marshall's reputation was as fragile as a house of cards. Being late for his first class would be the tiny flick of a finger that would topple it before he'd even begun his job as a professor at the tiny liberal arts college in Angel Falls, Ohio. Funny, but he'd imagined that if he'd ever returned to a college to teach, it would be with bright, eager MFA students, not a night class composed mainly of adults who were dabbling in creative writing for fun.

But as the saying went, beggars couldn't be choosers. He needed job security. *Tenure.* He wanted to live a responsible life with a decent job and provide well for himself and his almost-four-year-old daughter, Ava. Which was why he'd jumped when a job at the local college in his hometown had opened up.

Ava had started a new day care this week. She was exhausted after her long day and was crying up a storm when his mom had come to babysit, reminding him that he was the one responsible for uprooting his daughter.

He'd tried to console her, but when he left, she was still crying, each hiccupping *eh-eh-eh* ripping his heart out a little further.

Two doors down from his classroom in the administration building with the brick clock tower, Cade stuffed the windbreaker he'd used to cover his head from the rain back into his book bag, raked back his damp hair, and made sure his shirt was tucked in. The standard institutional clock on the gray wall read 6:59. He'd made it, thank God, but he felt guilty about his aggressive parking lot behavior. He wasn't usually an a-hole, but he'd supposed the high stakes involved with doing this job well had made him one. He vowed to do better—which seemed like his mantra these days. Falling short of everything but trying really hard not to.

There were ten students on his roster, and two of them, both women, were gathered around a desk, talking to the seated occupant. One of the women had short pink hair and arms covered with tattoos. The other woman was around fifty, with short gray hair and glasses. Scanning the rest of the class, he noted a woman and man, both above seventy, sitting on opposite sides of the room and a handful of middle-aged women, who he noticed had copies of his book on their desks.

He braced himself for the questions that were sure to come. In a few years, people would forget that he was a *New York Times* bestselling author with a one-hit wonder. But until then, his life was going to be hell.

The glory of hitting the *Times* list was followed almost immediately by claims by his ex-wife that he'd stolen her ideas. Claims she'd tweeted and posted on social media that had gone viral and had ended up in an interview on Page Six of the *New York Post*, the most infamous gossip column in the country. And once that story hit, his reputation had imploded. And his words had dried up.

He reminded himself he was here to teach, not run a damn book club. He would have to take charge and distract them from things he didn't want to share. And focus on the things he did want to share—teaching them the craft of writing. Even if he felt like a fraud.

"What's so funny?" Cade asked, clearing his throat and forcing a look of interest on his face. A look that would've come naturally just a few years ago but now felt forced. He reminded himself that he'd taught classes in grad school, so he wasn't a complete novice at teaching. It was just his ambivalence at being here, starting over doing something he wasn't quite sure he wanted to do. And the horrible realization that by returning to his hometown, becoming a professor at the exact same college where his father had taught, he'd somehow managed to become the father he despised.

Everyone looked up and automatically began to disband, making their way back to seats strewn with notebooks and laptops and coffee cups.

"Oh, hi, Professor," the middle-aged woman with glasses and short gray hair said cheerily. "I'm Helen. Gabby here was just telling us about some douchebag *idiot* who stole her parking spot."

His gaze swiveled over to the seat. The little crowd had dispersed, leaving a young woman in plain view. A woman with big brown eyes and lots of wildly curly dark hair wound up in a loose bun. Memorable, because she was beautiful. But mostly because he'd just seen her in the damn parking lot.

Oh, fuck.

For a second, he stared into her startled eyes. She was dressed in a dark gray dress and dangling earrings. Classy. She nervously twirled a pencil. A *pencil*, when most of the students had laptops—or at least notebooks and pens—in front of them.

The back of his neck prickled, causing the urge to rub it. What were the odds? This was an omen. Karma biting him in the ass. He'd never taken a parking space from anyone before, let alone a woman—let alone a *student*. Desperation had made him panic, and now he was going to pay. He was not meant to be here, in East Angel Nowhere, Ohio. Starting off on the wrong foot was certain to set the tone for the rest of his time here. And he could not afford wrong feet.

"I'm sorry for your trouble, Ms.—a—" He glanced at his class roster.

"Gabby. Gabby Langdon."

Langdon. He knew the family. Dr. Walter Langdon was a longstanding physician in town—had been his own doctor growing up—and Cade's sister, Beth, had just been hired into Dr. Langdon's practice to work with him and his daughter Sara. Cade had gone to school with one of the Langdon kids…Evie. They'd lost their mother young, as he recalled.

He looked up to find dark, fiery eyes spitting daggers at him.

Oh, shit. He called up his calmest expression. "Well,

obviously you found a spot because you made it here on time." *Before he did.* How on earth?

"Barely," she said.

Helen snorted. "Yeah, there's no courtesy—let alone chivalry—left in the world."

The old metal clock on the wall let out an audible click, as if it were tsking at him. His first impulse was to apologize. But how could he do that in the first minute of class? He'd be labeled as a jackass.

"Maybe it was someone in a rush for a good reason," he offered. Lame, but what could he do?

Gabby crossed her arms, a move that showcased her very nice breasts, which he certainly was *not* noticing. The fact that he was struggling not to notice added to his discomfort.

"You're awfully forgiving, Professor," she said.

The woman with the pink hair snorted. "Typical man, cutting another man some slack."

"Well, you never know when something's going on in someone's life that made them in a big hurry." He gave his nemesis from the parking lot a pointed look. "An extenuating circumstance." He hoped she wouldn't out him, even though he deserved it.

She narrowed her eyes. "Regardless of whatever is going on in *someone's* life, that doesn't give *him* an excuse to be a jerk."

"Go, Gabby," Ms. Pink Hair said, pumping the air with her fist.

He took a step forward and faced the pink-haired woman directly. "Maybe it was a fluke thing and the person's not really a jerk."

Gabby was not deterred. "Well, if one party injures another party, the second party should have some kind of recourse. Maybe in the form of an *apology*."

Lawyer. She *had* to be a lawyer. "This is a creative writing class, Ms. Langdon. The Con law class meets down the hall."

"Oh, this guy knew what he was doing, all right," the pink-haired woman said. "He tried to charm his way out of it too. I hope you let him have it, Gabby."

The woman—*Gabby*—looked him over with intelligent eyes that proved she was no pushover. He couldn't help but respect that, even though she could do him quite a bit of harm. Like all women. Life had taught him none of whom could be trusted.

"It's okay," she said carefully. "No harm done."

Oh, thank God. The knot in his neck uncoiled a little. She was backing down.

Then she smiled a little, a conciliatory gesture that threw him. And another thing: she was...pretty. Really pretty. She had soft curves and untamed hair and full red lips, and the cumulative effect made his breath hitch.

He tore his eyes away from her and glanced at his watch. "Speaking of time, let's get started. I'm Caden Marshall," he said to the class. "Taking over this class for Dr. Shreevesanan, who just found out she'll be on bed rest for the next two months until her twins are born."

A murmur rose up from the students. "Is Amira okay?" Helen asked. "She's my neighbor. She was the one who encouraged me to sign up for this class."

"But she's only thirty-three weeks," the pink-haired woman said.

"How do you know that?" Helen asked.

"I own the tattoo parlor downtown, and her mom came in last week."

Cade chose to ignore the information that Amira's mother, a sweet woman of around seventy he happened to meet earlier this week, might have gotten one or more tattoos. But the information also made him realize he was back home, where everyone knew everyone's business. It was a reminder to be careful about the information he shared. "Amira wanted everyone to know she's fine," he said. "The bed rest is just a precaution."

The class looked a little distressed. Amira was a sweetheart, but from what he'd heard, she had the reputation of being motherly in the classroom—kind, nurturing, and a very easy grader.

The gray-haired woman spoke up again. "I-I'm not sure I want to take this class if she's not the teacher."

"Well, Helen," Cade said, glancing at the paper he'd passed around and had everyone sign. "You're right, I'm definitely not Dr. S." He'd been a serious author, and now he wanted to be a serious teacher. "I know most of you work full-time jobs. Some of you are taking this class for fun. Others because you have a goal to publish a book one day. Regardless of your motivation, I want you to know that you'll work hard here. You'll stretch yourselves if you want to get something out of this class."

And maybe he would discover another serious writer with a lot of potential, just as his own mentor had recognized his talent and helped him along. That was a noble thing to do, right? Teaching *was* a noble profession. It just didn't feel exciting and gut-wrenching and heart pounding all at once, like his writing had once upon a time.

Something his father once told him a few years ago stuck in his mind. *Those who can't do, teach.*

He shook his head and turned his attention back to the multiple pairs of eyes staring at him.

"Okay. I thought we could go around the room and talk a little about ourselves. Feel free to say why you signed up for this class. I'll go first." Mentally, he dusted off the scrubbed version of his bio. "I teach creative writing but I did my PhD work on the writings of F. Scott Fitzgerald."

All true. But in the last year of grad school at the University of Michigan, he'd submitted a manuscript to the Iowa Writers' Workshop and had somehow gotten into the most prestigious writing program in the country—more difficult to get into than Harvard, where he'd studied as an undergrad.

One of the ladies held up a copy of his book, waving the stark black cover with gold lettering that he'd once been so proud of. "Professor Marshall, will you sign my book? And when's your next one coming?"

He forced a laugh. "Well. I'm glad you have such great taste in books. I'd be happy to sign it after class. And a publication date for the next one hasn't been set yet." He felt like an imposter, someone teaching writing who couldn't write. His eyes lit on Helen. "Why don't you go next?"

"I'm a librarian," she said, and Cade found himself exhaling deeply. "A year ago, my husband walked out after thirty years of marriage. That was scary, but in some ways, this is scarier. Writing exposes a personal side of yourself. It makes you vulnerable."

Cade nodded. "Hemingway reportedly said, 'There is nothing to writing. All you do is sit down at a typewriter and bleed.'" He got a few chuckles from that. "So you're absolutely correct. Writing *is* scary. Next."

His students were a ragtag bunch. There was the mother of a few young children who looked like she'd forgotten to comb her hair, which he could totally relate to; an older woman who thought she'd signed up for a poetry class; and a retired doctor who, because of his age, was taking the class for free and who was on his phone probably Googling the Hemingway quote and getting ready to challenge him about its accuracy.

Then came his pal from the parking lot. "My name is Gabby Langdon. I'm taking this class because I want to write a book."

Of course she did. "You and eighty percent of all people."

Her expression didn't fall, and something in her eyes flickered. He recognized it as a familiar look he got from Ava almost daily—defiance.

"Maybe so, Professor," she said. "But somebody's got to write them."

"What kind of books do you want to write, Ms. Langdon?" he asked.

She blushed. That threw him. "I—um—an emotional book that makes people feel things. And love. There has to be a love story." She pressed a hand over her heart.

Definitely a sentimentalist. Funny, though, that was what *he'd* set out to do—at the beginning. Write a book that made people *feel* something. Now he realized writing—and life—were so much more complicated than that.

"I've always wanted to write but I never thought it was an option for me. But now I want to explore that option, and I need the tools to do it. That's why I'm here."

"Aw, romance is all butterflies and ponies," the old doctor said from the back of the class. "Write something painful and real."

"Love *is* real," Gabby shot back.

"Yeah, real *painful*," Helen said, and that got a laugh from the class.

"Love is something Hollywood makes up to sell movie tickets," the old man said.

Cade silently agreed, but instead he said, "Any real experience—like love—can be translated into writing. That's why people read fiction. To feel something."

He'd given up his own illusion of romantic love a long time ago. He didn't need the heartache. The mental *bloodshed*. "Where do you get your ideas from?" a woman asked out of the blue.

"Maybe he gets them from his wife," someone whispered.

Cade pretended not to hear that, even while it shredded his insides. Instead, he walked casually to an empty desk and pulled it out a little, leaning against it in the aisle. "Stephen King said, 'Stories are found things, like fossils in the ground.' So to answer your question, I don't know how or why ideas take shape. But I want you to struggle with yours, and then come to class and share them with your colleagues. Each class, I'll be sharing a few pages of a student's work for instruction and critique. You may feel uncomfortable about that, but it's critical to share. Contrary to popular belief, writing is not a solitary profession."

In the early days, he'd trusted Emerson, his wife, implicitly—they'd shared everything about their writing in those early days, and it had been a heady, exciting partnership. He would never know for sure if he'd subconsciously taken something that wasn't his, and that haunted him.

The pink-haired student spoke up. "It's nice to know we're going to be reading each other's stuff. My name's Erin, by the way, and I write paranormal romance at night. Werewolves, vampires, and shape-shifters, mostly."

"Great. I'm eager to see your work." *Butterflies and ponies. Werewolves and shape-shifters. Fantastic.* "Okay, for next class, read chapter one of your textbook and come prepared for an essay quiz, which we'll have at the beginning of each class. Then starting this weekend, you'll each be writing fifteen hundred words a day and posting them to our class online portal. Anyone who can't meet that word count for five days a week should consider dropping the class. Any questions?"

Gabby raised her hand. "I have a question."

"Yes, Ms. Langdon?"

"Well, what if—well, what if we've never written that many words in a day before? And what if we work all day? I mean—do you have some suggestions on how to do that?"

Cade let out an impatient sigh. "Ms. Langdon, everyone in this class is an adult, and I'm not here to coddle anyone. I realize that word count might be a challenge, but it's meant to weed out the serious writers from those who don't care to work hard."

"But you didn't answer my question. I'm not trying to get out of the work, Professor. I'm only asking for suggestions on how to manage it."

"Clear your schedule, turn off the TV, decrease your social obligations, set a timer. Everyone has to develop their own style and find what works best for them."

As he approached the smart board to begin his lecture, he thought he heard a soft "Aye-aye, sir" behind him. When he turned, Gabby's eyes were trained on her notebook. But Helen, who was sitting across from her, was chuckling with her hand over her mouth.

"Ms. Langdon, perhaps you'd like to go first on Monday to read us your work, how does that sound?"

A hush descended, and he began his lecture. Okay, now they knew he was serious. And he was. He was going to keep everything by the book, strict, and on the straight and narrow. Just like he was going to rein in his life, which had veered completely off course. And he wasn't going to be sidetracked by any distractions—especially pretty, sentimental students who knew how to call him out for being cynical and unsympathetic. It was like she was holding up a mirror, and he didn't like at all what he saw.

Chapter 3

♥

As soon as class ended, Cade gathered his things, hoping to get home as fast as possible. He prayed Ava wasn't still lying on the floor, exhausted and sobbing. One of the seniors asked him a question about margins and font in her Word program, which he explained in detail. Sure enough, there came Gabby, headed toward him, book bag and coffee mug in tow.

He wasn't supposed to *notice* students. But Gabby wasn't an eighteen-year-old student, she was his age, and she knew how to put him in his place. He must be crazy, but even her defiance was sexy.

"Excuse me, Professor Marshall," she said, approaching his desk.

She was Trouble. Someone to avoid. But first he had to clear all these inappropriate thoughts out of his head. Including her light, fresh scent, which he'd just noticed as she'd walked up to him. He cleared his throat. "Ms. Langdon," he said, getting busy sorting his papers.

As he shoved his lecture notes into his book bag, he

decided that his attention on Gabby was only because it had been way too long since he'd had sex. It was time to change that, get out a little. Meet some people. Once he had Ava settled, he planned to do just that. He would choose someone simple, easygoing, and non-demanding. Someone who wouldn't compete with him, screw him over, and leave him for roadkill like his ex.

"I wasn't complaining about the word count," she said. "And despite what my question made you think, I am serious about this class."

"I wasn't implying that you weren't a serious student. It's just that I want to be clear from the beginning that this class will involve work, and anyone who doesn't have the time to put into it probably shouldn't be taking it." He glanced up briefly to see her gazing at him steadily, her eyes stubbornly narrowed.

"Oh, I'll devote the necessary time to it," she said. "I'm determined."

"I'm sure you are," he said. He stuffed the remaining papers into his book bag. When he looked up, he found she'd already turned to leave.

Oh, hell. "Ms. Langdon?" he called after her. He had to say what was on his mind, as quickly and painlessly as possible. She didn't deserve the crotchety, authoritarian treatment he'd been doling out in spades because he was struggling to get control of his life…and his reaction to her. Hell, it wasn't really working anyway.

She stopped at the doorway and turned back. "Yes, Dr. Marshall?"

"I'm sorry about the parking spot." There. He'd said it.

"You're sorry about taking my parking spot?" she echoed, a bit incredulously.

"Yes. There were extenuating circumstances, and I—well, I apologize. I was out of line. And—I appreciate that you didn't say anything in front of the class."

"That's all right. Because I guess now you'll have to give me an A for my silence." His face must've gone blank because she threw up her hands and said, "Kidding." A bright, wide smile spread across her face—unpretentious and so appealing.

In spite of himself, he smiled too. "Glad we can put that behind us." He paused. "Except I *did* see the spot first," he said, just to get her goat.

The blush rose into her cheeks. "Are you kidding—"

"Yes. Kidding."

She laughed. "Well then. Apology accepted." She held out her hand.

He glanced at her offering of peace. Something told him to glower and nod and leave it at that, but he couldn't do that. He just did the natural thing, reached out and shook her hand. But something happened between the shaking and looking into her big brown eyes, which had locked uncomfortably with his. A frizzle of awareness spread warmly through him, a wave of attraction he hadn't felt in years.

He had no idea how long he stared—too long. Finally he released his hand. Cleared his throat. Dragged his gaze back to his book bag and started digging for his keys.

"Well, I—um—yeah. See you Wednesday, Dr. Marshall." She gave a little salute before she turned on her heels and walked out of his classroom.

Cade watched her go. The old metal clock on the wall gave a loud click as the metal hand jolted forward, as if marking the moment that something in his life had just shifted.

* * *

Gabby walked down the fluorescent-lit hallway and out into the drizzly night. Professor Heathcliff had just the kind of aura of darkness she was attracted to—in a bad way. The urge to peel away those shadowy layers and see if something brighter lay beneath—that unexpected smile, for instance—was a temptation she had to ignore.

She gave herself a stern talking to. *I will not be attracted to guys with issues. I will not have the hots for my professor. This is my time to figure out who I am, not act on romantic whims*, which had clearly gotten her into trouble in the past.

In the glow of the iron lampposts that surrounded the Gothic brick building, a group of students had gathered. As she walked down the wide concrete steps, she recognized Helen's gray hair and Erin's pink spikes, which looked extra bright under the lamplight.

"We waited for you," Helen said, grabbing her arm. "Are you okay?"

"Yeah, we were giving you another ten seconds, then we were going to storm the classroom," Erin said, reaching in her denim bag for a cigarette. "I wish the offices were open. I'm dropping this class first thing in the morning."

"Yeah," Helen said. "I can't write fifteen hundred words in a week, let alone a day."

Gabby laughed. "Dr. Marshall's bark might be worse than his bite. But still, he's not exactly going to make this class a fun experience."

"He's scary," Erin said. "I don't feel like this classroom is a safe space for my muse."

"I don't think it's a safe space for my *ego*," Helen said. "It's already been trampled on by my ex."

"I work a lot of hours," Gabby admitted. "I'm not really sure how I'm going to find time to do all of this work."

"I thought this was supposed to be *fun*," Erin said.

An image of Gabby's dad suddenly came to mind. He was kindly and gray haired, but under all that pleasantness was a driven man who would not back down until each one of his children was settled and happy. She guessed his drive came from a promise he'd made to their mother before she died, that he'd watch over and guide each kid's future—except it had developed into a crusade. Her dad was hell-bent on having each of them be successful, self-sufficient human beings. The problem was that his ideas of success didn't always jibe with his children's.

She'd had many battles with her father as an undergraduate as she'd gone from major to major. Everyone in the family had breathed a sigh of relief when she'd finally settled into law school and, except for her bad choice of a fiancé, had molded her life into exactly how her father had envisioned it—a stable career, a decent income.

But the nagging feeling she just couldn't get out of her gut that something was missing in her life had only intensified once she'd found a box of her mom's things buried in a closet at her grandmother's house. In it were old college papers, notebooks full of writing, and a manuscript.

Her mother *wrote*. Maybe Gabby's dissatisfaction with her job and her own desire to write weren't quite as crazy as she once thought. In any case, she had to find out herself.

"We can't quit," Gabby said softly, and then again louder. "We're not going to quit. We can be strong together." She locked arms with Helen, who looked startled. Erin lifted a skeptical brow. "We're not going to let this guy get to us. But he's a big-time author. I think we can learn a lot from him. And maybe he's not as mean as we think." Because when he'd smiled just now, lordie, the angels practically sang.

Besides, Gabby was an optimist.

Heathcliff might be romantic and mysterious, but she would stay away from him, because no distraction was going to stand in the way of what this man could teach her about writing.

The group dispersed, and Gabby walked over to her car, which she'd parked directly in front of the administration building. She pulled off the soggy yellow ticket that was stuck under the windshield and smiled. She'd parked here as a last-ditch effort not to be late for class. Turned out it was so worth the thirty bucks she'd have to pay to see the look on Dr. Marshall's face when he'd discovered she'd made it to class before he did.

* * *

"How's my princess?' Cade's mother held out her arms for Ava, who leaped into them, while Cade looked on and smiled. It was a sunny Friday afternoon and they'd both survived their first week of class/day care, and now he and Ava were visiting his mom in the bookstore where he'd spent so many wonderful hours as a child.

This was the real reason he'd moved back home. To give Ava the experience of having a family, to show her that she was loved and cared for and adored even though things hadn't worked out between her mother and him.

"I have some picture books for you," Paige said to her only grandchild as she carried her to the back of the store. "Would you like to look at them while your dad and I talk for a few minutes?" Cade's mother was completely grandchild deprived and made no secret she fully intended to make up for every lost second by being lovey, warm, and by completely spoiling Ava. An arrangement Ava happened to be completely thrilled with.

Hell, Cade had to admit he was pretty thrilled with it too.

While his mom grabbed books for Ava and chatted, a big basset hound moseyed out of his corner bed and up to Cade's calf, nudging it.

"Hey there, Cooper," Cade said, stooping to scratch the dog behind the ears. "What's up, buddy?"

Cooper wasn't telling, but as Cade looked around, he noted not much had changed in the old building since his childhood: same painted tin ceiling, same brick fireplace from Victorian times surrounded by green and maroon tiles. He'd just walked over to inspect a cracked tile when his mom spoke.

"What a nice surprise," she said. "I thought they were keeping you too busy at the college to stop by, but I'm so glad you did." She clapped her hands together and spoke to Ava. "I'm so happy to have you and your daddy back in town."

"Me too, Mom," Cade said, and he realized he meant it. Even with all his mixed feelings about his new job, being back home just felt somehow very right.

"Me too, Grammie," Ava said with a sweet smile.

He stood from inspecting the tile. "I stopped by to order a few books for my research. Do you have time to help?"

"Of course." His mom led his daughter over to a window seat strewn with multicolored pillows, where a big yellow cat lay curled up enjoying the sun. She grabbed a small stack of picture books from atop a bookshelf and set them in front of Ava. The basset promptly climbed his personal little basset-sized staircase and plopped down next to her. "Here you go, sweetheart," Paige said. "You sit there with Mr. Buttons and Cooper for a few minutes while I help your dad, okay?"

Ava was more than content "reading" a story aloud to her new pals. Meanwhile, Cade followed his mom to the big wooden counter. The newest Harlan Coben lay on the counter, turned upside down with a pair of bifocals sitting on top. She snatched them up and perched them on her nose.

"How is that?" Cade asked, giving a nod to the book.

"Oh, terrific." His mom sighed. "Harlan is a wonderful writer. But not as good as you, though." His mom had never met a book she didn't like.

"Mom," Cade said with a warning tone. "I'm not here to talk about my writing. I'm here to order books for my research project. At my new job. As a professor, remember? I have a big meeting coming up with the New Faculty committee, and I have to tell them what research I'm going to produce and how that ties into my plan for tenure. If they approve, I'll be the new Fitzgerald Scholar."

"Well, that sounds very proper. Very structured," she said, pressing her lips together in that way she had when she didn't want to say what she was really thinking.

"I *am* structured, Mother. I have a real job now." He'd had a grant to finish his second novel, but he'd been unable to produce, and that was why he'd taken the teaching job.

"I hate to see you in a job that limits your creativity."

She failed to take into account the decent hours, great benefits, and, most important of all, the steady stream of income that was crucial when raising a child. His parents had been divorced since he was twelve, and lord knew they hadn't had a great marriage, but at the very least his mom had had his father's support in raising Cade and his sister, financially at least. His dad didn't do emotional support. Then or now.

"Most moms would be proud of the fact that I got this position at the college." Cade knew she was proud of him—she just would not stop campaigning for him to go back to writing. "And what have you got against professors? You were married to one."

"Let's not drag your father into this." She paused. "Cade, you know I'd be proud of you even if you were a beachcomber, if that's what made you happy. I just can't help feeling that your divorce sucked all the happiness from your life, except where Ava is concerned."

A glance over at Ava showed her happily turning pages while Cooper nudged his nose under her arm and the cat curled up in a ray of sunshine on her other side.

"Do you have time for a cup of coffee?" his mom asked. "Louisa brought us some new blend from the Bean. The tourists love it, so we decided to try it and now we know why—it's really good."

"That sounds great, but don't fuss." He was a coffee guy through and through. He smiled at his mom as she bustled around, starting the coffeemaker and then turning to a table heaped high with stacks of books. "Oh, this just came in and I snagged you a copy. Thought you might want to read your competition."

Reluctantly, he took the book she handed him. He recognized it immediately. It was the latest bestseller by Paul Blazer, one of his fellow students at the Iowa Writers' Workshop. His *third* novel since Iowa.

He set the book back down atop the pile. "Thanks for thinking of me, but I left that life behind. I really don't have time to write anymore."

He poured the coffee, and his mom grabbed a box of Thin Mints from a shelf below the counter and pushed it over to him, saying nothing, which spoke volumes.

His favorite cookie. Unable to resist, he dug in. And tried to steer the conversation back to a more neutral topic.

"You need anything repaired while I'm here?" He walked back over to the old fireplace. "I see you've got a couple of cracked tiles in the fireplace surround."

"Of course. The building is a hundred and forty years old. But Caden, I can't help thinking—"

"Mom. Don't."

"What kind of mother would I be if I can't speak my mind when I see that something's bothering my child?"

"Maybe the kind with an adult child who can figure things out on his own?"

She frowned. "How many years were you there for me when I was getting over the divorce? I hadn't had a job for fifteen years. I didn't know how to do anything, and I was so stunned and shocked that I had trouble functioning. Now I can offer support to you and Ava."

He squeezed his mom's shoulder. "You were and are a great mom. You picked yourself up and did great things. And I want you to know I'm doing fine. I have an opportunity for a good, stable job. And Ava will settle in. We're both doing terrific."

"You forget I've known you your entire life. And I know how much you love words. You were always scribbling in notebooks, making up stories, creating characters and worlds—"

"And then life happened, and I had to grow up."

"Sweetheart, I understand what you're going through, because I went through it myself. I'm afraid you're throwing the baby out with the bathwater. You're getting away from what you love to do."

"I'm fine, Mom." Cade smiled as gently as possible but stood at the same time, signaling that the conversation was done.

"I bet once you settle into a routine you just might

find joy in writing again. And maybe you'll start dating again too."

He gave her a warning look. Dating someone seriously was the last thing on his mind.

She suddenly reached over and grabbed his hand. "You've been suffering by yourself for way too long. You need to know your sister and I are here for you and for Ava because we *want* to be. We love you. Don't close yourself off from your family."

Cade nodded, because he was a little choked up. "I get it, Mom. It's good to be back home."

"Grammie, will you read this book to me?" Ava asked, holding up a book with a colorful painting of a little girl in pigtails holding hands with an older, balding man.

"Sure, Sweet Face, bring it over here."

Ava lifted the book up to the counter and Paige reached for it. The title was *Just Grandpa and Me*.

Cade exchanged glances with his mother. "Tell you what, sweetie," Paige said, holding out the cookies for Ava to take one, "let's pick another one."

"She'd be better off reading *Bad Grandpa*," Cade said as Ava disappeared around the bookshelves.

"You know your father is living in Gates Mills now."

A small bedroom community of Cleveland with rolling hills, plenty of acreage, and a lot of mansions. "No, I didn't know that."

"He stopped drinking."

"Don't tell me you're on friendly terms with him." Cade's voice came out sounding an octave higher than usual.

"I wouldn't exactly say friendly. More like cordial.

He's come into the shop a few times for books. You might just run into him yourself."

"I'll make certain that doesn't happen." Cade noticed his mother's frown. "You can't want me to have a relationship with him again."

She shrugged. "He's worked hard to get his act together. I believe he regrets things."

"Oh, Mom, come on. Surely you're not defending him."

"I'm not defending him. But I am old enough to realize holding on to old resentments poisons you. I'm over it. Maybe you should get over it too."

He thought about all the disappointments that they'd suffered over the years—his father's drinking, which his mother had struggled at first to cover up, the childhood events his father had never showed up for, the arguing. And, later, the myriad of young girlfriends his father had brought so nonchalantly to events he was actually sober enough to attend—the school plays, the ball games, the awards ceremonies. All that, and Cade had continued to believe the best about him. Had seen the brilliant literary critic—hell, he'd wanted to be half as brilliant as his father—and ignored the burned-out drunk who didn't seem to give much of a damn about him or his sister, Beth. Until...

"I might've forgiven him the awful things he said about my book. But when he accused me of selling out to buy fame... that was it."

"You had reason to be angry with him. All I'm saying is, I think your father feels remorse. Maybe you'll have the opportunity while you're here to reconnect."

"I don't need that kind of relationship, Mom," Cade said.

"Maybe not, but people change, and your daughter could really use a few relatives."

"Just not bad ones," Cade said.

His mom rolled her eyes and reached across the counter. "Hand over your list and I'll start ordering your books."

Just then the tiny tinkle of the bell over the door sounded, and the mailman walked in with a leather sack slung over his shoulder. He tipped his hat to Paige as he approached the desk and handed her some mail. Cade recognized him immediately as Matt McGee, or Matt the Mailman, as he was known when Cade was a kid. He was a little grayer, a little balder, but he had the athletic shape of a guy who walked a lot.

"Matt, you remember my son, Cade. And that beautiful little child over there is my granddaughter, Ava."

Matt shook Cade's hand with a strong, steady shake. "Hey there, Cade. Nice to see you all grown up."

"Hey, Matt. How are Anna and Connor?" Cade had gone to school with Matt's kids.

"Fantastic." He turned to Cade's mom. "This came for you, Paige. Maybe it's those tiles you ordered for your fireplace? I can come and fix those after my route on Saturday."

"Why, thanks," Cade's mom said. "Cade just offered to help out with that too."

Her tone sounded odd—nervous, maybe. Enough to make Cade look up. He wasn't completely sure, but his mother looked like she had some color in her cheeks.

"So you writing your next bestseller?" Matt said. "Your mom's impatient for it, you know."

"I just started teaching at the college," Cade said. "Not much time to write."

"Well, glad you're back in town. And I know your mom sure is glad."

"Thanks," Cade said. What was going on here? Things might look the same in his hometown, but only on the outside. His mother had apparently forgiven his dad, and was she dating? He didn't even want to think about that.

Matt gave him a pat on the shoulder and as he left out the door, Cade couldn't help noticing that he tossed a wink in his mother's direction, which brought color to her cheeks again. He'd started randomly flipping through one of the books his mom had handed him when the door opened again and he heard someone say, "Hello, Paige. Lovely to see you."

Cade jerked his head up at the sound of the too-familiar voice. Standing next to him at the counter was a broad-shouldered, silver-haired man. His father.

"Oh, hello, Elliot," his mother said cheerily. "We were just talking about you."

"I hope with sympathy," Elliot said. "Or at least a sense of humor."

"Neither," Cade said. "Just Mom being her usual kind and forgiving self."

"That book you ordered came in yesterday," his mother said, sending Cade a warning look that he interpreted as *try to be civil*. "I'll run back and get it."

His father stood there, scrutinizing him closely. Cade

had the sense that he was looking into a mirror at an image of himself years into the future. The same thick hair, his father's cut closely and tamed; the same thick brows, the same defined jawline, stubborn and unyielding. Yep, they were both definitely cut from the same cloth.

"You're looking well," his father said quietly.

Cade's first reaction was to move a step closer to the counter so that he blocked his father's view of Ava. As if that would protect her from this man who had wreaked so much pain and havoc on their family. He leveled his breathing as he decided his next move. His father looked fit and trim, all evidence of bloat or belly gone. He was dressed in a button-down shirt and dress pants, his blue eyes as bright as ever. The ravages of years of alcohol abuse seemed confined to creases around his eyes and mouth, which in his case was a look he wore well.

"Your mother tells me you're teaching at Glenn," his father said, trying again to engage him.

"Yes. Just started." He couldn't bring himself to make pleasant conversation. He told himself he was no longer the desperate adolescent boy begging for his father's love and attention. Elliot had failed horribly as a father, and Cade was not obligated to continue a relationship that brought him only disappointment and sorrow.

"I'd hoped you'd have another book out by now."

Anger made the blood whoosh in his ears. "Why would that even matter to you, Elliot?" His father had ravaged his book in the press and privately berated Cade for what he'd assumed was a depressing ending contrived to please the literary crowd. When Cade had finally done something his father had never managed to do—write a novel—his father's response had been that it hadn't been good enough. But then, nothing with their relationship ever was.

Cade braced for judgment. A critique, which Elliot did so well. Yet his father was uncharacteristically silent.

"Of course it matters to me. You're my son."

Cade controlled a snort, but just barely. Fortunately his mother walked out of the back room just then. "Here you go," she said, handing Elliot a brown envelope and placing another book on Cade's pile. "You're both all set." She looked nervously from one to the other.

"Thank you, Paige," his father said, the perfect gentleman.

Cade gathered up his books. His father was still staring at him with a shrewd expression. "Nice seeing you, Caden," he said.

"Take care, Elliot," Cade said. It was the most he could bring himself to say. "See you soon, Mom. Thanks for the books."

"I'm thinking dinner one day this weekend," she called after Cade. "With your sister. Check your schedule, okay?"

Cade nodded and turned to get Ava, but even though he'd left the counter, he could still see his father's face in front of him, and the look in his eyes. Maybe it was his imagination, or his brain playing tricks. But it was an expression he knew only too well. A longing. Except it was too late for that. Way too late.

Chapter 4

♥

It had been Gabby's dad's idea to head to the family's lake house that weekend for the Langdons' traditional Sunday dinner. The A-frame structure with cedar siding had been in their family for years, and it was just a short ferry ride away from Angel Falls. They gathered there often in the summer to eat, swim, and fish off her dad's small pontoon boat. In the evenings, there were fires near the lake and board games where they sat around the fireplace talking late into the night.

Some people loved the ocean, but for Gabby, nothing could compare to her time spent at the wooded retreat. Her earliest memories, from when she was seven or eight, were those of her mother, lying out on the dock while her father patiently tried to teach Gabby to fish (a lost cause, as she could never bear killing the worms). Sara usually had her nose in a book and Rafe would often try to one-up Gabby by catching as many fish as he could reel in. Evie, who was four years older than Sara and already a teenager, would be off by herself at the end of the dock having deep conversations with her best friend and loudly wishing she were away from her pesky younger siblings. One day Gabby remembered her mother setting down a dog-eared paperback, pulling her close and kissing her on the head, then reading one of Gabby's own books to her out loud.

Gabby remembered her mother's inflection as she read, how she always seemed to make everything more exciting, more scary, more...everything.

And years later, she remembered Rachel walking her out to this very same dock, telling her that she was so, so sorry about her mother, and how she would try her best not to replace her, but she wanted to be her friend and someone who would always have Gabby's back.

Sara had had more difficulty accepting Rachel into the empty spot her mother had left behind, but Gabby was hungry for a mother's love and affection, and she and Rachel had always had an understanding. But she missed the mother she barely got to know, and the very essence of her seemed bottled up in this old house.

If she stood on the dock and closed her eyes and breathed in the cool lake air, she could almost feel her mom here with them.

Tonight, rain had driven them inside, and her dad had brought out Pictionary. Everyone was playing except Evie's kids; Michael, who was three, and Julia, five, sat with crayons and coloring books by the fire. They didn't follow the rules perfectly, especially with Nonna tending to help both teams at random, but it was always a lot of fun.

Rachel teamed up with Evie and her husband, Joe, on one team, along with Sara and her husband, Colton.

Gabby was teamed up with Nonna, her dad, Rafe, and Kaitlyn. Kaitlyn, who owned the Bean, the coffee shop downtown, was good friends with Sara and Gabby. And lately, she'd been hanging around a lot with Rafe.

Except everyone but Rafe knew that Kaitlyn had a long-standing crush on him. Gabby's heart hurt for both of them—Kaitlyn, silently begging to be let in; and Rafe, still so wounded from the death of his long-time girlfriend when he was twenty-one that he was too closed off to even see it.

"Who wants coffee?" Kaitlyn asked, tucking a strand of blond hair behind her ear.

"Coffee sounds good," Rafe said, smiling a guileless smile, "but what's for supper?"

"Rafe, you just ate three pieces of lasagna," Kaitlyn said.

"I thought that was an appetizer," Rafe responded, patting his rock-hard stomach as he reclined on the couch.

"Ha ha," Gabby said. "I know this will excite you… we have strawberry shortcake too." She turned to her grandmother, who was sitting next to her on the couch. "We made it from scratch, didn't we, Nonnie?"

"And the whipped cream too," Nonna added.

"Oh, that sounds delicious," Evie said. "I've been so busy getting ready for the pottery exhibition that dinner's been hit or miss all week. The lasagna was amazing, by the way."

"Thank you," Rachel said. "I'm sorry things have

been hectic, but I'm so excited that you've started making pottery again. I was wondering if I could display a few of your pieces in my shop. I think it would be fun, and it might bring you some business." Part of the draw of Rachel's high-end antiques store was that she often showcased the work of local artists.

"Thanks, Rach," Evie said. "That'd be great. I'll make a few pieces this week."

"Evangeline," Joe said, a concerned look on his face, "aren't you busy enough for right now? Do you think you should just get through this exhibition before you take on more work?" Hearing Joe call Evie by her full name, accompanied by an edge in his usually very calm voice, caused Gabby to look from one to the other.

"Things *have* been a little hectic lately," Evie said in a placating voice.

"Yes, they *have* been," Joe said, punctuating that with a lift of his brows.

Gabby exchanged glances with Sara. Just fifteen months older than she was, Sara was her closest sibling in age and in sharing confidences. Her expression told Gabby she'd noticed the tension too. Evie had been thrilled to go back to work after some years home with the kids, but it looked like that major life change wasn't going quite as smoothly as she had let on.

"Okay, here we go," Rafe said. He nodded at Kaitlyn. "Katie, tip the hourglass. Everybody look up here." He drew something quickly on a legal pad and then rotated it so everyone could see. On the paper was a stick figure holding something long and tubular that coiled like a snake to the ground.

"A hose?" Kaitlyn said with a puzzled look. "You drew a hose?"

"Is it an Italian sausage?" Nonna asked, studying it carefully. "Or private parts? It looks like private parts." She dropped her voice and fake-whispered in Gabby's ear, "A very long one." Gabby bit the insides of her cheeks so she wouldn't laugh.

"Gabby, any ideas?" her dad asked.

"Hose, sausage, private parts...what's left?" Gabby said. "I can't even imagine."

"Time's up," Kaitlyn said, holding up the hourglass.

"Thank goodness," Nonna said.

"Okay, so what was it?" Rachel asked.

Rafe showed the card. "Equipment." He said it in a tone that indicated he thought someone should've surely figured that out.

Everyone groaned. "Equipment? What kind of equipment?" Sara asked with a fake-horrified expression on her face.

"Wait a minute. Is that *your* equipment?" Colton said. "If so, I think that picture's grossly exaggerated."

"Well, it's certainly not *yours*, Colty," Rafe said.

"Okay, boys," Sara warned.

"Let's do another one," Nonna said, clapping her hands.

"Good idea," Rachel said, picking up a card and drawing something on the legal pad.

"A mop. That's a mop!" Joe guessed.

"Yes. Correct," Rachel said, pointing excitedly at Joe. "Good job."

"I've been using one more often now, so it's more familiar to me," Joe said.

"Hey, my place needs to be cleaned. Feel free to bring it over sometime," Rafe said.

Evie narrowed her eyes at her husband. "I'm glad you finally learned what a mop is, sweetheart," she said in an overly pleasant voice. "Next week I'll teach you about Swiffers."

"Okay everyone, time for dessert," Gabby said quickly. "Kaitlyn, want to start the coffee?"

Gabby got up and began plating the shortcake, hoping that dessert would be enough to soothe whatever tensions were brewing. She and Kaitlyn served, and everyone was finally digging in to the shortcake with Nonna's perfectly stiff whipped cream and fresh strawberries when her dad spoke. "So, honey, Sara tells me you're taking a class at the college."

Gabby shot Sara a murderous look, but Sara merely shrugged. "I didn't think you'd mind that I told. We all know about Mom's manuscript and how excited you are about her writing."

Gabby let out a breath. It was only a matter of time before the entire family found out. "Well, actually, I'm really excited about the class," she said. "It's being taught by Cade Marshall, Paige's son. He's the one who wrote *Girl on the Edge*."

"Yes, he's one of *those*," Nonna said.

"One of those what?" Gabby asked.

"You know. Someone who writes *girl* books."

"What's a '*girl* book'?" Rafe asked. "That sounds dirty."

Kaitlyn smacked his arm. "It's not always about sex, Rafe," she said. She frowned at Rafe, but her eyes held that same soft look she always seemed unable to disguise in his presence.

"Sorry," he said with a grin.

"How do you know about *girl* books, Nonna?" Gabby asked. Nonna had always been a fierce reader, but since her dementia diagnosis, she hadn't been able to maintain the concentration to read a book.

"*Gone Girl*," Nonna said. "I just saw the movie."

Rachel laughed. "*The Girl on the Train*."

"*The Girl with the Dragon Tattoo*," Colton said.

"'Uptown Girl,'" Rafe said. "'Brown Eyed Girl,' 'Big Girls Don't Cry.'"

Kaitlyn rolled her eyes.

"What?" Rafe said. "Don't songs count?

"Books, Rafe," Kaitlyn said. "We're talking about popular books."

"Okay then, how about *The Woman in Cabin 10*?" Rafe asked.

"How do you know about that book?" Kaitlyn asked.

"I read it," he said simply. "Randy had it at the station."

"Nice," Colton said, slapping him on the back. "I always knew you were literate."

Kaitlyn looked a little surprised at Rafe's answer, and she cracked a smile. Rafe smiled back. For a moment it seemed like those two weren't paying much attention to anyone else in the room.

"If Cade Marshall writes bestsellers, what's he doing teaching writing classes?" Gabby's father asked.

"He's a professor, Dad. I guess he teaches and writes," Gabby said. When he wasn't standing around being such a hottie.

Oh my gosh. Gabby startled. She didn't say that out loud, did she?

"Honey," her dad said, setting his dessert plate down on the coffee table, "I know you've been fascinated with that box of your mom's writing that you found, but you just made partner. That class seems like a lot on top of work."

The class meant so much more to Gabby than, as her father believed, a way of trying to understand her mom more. It was about trying to understand herself in ways she couldn't even fully fathom. And yes, she was always looking for a connection with her mother, but she didn't even know how to begin to put all of that into words. "Don't worry about me, Dad. I've got the time."

"Well, all right, but this isn't like flower arranging or cake decorating or any of those other things you've signed up for."

Gabby tried not to wince. In her father's eyes, she'd always be that lost kid, always searching for something more.

"Gabby's always been a writer," Rachel said. "I say go for it. Who knows, maybe *you'll* be the one to write the next big *girl* book."

As Gabby got up to take her turn, she smiled at Rachel, who really did tend to have her back. She wanted to see herself as one day writing a bestselling book. But she couldn't help thinking that the title would be *Girl Confused.*

* * *

What a week, Cade thought, as he pulled up to the babysitter's house at three the next Friday to fetch Ava. As soon as he opened the door to the small yellow ranch, which was sticky with fingerprints, his father's intuition prickled at the back of his neck.

Despite Mrs. Arcadian, the babysitter, being recommended by one of his colleagues, he was less than thrilled with the arrangement, because chaos seemed to run rampant whenever he dropped by. Ava had been unhappy this whole first week, despite all his encouragement that a brand-new day care would be wonderful once she got used to it.

Ava was a resilient child. She'd adapted surprisingly well to her mother leaving when she was one. Emerson tended to flit in and out of her life at random, something that gave Cade ulcers and which he would never be able to understand.

He'd seen a counselor regularly since the divorce to help him keep his own head straight and be able to say and do the right things for Ava. He wanted to make sure Ava understood that he would always, always be there for her. Despite her mother's capriciousness, Ava was a happy, sweet, loving child, and Cade would do anything in his power to keep her that way.

Cade realized that he himself was a worrier about practically everything as far as his daughter was concerned and constantly reminded himself to relax, to not demand perfection. But Mrs. Arcadian was a bit too laid-back as far as supervision went and appeared, even in his limited interactions with her, to be too strict with other matters. She didn't seem to have time to really work with Ava on things like being kind, apologizing, and saying thank you. Plus, he couldn't stand the sticky doors.

He missed their old babysitter, Mrs. Clapstone, a saintly woman with snow-white hair who used to wash and iron the altar cloths at her church every week. She'd been the closest thing to an honest-to-goodness grandma Ava had had in Michigan, where they'd lived before returning to Angel Falls. Mrs. Clapstone had been a stable influence at a very unstable time. Hell, he'd offered to relocate the woman, but she had her own grandkids and wouldn't dream of it.

Being a single dad was terrifying at times, but he was getting better at it. He could make mac and cheese with his eyes closed, and while his braiding technique pretty much sucked, it was passable. Enough.

"That boy bit me!" Ava said, running to the front door and twining herself around his leg, pointing an accusing finger at a tow-headed boy with innocent blue eyes whom he recognized as his colleague Paula's son. The room was noisy with the sounds of a baby crying. An infant, surely less than a year old, was crawling across the carpet, a trail of bright green snot snaking under his nose. Two toddler boys were pushing one another. Mrs. Arcadian, a stout woman of around forty, ran after the baby and scooped him up, balancing him on her hip, as she ran after the biter in question, who had bolted behind the couch. The baby, who was facing outward, coughed in Cade's direction.

Instinctively, he nudged Ava behind his knee, out of the line of fire.

"Hi, Mrs. Arcadian," he said to the visibly frazzled woman.

She barely managed a nod. "Brayden, did you bite Ava?" the woman asked. To her credit, she sounded appalled.

"No!" Brayden said emphatically. "I did not bite her."

"Yes, he did, Daddy," Ava said, patting Cade on the thigh. "But don't worry, I bited him right back."

Cade felt his face flame. As she bent to lift up Ava's pants leg, he saw the round imprint of a mouth with tiny pinpricks, the outlines of sharp teeth, sunk into his daughter's tiny calf.

Oh, shit. It certainly didn't look like a life-threatening injury, but what did he know? Didn't bites get infected? He remembered seeing a picture of a horrible, red, swollen limb in freshman biology, which caused him to know beyond a doubt he wasn't cut out for medicine, as his sister was. Or maybe there was cause to worry about whatever germs Brayden had just inoculated into Ava's bloodstream? Regardless, it was an automatic doctor's visit. Something else he'd have to squeeze into his already over-packed to-do list today. There were not enough hours.

At the same time, Brayden held out his arm. Similar marks were visible on his forearm.

Ava was not lying. She'd sunk her teeth right into Brayden too. Should Cade be proud of that? Because he was, a little. That was the thing about being a parent. It made you cross moral boundaries you'd never think of crossing before.

"These kids are biting each other, and no one noticed?" Cade worked hard to control his tone—and his temper.

"Well, I am short on help today, Professor. And sometimes it's good for the children to work out their own battles, you know what I mean?"

Cade sighed. Biting, strike one. What she'd just said, strike two. *Please, God, he prayed. Don't let there be a strike three.* He really needed this day care to work out. He understood it wasn't perfect but he had no good alternatives. "No, I don't know what you mean. Biting is…harmful." He stooped down to the kids' level. "Brayden and Ava, we never bite anyone. Biting is mean and can hurt people."

"I can punish them both tomorrow," Mrs. Arcadian said. She wagged a finger at the children. "No snacks for you two tomorrow."

Oh, hell. Strike three. Caden stood. "Mrs. Arcadian, it's—it's just wrong to withhold snacks from children. Ava won't be back tomorrow. And I work with Brayden's mom. Rest assured I'll be talking about this with her as well."

He rubbed Brayden on the head. The boy looked as if he were about to cry. "It's okay, buddy. We all make mistakes." He was about to turn to his daughter and tell her to say she was sorry when she bolted out from behind his leg and hugged Brayden tightly. "It's okay, Bwayden. I know you didn't mean to hurt me and I'm sorry I hurt you."

She looked up with enormous blue eyes that reminded him of...himself. Where she'd acquired the compassion he saw there was anyone's guess.

"There, Daddy, see? All better now. Let's go home now, 'kay?"

"It's all better now," Mrs. Arcadian echoed. "You come back tomorrow, Professor, all right? Everything's fine. The kids worked it out."

God, he needed to say yes. *Say yes*, he commanded himself. "I'm sorry, Mrs. Arcadian." Looking from the tearful little boy to the frowning babysitter, he scooped Ava up, opened the sticky door, and left.

He had no babysitter and three classes to teach tomorrow. And no clue where he would even find another one, let alone find one *fast*.

Chapter 5

♥

I'm hungry," Ava said in the doctor's office examination room, stopping her ceaseless state of motion long enough to lean her elbows on Cade's knee, imploring him with eyes the color of a cloudless summer sky.

Something inside him melted at her innocence, her trusting nature, her sweetness. He would protect all of that to his grave. Cade didn't ever want to let Ava down, even though he felt like he did every single day.

"Why do I haveta go to the doctor?" she asked.

Because *bite marks*. "Because we're going to have Aunt Beth check your leg and make sure everything's okay." Cade had no idea what bite marks meant from a medical standpoint but it couldn't be good, and he wasn't taking any chances. He'd been nervous enough to rush right over despite knowing Ava hadn't eaten much lunch. Now it was nearing three thirty, and this was the third time she'd mentioned food during their fifteen-minute wait.

For the entire time, he'd been staring at a life-sized

painting on the wall of a ballerina in a pink tutu, waving a trail of sparkly stars with her hands. It had captured Ava's attention, and she'd been trying to pose the same way.

There was something about the painting besides the fact that it was done in bold, bright colors, pinks and purples and deep blues, with a trail of glitter around the little ballerina as she twirled. The artist had captured the face of the child dancing—an expression of pure joy that instantly made him feel a little melancholy. There was a time in his life not long ago when he'd felt that joy—writing had brought it. He might not be able to feel that freedom of spirit anymore, but he'd be damned if he'd let Emerson take it away from their daughter.

At last, the door opened. "Hi, big brother," his sister said as she walked into the exam room. She immediately stooped to Ava's level. "And I see Tiny Dancer is here."

"I'm not Tiny Dancer," Ava said, a big grin spreading across her face. "I'm big dancer! And I wanna be a ballerina."

"Tell your daddy you want dance lessons," Beth said as she picked Ava up and looked at Cade. "You heard my princess niece."

Cade had no problem with that, once things settled down. But first, the bite marks. "Thanks for squeezing us in. Some kid at day care bit Ava on the leg."

"Did you bite him back?" Beth asked, ignoring Cade's formidable frown.

"Yes!" Ava said, running her hand down Beth's long ponytail. "You have pretty hair, Aunt Beth."

"So do you, Sugar Muffin," Beth said, kissing Ava on the forehead.

Ava laughed. "I'm not a sugar muffin."

"We don't bite back, Ava," Cade said, trying to keep things on track. He shot his sister a glare. "Is that how they're training doctors now, an eye for an eye?"

"No, but maybe growing up with our cutthroat critic of a father had something to do with that."

Cade gave her a don't-even-go-there glower.

"I hope you don't look at your students like that. You probably scare the living daylights out of them."

"And I hope you don't give patients advice like that, being new here and all."

Beth had gotten hired into the town's family practice as a pediatrician when Walter Langdon, the founding partner, started to decrease his hours.

Walter Langdon—Gabby's father. Who was, technically, his sister's boss. Another reason to stay away from the student who pushed all his buttons.

Cade focused on his sister, whom he'd once been very close to. But in the past few years, embarrassed from the bad publicity and hurting from the death of his marriage, he'd withdrawn instead of reaching out. He wanted to try and fix that with Beth. "Look, I really appreciate your fitting us in and letting us bypass the waiting room. Can you just take a look at the bite?"

"Sure can," Beth said, smiling broadly at her niece. "Ava, sweetheart, I'm so glad you live closer to Auntie Beth now. We can do fun things together. Like torture your dad."

"I like to torture Daddy," Ava said with a gleam in her eye.

Cade couldn't help smiling. "Yes, you both are good at it too."

As Beth perused the wound, Cade stood behind her shoulder. "Is it bad? Hepatitis? Infection? Rabies?"

"Yes, I think we need to do an amputation." She rolled her eyes at her brother. "Geez, you're worse than Mom."

"What's ampanation?" Ava asked.

"It means we just have to wash it off, sweetheart," Beth said, and proceeded to do so with an antiseptic cloth. "There's no broken skin," she said to Cade. "She'll be fine." To Ava, she said, "You can do ballet anytime you want."

"Yay," Ava said.

"There's a dance studio right downtown, you know that, don't you?" She dropped her voice. "Lots of cute mommies go there too."

"Not interested," Cade said quickly. "In the mommies. The dance lessons, we'll consider."

"Time for McDonald's, Daddy," Ava said.

"McDonald's is fine once in a while but only as a special treat," Beth said. Then to Cade, "You can cook, can't you?"

"Of course I can cook. It's just been a hard week." He didn't want to belabor the fact that his house was still mostly unpacked, that he'd added two classes on last-minute notice because of Amira's pregnancy emergency, and that he no longer had a day care, a situation he decided not to speak of in front of Ava.

"Don't take offense, I'm just checking. Maybe you can come over next weekend for dinner. I can invite Mom. And Dad."

One look at her told him she was teasing about his parents being together in the same room, even if his mother didn't seem to mind.

"Okay," Beth said, clearly taking in his scowl. "How about just Mom? She'd love seeing Ava, and I cook a mean mac and cheese. And I just got a grill—I was thinking you could help me set it up." Beth turned to Ava. "Want to come to my house for dinner this weekend? We could make ice cream sundaes."

Ava perked up and nodded.

"I'll bring the ice cream," he said. "Thanks for the invite."

Ava was tugging on his pants leg. "C'mon, Daddy, time for a Happy Meal."

"Bye, Squirt," Beth said. "See ya soon, 'kay?" She did a fist bump with Ava. "I'm glad you're back," she said to Cade, giving him a sudden hug. "Mostly because Mom will split her attention trying to find both of us a spouse. And you know, you have support here. You don't have to do everything all on your own."

"Yeah yeah," he said, smiling. But then he thought of something as Beth held out a sticker box, which Ava trolled through with great enthusiasm. He reminded her to only take one, then lowered his voice to speak just to Beth. "Actually, I do have a favor. Do you know of a day care that might take Ava on short notice? Like, tomorrow?"

"I can call a few of my patients' moms. Let me get back to you."

"Thanks. Hey"—he tilted his head toward the wall—"the painting's great. Did a local artist do it?"

"You'll never believe it. The person who painted this isn't an artist at all. Sara Langdon got her dad to agree to redo the office décor before they hired me, and her sister did it. She's actually a lawyer. Someday when no patients are here, I'll show you all the patient rooms. She did murals in every one of them, and they're all different."

Whoa. Wait a minute. His muddled brain put together the pieces. *Gabby painted it.* The jubilant, carefree expression on the child's face in the painting hit him again in the gut.

The painting *felt* like her. The determined look on the dancer's face, the brightness, the love of dancing. He didn't know Gabby at all, but the vibrancy, the life and passion, just seemed to . . . fit.

Beth walked them past the billing desk, where a kindly-looking, gray-haired woman immediately started chatting with Ava.

"Why, Cade Marshall," the woman said. "I haven't seen you since you were eighteen and left for college. It's great to have you back."

"Thanks, Mrs. Hendricks," he said. She'd worked in the office since Cade was little and Dr. Langdon was the only physician in town. He'd also played baseball with one of her sons. "How's Jerry?"

"Two kids and a third on the way. And call me Leonore."

"Let me pay for the visit," Cade said to his sister.

"You're family, and this wasn't even a real visit."

"I insist."

His sister dug her heels in. "Cade, you big lug. Remember when you drove an hour to get me when my date let me out in the middle of the night on Route 77? Remember when you helped me rent a UHaul and load up all of my junk and moved me into my college dorm when mom had that big conference?" She held him by his arms and shook him a little. "Let someone do something for you for once. I'm just so damn glad you're close by again." She gave him a squeeze. "Besides, I know you can fix anything, so now that you're in town, I'll be taking total advantage of you."

Cade hugged her back. "Okay, fine."

She rolled her eyes. His sister wanted to reconnect. Be close again. He got what she was saying. He had to learn to let people in again.

"See you soon, Ava," Beth said as she stood waving from the doorway. "Can't wait."

"Can't wait," Cade said, giving his sister a wave as Ava pulled him toward the door.

* * *

The first sign that Ava's mood was fading fast was when she'd started rubbing her eyes the second they left Beth's office. Cade picked her up and carried her the rest of the way to the car. As he buckled her in, he kissed her forehead.

"You've been a real trooper, honey. I know you've had a long day."

"Hungry, Daddy. I want chicken nuggets. And a toy."

At this point, he felt like he could eat the cardboard on the Happy Meal box himself. "Coming right up."

He drove down the main thoroughfare, away from the quaint one-of-a-kind shops, another couple of miles to the edge of town, where the McDonald's was secretly tucked. As he pulled into the drive-through line, he reached in the car door for his wallet.

Ava was starting to whine. "Brayden bited me. And Mrs. Awcadian is mean. I'm hungry! I miss Mrs. Clapstone. Why can't she come and babysit me? I wanna see Grammie. And I want a puppy."

Great. Only three more cars before him in the line. Cade was trying to come up with something comforting to say when he realized his wallet wasn't in the door. A growing sense of dread sank into his stomach as he struggled to put together the pieces of his afternoon. Wait—he remembered tucking the wallet into his book bag before he left the office. He whipped his head around, praying he'd dumped his bag into the backseat like he usually did, but he already knew the answer—in his rush to be on time to get Ava, he'd left the bag on his desk chair.

Fighting a mild sense of panic, he started scrabbling for change. He searched his jeans pockets, the glove box, and the compartment between the seats. He even flipped up the floor mats but couldn't come up with more than fifty cents. There was a box of animal crackers on the floor, which he picked up and shook. Dammit to hell, why had he eaten the three remaining ones on his way to the day care anyway?

"What's wrong, Daddy?" Ava asked, alerted that something was not quite right. "What are you looking for?"

"Daddy forgot his wallet at work, so we might have to stop and get it because I don't have any money." With that, she started to cry. Oh God. In a last-ditch move of desperation, he slid his hand between the back of his seat and the bottom. His fingers closed over a flat, rectangular card—maybe his bank card, which he'd looked all over for last week. He pulled it out, only to find it was his new campus ID card instead.

Cade pulled away from the drive-through line, which increased Ava's desperation. "I want McDonald's now!" she cried. "Why can't I have it *now*?"

An idea suddenly occurred to him. If he walked into the bank, which was half the distance to his office, he might be able to withdraw some money using his campus ID. Angel Falls was a friendly town, and surely someone working in the bank would know him. And as a last resort, everyone in town knew his mom.

"Daddy's just got to stop at the bank for some money. It'll be so quick, I promise." Feeling like the worst dad in the world, he exited the McDonald's parking lot and drove back to town, while Ava's crying started to take on a pattern of gasping inhalations and loud, long exhalations. He pulled into a diagonal parking spot right in front of the bank, which was located in the center of the town between the hardware store and the florist's, undid Ava's car seat, and picked her up, rubbing her back a little to calm her.

"Just a few minutes more, honey, okay?" he said. But picking her up didn't help, as she was at the end of her rope. She was sobbing now, throwing her head back and kicking him in the thighs. Her sobs turned into screams, and her face turned radish red, one braid completely undone.

In the bank lobby, Ava's cries seemed to echo off of the high ceilings and old marble tiles on the walls and floor. He got in the nearest line, but the woman in front of him turned to stare, sending him a nasty look, like this was all his fault. Which, he had to agree, it sort of was.

Oh, shit. His pride all but gone, he opened his mouth to beg the woman to let him go next, but just then she said, "Children should be left at home when they're tired like that."

He stared incredulously at the awful woman and bit down hard on the insides of his cheeks just in case he was tempted to say what was really on his mind. "Just a few more minutes, baby," he said, rubbing the back of her head, a move that ordinarily would have soothed her. "Please don't cry."

"Daddy, I wanna go home!" she said between raspy breaths.

He turned to the woman in front of him and sucked up his pride. "Excuse me, ma'am, but would it be all right to go in front of you? My daughter is a little cranky, and all I have to do is—"

The woman ignored him. Or maybe she did say something. How could he tell with Ava screaming in his ear? In one final insult, Ava somehow made her body go limp, wanting to be let down. Then the kicking started up again, harder this time, and fearful of her aim, he complied.

"Just another minute, sweetheart," he said, but the screaming was so loud he was certain she couldn't hear. He should just drive her home and pull out the PB and J.

Suddenly it was his turn. "I'm sorry, sir," the teller said. "We can't accept a college ID as a primary form of identification."

Cade knew when to accept defeat. He thanked her, scooped Ava up, and exited the bank. As soon as he got outside, Ava did the limp thing again. Then the kicking started up, harder this time. He had no choice but to let go, and this time when she hit ground, she dropped and lay down in the middle of the sidewalk. He tried grabbing her arm, but it was dead weight. People walked by staring, some sympathetic, one man covering his ears. Cade had just bent down to pick Ava up again and head for his truck when a woman on an old-fashioned red bike with a basket on the front came pedaling down the sidewalk. How he even noticed anything in the middle of this crisis he wasn't sure. It wasn't so much because of the antique bike, which was unique, but because of her hair—curly, kind of wild, one-of-a-kind hair. *Gabby.* How was it that this woman always seemed to see him at his worst?

He found himself hoping she wouldn't recognize him and just pass by like everyone else, but she hopped off the bike, kicked down the stand, and headed toward them. She took a quick glance at Ava, who was now sitting on the ground at his feet and crying so hard she was making little *he-he-he* noises accompanied by her chest shaking every time she breathed in.

Gabby sized up the awful situation. She was wearing a gray sweatshirt and jeans, nothing fancy, but something shot through him like a fresh breeze blowing from the ocean. A clean breeze, blowing away all the bullshit of his life.

The sensation only lasted an instant. It was a wish, a fantasy—surely the result of a desperate situation. But for that one instant, it almost made him believe in miracles.

"Hi, Professor," she said with a concerned look, just as he'd managed to peel his daughter off the cement.

Ava was oblivious to everything and was now pounding her forehead into his shoulder. He inserted his hand over his shoulder to keep her from knocking herself out.

"What's her name?" Gabby asked. At least he thought that was what he heard.

"Ava. Her name is Ava."

"Ava, guess what?" Gabby said. "I have chicken nuggets. Want one?"

What the—she had chicken nuggets? Cade's entire body froze. So did Ava's. At first he thought she'd stopped breathing because the steady stream of gasping hiccups had simply...stopped. But no—the kid was just as shocked as he was.

Gabby looked up at him with guileless brown eyes the color of rich black coffee. "May I give her one?"

"Sure," he said incredulously. *Give her two. Or ten. Whatever it takes.* "Yes. Of course. Thank you." His daughter was calming down, though she had tears streaking down her face and her shoulders were still heaving.

"You don't think she'll choke on that, do you?" Cade asked.

Gabby smiled at him. Sort of a you-silly-man kind of smile. She laid her hand on Ava's forehead and pushed the girl's damp hair back. That tiny gesture of compassion did something to him. Thawed a layer of ice around his heart. Who would be compassionate to someone else's screaming, sweaty, melting-down kid? Certainly not anyone in the damn bank, that was for sure.

His daughter had gone silent, chicken nugget at her lips. The scent of salt and fried coating wafted up to his nostrils, and his stomach grumbled. "Chew slow, okay?" he said.

Ava bit into the nugget, and oh, the resulting silence was joyous. Cade, in a sneak-attack move, walked over to his truck, and quickly buckled her into her car seat, which was a lot easier now that she had muscle tone.

"Poor thing," Gabby said in a soothing voice over his shoulder. "You must be starving. Your daddy forget to feed you today or something?"

Cade straightened in time to see Gabby flash a wicked smile. Except it made him smile too. And something else too—her act of kindness made him want to kiss her feet in gratefulness. No, not her feet. Her lovely full lips.

Fortunately he became preoccupied again with the car seat. When he finished, Gabby had just returned from pulling a soft drink out of her bike basket.

"Thanks for helping out," he said. "We were in the McDonald's line when I realized I'd forgotten my wallet. I thought the bank would let me get some cash with my work ID, but..."

"Oh, wow, here." Without hesitation, she reached into her jeans pocket and handed him a twenty. "Hey, sweetie," she said to Ava, holding out her drink. "Want a sip of my Coke?"

Ava nodded vigorously.

"Just a sip," Cade said. All he needed after this was a wired kid running circles around his desk at midnight while he tried to grade papers.

Gabby gave Ava another nugget. The Coke was ice cold and soothing. He nearly grabbed it and took a swig himself.

As if Gabby sensed his hunger, she held out the packet of nuggets. He took one and popped it into his mouth. Which may have been unchivalrous, but hey, desperate times.

"Tell you what," he said, practically swallowing it whole. "I'll borrow your twenty. But I owe you another Happy Meal. Would you like to drive through with us?"

She quirked a gracefully arched brow. "Would it give me more points on my latest paper if I said yes?"

He frowned, which made her laugh. "Just kidding, Professor," she said. "I'd love to drive through. I'm starving." She paused. "Although this is the second time in a week I've saved your butt. This has got to be good for extra credit or something."

Cade laughed, which sort of surprised the hell out of him. After all the trauma and tears, he felt almost giddy. Must've been the hunger. "Is it okay to leave your bike here for a few minutes?"

"No problem." Gabby turned to Ava. "Can I sit next to you?" Ava nodded. Dirty tear tracks ran down her cheeks, her face was flushed, and her braids had come undone. Gabby settled into the seat next to her and buckled her seat belt.

"Can I have more Coke?" Ava asked.

"A little," Gabby said, then lowered her voice. "If you don't tell your dad." In the rearview mirror, Cade caught Gabby's mischievous smile as she held the cup for Ava. For a moment, their gazes held and locked. His daughter took a sip and even said thank you. Gabby took a French fry, gave Ava one, and passed the box up to Cade. He took three fries from the packet.

"Guess you're our chauffeur, Professor."

"What's a chauffeur?" Ava asked.

"When you're really rich, you don't drive your own car, so you have someone who drives you while you relax in the backseat."

He chuckled a little, and that made him think that maybe *he* was the one who'd relaxed, thanks to Gabby. Even without the Incident from Hell that he'd just been through, it had been a long time since he'd really done that. A few minutes later, he approached the drive-through window. "What'll it be, Ms. Langdon?" he asked.

Gabby hesitated. "Call me Gabby. And . . . I'm thinking."

He was thinking too. That when she smiled, her entire face seemed to light up. She had warm, sparkly brown eyes, and pink, kissable lips, and just looking at her in the mirror sent a warmth coursing through him that had nothing to do with the late August heat. He hadn't been attracted to a woman in a long time—not like this. Except this woman was off-limits—his student—regardless of the fact that she was near his age.

"Can I take your order, please?" a voice said impatiently from the speaker.

He turned and ordered food for him and Ava, including a double cheeseburger for himself.

"Oh, that sounds good," Gabby said, tapping him on the shoulder. "One for me too, please. And a chocolate shake." She paused. "Are you having a shake too?"

Their eyes caught again in the mirror. He couldn't remember the last time he'd eaten a milkshake. But suddenly that sounded too good to pass up. "Yeah. I think I will. Good idea, Gabby." As he finished ordering, he couldn't help thinking that spending time with her was also something too good to pass up, even though there were a million reasons why it was a very bad idea.

* * *

On the way back from the drive-through, Cade stopped to get Gabby's bike, and Gabby watched as he lifted the old, slightly rusty antique and placed it with care in the back of his truck, a move that not only (a) showcased his muscles and his great body, but also (b) made her like him even more, even though she was trying hard not to. His life seemed complicated in ways she couldn't imagine.

But she decided she was going to enjoy the burger, shake, and fries and not think much beyond that, and the pleasure of his company. Because she was finding him, unlike his Heathcliff-ish personality in the classroom, very funny—able to laugh at himself and Ava's meltdown, and he'd already demonstrated that he was able to keep his head together in the midst of all that stress. He had a spontaneous, booming laugh that was…amazing, and seemed to vibrate deep down inside of her. And it was clear he was totally in love with his little daughter, a trait she found very appealing.

From the inside of the car, she learned that the stickers she'd seen that first evening in the parking lot were Disney princesses. More stickers were on Ava's car seat, these being pink hearts and sparkly stars. Gabby couldn't help noticing that Ava herself wore brown leggings and a faded orange T-shirt—an outfit that seemed inconsistent with her sparkle-loving persona. With all Cade had to contend with, probably the last thing on his list was picking out cute clothes for his daughter.

They drove the few blocks to his little rented clapboard house, sandwiched closely in between other unique homes on Elm Street. Gabby knew the area. In town it was called Professors' Row. The quirky old houses displayed a mix of colonial or craftsman or Victorian architecture. As a kid, she'd loved to imagine that they all had faces.

Ava was silent the whole way back, happily scarfing down French fries.

Gabby couldn't help sneaking a couple of surreptitious glances at her enigmatic professor. Strong, set jaw. Thick, wavy dark hair a woman would kill to tangle her fingers in. His muscular forearms on the wheel and his lean body indicated that he worked out regularly, so clearly Professor Hardbody had an athletic side that would put the guys on her Australian Firefighter Pinup Calendar (compliments of Rafe) to shame.

After Cade pulled into his driveway, he helped Ava out of her car seat while Gabby grabbed the bag of burgers. Then she followed them through the side door of the little house.

In the living room, there were still boxes scattered everywhere, many of them filled with books, which reminded her of all the boxes she had waiting for her at her own place. Beside one of the boxes, a row of dolls lay in a semicircle on the floor, covered by a faded yellow flannel blanket.

Ava went to the bathroom, and Cade went after her to make sure she washed her hands. When they returned, Gabby noticed he'd washed the tear streaks off Ava's face. That small thing tugged hard at something deep inside her. Then they all sat in the living room, where Ava sat at a little plastic picnic table. Cade opened a couple of canvas spectator chairs, because his couch was still wrapped in plastic.

"Wow, you've still got a lot of unpacking to do," Gabby said, taking a seat. He handed her a burger wrapped in waxy paper. The smell alone was making her quiver, not to mention the fact that when their hands grazed, she couldn't help but notice he had lovely hands—long-fingered, elegant, competent hands with a few calluses that looked like he did a lot more with them than type on a keyboard.

"I've got a big research presentation coming up that I've been preparing for in my spare time. The unpacking has been a little slow because of that."

Ah yes, she understood all about being busy. "I just moved too—into a little carriage house outside of town.

It belongs to a client of mine who owns a very stately, century-old farmhouse."

"Why outside of town?" he asked.

She shrugged. "Peaceful, quiet, beautiful." She was tempted to mention the fact that she'd been looking for a slightly out-of-the-way place to be able to write but she thought that might sound silly.

"Good inspiration."

Somehow, he'd managed to say what she was thinking anyway. "Yes! Exactly. I hope so."

They ate in silence for a few minutes—and maybe it was just the effect Cade was having on her, but the burger tasted incredible. Ava ate more nuggets and managed to get a glass of milk down before she started rubbing her eyes.

"I think it's bedtime, Half Pint," he said, standing.

Gabby's heart stuttered at the fact that he'd called his daughter Half Pint, just like Laura Ingalls Wilder's Pa. Oh, man. Were fathers sexy? She'd never thought of it before. But this one sure was.

"No, Daddy, *full* pint," Ava said, as Cade lifted her into his arms.

He kissed the top of her head. "Say good night to Ms. Gabby."

"Are you coming back?" the little girl asked, rubbing her eyes.

"I'd love to," Gabby said, taking Ava's hand and kissing it. "Good night, girlfriend."

"I'll be back in a few minutes," Cade said. "Finish your dinner."

Common sense told her it was time to go. But being

here was like being under a spell—an adorable little girl, a mysterious and intriguing single dad, and cheeseburgers—delicious, greasy cheeseburgers. A spell that she didn't want to break. "Of course," she said. "Take your time."

While Cade carried Ava upstairs, Gabby looked around quickly. A fireplace with a white-painted mantel sat in the center of the room, bookshelves on each side. A paned window overlooked a big porch and the street beyond. Down the hall, she'd noticed a study with more bookshelves, but she saw there was a desk already set up in the corner of the living room, perhaps Cade's way of keeping an eye on Ava while he worked? She liked that thought.

Cade's voice behind her made Gabby startle. "I need—she's asking for her special doll."

Gabby set down the photo of Cade and Ava she'd picked up from his desk, heat infusing her face. Perusing the lineup of dolls on the floor nearby, she bent and picked up a very well-loved doll with matted blond hair and big blue eyes.

"This one?" she asked.

"Miss Amelia. The one and only."

When he returned ten minutes later, Gabby had taken a seat and was leafing through a very old edition of *The Great Gatsby*. A card sitting just inside the cover was inscribed, *May you be rich as Gatsby but in the things that count. Love, Dad.*

"That's from the original printing," Cade said as he reentered the room. "It's a first edition."

"It's a beautiful dedication," Gabby said.

Cade shrugged. "My father knows how to write

beautiful sentiments. Much moreso than he knows how to be a father."

Gabby closed the book cover. "I'm sorry."

"No, I'm sorry. It's no secret we're estranged. I didn't mean to mention it."

"That's okay," Gabby said, carefully setting the book back atop a box. But she couldn't help but wonder about Cade's relationship with his father. She knew from Rachel the man was a famous literary critic whose work appeared frequently in the *New York Times*. But according to Rachel, he'd left a lot to be desired as a husband and father. Yet the book inscription she'd just read seemed to be clear evidence that he loved Cade.

"Is Ava asleep?" she asked.

"Went down like a stone," he said. "Thank God."

She noticed how his mouth quirked upward, and his eyes sparkled, both signs of a good sense of humor. She was starting to like this guy way too much, so she stood up. "Thanks for talking me into getting the food. It was delicious."

"Ava thought so too. Two Happy Meal toys—yours and hers—in one day. It didn't end so badly after all. Thanks for saving my butt. And I'm good for the loan." He paused. "Now that you know where I live."

"No problem, Professor." Their gazes collided again, both of them looking uncomfortably away. Gabby felt her cheeks heating again. She busied herself with gathering up the trash.

Gabby had dated enough men to know what attraction was, and oh, lordie, she was definitely feeling it now. And, if her guess was correct, he was too.

He might look like a hunky, overworked single dad but…well, who knew? If she were younger, she might've thrown caution to the wind. But she was thirty, and being in his class mattered more than she could put into words. Mattered too much to screw up.

He took the bag from her. "Please—I can clean up." Something about the slightest smile he wore made her suddenly envision what it would be like to crack open a bottle of wine, sit on his big covered porch listening to the sounds of birds as they chattered their final night song, and watch the moon as it rose over their quiet town.

Who was this man, who seemed kind of uptight and strict in the classroom but seemed so wonderfully vulnerable and human—not to mention sexy—after hours?

"Ava had a tough day," he said. "Someone bit her at day care, and I had to take her to see my sister—at your dad's practice."

"Oh—Beth, right? I've met her. She's nice."

Cade nodded. "Afterward, Ava was tired and starving and I didn't have any snacks in the car. Hence the meltdown."

Gabby stared at him. "Did you say *bit*?"

"Yes. And apparently Ava gave as good as she got."

Gabby couldn't help laughing. "Okay, I just wanted to make sure I heard that right. So did you get the situation straightened out at the day care?"

He shrugged his big shoulders. "I understand kid stuff happens, but I'm not really happy at the way the person in charge handled it. She watches five other kids, and it's not an ideal situation."

"Well, if it doesn't work out for you, I have a good friend who runs a day care on the other side of downtown. My sister's youngest goes there two days a week while she's getting her business off the ground. It's called Happy Daze."

He frowned. "There wouldn't happen to be any immediate openings, would there?"

"Hand me your phone, and I'll punch in the number. My friend's name is Lucy. You're welcome to call. And I'm happy to vouch for Ava if you need me to."

As he handed over his phone she couldn't help but notice the screen displayed a photo of Ava with a big basset hound licking her face. Adorable, dog and child both.

"Thanks," he said, as she returned the phone.

"I saw one of the murals you did at the office—the ballerina. It was really good."

Gabby felt heat rush into her face. "Oh, thanks."

"Do you paint much?" he asked.

She shook her head. "Not really. I did that when I was taking a mural painting class. Sort of as a last-ditch effort to make my job bearable."

"It had a lot of life—of spirit." He sounded like he meant it.

"Thanks. I really enjoyed doing it." Feeling awkward now, she said, "Well, I'd better go get started on my homework." She made a go-get-'em sign with her fist as she headed to the front door.

"Why are you in my class?" he asked as he walked her out.

"I'm in your class because I might want to be a

writer." Just saying that made her pulse accelerate. She braced herself for the judgment she was certain would come.

She was standing opposite him now, and for the first time she realized how tall he was; he had her by at least six inches. And his shoulders—impossibly broad. Strong. Full of lean muscle. She had to focus to hear his next words. "You work as a lawyer?"

"I just made partner at my firm."

"Oh. Well, congratulations. And I look forward to reading your work."

That was it? He wasn't going to chide her, or tell her she was ridiculous, or that the whole thing was too impossible, or what most people might say, *good thing you've got a great day job, LOL*, which was why she'd stopped telling people about wanting to write anyway.

"Did I say something wrong?" Cade said.

"No, you just—made it sound like I didn't say something that came from left field, which is the usual reaction. And why I don't tell many people that I want to be a writer."

"I don't see anything left field about wanting to be a writer."

She laughed. "That's because you defied the odds and made it." He looked a little uncomfortable at that. "You must've had a lot of encouragement growing up."

He thrust his hands into his pockets, which made him look both boyish and very sexy. "Well," he said, "my mom was constantly reading and she owned the bookstore, of course. She taught me to read when I was three. And my dad was in the business too. So when I started to write stories, yes, I got a lot of encouragement."

"My dad equates entering a field as volatile as writing as akin to signing up for an unemployment check. You must have had exceptional talent to succeed like you did."

He laughed. "It's not so much talent as persistence. The ones who succeed are the ones who don't quit."

"I wish I could believe that. Also, easy for you to say."

"No, not so much." He gave her an assessing look, which made her feel even more unnerved. "Everything in life is hard. That's why you've got to spend your working hours doing something you really want to do."

What *did* she really want to do? She wished for the thousandth time she loved helping people create their wills, finding ways to give their money to people and charities where it would do a lot of good.

Anyway, it was time to go, not stand here and fret about her life in front of her hot teacher. "Well, thanks again for dinner, Professor."

She opened the front door and walked out onto the porch. The night was just a little cool, the first sign that the season would soon change. The dark outlines of trees that lined the old street were silhouetted against the deep blue twilight sky.

"Wait a minute," he said, catching her by the elbow, then dropping it suddenly. "I mean—it's dark. I don't want you going home on your bike."

"I'll walk my bike—it'll be fine. This is Angel Falls."

He pulled out his phone. "Let me call you an Uber."

"My parents don't live too far from here. I can leave my bike with them and they can give me a ride home."

"I'd take you home myself if I could. But if you let me call the Uber, I can return your bike in the morning." Then he added, "Please. It's the least I can do."

Something made her give in. Maybe it was the sincerity in those interesting eyes of his that made her say, "Okay. Thank you," and tell him her address.

The next three minutes were awkward. Especially when compared to the easy way they'd conversed earlier. At last, a car turned onto the quiet street, indicating that the Uber was arriving. Gabby moved to cross the porch at the same time he did, and their arms grazed, sending a bevy of tingles up her arm. Oh dear, this was terrible. She hadn't felt this graceless since high school. What was it about this guy that was making her freak out so much?

"Well, thanks, Gabby, for your nuggets—I mean, *the* nuggets. The *chicken* nuggets. And for spotting me a twenty. I promise to pay you back as soon as I get to the bank."

She smiled. "Thanks, Professor. I'll see you in class."

"Night, Gabby," he said, leaning his long body against the door frame.

She ran down the steps before she could think about how nice her name sounded on his lips.

Chapter 6

♥

Gabby woke up after her first night in the carriage house nestled in her thick down comforter atop the mattress on the floor. She was toasty and warm, and sunlight was flooding in from the big window next to her. When she cracked open an eyelid, she saw the branches of a large oak tree right outside her window and a peek of bright green fields and woods beyond. But as consciousness dawned, the reality of a room full of unpacked boxes sent a jolt of reality through her.

A knock on the door jarred her fully awake. She heard her grandmother's voice. "That child always could sleep through an earthquake. Knock louder, Walter."

It suddenly dawned on her: it was Saturday morning, and her family was here to help her move in. She bolted out of bed and ran across the thick, knotty pine floors to the door and opened it. In front of her stood her father, Rachel, Nonna, and Rafe.

"Good morning, family," she said, opening her arms

wide and hugging her dad. "I'm sorry I overslept. I swear I set my alarm. Come in."

Rafe entered first, carrying a rectangular donut box. Rachel carried a drink holder filled with cups of coffee from the Bean. They all piled in and headed for a tiny, whitewashed table next to a window.

"Nice digs," Nonna said, looking around. "But why are there barn doors in here?"

"Because that's the style now," Gabby said, kissing her on the cheek. "Want a donut?" She reached into the box. "Jelly or cream stick?" she asked.

"Raspberry jelly, please," Nonna said definitively, taking a seat. Gabby busied herself placing a donut on a napkin and dumping a creamer into Nonna's coffee.

"Thank you, sweetie. Now you sit and eat," Nonna said.

Gabby went to check her phone, which she swore she'd set an alarm on, and found it to be dead. "I forgot where I packed my charger."

"No need to apologize," Rachel said. "It's Saturday, and you've just finished a long work week."

"When I was young like her, I was on call every third night," her dad said. "No sleeping in."

"Walter, you're a recovering workaholic," Rachel said. "Do you really want to make your daughter feel guilty for sleeping in a little on a Saturday?"

Her dad took a sip of his coffee. "I didn't mean it as an insult. Just that I was never allowed to sleep in."

"You poor thing," Rachel said, smiling at Gabby. Gabby loved that Rachel always knew how to handle her dad's rough edges.

Rafe ruffled her already disastrous hair. "Hey, Gabs. You look beautiful this morning."

"Shut up," she said, biting into a cream stick.

In response, he flexed his biceps. "Hey, I brought the brawn power to move your shit—I mean stuff. And we brought you Mom's desk."

Her anger dissolved. She was grateful Rafe and her father would help assemble her bed, arrange her furniture, and do the heavy lifting on anything she needed. "You brought me Mom's desk? From the attic?"

A scratching sound at the screen door made everyone turn. A little black cat had stretched its lithe body the length of the screen and reached up as if it were reaching for the doorknob. Gabby jumped up and let it in. It ran right in and wound itself around Gabby's legs. She grabbed a paper bowl off the counter and filled it with water. And poured some cat food into another bowl.

"You can't find your phone charger or get dressed, but you have cat food?" Rafe asked.

She shot Rafe another look. Of all her siblings, she and Rafe had always fought the most passionately, yet they seemed to understand each other just as fiercely too.

Or at least it used to be like that. These past few years, Rafe didn't seem to really open up to anybody, despite their best efforts.

"I bought some on the way home from work yesterday, okay?" Gabby said. "She's been hanging around every evening this week when I was here cleaning and hauling over a few boxes. Meet Midnight. My new cat."

"Maybe you should call her Twilight. Or Eleven

O'Clock," Rafe said, examining one white paw as the cat rubbed affectionately against his calf. "She's a little odd looking."

"So are you, and we kept you," Gabby shot back.

"Honestly, you two," Rachel said. "I sometimes feel like you're back to being teenagers again."

"You hurt her feelings, Rafe," Gabby said, bending down to stroke the cat. "She's a beauty."

"She is a beauty," Nonna said, stooping over to stroke the cat's back. "I used to have a black cat when you kids were small."

"What was its name again?" Rafe asked. "Hershey?"

"No," Gabby said, "that was the little mini pinshcer we found that one time."

"Coco," Nonna said quickly—and accurately. Amazing how she could remember things so precisely from many years ago yet forget the simplest things from five minutes ago.

"This place is beautiful," Rachel said, looking around with her usual discriminating taste at the exposed brick walls, the big windows, and the cute little kitchen.

"I've got the perfect place for Mom's desk." Gabby pointed to a little alcove with a window that overlooked rolling hills of pastureland surrounded by a white fence and forest and a little lake in the distance.

"What a beautiful view to inspire you," Rachel said.

"Yeah," Rafe said, peeking out the window. "And here comes something else inspiring for Gabby. Looks like he's about six two, thick, wavy hair, tall, dark, and handsome..."

"Ha ha. Very funny."

Then a knock sounded at the door.

Gabby looked at Rafe. "Not joking," he said smugly.

Panic set in. Gabby told herself, *No, it couldn't be*—and yet somehow, she knew in her heart it was. She ran to the window and pushed aside the curtain. Cade was standing on the tiny front porch. She dragged her fingers through her tangled hair, which would take a good shower and a heavy hand to tame. "I can't open the door looking like this!"

"Why not?" Nonna asked. "Is it somebody special?"

"It must be," Rafe said. "Because Gabby wouldn't comb her hair for just anyone."

Gabby shot him a glare.

"Go change," Rafe said. "We'll get it."

Rafe, although annoying, usually came through when she needed him. Gabby ran to the bedroom area and started digging through a suitcase of clothes. She'd finally found a pair of undies and was rummaging for her jeans when she heard the door open and Nonna say, "Oh my, you *are* a hottie."

"Hi. I'm Cade," a familiar deep voice said. "I'm looking for Gabby Langdon."

After uttering a curse under her breath that only Rafe heard, based on his chuckle and the fact that he was standing nearest to her, Gabby turned to see Cade's tall form gracing her doorway. He was wearing a T-shirt and jeans and had one hand on her bike as he bent to pet the cat with his other hand. The rolling fields and the lake framed him in the distance.

The sight of him made her breath catch. He caught

her gaze and smiled. She dropped the undies like they were on fire. A flash of heat surged clear through her and bloomed on her cheeks, her throat went cotton-dry, and her palms got so sweaty she had to wipe them off on her pj pants. How long had it been since she'd had such a visceral reaction to a man? She couldn't remember.

Her reaction completely rattled her, which made it all the worse. She became aware that Rachel was staring at her, although Rafe and her dad seemed oblivious, thank God, and Nonna, her priorities clear, had gone back to finishing her donut.

Professor, Gabby reminded herself, as she tried to reconcile the gorgeous man who was sending her into heart attack mode with all the male teachers she'd had in the past. Distinguished professors had beards like Walt Whitman's, which they thoughtfully stroked. And little wire-rimmed glasses. And far less brawn. And maybe even little paunches. And they *definitely* didn't look at their students like Cade was currently looking at her.

Cade's mouth quirked up as his gaze swept over her calmly and slowly—her old T-shirt from law school that said "Make Love Not Law Review," plaid flannel pants, and bare feet. Yet even in her embarrassment, Gabby felt his gaze boring through her in a way that made her suddenly aware of every muscle and bone. He was looking at her like a *guy*. An interested guy. Not like Walt Whitman. Or any other teacher she'd ever had.

Whatever she'd seen on his face, it was gone in an instant, making her wonder if it was a figment of her imagination. Rachel stood to shake Cade's hand.

"Come in," she said, guiding him through the doorway before he had a chance to protest. At least someone had remembered how to speak and be polite.

Her dad, always friendly, shook his hand too.

Gabby walked over. "Cade, you know my dad. Meet my stepmom, Rachel, my brother, Rafe, and my nonna. Cade is a writing professor over at the college."

"Nice to meet you all," Cade said. "I'm just dropping off Gabby's bike."

"Help yourself," Rafe said, opening the donut box in front of Cade.

"Thanks, I think I will." He chose a cream stick, Gabby noted, her favorite.

Rafe pulled up a wooden chair that had been leaning against the wall, and Cade took a seat.

"So you're Gabby's teacher?" Rachel prompted.

"Is he her boyfriend?" Nonna fake-whispered to Rachel, loud enough for everyone to hear. Nonna pulled her eyeglasses down her nose and took a long look at Cade.

"I *am* her teacher," he said, smiling at Nonna.

"And tell us, Cade, why do you have Gabby's bike?" her dad asked with an interrogative tone reserved for suspected criminals, bill collectors, and potential boyfriends of his daughters.

"My daughter was having a little meltdown yesterday, and Gabby happened to drive by with chicken nuggets," Cade said. "She left her bike at my house so I'm just returning it."

"You had chicken nuggets and didn't bring me any?" Rafe said.

Gabby frowned, sending him the message *Just behave already, will you?*

"Oh, you have a daughter?" Rachel asked, raising a brow. Gabby could practically hear her thoughts. *Divorced, has a kid. Time to meet the minister.*

"She's three," he said. "We just moved here."

Nonna came to sit beside Gabby and whispered—in a very loud voice, "Who *is* he, Gabby?"

"Just a friend, Nonna," Gabby said, but the next thing she knew, Nonna was leaning forward and tapping Cade on the knee.

"Hello," Nonna said.

"Hi," Cade said good-naturedly, extending a very masculine-looking hand.

Nonna took it and smiled. "Nice, strong handshake," she said. "Just like Jacob's."

Gabby wondered if she should warn Cade that Nonna sometimes said inappropriate things. Well, make that *a lot* of times. "Who's Jacob, Nonna?"

Nonna wasn't letting go of Cade's hand, but he didn't seem to mind. "Jacob was my first love," she said.

"You never told us about him before, Nonna," Gabby said.

"He had eyes that same color," she said, peering into Cade's eyes. "Sometimes they were green, and sometimes they were blue-gray. Pretty eyes. Just like yours."

"Well, I'm glad you like them," Cade said, smiling sweetly at Nonna, and that made Gabby like him even more.

"You're adorable," Nonna said. "Are you married?"

She tipped her head toward Gabby. "She's thirty, and she needs a husband."

"Okay, Nonna, he's just here to return my bike," Gabby said, hoping that would stop conversation. "Thank you," she said to Cade, giving him a hint to exit.

"No problem," Cade said.

"She was engaged to someone we didn't like too much," Nonna said, now on a roll. "Thought he was all that."

"Oh, I'm...sorry to hear that," Cade said. Okay, so it wasn't enough Gabby's hair looked like Helena Bonham Carter's in *Sweeney Todd*, but now she was also getting embarrassed by her own family.

"How did Gabby meet you?" Nonna asked.

"Gabby's my student," Cade said, not seeming to mind the information was a repeat.

"What class are you taking now?" Nonna asked Gabby. "She's always taking classes."

"I'm taking creative writing, remember?" Gabby said, feeling heat burn her cheeks.

Rafe intervened. "Gabby loves learning things. First it was bartending, then photography, then EMT classes—"

Gabby couldn't meet Cade's gaze. Rafe was trying to be kind, but could she possibly be more embarrassed? "That's enough, Rafe," she said.

"We have a lot of different professionals in the class," Cade said. "A lot of people with diverse backgrounds have an interest in writing."

"I hope Ava's better today," Gabby said, steering the subject into safer territory.

"Much, thanks," he said, flashing a smile. "Amazing what sleep and food will do for a three-year-old." He wiped his fingers on a napkin and said, "Well, I'd better be going. Great to meet you all. And thanks for the donut."

"I'll walk you out," Gabby said, which also sounded crazed because the carriage house was, like, one room.

Once they were outside the door, Cade walked over to where he'd parked Gabby's bike. "I hope you don't mind but I went over it a little. Put some air in your tires, tightened your seat, greased the chain."

Gabby felt another rush of heat blaze into her cheeks. He was being perfectly nice but why did it all sound so…dirty?

As if to confirm her thoughts, Nonna, from inside, suddenly said, "Did you hear that? He greased her chain."

"Thank you," she said, ignoring the fact that her family was listening to every word. "That was very kind." She was coming to think he *was* very kind—to melting down toddlers, to her, not only bringing back her bike but returning it in better condition than she'd left it.

"See you in class," he said. "Have a nice weekend."

She stopped him from walking away by saying, "I—just moved in. I was up late packing. I don't usually sleep until noon." She needed to stop blathering, but for some reason, she didn't want him to leave just yet.

He smiled, and she couldn't help noticing it reached all the way to his eyes. Today they looked gray-green, the same as his T-shirt. She wondered if they always tended to take on the color of his clothing.

"Hey, it's Saturday," he said. "No one has to get dressed—or brush their hair—if they don't want to, right?" His mouth twitched, and his gaze swept over her again in a way that made her shiver despite the warm day. Then he raised his hand in a little wave and, with a last glance, headed for his truck, which was parked in the long gravel drive.

"Why did your professor have your bike again?" her father asked as soon as she'd stepped back through the door. "You went over to his house?"

"More importantly, why is he checking the air and tightening your seat? Oh, and greasing the chain?" Rafe said, laughing.

Gabby smacked him on the arm. Playfully. Mostly. "His daughter ate my Happy Meal, so he offered to get me another one and he ended up putting my bike in his truck. By the time we were done eating, it was too dark to ride it back home."

"Is it a good idea to be on such friendly terms with your teacher?" Rachel asked. "Not that it's my business."

That was Rachel's typical I'm-not-butting-in but-I'm-really-butting-in line that she'd perfected over the years.

"I just helped out his kid, no big deal," Gabby said. "So can we get that desk now?"

"I'd eat chicken nuggets with that guy anytime," Nonna said, going for another donut.

"Nonna, I'm not sure if you should have a third donut," Gabby's dad said.

Rachel gave him a dirty look.

"The sugar," he said defensively. "The cholesterol."

"When you're eighty-nine years old," Nonna said, "you can have all the donuts you want."

"Aren't you, like, only eighty, Nonna?" Rafe asked.

"I don't know, but I'm old enough to have another donut if I want one."

Rachel smiled at Gabby's dad. "You heard her, Walter."

Walter shrugged. "I know when I've lost a battle," he said. "All right, Rafe, let's go haul that desk out of your truck."

As Walter and Rafe left the room, Nonna licked some cream off her thumb. "Don't ever let anyone tell you not to eat donuts," she said.

"Malcolm used to hate it when I ate junk food," Gabby said. He never said anything if she went for seconds, but she could always see the disapproval in his eyes.

That bad thought was interrupted by the sound of the screen door banging. The men walked in carrying the desk and set it into the little alcove. It was a battered antique made of dark, polished wood and was badly in need of refinishing.

"So, Dad, what's the story behind this thing, anyway?" Gabby asked. "Is it a family piece?"

"That old thing?" Nonna said, looking it over as the men set it down. "It's an eyesore. Maybe you can donate it to Goodwill. Aren't you a lawyer? You can afford a nice desk."

Her dad stood up and smiled. "Your mother bought it at a garage sale back in the day when everything we owned was secondhand. She set it up in the living room of our apartment so she could work and watch you kids."

Gabby could only imagine how that worked out—Evie and then Sara, two rambunctious little kids, with two more to follow.

"She'd want you to have this, Gabriella," her dad said, wiping off the thick coating of dust from its surface. "Maybe you'll do what your mother never got the chance to accomplish herself."

Ah yes. Because of the cancer. That hung in the air and made everyone go momentarily silent.

"Thanks, Daddy," she said, giving him a hug. Her dad rarely spoke about their mother, and especially not in front of Rachel, but lately he seemed to be making an effort.

"Have you opened the box of your mom's writing yet?" Rachel asked, looking at the myriad number of boxes that covered the floor of the small space.

"Um, no." Gabby pointed to a medium-sized brown box near her bed that was stamped with a Corn Flakes logo.

"But you found that months ago," Rafe said.

"And you were so excited," Rachel added.

"Open it," Nonna chimed in. "It's like a box of chocolates. You don't know what you're going to get until you open it." She paused thoughtfully. "What poet said that?"

"Forrest Gump, Nonna," Dad and Rafe echoed at the same time.

"Well, when the time is right, the time is right," Nonna said.

"Can't argue with that," Rachel said with a shrug. "When you're ready, it will feel right."

Before everyone left, Rachel insisted on taking a photo of all of them together in front of the desk, which was corny but also sweet.

Then Rachel looked at her watch. "Oh, I've got to go. I'm meeting a client at the store to let her look through some boxes of antique china."

Rafe picked up the leftover donuts. "I'm happy to find these a home, if no one wants them," he said, closing the lid.

"Right. In your stomach," Gabby said. "I don't think you should take those. You need to keep yourself in tip-top shape, ready for any emergency."

"I'm a growing boy, Gabs. And be nice to me. I can stay and set the glass back onto the desk for you."

"Fine. The donuts are yours."

Rachel cornered Gabby on her way out. "I'm really excited about introducing you to our brand-new minister. He's very good-looking and your age, and I think you two might just hit it off."

Oh no, there it was. Rachel had been building up to this for the past several weeks, and there was no avoiding it. Gabby decided to be firm and snip the issue right in the bud. "Oh, thanks, Rachel, but I'm really busy right now, what with work and class—"

"He's very busy too. I think you might find you two have quite a lot in common. Check your calendar for the next few weekends, okay?"

"Rachel, I—" Gabby could tell from the determined look she wore that she wasn't going to back down.

"You've got nothing to lose," she continued, nonplussed.

"Okay, fine," Gabby said on a sigh.

Rachel kissed her and gave her a squeeze. "I'll have him call you," she said, a little too eagerly.

Nonna gave Gabby a hug and then they were gone.

After everyone left, Rafe cleaned the glass top of the writing desk with Windex. She dusted off the top of the desk and helped him place the glass on. Then they sat around talking, Rafe in her desk chair, Gabby on the couch. The box of her mom's stuff sat a few feet away and Gabby couldn't help but occasionally glance at it.

"Just open it, Gabs," Rafe said, reaching into a box and pulling out a paperweight that Gabby had made in glass-blowing class, which he began to toss from hand to hand.

"How do you know I'm thinking about the box?"

"Because every other box around here is open except that one. What's the problem?"

She shrugged. "It's too weird to talk about."

He leaned back in the desk chair and kept tossing. Maybe that was why Gabby always felt she could talk to Rafe. He didn't judge, and he had this relaxed way about him that made him easy to talk to.

"Expectations, I guess. Nervous of what I'll find. Afraid she was writing about some old love or something I don't really want to know about—private stuff, you know?"

"On the other hand, it could be a great opportunity."

"For what?"

"To see a side of our mother you've never seen before." He paused. "Is that why you're taking a writing class? To feel closer to Mom?"

She shrugged. "It's just something I'm doing in my spare time."

"Gabby, technically you don't have any spare time. Try again."

"Okay, fine, I guess Mom inspired me. I've always wanted to see if I'd be any good as a writer, and I thought now would be a good time to find out."

"Well, I hope you at least find what you're looking for. In the class and in that box. I hope whatever Mom wrote speaks to you in some way."

"Thank you, Rafe." She was getting a little teary eyed.

"So what's the deal with that guy?" Rafe asked. He pulled out a penknife from his pocket and gestured to Gabby to push their mother's box toward him.

She did, and Rafe split the top of the box open. The scent of old papers wafted up, always a comforting smell. But along with it came a whiff of fear. What if there was just some dull, old manuscript in there? What if it was...amateurish and not very good? What if there were no insights, no discoveries about her mom? Even worse, what if there were *love scenes*? She would definitely skip those.

"He literally is my writing professor. The chicken nugget story is true. That's all."

"I don't see anything wrong with taking a class. Just that the man looks at you like a hungry wolf."

"He does not."

Rafe shot her a look that said, *Trust me, I know what I'm talking about*. "That's not flattery, by the way. It's a warning. Take it as a recommendation to stay away."

"Why doesn't anyone in our family think I can handle myself around men?"

He shrugged. "Because Malcolm wasn't the greatest guy, and we all saw it before you did."

"Okay, fair enough. But I've got my eyes wide open. What about you?"

"What do you mean, what about me?"

"I don't know. You seem...lonely."

"I love my job, I'm working on getting another side job, and I'm a single male in the prime of life. What more could I want?" Her brother was handsome and charming, with a disarming sense of humor, but she couldn't help feeling that he was hiding something behind that happy-go-lucky, carefree attitude.

She wished Rafe would talk to her, but he never did, really. "If you ever want to talk about anything, I'm here."

He smiled, his big, wide Rafe smile with dimples that made women sigh and fall at his feet. "I'm fine. But I appreciate your concern." He got up and kissed her on the head. "I gotta go."

"Where are you going?"

"I'm helping somebody's mother move some things into her attic."

"Wait. Could that be Kaitlyn's mom?" More evidence that Rafe was getting tangled up in Kaitlyn's life.

Rafe rubbed his neck, looking uncomfortable. "I promised Kaitlyn I'd help move a few things." He added quickly, "Then I'm going out with the guys."

"You seem to be spending a lot of time with Kaitlyn," Gabby said, not quite ready to let it go.

"Yeah, so what? We're just friends."

"Friends with benefits?" Gabby asked.

Rafe's thick brows knit down as he frowned. "Absolutely not."

Gabby held her hands out in defense. "Okay, don't bite my head off. I'm just asking."

"She's been a friend for a long time. I wouldn't do anything to jeopardize that." He paused. "Hey, do you have a date for cousin Stephanie's wedding?"

"I was planning on going with Kaitlyn. Why?"

"Well, I was going to ask her. As a friend, you know? Because she broke up with that guy she was dating."

"Steve."

"Yes. But I don't want to give her the wrong idea."

Wait…is it possible he could want to ask Kaitlyn to be his date? "What's the wrong idea?"

"That I'm…interested. That would definitely be the wrong idea."

"Why would it be the wrong idea, Rafe?"

"Because I'm not interested in anyone, okay, Gabriella?" He tugged her hair, as if he were ten again. As if that would be enough to distract her from the truth, that maybe after all these years, Rafe finally liked somebody more than just to sleep with her but was too terrified to ask her out.

"Bye, Gabs," Rafe said, heading for the door.

"Goodbye," she called after his retreating from. "It's okay to be human, you know that Rafe? Kaitlyn's really nice. And God knows why, but she might actually like you back."

Rafe disappeared with a wave of his hand. The door

clicked shut behind him, leaving Gabby alone in a space that was suddenly silent.

She sat down in the desk chair and traced her fingers along the desk, imagining how her mother must've done this same thing. Then she opened the drawers one by one. In the bottom right was an old manila folder. In it was a bunch of newspaper clippings. The first one showed a formal picture of her mother in a black V-neck sweater with a string of pearls. Her hair was curly and wild just like Gabby's, and it was all poufed out and curled in a typical eighties style.

Her dad had often told her she resembled their mom the most, in looks and personality. She wondered if her mom had ever had man troubles. Or confusion about men. What was it like when she met her father? What had caused her to start writing?

Impulsively, Gabby reached into the box and pulled out a bundle of papers. Bound by a rubber band was a series of papers, like the kind one would turn in for a college class. Sure enough, the corner of every paper read, "Professor Bowman, Creative Writing, Section 10701." Gabby flipped quickly through the papers. Nearly every single one had a big red "A" on the top and words like "Excellent!" "Fabulous job," and "Fantastic." One said, "Shows great promise—dig deeper!" Great. So her mother was an amazing student.

At the bottom of the pile was a little blue final exam booklet with an inscription on the cover: "I've enjoyed having you as a student. I hope you will continue writing after class ends because I see real promise in your work."

Oh, wow. Her mother was talented—at least, her professor thought so. And she was lucky enough to have an encouraging professor—maybe a mentor, who seemed to believe in her. Wasn't that everyone's dream?

She thought about her mother. There was so much she would never know about her. Or about Rafe, who in his own way had closed himself off so it was only possible to know him to a point.

She refused to accept that on both counts. She would find a way to learn more about her mother. And Rafe—he didn't look from the outside like he needed help, but he did. And she was going to be the one to crack his shell.

Chapter 7

♥

I need a drink, and I don't mean coffee," Gabby said after her friend Lucy had opened the door to the coffee shop downtown to let her in.

It was 9:15 at night. She'd spent the whole day working on her story for Cade's class. Well, she'd actually spent 90 percent of the time staring out the window at the lush green fields and 10 percent typing away at her laptop—and when the afternoon was over, she'd only made half of Cade's mandated word count. To make matters worse, the carriage house was practically in the same unpacked state as Cade's barely moved-in house. At this rate, she wasn't sure how she was going to find the time to make it the homey, lived-in space she wanted it to be.

Lucy waved her in as she talked on her cell phone. Spread out across two small tables that had been pushed together were packets of tissue paper, scissors, a ball of yarn, and pipe cleaners. Sara and Kaitlyn were arranging another set of tables for a work area. All

Gabby knew was they were working on some kind of art project for Parent Night at Lucy's day care.

"No, Alex, I mean it," Lucy was saying into the phone. "I'm not coming over tonight. Goodbye." She pushed the *end* button. "There are no good men," she said. "I hate men."

"Oh no," Gabby said. "What happened with Alex?" Alex and Lucy had been dating for years. He was the best guy on the planet—kind and considerate, and he had a great job as a high school math teacher who also coached soccer.

"It's his mother. We walked into her house before church last Sunday, and she gave me all kinds of grief about my yellow sundress."

"That's a pretty dress," Gabby said. "I'd say it was very appropriate for church."

"It has an opening in the upper back around three inches wide, but nothing too terrible, right?" She held the fingers of her hands together in a big O. "No bra strap showing, barely any skin...Well, she asked me to change. Or put a sweater on. And I didn't have a sweater."

"What did Alex say?" Kaitlyn asked.

"He offered to jokingly help me take it off—and he said that in front of his mother, which didn't make things any better. But I still had to cover up the dress. He didn't stand up for me."

"Well, maybe he couldn't," Sara, the voice of practicality, said. "Maybe that church is very conservative."

"A guy should stand up for his girlfriend," Lucy said, crossing her arms.

"Did you say that?" Gabby asked.

"He said to just please cover up. So we had to go back to my place and get my sweater."

"Well, chalk it up as a little sacrifice?" Gabby said, trying to smooth things over.

"It's just that his mother is always doing stuff like that. She doesn't like me. We're not even engaged yet, and it's like she's...she's trying to get rid of me before he even pops the question."

Gabby hugged her friend. "I know one thing. Alex loves you, and he's a great guy. But you're right. If his mom's doing stuff like that to push against your relationship, Alex is going to have to take a stand."

"I know, right? He made light of it. Told me he loved the little peephole for my back. And helped me take it off. In fact, we were almost late for the service."

"Lucy, Lucy, Lucy," Gabby said in mock horror, covering her mouth. But secretly, she wondered what that would be like. Having a guy who could made you late for things.

Kaitlyn handed Gabby a glass of white wine.

"Anything going on with you?" Gabby asked.

"Steve wants to get back together."

Oh, wow. Kaitlyn had broken it off with Steve a year ago because she'd felt that staying with him would be settling, a move Gabby thought was pretty courageous.

"Steve is such a great guy," Lucy said. "He coaches with Alex. Alex says he's formed an after-school basketball league that's also a confidence-building program for kids who are academically struggling."

"He *is* a nice guy," Kaitlyn said. "But he's not the guy for me."

Sara exchanged a look with Gabby. They all knew Kaitlyn's real problem. For the thousandth time, Gabby wondered why Kaitlyn would set her sights on Rafe, who was about as determined to stay single as Leonardo DiCaprio.

"Oh, I almost forgot," Gabby said. She took her backpack off her shoulders and pulled out a plastic Tupperware container. "I made brownies."

"Not those killer brownies with the caramel and dark chocolate chips?" Sara asked, her eyes widening.

"Yep," Gabby said.

"I love your brownies," Kaitlyn said. "You're such a good baker."

Gabby took that as a sincere compliment, not only because Kaitlyn owned the Bean but also because she baked all the goodies for the coffee shop every day. If Gabby's baking was passable, Kaitlyn's was amazing.

"You sure you don't want to give Steve one more chance?" Lucy asked quietly.

"Nope," Kaitlyn said, waving her hand in the air. "No more chances. I've had a couple of dates with a guy from the Richardson fire department. He's pretty nice...and he wants to take it to the next level."

No one said what they were thinking, which was that the guy from Richardson was *not* Rafe. Gabby suspected Kaitlyn was trying to force herself to forget about her brother. That was a good thing, right?

Kaitlyn studied their faces. "Don't look so shocked. I'm not going to spend my whole life pining after Rafe."

"What are you going to do?" Sara asked.

"I'm going to sleep with the new guy," Kaitlyn said. "I can't get past the friend zone with Rafe, though God knows I've tried. I've got to do something to forget him." She tossed a ball of yarn into the middle of the table. "It seems like just when I try to move on, he's right back there, doing something that makes me hang on for longer."

"What did he do this time?" Sara asked.

"I mentioned the firefighter and he got all red under his collar. Then he asked me to be his date for Stephanie's wedding."

"Hey, you were supposed to be *my* date," Gabby said.

"Sorry," Kaitlyn said. But she didn't sound sorry.

"So you're going as Rafe's date?"

"Yes. As friends. *And* I'm going to sleep with the firefighter. So see? I Have this handled."

Yikes. Gabby had doubts about that.

"You're going to have to confront Rafe and tell him how you feel," Lucy said. "It's the only way you're going to get him out of your system."

Gabby wasn't so sure about that either, and from Sara's pointed looks in her direction, she agreed. Rafe seemed...clueless. She wasn't sure how he would react to the truth.

"We're good friends," Kaitlyn said. "And right now...I don't want to lose that. I feel like I can tell Rafe anything. He...gets me. But when I try to get closer, he just shuts down. I swear, after this wedding, maybe I should cut things off. For my own mental health."

Lucy raised her glass of wine. “Let’s drink to mental health. After a week with all those little monsters, I need it. Plus, I had to get treated for pinkeye this week.”

“You love those little monsters,” Sara said. “Don’t lie.”

Lucy shrugged. “Sometimes. And also, some of their parents are awful. I wish they’d just let us do our job, you know? I had a run-in with a dad this week. He was upset about the type of classical music we played for his baby. Little did I know he’s chairman of the music department at the college. How was I supposed to know all classical music stations are not created equal?”

“Well, we’re ready to do arts and crafts,” Sara said. “Just tell us what to do.”

“I have to make a hundred tissue paper flowers and glue them to that poster board over there. And I need our resident artist to write ‘Welcome Parents’ with some kind of fancy lettering.” Lucy handed Gabby a handful of markers. “You don’t mind, do you?”

“Of course not.” Gabby got to work lettering the sign. “I had an interesting run-in with someone this week.”

“Well, why didn’t you say so?” Kaitlyn said. “Who is he? Is he hot? Do you want to do him?”

“I just *met* him,” Gabby said. “Geez.”

“The sooner you move on after Malcolm, the better off you’ll be,” Kaitlyn said.

“I’m over Malcolm. I dumped him, remember? Besides, this guy is someone I could never sleep with. Someone I can’t even date. I’m just having . . . thoughts.”

"Dirty thoughts?" Lucy asked. "That's definitely a start."

"Yeah, Gabs," Sara said. "Why can't you date him?"

"He's my professor."

"Gabs is hot for teacher," Lucy teased. "What class are you taking again? And can I take it too?"

"What is it with you and the classes?" Kaitlyn asked. "Aren't you tired enough after the hours you put in at that firm? And aren't you sick of school after all those years?"

Gabby shrugged. She really should've kept her mouth shut.

Because she understood how great her life looked from the outside. Even her friends didn't get why she felt so unsettled. How could she explain it to them when she didn't understand it herself?

"I mean, we *are* grateful for that bartending course you took back in college," Kaitlyn said.

"And the EMT courses really came in handy when you saved that woman from choking in that restaurant," Lucy said.

"The photography lessons will always be a good life skill," Sara chimed in. "Plus those framed prints you gave me for my wedding look great in our foyer." Her sister was in on this too. Ugh.

"Didn't you start flight lessons too, a couple of years ago?" Kaitlyn asked.

"Our dad put the kibosh on that pretty quick." Sara looked over and must've noticed Gabby was looking a little panicked, so she gave her a little nudge with her elbow. "We're just teasing you a little."

"Yeah," Lucy said. "You can do whatever you want in your spare time."

Yes, of course. In her spare time.

"Tell us about the *guy*," Lucy said.

"He's not a *guy*. He teaches creative writing. You may know him, since he's a local. Cade Marshall."

"Oh, I remember him," Kaitlyn said. "He got taken down by his ex. Stole her ideas and she sued him for it."

"Did she win?" Lucy asked.

"The judge dismissed the case," Sara said. "But his reputation has suffered."

"Wow, that's pretty tragic," Kaitlyn said. "So did he do it? Steal his wife's story?"

"I don't think he did," Gabby said, realizing she had no basis for saying that, just a gut sense she had about Cade. But they all knew her gut sense about men was totally off.

"You're too trusting," Lucy said. "You think the best of everyone."

"Cade's sister just joined our practice," Sara said. "She's alluded to his ex as being needy and jealous. She rarely sees their daughter."

"Paige stands by her son," Kaitlyn said. "She gets really upset if anyone brings that whole scandal up. But he hasn't written anything since. I know because my mom wants to read the sequel, and there isn't one."

"He may call you, Luce," Gabby said. "His daughter's in a sketchy day care situation, and he wants to switch her somewhere else. I didn't know if you had any openings, but I gave him your number."

"Already taken care of," Lucy said. "His little girl is

officially enrolled and starting Monday." She paused. "And by the way, he *is* hot."

Gabby ignored the last comment. "Thanks for doing that."

"Wow," Kaitlyn said. "You just met the guy, and you're already playing mom. This sounds serious."

"It's not like that. I was just being helpful."

"Help me set these down over there, would you?" Sara asked, picking up a bunch of finished flowers and giving Gabby a nod. As soon as they were far enough away from the others, she dropped her voice to a concerned whisper. "Oh, Gabby. You know I always love and support you but I have to speak my mind, and I can't help seeing red flags all over the place—divorced, a kid, and a scandal. And your *professor*. I mean, the potential for getting hurt if you got involved with someone like that—"

A very familiar feeling rose up like tidewater in Gabby's chest. It was as if she were already disappointing everyone, even though she hadn't even done anything yet. "I'm not involved. I just helped him out and thought he was cute. I shouldn't have said anything."

"I just worry about you," Sara said. "I want you to meet someone wonderful who deserves you, that's all."

"I know I've made some mistakes in the past, but I understand he's off-limits. It was just that I saw him being an amazing father. I mean, his kid was completely freaking out. Remember when Michael dropped to the ground in the grocery store that one time? He completely lost it, and Evie actually called us to come help because she was afraid she was going to murder someone. It was like that, but Cade just handled it really well."

It wasn't just his fatherly skills, and Gabby knew it. It was attraction, as pure and raw as a shot of tequila burning down your throat. And the way he looked at her when he'd dropped off her bike. The earth had stood still, just for a few seconds, as if they were the only two people in the room.

And the way he'd responded when she said she wanted to be a writer. He was the only person on the planet who thought becoming a writer was actually a rational possibility, something she could barely admit to herself, let alone out loud.

Back at the table, their friends were still talking about Cade. Oh, why had she opened her mouth?

"Aren't there rules against that?" Lucy asked. "Sleeping with a student?"

"It's unethical," Gabby said, anxious to stop talking about it. "Because there's a power differential. He controls my grade."

"Big deal," Kaitlyn said. "You don't need a grade. I say go for it. You need some fun in your life— Ow!" she exclaimed, as Sara glowered. "You didn't have to poke me with your elbow!"

"Gabby, you deserve to be happy," Sara said. "Just focus on someone uncomplicated."

"I'm thirty years old," Gabby said. "Everyone's complicated by now."

"Good point," Lucy said. "Okay, ladies, here comes the last batch of flowers." She carried over the last piece of poster board. "The sooner we get done, the more we can drink. And after an entire week with those little monsters—I mean sweet, adorable children—I'm going to need several."

As Gabby set to finishing the tissue paper flowers, she couldn't help thinking that everything her friends said reinforced the fact that Cade Marshall had a lot of caution lights flashing everywhere.

They were right, of course. She wasn't going to go looking for trouble. She was going to stay on the straight and narrow for once, let her friends and family help her this time and steer clear from any man likely to crush her heart.

Chapter 8

♥

The following Tuesday during office hours, Cade reached into his book bag for his ringing phone. Instead of the phone, however, he pulled out a plastic rabbit Happy Meal toy on wheels. He sat back in his chair for a moment and rolled the bright blue plastic thing on his desk. As he did, the bunny's ears wiggled and its head bobbed up and down.

Despite himself, he smiled. The toy brought back memories of Gabby coming to his rescue with chicken nuggets. She had this way about her, of making people smile. It had certainly worked with his daughter. And, he hated to admit, with himself.

His phone screen said Joanna Devereaux, his literary agent, was calling. He debated letting the call go to voice mail, but experience taught him she didn't give up easily.

"Hello," he said.

"Cade, hi," she said. "How's life in Ohio?"

"Great. Getting settled," he said. A familiar sense of

dread settled in his gut, because he knew why she was calling. And it wasn't to talk about Ohio.

"So I'm wondering if you've got any pages for me."

"Joanna, we talked about this. No pages. I'm sorry."

He heard her sigh. "Your publisher hasn't given up on you yet. There's still a chance to keep your foot in the door."

"I took a teaching job, and I'm on the research track for tenure." He tried to sound optimistic, focused, and confident. "I'll be too busy to write. I'm sorry."

"I can't believe you're ever too busy for something you have a real passion for, and I know you. You *are* passionate about writing."

He used to be. "I've started a new life. Lots of people do it."

"You had a few bumps in the road." Her voice held a note of pleading, which slayed him. "All I'm saying is consider it."

He'd stopped making money for Joanna, yet she still called to check in. And to encourage him. "Joanna, I really appreciate your . . . concern."

"You have talent, Cade. You're a good writer. Call me when you've got something for me. Okay?"

"Got it." If only he could. He'd tried—for three years.

Cade hung up the phone and heaved a sigh. He was dry . . . a one-hit wonder. Washed up at thirty-two. He hated disappointing Joanna, who had believed in him from the start. Even worse, he hated disappointing himself.

Well, he had other things to focus on. Building a life for Ava, for one. Their house might be charming, but it was more like a charming train wreck. Just this morning he'd found a puddle of water in the kitchen, even though he'd just had the roof inspected before they'd moved in. Old homes always needed work, but honestly, he found fixing things to be relaxing. Unlike his real life trials and tribulations, those kinds of problems actually had solutions.

Work was busy too. Today, he'd had a meeting with the chairman, Jake LaGuardia, who'd hired him, and the committee that decided tenure. They wanted to make sure he was on the right track. And they wanted to meet again, next time with a full proposal for his planned research project. If he didn't have a solid plan for his research and put some kind of positive spin on the fact that he was no longer writing, they'd soon flag him for the fast track...right out on his butt.

He needed to leave behind the capricious, backstabbing, muse-killing literary life and focus on cold, hard facts. He loved writers of the Jazz Age—Fitzgerald, Hemingway, Faulkner, Stein—and planned to expand on his PhD research about the great literature of the past rather than bleed himself trying to write fresh stuff. Besides, critics could string up an author by the balls for his or her writing, but research, if it was sound, rarely got critiqued in the same way.

He shook the negative thoughts off and took a sip of his leftover coffee. It was cold and very, very bitter.

A knock sounded at the door. He opened the door to find a man who, with his longish, dyed black hair and tight skinny jeans, gave the impression of wanting to look younger than he was. "Hi," his visitor said, walking in and making himself at home in one of the seats, "I'm your neighbor from the office next door. Name's Tony. Tony Livingstone. I teach American writers of the nineteenth century but I also write historical fiction. Great to meet you." He extended a hand, which Cade shook.

Tony seemed nice enough. But three other professors this week had already told Cade he was a snake and had probably used grades to bribe students to sleep with him. Tony hadn't been caught yet, but Jake was aware of the situation.

"Hey, you're good friends with Jake, aren't you?" Tony asked.

"I worked under him in grad school a few years ago," Cade said, alarm bells going off. He'd known Jake a long time, and Jake had given him this job when he was floundering. Cade wasn't about to do anything to risk that or to screw the one person who'd helped him when few others would.

"As one fiction writer to another, you know how hard it is to get academic grants for writing. We should stick together. And maybe we could help each other out."

"Help each other out?" Cade asked, trying to squash his suspicion that this guy was asking him for favors already.

"Yeah, you know. I could sure use a good word whispered in Jake's ear from a fellow author that I'm worthy of the fiction fellowship that's being given out next semester. It allows an author to have a reduced class load to be able to have time to write. In return,

I could help you too. I sit on a lot of influential committees."

"Well, I'm new here, so I'm not in a position to recommend anyone," Cade said in a definitive tone as he ushered Tony out. "But it was nice to meet you."

A little later, the sound of shuffling papers made him look up. Carol Cartwright, the department secretary, had walked in. She'd been a fixture in the English department for fifteen years, and from all accounts basically kept the whole place running. Every day she wore a different-colored suit with matching shoes—today's were orange—and had a short, practical haircut that she wore in an unchanging style.

With her usual no-nonsense stride, she approached his desk. "Good morning, Professor Marshall." She glanced down at his coffee. "You do know there's a fresh pot brewing, don't you? Want a cup?"

"Thanks for letting me know. I'll get one later."

Jake popped his head in behind Carol. "Ah, Cade. Glad you've met Carol, our secret weapon that keeps the department together." He walked in and shook Cade's hand and gave him a friendly pat on the back. "I just wanted to say it's great to have you here, son." He glanced at his watch. "I've got to run to a meeting. Let me know if you need anything, okay?"

"Thanks, Jake," Cade said, grateful to have Jake as his boss as well as his friend.

Jake ran out, leaving Cade with Carol, who set down some papers in front of him. "We've got a couple of great graduate student candidates if you're looking for help with your research. And one community professional who wants to work with a professor as part of her classroom experience this semester."

There were a slew of literature and creative writing grad students who needed to earn their tuition, and it was customary for professors to keep one busy for a semester. Cade understood how the system worked; he was once one of those eager students himself. But he certainly didn't want a student to help with his research for The Book That Refused to Be Written, as he called it. And as for his proposal... well, he had a lot of thinking to do on that.

He hadn't done research since his PhD work five years ago—he'd gone from there into the MFA program at Iowa, where he'd written *Girl on the Edge*, and his career had taken off. He never thought he'd be doing academic research again. At one time, he'd loved the power of fiction to break the rules, to free him to feel deeply beyond the constraints of facts, and to say something he felt was important about life. Yet here he was.

"I may—um—pass on that opportunity until next semester. Since I'm new and jumping into Professor Shreevesanan's classes and all."

"You sure about that? Grad students are usually very eager to do extra work, like grade papers. And they're pretty good at it."

He smiled. "I'm sure. I'd rather get my feet wet myself, if that's okay." He was determined to go this alone until he found his footing.

A few minutes after Carol left, there was another rustle at the door. He looked up from his paperwork to see Gabby standing in his doorway. She wore a bright yellow rain jacket with clingy athletic pants that showed off shapely legs. Raindrops rolled off her hood, her wet hair curling crazily. Judging by the pink flush in her cheeks, he'd guess she probably rode her bike onto campus again.

Wow. Just wow. What *was* it about this woman that hit him without warning right in the gut? An image entered his mind, of her hair tussled from sleep, cute toes peeking out from beneath worn flannel pj pants, and the shapely curve of her breasts visible under that "Make Love Not Law Review" T-shirt. It made him think of things he'd rather not think of. Like how she would look after being made love to, thoroughly and well.

"Hi, Professor," she said with a frown, then broke into a little smile. Even the smile floored him. With that and the raincoat, she literally looked like the sunshine coming out after a cloudburst. He imagined rising up from his desk chair to kiss her, good and hard.

He cleared his throat and sat up, trying to act like a professor. "Good afternoon, Gabby—I mean, Ms. Langdon."

"Good afternoon, Professor," she said tongue-in-cheek, and he could tell she was biting down on the insides of her cheeks to keep from laughing. "You can call me Gabby, you know. I wanted to thank you for returning my bike the other day. And for looking it over. I like what you did to my seat. It feels really good now." Gabby broke out into a bright crimson blush.

"You're welcome." He loosened his collar, because dammit if he wasn't sweating. She sat down in the seat across from his desk, slipped her bag off her shoulder, and pulled out some papers. "I'm sure you didn't come all the way to campus just to thank me. What can I help you with?" he asked. In his heart, he already knew why she was here, and reminded himself, no matter how much he liked her as a person, his job wasn't to blow smoke up students' butts.

"I stopped by to discuss your comments on my homework."

"Certainly. I'm always happy to discuss."

She held up the first page of the paper so he could see. "It looks like the Red Wedding." His eyes flicked up at the *Game of Thrones* reference, and he found that the corner of her pretty mouth quirked up a little. It made him want to laugh it off too, but he forced himself to keep his expression serious. She continued, "I—um—I didn't notice anyone else's paper looking quite so... injured."

Cade was torn. Yes, he'd been tough on her. But yes, her story did have major problems.

He reminded himself that his writing class was comprised of adults who had other jobs, who were taking this class for their own reasons—to explore writing or for fun. Most, maybe all, of these students would never develop the talent or drive it took to be a bestseller or to survive as an author. Hell, even with all his special training, he himself couldn't sustain his own career.

"Excuse me, did you just hear what I said?" she asked. She was leaning forward in the chair. He hadn't heard a word but he could smell her. Strawberries, maybe? Something sweet and delicious. Oh no, did he just think that?

"I'm sorry, come again?"

"I said, I read through all of your comments, and I'm still not clear on how I can improve my story." She flipped through the pages. "'Cliché,'" she read off. "'Been done a thousand times before.' I can't help feeling you hated my story." Having punctuated her remarks with a final flap of her paper, she sat back and waited for him to answer.

"It doesn't matter how I felt about it," he said. "How do *you* feel about it?" He rotated his desk chair and pointed to a print that was hanging on the wall behind his desk. It was a photograph of Ernest Hemingway sitting at a desk with a pen poised in his hand, leaning his elbow on a book. The quote above his head read "There is nothing to writing. All you do is sit down at a typewriter and bleed." It was the cold hard truth, and Cade's favorite quote.

Her eyes widened in surprise. She sat forward again. This time she spoke animatedly with her hands. "I realize you don't know me at all, but I graduated summa cum laude. I also graduated in the top ten percent of my law school class, and I *don't do below-A work*. So if there's a problem here, I want you to know that I will do whatever it takes to fix it."

That was unexpected. Underneath the bubbly, effervescent exterior lay a crouching tiger. Intriguing.

"I appreciate that you're a good student. But you still haven't told me what *you* like about your story."

"Well, it's got magic, a smart teenage girl wizard, and a tortured vampire who can't ever have her. There's tons of angst and emotion. Isn't that good? Plus, it's light, upbeat, and hopeful. I'd like to think that's also my attitude about life."

"Pain and suffering are at the root of every human experience," he said.

She rolled her eyes. *Rolled her eyes.* "You're kidding, aren't you? I mean, life has good things in it too, Professor." He felt his professorly edge eroding faster than the truth, which was hard to deny. That this student was not like any student he'd ever had. She was fearless, annoying as hell, and . . . off-limits.

He tried again. "Your story is a cross between *Harry Potter* and *Twilight*. Both have been done before." Now *he* wanted to roll his eyes but decided to take the high road.

"Isn't that a good thing?" she asked. "Catchy, high-concept? That's how they pitch movies, isn't it?"

"For someone doing this for fun, the story is fine. If that's your goal, then we can work with that."

She stood up and approached his desk. "I'm not doing this 'for fun.' I spent all weekend on this assignment. I want to learn how to make it better. So please don't hedge on your answers."

He sighed. "Your writing itself is very good. You have a great command of language, but the story has problems. Novice problems. If you're serious about writing, they'll have to be addressed." He paused, debating whether to continue. "This story doesn't feel like the story you were meant to write."

Cade swore she went pale. Her hands fluttered in her lap. Clearly he'd hit a nerve. "I'm going to be brutally honest with you, if that's what you'd like me to be."

She crossed her arms and braced herself to take one on the chin. "I want honesty. I'd *appreciate* it."

He shouldn't have walked around to the other side of the desk, because he was close enough now to see that she had the tiniest mole near her mouth. "All right then. What you turned in is technically correct writing but there's no underlying...excitement there. I had the sense that the writer was waiting for an IRS audit instead of truly wanting to tell a story."

For the flash of a second, she looked upset. But then anger lit in her eyes. "You're saying my story is *boring*?" She tossed up her hands. "How could it be boring? There's a vampire chase, the heroine gets a concussion, and the hero and heroine get attacked by a pack of werewolves."

Carol stuck her head into his office. "Is everything all right in here?"

Cade looked from Gabby to Carol. "Yes, Carol, we're just...discussing a class matter. Sorry. We got a little...passionate. I mean, loud. We got a bit *loud*. In our *discussion*."

"It's okay, Carol," Gabby said, biting down on her lip to stay serious. "Professor Marshall is chewing my writing out a little. We can close the door."

Carol looked at him and cocked a brow. "Professor?"

Do not close the door, he said silently to himself. *Do not—*

Yet Carol gave an efficient nod and did just that.

He rubbed the back of his neck, which had suddenly developed a crick, and tried to gather his thoughts. "That's all very exciting, but it feels like the story you *think* you should write, not the story that's in here." He rapped his chest with his fist. Now *he* was getting emotional. He took a breath to make himself calm down. "I believe you're capable of more."

There, he'd said the truth. Maybe she'd get teary and upset and leave, but based on her earlier reaction, he doubted it. He almost hoped she would, because she felt dangerous to him in ways he didn't quite understand.

Gabby broke eye contact first. She swallowed. He hoped she wasn't a crier. When she looked up, he could see she was not taking his criticism well. *Dammit*, he should have known better than to be brutally honest, regardless of what she'd said about wanting the truth.

She shoved her papers back into her book bag.

"I'm sorry if I upset you," he said softly.

She shook her head. "I'm not upset at you. Although it does feel like you're being unnecessarily harsh. Or at least harsher toward my work than you've been with the other students."

"You're misunderstanding me, Ms. Langdon," he said.

"And I think you're misunderstanding me," she responded. "I just want to prove to myself that I can do this. I *need* to."

Just then, there was a knock on the door. Carol's short bob reappeared in the doorway. "Yes, Carol?" Cade said.

"I've got some paperwork for Gabby. If you're done with her, Professor?"

"I'm so done you can stick a fork in me and serve me on a turkey platter," Gabby said. He hoped her attempt at humor meant she wasn't too upset by his criticism.

"Look," Cade said. "My comments weren't meant to discourage you from writing. Only to make you think about *what* you're writing. To make it yours and not a mash-up of what someone else has done."

"Don't worry. It's going to take more than one terrible grade to make me give up."

"It's not personal, Gabby. One of the first things a writer has to learn is how to develop a very, very thick skin." Funny, but everything seemed personal about his interactions with her.

"Well, I'd say thank you," she said, smiling again, "but that might be pushing it." She zipped up her bright yellow jacket.

Carol turned to her and said, "Before you go, Gabby, I wanted to show you the professor we've assigned you to for a research experience. He's next door, and you can meet him now if you want."

"That's great, thanks."

"He said to bring you right over." Carol glanced at Cade. "As soon as you're done with Dr. Marshall, that is."

"You applied to do research?" Cade asked. "How is that, when you're not a graduate assistant?"

"I just wanted the experience of working with someone who writes fiction. I've done a lot of research during my work in law, so I'm qualified to help."

Cade picked up some random papers and feigned disinterest, but his heart was pumping so fast he heard the blood *whooshing* in his ears. Tony Livingstone's office was next door. The thought of Gabby working with someone surrounded by so much suspicion made his stomach churn. And the brief interaction he'd had with Tony today had roused the hairs on his own neck.

Cade decided to stay out of it, to let it lie. Gabby was an adult, and certainly not defenseless. And hadn't he already had a heated enough exchange with her? Besides, maybe she hadn't been assigned to Tony. The hallway was long and full of professors' offices. "Who is Ms. Langdon set to work with, Carol?"

"Dr. Livingstone."

"Absolutely not," Cade said a little too quickly. *Fuck.*

Gabby and Carol both stared. Gabby's mouth dropped open in a little O that was a bit too appealing. A strange thought occurred to him—that he was worried about Tony overstepping boundaries, when perhaps he should be worried more about himself.

"I beg your pardon?" Gabby said, indignation lacing her voice.

"I mean...what I mean is, Ms. Langdon, how can you possibly have time to do research with your demanding work schedule and the time you need to devote to my class?"

"As I said during our—*discussion*—I'm used to working hard, Professor Marshall. I don't think it's any of your bus—"

Tony suddenly appeared at the door, tossing back his boyishly long hair, his eyes lighting on Gabby like she was a steak dinner complete with baked potato and chocolate fudge cake. "Are you Gabriella?" he asked in his deep, charming baritone.

Cade took a deep breath. Told himself he was new here. No one had any proof on this guy. Even Amira

Shreevesanan had let him know they were all watching him carefully.

"I understand you have an interest in writing fiction," Tony said, leaning on Cade's desk and inclining his body toward Gabby.

Cade cleared his throat. "I don't think your research interests are a good fit with Ms. Langdon's." Considering that the only research Tony might possibly want to do was the kind under the sheets. "What I mean is, she should be with someone who writes contemporary American fiction."

That certainly wasn't Cade because he wasn't writing any fiction, was he?

"Oh, I'm confident I could satisfy Gabriella's interests," Tony said. "She's a mature student, and I'm certain I can be very flexible in meeting her needs."

Okay, that was it. This guy was not meeting anybody's needs, much less Gabby's. Before Cade knew what he was doing, he'd stood up and leaned over his desk. "Actually, I just offered Ms. Langdon a position working with me and she's...considering it."

"Oh, is that right?" Tony said. "Funny, but I was passing by in the hallway a little while ago, and I overheard you telling Carol you were too overburdened this semester to take on a student."

"I changed my mind," Cade said with a pointed look at Gabby. "I could use some extra help this semester. If Ms. Langdon's willing, of course."

His gaze met hers. She was frowning a little, as if she couldn't really figure him out. Hell, he couldn't figure himself out.

"Well, I'm excited to have two amazing options," Gabby said. "I'd like to think this over, if that's okay with both of you."

"Feel free to come speak with me more if you have any questions," Tony said, his crocodile gaze sweeping her up and down as he walked over and shook her hand. "I look forward to seeing you around the department, Gabriella."

Tony and Carol left, and Cade took a seat in the battered wooden chair next to Gabby. He would have to bring some real furniture in here, because the stuff that came with the office was really uncomfortable.

"Why—" she began.

He shrugged. "I won't speak badly about a colleague who's innocent until proven guilty," he said, thinking of his own situation, when so many of his colleagues had seemed so eager to believe his ex over him.

"But?" Gabby said.

"There are... allegations. There's no proof of wrongdoing yet, but we're all on high suspicion. And I didn't like the way he looked at you."

"I see." She looked at him with clear, honest eyes. "I know you don't really want me as your research assistant. I'll ask Carol for another assignment."

"No, I—I have plenty of work to keep you busy. But it's research, not fiction writing. I can, however, work with you on your fiction if that's what you want."

"What's your research?"

"I'm exploring the letters of Fitzgerald to his editor. They talk a lot about his novels."

"That sounds interesting."

"And about before. I probably was a bit harsh. I'm not used to teaching writing. I forget to hold back."

"I'll rethink the story." She blushed again.

"Okay, so I expect you to see me after our next class for your first assignment. And we may have to work around your schedule to make time to talk about things. If that's all, I'll see you in class."

"Yes, Professor," she said, saluting him and standing up. Just as she reached the door, she turned back. "Thanks for the opportunity—and for telling me the truth about my writing." She paused. "I think."

Their gazes collided again for one last, lingering moment before she was gone.

Cade got up, closed the door, and leaned against it for a moment. Outside the palladium window, the campus was rainy and wet, the first sign that summer was about to end and change was on the way. Students rushed past with multicolored umbrellas and rain gear. Then an old-fashioned red bike passed by, driven by a woman in a yellow rain jacket.

Cade closed his eyes. He'd been hard on her, but he hoped encouraging too. Yet he could not help but know that the story *he* was meant to write was trapped beneath layers of bullshit he'd been unable to wade through for the past three years. What kind of teacher was he, who could not practice what he preached?

Plus he had a serious problem with this woman. She was gorgeous, and now he would have to figure out a way to not only have her in class, but to work with her outside of it as well. What had he done?

Chapter 9

♥

The minute Gabby stepped into the lodge at Crystal Lake for her cousin Stephanie's wedding the following weekend, she knew she shouldn't have shown up without a plus one.

Granted, the view out the magnificent floor-to-ceiling windows was spectacular—a lush, piney forest wrapping lovingly around a lake so pure and blue it took her breath away. To her left was a huge fireplace with a roaring fire and cozy couches with couples gathered around laughing. A giant moose head mounted atop the fireplace had eyes that seemed to follow Gabby around the room and appeared to be looking at her judgmentally. *Still single?* it seemed to ask with a mocking smirk.

Then there was her own family, all conveniently paired off: her dad and Rachel, Evie and Joe, Sara and Colton. Even Kaitlyn had abandoned her to hang out with Rafe. That left her. By herself. And Nonna, who was always a social butterfly at weddings. Except now with the Alzheimer's, she tended to talk to anyone, even strangers, and easily forgot how many drinks she'd consumed.

That left Gabby open to the well-meaning questions of old aunties and distant cousins and to be hit on by Rafe's friends from the fire department, all of whom had gone through school with the groom, Everett, who was a member of the fire department of a neighboring town.

Everyone was gathered in the lodge lobby, getting the keys to the cabins where they'd be staying tonight and chatting a little before getting ready for the wedding. Sara walked by and gave her arm a little squeeze. "You should've let Rafe fix you up with one of the guys from the station," she said. "Rambo's looking at you."

Rambo was their affectionate nickname for Randall Ames, who'd always seemed to have a little crush on Gabby that had magnified since his girlfriend had recently dumped him.

"I remember Randall before he was Rambo," Gabby said. "I can't seem to get over seeing a scrawny kid chewing with his mouth open at the dinner table and trying to gross us out whenever Rachel turned her back."

"I wish Kaitlyn shared that same sentiment about Rafe," Sara said.

One glance showed Kaitlyn and Rafe laughing it up with a few of Rafe's friends.

"That's a disaster waiting to strike," Gabby agreed.

Just then Randy caught her eye. "Hey, Gabby! Come on over here," he yelled. There was another cluster of guys, probably friends of the groom's, all laughing and talking. A couple of them looked up when Randy shouted across the lobby.

"Sara," Gabby said, grabbing her sister's arm, "if anyone asks, tell them I'm seeing someone, okay? Promise me."

Sara chuckled. "You might meet someone really nice who's not in Rafe's firefighter group," she said, but she must've seen the threat of death in Gabby's eyes because she relented. "Okay, okay. Don't panic. I've got you."

"Gabs!" Randy came running over and enveloped her in a big bear hug and spun her around. *That* certainly didn't attract any attention.

"How's my second baby brother?" she asked, trying to stress the *brother* part as she tried not to get squeezed to death in his viselike arms.

"You're so easy to pick up," Randy said with a big, booming voice as he set her down. "You're not heavy enough to give a guy a good workout." Randall was six four and stocky, with the arms of a lumberjack. "Rafe told me you haven't got a plus one. What do you say we hang out later?"

Gabby looked to Sara for help, but she'd already turned away and into the arms of her loving husband.

One of the other guys in the circle had turned around as a result of the commotion. He had his hands in his jeans pockets, and he was laughing at something someone had said. He had a long, lean frame—a runner's build, but strong, and turned with an ease of movement that indicated athleticism. His hair was dark and wavy and...freshly cut. And he was staring at her.

Holy Hell. *No.* Impossible. Those same stunning hazel eyes, the same determined jaw, those dark brows that tended to give him a sexy, brooding look—all these features were familiar. Except she barely recognized him because he was *smiling*. It was none other than Cade Marshall—talking and joking with a bunch of buddies, showing that same side of him she'd seen before with his daughter.

The reaction slammed into Gabby all at once—hitting her straight in the abdomen—no, lower. A blush crept hotly into her face and made her forget she was gripping on to Randy tighter than a steering wheel on a slick road.

"Gabby?" Randy said. "You okay?"

"Oh, hey, Randy," she said. "It's great to see you. My...my date's calling me," she said, patting him on the arm and smiling. It was just a little white lie. She was counting on enough liquor flowing freely between all of those guys and enough shenanigans going on that that he wouldn't really notice who she was with.

Randy looked puzzled. "Rafe told me you weren't bringing a date."

"Last-minute decision," she said with a shrug and kissed him solidly on the cheek. "Catch you later."

By the time Gabby reached Cade across the lobby, he was deep in conversation with another guy. *That* guy noticed her and smiled, and she gave a polite smile back. Before Cade could turn around, she tapped him on the shoulder, then wished she had a camera for the please-God-no expression on his face when he turned around. Except there was something else beneath the torment, a flash of something hot-blooded-male-dangerous in his eyes, but it was gone in a flash.

"Hi, Teach," she said with a grin.

He rolled his eyes.

He smelled…amazing, like some foresty, piney-scented cologne that seemed to fit perfectly with the natural setting outside. Suddenly she wondered if he was the kind of guy who would look for a wedding hook-up, something she was certain many of Rafe's single friends were doing.

She hoped so. Not! She hoped *not*. Oh, what was she thinking?

"Cade, who's your friend?" the guy next to him asked. A cute guy, Gabby noted, with sandy hair and nice blue eyes.

She smiled and held out her hand. "I'm Gabby. Gabby Langdon." She shot Cade a look, thinking that turning her attention to someone else would make him happy, but he was scowling.

"Well," Cute Guy said, "I'm Jack. And are you here with a date, Gabby Langdon?" He was not letting go of her hand. "Because there's a bunch of us who all came stag, and we'd love some company tonight."

Cade reached over and tugged Gabby closer. So close she bumped into his side, which happened to be as solid as a barn door. Heat seemed to radiate off of his muscular body, and the feel of his fingers on her elbow felt…warm. Possessive. Make that *hot*. "Back off, Jack," Cade said, practically growling. "She's taken."

Something inside her melted. One, because the crazy nuclear reaction that had begun from the first moment she'd seen him in class—make that the parking lot—was continuing, and it was even worse now that they were *touching*. Plus, he'd said she was *taken*. Taken, as in *by him*?

She nearly missed what Cade's companion said next.

"I can't talk much about books like Cade can," Jack said, his gaze flicking up and down her, "but I know all about the human body. Much more interesting."

"He's a doctor," Cade said, his mouth quirking up slightly but his eyes still narrowed down to pounce. "Studying to be a gastroenterologist." To Jack he said, "Trust me, she doesn't want to hear about people's butts."

"Bye, Jack," she said with a little wave as Cade pulled her away. "I'm not taken," she protested to Cade, just in case he thought she would fall at his feet at his suggestion that she might be his date. Which she was afraid she totally would, but still. "I'm single, and he was cute. And I think butts are very interesting." They stopped next to a big sign in the middle of the lobby announcing kayak tours, bird watching expeditions, and hiking trails.

"Are you always so difficult?"

She shrugged.

"You think butts are interesting?"

"Not all butts. But I liked *his* butt," she said, then lifted her brows, waiting for his reaction. And to that he shook his head and laughed, a big, resonant kind of laugh, which she loved because she knew she'd gotten to him. There was a warm-blooded man under that deathly serious veneer. She kept seeing peeks of him, and she suddenly decided it was going to be her mission to make him laugh more. "I'm just enjoying how easy it is to get a rise out of you. And also, you have *friends*. Shocker."

He laughed again, a soft chuckle this time. That was when something happened inside her chest. Her heart cracked open just a little more. Damn him anyway.

"Don't do that," she said. The rush of adrenaline coursing through her was making her giddy.

"Don't do what?"

"Laugh. It makes you far too appealing."

He didn't laugh at that. Instead, their gazes caught, and for a second, Gabby saw pure, undisguised heat there. Her breath hitched.

"Um—why are you here, anyway?" she asked. "Do you know Stephanie too?"

"In my case, it's Everett. I'm a friend from college." He took his eyes off of her to scan the big rustic lobby. "You seem to have a lot of male admirers here."

He tipped his head to where Randall was leaning against the check-in counter, looking their way.

She put her thumb and forefinger close together. "One of my brother's friends has a tiny crush on me. I'm sure it's temporary."

"Those guys are all waving at you," Cade said. Gabby looked over to see a group of Rafe's friends had gathered around Randall.

"All firefighter friends of Rafe's. I've known them forever. We all used to hang around together. I was much more...carefree then." When he raised a brow, she sighed. "Okay, I was a little bit of a flirt. Before I knew better. Now I'm not nearly as much fun as I used to be."

Nearby, a good-looking guy in an expensive suit was talking with a beautiful woman dressed in a silky strapless dress and heels. "I used to be that woman—with a handsome, shallow boyfriend."

"What saved you?" he asked, leveling his quietly assessing gaze on her.

"Turning thirty. Finally waking up and deciding I deserved better."

He looked...interested.

"Well, that must've been a big improvement—getting rid of the bad guy."

"I grew up. Made partner. Now I'm serious." She tried to pull a serious face.

"You seem a little sad about that."

She shrugged. "In some ways, my life didn't turn out to be the exciting adventure I thought it would be. But I'm working on that."

"Life isn't a fairy tale, Gabby. It's hard."

"I understand that but we all make certain...choices. Sometimes we make the wrong ones. But that doesn't mean we can't correct them, right?" At least she hoped she could. Before it was too late and she was stuck at Lock 'em, Stock 'em, and Fleece 'em forever.

"Life is going to be difficult regardless."

"You sound like everyone I know. My family, in particular." She shrugged. "I just don't share your cynical view. Does difficult have to mean joyless?"

"I'm all for pursuing what makes you happy. It's just that the older you get, the more people depend on your good decisions."

"True, but I also like to believe that sometimes you get a second chance to figure out what makes you happiest."

Before he could answer, Sara walked by. "Hey, we're going to get settled in our cabins now. Kaitlyn said to tell you she's going to pick up your key, and you're in cabin number seventeen."

Across the lobby, Kaitlyn waved. "I better go," Gabby said. "See you tonight?"

"You bet," he said. His slightly sarcastic tone didn't match the flare of desire so evident in his eyes.

"I don't know about you," Gabby said, "but I'm really looking forward to seeing you act like a normal person." She started to walk away but slowed her steps. "Oh... you don't have a date, do you?"

He shook his head carefully. "Nope. No date. And since you don't either, I guess you can't get out of dancing with me."

Her heart tripped. Did he just...? He did. He'd asked her to dance. Gabby's mouth fell open. "I *love* to dance," she said.

"Somehow I would've predicted that." Cade winked before he turned away, leaving her standing there in the middle of the lobby with a silly grin on her face. But only the moose saw.

* * *

Gabby rolled her suitcase out of the lodge and down the long, winding driveway that led to the cabin area. Kaitlyn had gone ahead to the cabin she was sharing with Gabby, but Sara walked alongside her with her own suitcase.

"So, Rachel pointed out your professor," Sara said. "He's cute."

Gabby couldn't think of anything to say to that that wouldn't be incriminating, so she stayed silent.

"Aha, so you *do* think he's cute."

Incriminated anyway. "Of course I do, because he *is* good-looking. So what?"

"I thought maybe you'd be off somewhere with him, exploring the grounds—or each other."

"It's not like that," Gabby said, not laughing. "This isn't a joke. This guy's on the straight and narrow. He won't step over the line to date a student."

"Well, that sounds responsible. I like him already."

"Last week you were warning me not to go near him."

She shrugged. "That was before I found out he fixed your bike."

"What about his complicated past—the ex, the book scandal?"

"Maybe it's not that complicated." Sara looked at her kindly. "But that might also mean it's better to wait until you're done with his class."

"I thought you were all for me dating simple guys without a lot of history. You do know Rachel's fixed me up with the new minister, don't you?"

"She's really excited about that. Try to keep an open mind."

"I have an open mind. I'm not judgmental."

"I always thought that was part of your problem with Malcolm. You seem to accept everyone without considering their faults. I'm kind of the opposite. I had a lot of preconceived ideas about Colton."

"What changed your mind about him?"

Sara shrugged. "Mostly, he was irresistible." She smiled. "But this isn't about me. You're a kind, loving, spirited person."

Yes, *spirited.* That was the part that always got her into trouble.

"Love is going to happen to you too. I just know it." Sara gave her a big hug. "You know what Grandpa used to say."

"What's for you will find you."

"I've always interpreted that to mean just live your life. Be yourself and the rest will follow, you know?"

Gabby laughed. "But you and I both know, *nothing comes to anyone who does nothing*—which is straight out of Nonna's mouth."

"So maybe the strategy involves a little of both, right?" They'd reached the cabin area, where a double row of the little wooden buildings stretched out on both sides with a grassy space in between. Before Sara turned off to head to her own cabin, she said, "I need to ask you a favor."

"Sure. What?"

Sara paused and clutched the handle of her rolling bag with both hands. "I just see this thing between Kaitlyn and Rafe ending badly. I—I don't know, I just have a horrible feeling that Kaitlyn's going to get her heart broken."

"Kaitlyn understands how Rafe is," Gabby said. "I've tried to talk with Rafe about this. Truthfully, I think they'd be cute together, but he won't hear of it. I'm going to stay out of it."

"I just feel really nervous," Sara said. "You know how people get carried away at weddings."

"They're adults." Gabby edged her suitcase in the direction of her cabin, eager to leave the sidewalk and the conversation. "It's not our business."

Just as she started backing away, Sara said, "Say something to Rafe."

Gabby halted. "What? No! I'm not his babysitter. If you feel that strongly, *you* talk to him."

"I'm always the older sister with him. He tunes me out. You have a...rapport with him. Tell him to be careful. She's rebounding from her breakup and I don't want him to take advantage of that."

"I don't think she's rebounding. I think she dumped Steve because it wasn't the relationship she wanted."

Sara sighed. "Rafe is never going to get serious, and I'm afraid he's going to break her heart. Please, just mention it to him. One time. For me."

"I'm not sure interfering is a good idea." But she could already hear the wheels on Sara's wheelie bag bumping along the crude asphalt walkway as she fled the scene. Then suddenly the cabin door before her opened. Rafe appeared, wearing tuxedo pants and suspenders and no shirt. Half of his face was covered in shaving cream. And he held a razor in one hand. "Hey, Gabs. I thought I heard voices out here." He looked in one direction, then another, then gave her an assessing look, his eyes brightening. "You're not here to iron my shirt, are you? Because that would be great."

Gabby walked into the cabin, which had a retro vibe consisting of knotty pine paneling, an oak dresser and matching bed, floor-length floral curtains, and stock watercolors of trees and rivers and waterfalls. It was cute in a rustic kind of way, but she preferred something a little farther from bugs and critters, which she was certain were plentiful here.

Gabby flopped down on one of the beds while Rafe went into the bathroom. When he returned, the shaving cream was gone off his face but a towel was wrapped around his neck.

Rafe sat down on the bed opposite and stretched out his long legs. "To what do I owe the pleasure of your visit?"

"Rafe, I—" Oh, this wasn't going to be easy. "You know I love you."

His ruggedly handsome face paled. "Oh, this is bad, isn't it? What happened?"

"Nothing happened. I just want to have a little sister-to-brother chat."

Rafe didn't have frown lines, but he did have a few little maturing crinkles around his warm brown eyes, which women seemed to find fascinating. "The last time you started a talk with *I love you*, you guys warned me you were going to tell Dad I was sneaking out of my bedroom window after curfew. And then you did it."

"Oh, come on," Gabby said. "You were only grounded for a year."

He lifted his brow pointedly.

"And besides, you found other ways to sneak around

and see Claire," Gabby said. As soon as the name of Rafe's first love was out of Gabby's mouth, she knew she shouldn't have mentioned it. His grin instantly faded, and the same old hurt entered his eyes. The fact that he still couldn't bear talking about her after all this time spoke volumes.

Still, he made a valiant effort to pretend it didn't matter. It frightened Gabby that, after all these years, it was pretty apparent that it still did. In the back of her mind, the romantic in her hoped that Rafe would overcome his grief and see that Kaitlyn was a fantastic person. But now she wondered if Rafe's wounds just went too deep.

"I came to talk to you about Kaitlyn. About your relationship."

"Um, I don't have a *relationship* with her," he said defensively. "We're friends. You know, like family friends. I mean, she's been hanging around our house so long she's practically one of us, right?"

Gabby frowned. She was pretty intuitive, and Rafe was red under his collar, a sure sign of discomfort. He was also rubbing the back of his neck and not making solid eye contact. The years had taught her he wasn't telling the full truth.

She walked over to the bureau where a six-pack sat among his car keys, wallet, and room key. He was probably planning to spend the night reunited with his guy friends, reminiscing about old times. He wouldn't have much time to spend with Kaitlyn, much less have a romantic rendezvous with her. Sara was probably worrying about nothing.

On the other hand, he and Kaitlyn had been pretty chummy in the lobby earlier. And there was just something about the way Rafe looked at her that made Gabby think…

Made Gabby think of the way Cade had looked at her across the lobby. After the initial shock had worn off, of course. It was like the professor-student thing had vanished, and he'd seen her simply as a woman. A woman he'd thought was pretty hot.

"We love Kaitlyn," Gabby continued. "I just want to make sure you…behave like a gentleman. She's not someone to fool around with, Rafe. Don't do something stupid that will ruin what you have with her. Plus, you're right. She *is* part of our family."

"Why are you warning me about this now?"

"Because it's a wedding. Because we all know what happens at weddings. There's fun and shenanigans and drinking, and one thing leads to another…"

The picture in her head was not of Rafe and Kaitlyn getting carried away. It was of a flash of dark hair, the image of Cade laughing with his friends and then turning to look at her, of feeling his gaze follow her across the room, burning a trail along the way.

"I get it," Rafe said, not protesting at all, which Gabby thought was odd. Rafe rarely took forced advice from anyone without fighting back.

At a loss about what else to say, Gabby looked around. There was a pair of navy boxers on the floor beside Rafe's suitcase, and his wedding tux was laid out carefully on his bed, the shoes at the foot. His suitcase was jumbled, but an object lying in the middle of the clothes caught her eye. There, mixed in with the scattered items of clothing, was a box of condoms. Like any decent sister, she reached down and plucked it out. "What is this?"

Rafe reached her in two strides and snatched the box out of her hands. "Sorry if you haven't seen these in your own life in a while, but it's none of your business."

She crossed her arms. "I know what they are. But a *box*, Rafe? Of thirty-six?"

"There are lots of bridesmaids," he said with a devilish grin.

"Rafe!"

"I'm joking," he said, holding out his hands in defense. "Will you chill, please?" He tossed the box on the bed. "Randy threw it in there as a gag. You used to be fun, but now you take everything so seriously."

Whoa. It was one thing to admit this to herself, but to hear it from Rafe took her aback. What had happened to the person she used to be, someone spontaneous, excited about life? She used to look forward to having adventures, letting loose a little, but it was like someone had come in and turned the volume down on her life. Way down. Becoming an adult had dampened more than her sense of fun…it had dampened her spirit too.

"Life is short," Rafe said. "YOLO, you know?"

You Only Live Once. "Life isn't all YOLO, Rafe. Life is responsibility. Settling down. Doing the right thing."

"But settling down doesn't mean settling."

Ouch. Rafe could always hit the bull's-eye on her biggest fears. That had been exactly her thing with Malcolm. Settling. She'd literally talked herself into believing that he could be the man she wanted. She made every excuse for his behavior to give him the benefit of the doubt. In fact, she'd tried so hard to do just that, she'd almost believed it herself.

"Look, Gabby," Rafe said, "don't get hung up on your past. Have a little fun. Loosen up." He massaged between her shoulders at the tense muscles there. "Everything will work out, you'll see."

Rafe steered her to the door, and before Gabby knew it, she was standing outside again on the tiny covered porch, next to where she'd left her suitcase. "I'm going to finish getting dressed," Rafe continued, "then I'll see you at the wedding. You need anything?"

"I'm fine. Thanks, Rafe."

As he shut the door, Gabby shook her head to clear it. What had just happened? Wasn't she the one supposed to be giving *him* advice?

Chapter 10

♥

The wedding took place at the edge of the lake at sunset, but Cade wasn't really interested in the ceremony. Since his own marriage had ended, being at any wedding tended to make him want to bolt as quickly as possible.

From his vantage point several aisles behind Gabby, he watched her interacting with her family. She appeared to be in charge of her grandmother, who was apparently a wild card. He could hear the older woman exclaiming about the bridesmaids' strapless dresses and, pretty loudly, about a tattoo of an eagle on one of the bridesmaid's backs.

Gabby seemed to take it all in stride, trying to distract her grandmother and at one point sending a fierce glare in the direction of someone who seemed to have reprimanded her.

Gabby herself looked amazing in a purple dress that hugged all her curves. Her hair was piled up on top of her head, but little tendrils escaped and grazed her pretty neck.

Kissable. Her neck was very kissable.

Maybe staring at her for an hour had loosened his will and his tongue, because the first thing he said when he caught up to her at the reception was, "So I take it you don't have any tattoos? Since it seems like your grandmother doesn't approve."

She looked a little surprised he'd sought her out, but she smiled, which he took as a good sign. "Well, not on my *back*," Gabby said.

He raised a brow. "I'm not even going to respond to that." It would only get him into deeper trouble.

"Do I strike you as someone who might have a tattoo?" Gabby asked. "Even if my grandmother didn't approve?"

Cade thought about that for a second. "Yes. I think you just might. Probably a small, symbolic one in a place not everyone notices. A quiet statement to yourself."

She sipped her drink, but the color that rose into her cheeks told him he may have hit the mark. Then she cleared her throat. "What about you?"

"The only ink I partake in is pen on paper."

She eyed a waiter who was passing by with some bacon-wrapped scallops and flagged him down. "Oh, those look delicious," she said, taking one and popping it in her mouth. She closed her eyes and savored it for a moment. "Oh, wow. That is so damn good. Cade, try one."

Cade. She'd called him by his first name without even realizing it. The sound rolling so easily off her tongue did something visceral to him he couldn't quite describe. So he focused instead on taking an hors d'oeuvre from the offered tray. It was decadent, buttery, and flavorful. "Wow, that *is* good."

"Told you," she said, taking a last bite. "My goal at weddings is to hunt down and taste every single appetizer so that my appetite will be completely ruined before dinner. Want to join me?"

He laughed. "I can see why Ava can't stop talking about you," he said. "You're…fun."

She looked at him, seeming a little startled. "You think I'm fun?"

There was something in her eyes that looked like she was hoping for a yes. Gabby with her antique bike and her chicken nuggets and her quiet teasing. And her kindness to Ava and to her grandmother. And to him.

"Yeah," he said softly, "I think you're fun." He held out his plate. "Have another. You know you want to."

"Hmmm." She tapped her chin with her forefinger, pretending to be deep in thought. "Okay, if you insist," she said before snagging the last one from his plate. She popped the whole thing in her mouth and groaned from pleasure.

He chuckled, then grew quiet. Because the look on her face reminded him of another pleasure entirely, and it wasn't culinary.

"Don't laugh at me," she said.

"I'm smiling because you have no idea how beautiful you are." Oh, hell. Had that just come out of his mouth? And he'd only had one drink so far.

She sucked in a breath. "Wait, am I hallucinating? Did Professor Heathcliff just pay me a compliment?"

A sort of inappropriate one, and he'd better watch himself. "Professor Heathcliff?"

"Yes, you know. Dark, mysterious... a little cranky."

"I'm trying to decide if *that's* a compliment."

"Well, you do sort of have a different personality in front of our class than you do in the wild. Much more intimidating."

He shrugged. "I wish you'd tell that to my daughter. She's not intimidated by me at all." In truth, Gabby had called it exactly right. The fact that he couldn't screw up his teaching gig, and the stress of returning to town with everyone knowing—and many believing—the scandal about him, had made him crotchety.

He assessed her as she looked around at the crowd. If she hadn't been in his class, he'd be taking her off to the dance floor or maybe they'd forget the dance floor altogether and just head straight back to his room. This was the first time since his divorce he'd felt such powerful attraction—and wanted to act on it.

All the more reason to go back over to his friends and enjoy the evening with any of a number of women who were single, eligible, and *not in his class*.

Cade looked around. "Everyone's taking their seats for dinner. I should go." Funny thing though, he didn't want to. But he'd already overstepped his bounds.

In the second that he hesitated, she grabbed his elbow. His forearm muscles contracted under her touch. "Wait. Don't go."

He shot her a questioning look.

"I saw you fooling around with your friends earlier and I think you've got the moves," she said. "Prove it to me."

Dancing. She was talking about dancing, he reminded his sex-deprived brain.

"You promised me a dance," she reminded him.

"I did, but now I'm thinking maybe that's not such a good idea."

She frowned. "Why not? Are you a klutz? Two left feet?"

He smirked. "No, I'm a great dancer."

"Sprained your ankle? Pulled a muscle?"

"No."

"Is it me?" She pulled a face. "You don't want to be seen dancing with me in front of your friends? I promise I'll behave from now on with the hors d'oeuvres."

"Stop. None of that. It's just that I'm...your teacher."

"Oh, for God's sake, we're an hour from Angel Falls. No one cares about that."

He shrugged. "I care."

She scanned his face. "Okay, I get it. I respect that." Her hand dropped from his arm.

He was suddenly free to bolt, the safe thing to do. Yet his body refused to comply. In the background, the clinking of silverware against glasses grew louder throughout the room as people called for the groom to kiss the bride.

"I-I'd better go," she said with a small smile.

She started to walk away. He noticed the fire department guys watching her, one in particular. And there was his friend Jack, holding a drink, ready to pounce.

"Gabby," he called after her. Applause and cheers sounded through the room as the bride and groom acquiesced to the crowd's demand.

She turned and lifted her brows. "Yes?"

"You're right. I'm taking things too seriously. Will you save me a dance?"

She tapped her index finger on her cheek. "Okay, fine, but you seem a little fickle. And my dance card *is* almost full."

He laughed out loud. She was gorgeous, spirited, irresistible. Who could blame him for wanting to spend more time with her?

And it was only a dance, right?

Chapter 11

♥

Gabby had been starving all day even with the appetizers but when dinner finally came, she'd lost her appetite. Out of the corner of her eye, she saw Cade sitting with his guy friends, laughing it up. Several times, he'd caught her staring and smiled.

Oh, lord, she was in trouble. Because she liked this looser, more relaxed side of him that he seemed to display everywhere except in class. She liked it way too much.

"So, Kaitlyn," Rafe said, drumming his long fingers on the table, "Have you had any coffee yet tonight?"

Kaitlyn looked at him like he'd had too much to drink already. "No, Rafe, I have not."

"How would you like to go over to the dessert table and check out the coffee?"

"I'm sure it's top quality here at Lincoln Lodge," Colton said with a grin. Rafe shot him a dirty look as he walked off with Kaitlyn. "That's the worst pick-up line I've ever heard in my entire life," Colton said when they were out of earshot.

"And yet it worked," Rachel said with a smile.

"C'mon honey, let's dance," Joe said to Evie.

"Sure," she said, taking his hand. "Since it's after nine and we're still upright."

"What do you say, Sara? They're playing our song," Colton said, standing up and walking over to Sara's chair.

"I've never heard this song before in my life. And you always say that. You just like to dance."

All the cute couples left. That left Gabby at the table with her parents. And spinsterhood staring her in the eye.

She hoped Cade would ask her to dance, but he was so nervous about it, she wasn't sure he would. That left Randy or her female cousins as potential partners. Which was worse? Hmm. Toss-up. "C'mon, Nonnie," she finally said, "let's go get some of those delicious Russian tea balls and a cup of coffee." And maybe a gin and tonic for herself. Sounded great, dousing herself with drink and eating cookies and passing the evening with her grandmother and her friends.

Gabby grabbed a plate and started piling on cookies, her favorite part of any proper Italian wedding and probably the most fun she was going to have all night. "That bride has a tattoo," Nonna said loudly from behind Gabby. "Why does everyone have a tattoo? And her boobs are hanging out of that gown."

"Shhh, Nonna," Gabby whispered. People were shooting them dirty looks. She noticed Stephanie's mother standing a few feet away, so she steered Nonna out of hearing range. "Here," she said, holding out a plate. "Tell me what cookies you want."

"What I really want is a drink. But don't tell your father."

Gabby couldn't help smiling. There was the Nonna she knew and loved. The subversive spirit that was so like Gabby's own.

"Okay, what would you like?"

"Whiskey sour," she said. "And tell the bartender not to use cheap whiskey."

"Gotcha. I'll be right back."

Nonna began to look over the beautiful plates of homemade cookies that all the relatives had baked in celebration. Gabby walked over to the bar and stood in line, careful not to make eye contact with any of Rafe's friends and glancing back at Nonna frequently. Thankfully Nonna had taken up a conversation with a couple of cousins from Italy and was staying out of trouble.

"Put that on my tab," a deep voice said when the bartender handed her the drinks.

Gabby turned to find Randy standing so close behind her he could reach out and lick her ear, the thought of which immediately made her step away. "Randy, you know there's no charge at a wedding."

"I know that, but that's the only way you'll let me get you a drink."

Gabby sighed. He just was not going to give up. "Look, I know you're going to find somebody but it's not me, and deep down you know that."

"Just give me a shot, Gabs."

"I'm sorry, Randy. You'll always be like a brother to me."

He put a hand over his heart. "You're killing me, you know that? How about a dance?"

"I can't now. I'm just getting something for my nonna and—" She glanced back at the cookie table only to find Nonna was...gone. "Oh no, I've got to go." Without saying goodbye, Gabby left the line, searching the crowd. "Have you seen Nonna?" she asked the Italian cousins, but all she got was "*Scusi, non capisco.*" Dread churned in her stomach. There was another wedding going on down the hall. What if Nonna had wandered in there?

Gabby pushed her way back to her family's table, stopping by her father's chair. "Dad, I lost Nonna," she blurted out.

Rachel gave a little gasp, but her dad chuckled, his usual initial response to any crisis, which had a remarkable way of breaking the tension. Years of being a physician had given him nerves of steel, but he immediately stood and began scanning the room. "Where did you leave her?"

"Near the bar. I left her chatting while I went to get us a drink, but I looked over and she was gone."

The "Chicken Dance" melted into another song with the strains of an accordion, something Gabby hadn't heard in ages.

"Well, look at that," Colton said, pointing to the dance floor.

"No, get out," Evie said.

"Nonna's still got the moves," Rafe said.

Suddenly Nonna whizzed by, waving to all of them, led by none other than Cade, who gave Gabby a wink as they passed.

Gabby stood watching in shock a few feet from the dance floor, Colton laughing at her side. "She dances a hell of a polka," he said.

Gabby clutched her stomach. Relief that Nonna was okay, anger at herself for letting her out of her sight, and shock at the sight of Cade dancing with her grandmother all mixed together, too many feelings at once.

"No one would've blamed you if she really took off, you know that, don't you?" Colton said kindly.

Suddenly Nonna was taking the empty chair next to her, a little out of breath. "I haven't had so much fun since I used to go dancing with your grandfather. I love the polka!"

Cade was smiling. "I hope I didn't cause a problem. She was standing on the sidelines clapping her hands, then she grabbed my elbow and said, 'C'mon let's go!'"

Colton shook hands with Cade and introduced himself.

"That was so much fun," Nonna said. "Thank you, young man."

"You're welcome," Cade said.

"Gabby, where's my drink?" Nonna asked.

"C'mon, Rose, I'll get you one." Colton winked at Gabby. "You two can take a spin around the dance floor."

"Oh, I—well, I—I can't polka," Gabby said, suddenly unable to form real words.

Cade glanced over at the band, which was back to playing popular songs. "No worries. I think you're safe."

"You never know in Ohio," Gabby said. But she took his outstretched hand.

They'd almost made it out to the dance floor when Rafe took hold of her arm. He addressed Cade. "Are you sure you want to go out there with her?" he asked. "Because Gabs gets a little crazy when music plays, just warning you."

"Rafe, go chase girls or something," she said, pushing his hand off gently like she was swishing away a bug. "C'mon, Cade. Don't listen to him."

He guided her onto the dance floor and pulled her close. The adrenaline from Nonna being lost and the relief at finding her, and now this...well, it was all too much. Gabby's knees seemed to have forgotten how to hold her body up, and every limb felt heavy and clumsy.

"I thought I lost my grandmother," she said.

"I'm sorry for the worry. It was kind of hard to refuse her."

"Well, she looks so happy."

"Your nonna can certainly polka it up."

"Apparently, so can you."

"Well, I did study in Poland for a semester."

"Really?"

"No," he said with a grin. "My mother taught me when I was a kid."

She shook her head and laughed. But then their gazes tangled, and the beat of the music shifted to a much slower one.

"Well, I'm glad she felt comfortable with me," he said. They danced quietly for a few minutes. "You, on the other hand, are very tense." He held her gently at the waist, pulling her near enough to feel his body heat radiating out from all that hard muscle.

That move somehow didn't make her any less tense.

She froze, lost in his woodsy scent: menthol from shaving cream and clean man. He drew her closer until the stubble of his cheek brushed a bit coarsely against her temple. When he drew back to look at her, if she wasn't melting before, she was a veritable puddle now.

"Don't move," he said softly. She couldn't even if she wanted to, because she was paralyzed, blinded by her attraction to him. And she understood exactly what he was saying. They were under a spell, and neither of them wanted it to be broken.

Time stilled. The noise around them faded away until she was aware of only him, and she swore she felt his heartbeat as she stood there wrapped in him, his hand wound around her waist, his other hand entwined with hers.

He bent his head, and she thought he was going to kiss her, right there on the dance floor. But just then the music changed again to a rapid, popular beat.

Then he surprised her again. His moves were smooth and easy, not the jerky, self-conscious shuffling with a drink in one hand that a lot of guys did. He must've seen the surprise on her face because he looked pleased. And then it happened—he grinned.

That was the moment Gabby knew she was a goner, that if tonight he said the word, somehow, somewhere, they would end up in bed together.

"Wow, you can dance," she said, more to lighten things up than anything else, He was a really good dancer. Graceful, crazy, and *fun*.

"How about we get something to drink and cool off a little outside?" Cade asked.

"Sure," she said.

Cade walked by the dessert table, where pieces of cake and flutes of champagne were sitting for anyone to take. He handed her two flutes and snagged two pieces of cake, and they made their way out of the hall.

Night had fallen, and with it a slight chill had filled the air. The clouds hung low and heavy, and a streak of lightning flared in the distance, followed by a rumble of thunder.

Suddenly she felt his coat being draped around her shoulders as they sat at an iron patio set, one of several on a terrace that overlooked the lake.

"Thank you." She pulled it closer around her. It smelled heavenly. Like wonderful man. *Was* he a wonderful man? He might be. She hoped with all her heart that he was.

A lot of guys would have taken the opportunity to suggest something by now—inviting her back to their cabin, for example—but she didn't see that happening with him. She longed to reach up and smooth the creases between his strong brows, feel the stubble of his beard as their lips finally met, but she didn't dare cross that line.

As if sensing her thoughts, he grabbed her hand and brought it to his lips to kiss her fingers, slow and deliberately, and she wondered if that was how it would be with him—savoring every moment, taking his time. Or would he kiss her passionately and with abandon?

All too soon, they'd finished their cake. "Gabby, I had a great time dancing with you," he said. "But... I think I'd better walk you back inside."

Damn, damn, damn. Was it her? Was she imagining all this, that he was just as intensely attracted to her as she was to him? Another lapse of judgment, like in her past?

He'd eased her hand down but was still holding on to it. "It's not that I don't want to, but I can't."

"I'm thirty years old, Cade. I'm an attorney."

"I can't take the risk, no matter how much I'm tempted."

That made her smile. "You're tempted?"

"God, yes."

She would have slept with him on the spot. Dammit, why did he have to be so . . . upstanding?

"I'll walk you back to the reception."

She sighed and gestured in the opposite direction. "Thanks, but I think I'll head back to my cabin. I don't need an escort."

But he was already next to her, his hand on her elbow as she stepped in her high heels over the uneven pavement.

Halfway down the hill, another crack of thunder rent the air, and the sky let loose. Buckets of cold rain were dumped from the sky. Cade grabbed her by the hand and led her under the tiny porch of a close-by cabin. *His* cabin, she discovered, as he was soon fumbling with a key in the lock as the water from their wet clothes dripped onto the small concrete slab in front of the door.

Then they were inside. Cade flipped on a light and tugged off his shoes. He ran into the bathroom and returned with a fluffy white towel. She slipped off her shoes and toweled her hair and face first. What to do with the rest of her she had no idea, but she was shivering. He'd just wrapped another towel around her shoulders when a loud crack of thunder hit, and the lights went out.

"Cade?" she whispered.

"Here," he answered on an exhale. The dangerously sexy edge in his voice sent another shiver through her that had nothing to do with being soaked to the bone.

He was right there, next to her, still clutching the ends of the towel. She couldn't see him in the thick blackness, but she could feel the heat radiating off of him, and more—she swore she could sense his wanting her. For a moment, they both froze. Gabby held her breath as thoughts began to overtake her brain—of kissing him. Of wrapping herself around him until all his upstanding defenses crumbled. Of dragging him over to the bed and having her way with him.

His clothes rustled quietly as his weight shifted, his fingers reflexively tightening on the towel. For a moment, Gabby thought he was going to tug her into him and kiss her.

I slept with him, Gabby imagined herself telling Sara tomorrow. *I couldn't help it, really. I mean, we were drenched, and the lights went out, and his hands were all over me...*

Except Cade's hands weren't all over her. In fact, he'd dropped them from around her shoulders and now he appeared to be...gone. He'd turned on his phone flashlight and began rummaging through his suitcase. In the dim light, she could see him shrug out of his suit jacket and toss it to the floor.

The broad planes of his shoulders were outlined in shadow, the thick wave of his hair, the muscles of his forearms as he dug through his clothes.

She realized that for the first time since her breakup with Malcolm, she wanted someone badly. She'd tried so hard these past months to school herself in not making the same mistakes, but what if Cade wasn't a mistake? Maybe it was time to take a risk, as Rafe had encouraged her to do. "I should go," she heard herself saying instead. *Some risk taker.* "My cabin's just across the way."

Seeing the way he looked at her just then made her breath catch. "Don't go yet," he implored. "I mean—there're no lights anywhere." He walked over to a window and pulled the curtain back to stare out at the double line of cabins, but there was only a wall of darkness and the persistent patter of raindrops on the glass. Then he walked over to her and pressed something into her arms—dry clothes. "Here, take my phone and go into the bathroom and change. We can wait out the storm."

The urge to protest withered away and she did as he'd instructed. His sweatshirt smelled clean, like laundry detergent, and a little bit like him, something she found both comforting and disturbing at the same time. She imagined him throwing this and his daughter's wash in at the little wood-slab house back in Angel Falls, and it struck her with a strange, warm feeling deep inside. Was the thought of a man doing laundry arousing? Apparently so.

She changed quickly and groped her way back to the

bedroom, finding him dressed in a T-shirt and shorts. Under the dimness of the phone light, she had the quickest glimpse of his legs, lean and muscular, and his bare feet. She couldn't see very well but from what she could tell he was…delicious.

They ended up sitting on the floor propped up against the bed talking. About thunderstorms and Angel Falls and how they'd both snuck books to read in favorite places, Gabby under her mom's desk and Cade on the window seat after hours in his mom's bookshop.

Until there was a huge flash of lightning and a bongo-drum boom of thunder that made her jump. Instinctively, she put her hand on his arm. "Oh, sorry," she said, half-laughing, half-jumping out of her skin. She instantly jerked it back but he took hold of it. For a few beats, she froze, feeling the strength and warmth of his grip, sensing rather than seeing his long-fingered and beautiful hand. He slowly kneaded her fingers, as if he were deciding, deciding, while she sat next to him freaking out. The velvet warmth of his skin felt wonderful, thawing her cold limbs to the consistency of butter.

With one of her senses taken away, being next to him in the dark seemed to elevate his touch to the level of foreplay. Every movement of his fingers, every slide of his hand against her palm, sent stabs of arousal through her. She wanted to curl up against his solid chest and lose herself in exploring all the different textures of him—his silky hair, the hard plains of muscle, the rough grain of stubble.

She could feel everything between them, magnified a thousand times—the aura of energy, the held breaths, the pounding pulse of their heartbeats. The moment seemed to stretch on forever, full of unspoken words distilled down to a single touch that thrilled her to the core.

"Kiss me," she whispered without thinking. He went still. "Kiss me," she said, more steadily now.

Suddenly she felt the inexorable draw of him as he tugged her to him, bringing them so close together she could feel his breath on her cheek. His hand curled softly around her neck and pulled her in until finally, finally his mouth was on hers.

His lips were feather light, his kisses slow and measured, as if he were using them to memorize the shape and feel of her mouth. Then they became deep and unrestrained, the kisses of a man whose careful control was all but lost. His tongue slid against hers, every tentative exploration sending sparks of fire all through her that coiled and flamed in her core.

She ran her hands up his arms, over the solid bands of muscle. Then up, over the curve of his shoulder, to curl around his neck, brushing the ends of his hair. The way he drew her close undid her, his arms reaching around hers, dragging her into his hard warmth. His touch was sure, confident, experienced, a man who knew his way around a woman's body.

That was when things got a little crazy. Maybe it was the fact that all their senses were focused on touch and taste and little else. Or the fact that the darkness was the perfect excuse to push limits where rationality would have prevailed otherwise.

Somehow, she found herself in his lap, her hands

on his shoulders, her legs wrapped carelessly around his thighs, lost in deep, sensual kisses as their tongues and limbs tangled. Then he was kissing her deeper, more passionately, his hand under the borrowed sweatshirt, caressing the sensitive skin of her back, and oh my God, they were going to do it right here on the floor and she wouldn't be able to move because, with a few kisses, he'd reduced her to a trembling blob of goo. All this and they hadn't even gotten past first base.

Her last rational thought involved Rafe's supersize box of condoms. Instead of being so censoring of her brother, she probably should've grabbed a couple.

"Your skin is so soft," he whispered in her ear, and the sound of his voice sent a shudder shimmying through her. "Are you still cold?"

What, are you kidding me? Heat was rolling off of her in waves, threatening to burn this place up in flames. "I'm good," she managed. "You?"

She pushed against him and he yielded, and somehow they both ended up on the carpet, her over him. Under her hand, his heart beat boldly and strong. Her fingers brushed coarse-soft hair. She learned the contours of his chest by kissing her way up it, exploring every hill and valley, the hard muscles covered by a layer of smooth, soft skin, which was such a contrast to all the hardness of his body. She felt his rumble of laughter as he lifted her up until their lips met.

"What are you doing to me?" he whispered. "It feels so damn good."

She was afraid to say anything to break the spell

between them so she poured herself into giving him more kisses.

"Don't stop," he said, curling his fingers around her wrists and tugging her upward so she was fully atop him, his erection pressing into her at exactly the right place, his kisses deeper and harder, his hands running up and down her back. He traced his fingers over her bra clasp, mapping it out with his fingers.

This was really going to happen. And that was fine with her, because she wanted him more than anything.

And then the lights flickered on. Suddenly they were bathed in fluorescent lighting, blinking against the harsh brightness. Gabby became aware that she was straddling him, her legs wrapped around his, her clothing askew. Cade was lying on the floor, bare chested. The kissing stopped, of course, and she couldn't quite tell what exactly the look in his eye meant, but it was probably a big dose of *Oh no, what am I doing* and *Oh my God, this woman's hair is a disaster*.

She pulled back, disentangled her legs, and knelt at his side. He was panting a little, still looking at her in that strange way.

She had no words. When she glanced at him again, his face said it all. Guilt and confusion had taken hold. And then he opened his mouth to speak.

"Don't say it, Cade," she said.

"What?" he managed.

"Whatever you're about to say. Because that was... wonderful. And I don't want to hear you say that it wasn't. Please, just don't, okay?"

"It *was* wonderful," he said, and that surprised her.

"But I didn't mean for it to happen. I'm still your teacher and I want to do the right thing here."

She managed a nod, even though she didn't want him to be logical. She wanted more kisses. But she didn't say that. Her eyes grew watery because... well, because she couldn't help it. She was frustrated and a little embarrassed and she still wanted him so badly.

Cade stood. "I'm walking you back to your cabin."

"I don't need you to do that." She wished she could just leave already, but her limbs felt as if they were moving in slow motion.

"Look, Gabby, even outside of the professor thing, I'm not the kind of man who's looking for a relationship," he said softly. "My entire focus is on my daughter right now. It's a good thing this didn't go further because I would never want to hurt you."

Oh, great. He was basically telling her there was no hope for them even after the class was over. Good to be clear on that.

She had one hand on the battered doorknob, and she should have just left, but then she made the mistake of looking at him. And that was when it suddenly hit her, that he was... lying. Oh, perhaps not the part about not wanting a relationship, but he couldn't hide the fact that he still wanted her. She saw it in his eyes. In the tight set of his jaw, and the way he pressed his lips into a straight line. He couldn't hide what they both knew. That there was something combustible between them, something bigger than both of them.

"I can walk myself." She started to open the door to let herself out, but something made her pause. A streak of courage, maybe. Something she felt deep in her gut, as strongly as she'd ever felt anything. The certainty with which she felt it shocked her. "By the way," she said, looking him straight in the eye, "I'm not sorry. For any of it. I'm old enough to do what I want. We're equals. That's where I stand with this." She released a breath. At least for once she'd said what she needed to say. And she'd said it with conviction, which for her, felt really good.

Then she opened the door and ran out into the rain.

* * *

Gabby was relieved that Kaitlyn wasn't back in the cabin. Yet at the same time, she could've used someone to talk to. It was still raining, though not pouring, and as soon as she got inside, she stripped off the borrowed clothing and took a shower, letting the hot water beat away her worry.

It didn't work. She tried to console herself with the fact that, even if Kaitlyn were there, she probably wouldn't confide in her about what had happened between her and Cade. She felt fairly certain no one had seen them together, and she made a silent vow that she would never say a word. Secrets had a tendency to get out. People saw, they overheard. She didn't hold either one of them to blame for what had happened, and she would never want Cade's reputation to suffer for it.

Resolutely, Gabby closed her eyes and lay back on the bed. She stuck her nose down under the collar of Cade's sweatshirt (which she'd put back on) and breathed in the scent of him. Oh, those lips. Those hands. If the lights hadn't come on, she would've made love with him right there, without hesitation. If he came back now and knocked on the door, her answer would still be the same. He was good-looking and charming and...nice. When he wasn't in front of the classroom being all dark and broody, he was a normal, fun human being who was...irresistible. And he definitely wasn't ever getting his sweatshirt back.

But he was her teacher. Gabby knew that she'd crossed a line she'd never crossed before. A line that would blur the lines between fairness, favoritism, and power.

She lay awake for what seemed like hours. She debated finding Sara, but she knew Sara and Colt had been looking forward to this weekend away and didn't want to burden her. Plus, nothing had really happened, and it would be best to just forget everything, not call attention to it.

At around two in the morning, Gabby was startled from her half-awake state. She heard voices from outside the door.

"Kate, please. It's not like that." It was Rafe.

"Gabby's probably sleeping," Kaitlyn said in a hushed voice. "Please go before you wake her up."

"Don't be angry with me," the first voice implored.

"I'd rather you not touch me right now," Kaitlyn said.

Uh-oh. Did that mean Rafe *did* touch her...before?

"I can't help it those women were texting me," he said. "I swear I didn't give them my number. The guys must've put them up to it."

"Admit the truth. You came here for an easy lay. Not to spend time with me. And those floozy girls know it."

"That's not true."

Gabby froze under the covers. She shouldn't be listening to this, yet part of her could not wait to hear what was next. And for once she had the perfect excuse to eavesdrop—she was literally stuck in place.

"Then why did you keep looking at your phone when we were . . . you know?"

"Kaitlyn, I'd rather kiss you than look at my phone any day of the week."

Kissing? Oh my God, they'd been kissing.

"I don't believe you."

"I'm sorry I seemed distracted," Rafe said. "Look, I care about you a lot. You're just . . ."

"I'm just *what*?"

"You're just a settling-down type of girl, and I'm . . ."

"Don't even finish that sentence, okay? Good night, Rafe."

Gabby heard the door click and froze in place in her bed. She heard Kaitlyn's long, drawn-out breath as she latched the chain. Heard her tiptoe to the bathroom and the water running as she brushed her teeth.

A few minutes later Kaitlyn sank into the bed beside her.

"You okay?" Gabby asked.

"No," Kaitlyn said, her voice sounding muffled and strange.

Gabby clicked on the light. Kaitlyn had clearly been crying, judging by the mascara stains under her eyes and the wad of Kleenex clutched to her chest. She blew her nose loudly before dropping her head back onto the pillow.

"I'm sorry I woke you," she said.

"I was awake," Gabby said. "I heard you and Rafe. Is everything all right?"

Her eyes got teary again and she shrugged. "I don't want to talk about it, if that's all right." She blew her nose again. "How about with you? I saw you with your cute professor." Why did everyone refer to Cade as *her* professor? It reminded her of Professor Bhaer in *Little Women*, a character she desperately tried to love. But after Laurie, anyone else in the world would be second-rate for Jo.

"Oh, sure. Nothing to say. He's pretty much a straight arrow about not mixing business with pleasure."

"Is he gay?"

No. Definitely not gay. "Maybe," she found herself saying, going a little overboard to avoid suspicion. "You sure you don't want to talk about it?"

About the kissing. And touching. Or lack thereof.

Kaitlyn gave a tired sigh. "I felt like we were getting somewhere. He seemed really into me. We did a slow dance, and I don't know, I just felt this…electricity. It was powerful, and I could tell he felt it too." She tossed a skeptical look at Gabby. "I know you don't believe me, but don't pity me, okay? This time I learned my lesson."

"I don't pity you," Gabby said softly. Just the opposite. She knew *exactly* what Kaitlyn was talking about. "I just don't want you to get hurt."

Tears leaked out of Kaitlyn's eyes, and Gabby felt at a complete loss for words.

"Look, you've got a great brother," Kaitlyn said. "But he's an emotional black hole. I mean, he's so damn charming, and I'd had a few drinks, so he was probably even more charming than usual, and I was at the point where I'd do anything to have him for one night. So we started making out in his cabin, you know? And then..."

"The lights went out?" Gabby offered. She really didn't want to hear the private details. She was *afraid* to hear the private details. And as for Rafe, she was going to kill him at the first light of dawn.

"Yes, but we barely noticed that, and things were really fantastic until his phone kept flashing. Not once or twice, but like, continuously. I couldn't help but notice it with the lights out. Finally I looked at it and it was all texts from women."

Gabby frowned. "What kind of women?"

"Apparently half the single women at the wedding were trying to hook up with him. *And he kept looking at the texts.* Honestly, I almost threw the phone at him."

Gabby believed Rafe when he said Kaitlyn's friendship was important to him. So he wouldn't...he didn't...oh God. "Rafe would never go out of his way to hurt you." No, but he could hurt her in a careless, not-really-getting-it Rafe way. But surely he wouldn't have...slept with her?

Kaitlyn gave a sad shrug. "It's all right, Gabby. I was hoping he thought of us as something different. Before this weekend, he was acting like that was possible, and when he asked me to take a walk and one thing sort of led to another... Well, I was wrong. I've been wrong this whole time."

"Kaitlyn, did Rafe—did you—I mean..."

She shook her head. "It doesn't matter."

"Maybe if you two can talk it out..." Oh, she was not being helpful or consoling. Rafe? Talk it out? She couldn't picture it. "Forget what I just said. Rafe needs to get his act together, and I'm not sure you—or anyone—can help him do that."

"I'm done," Kaitlyn said. "It's never going to work out between us. I don't have any more time to wait until he grows up." She blew her nose again. "And he has problems but I'm not his shrink! I'm not anyone's shrink. I just want a normal guy without... intimacy issues."

"Oh, honey." She reached out to pat Kaitlyn's shoulder.

"It's all right, Gabby. I'm sorry. I know Rafe's your brother, and I don't want you to think badly of him."

"Don't be sorry. I know Rafe has his issues."

At least Kaitlyn had thought this out before she'd slept with him. She hadn't, had she? Gabby hoped to God she hadn't.

Chapter 12

♥

The following Wednesday morning, Gabby found herself at the bottom of a winding drive that led to a magnificent country estate. The mansion could've come straight from the pages of *Architectural Digest*, complete with its French country-chateau look and its rolling fields bordered by white wood fencing, which encircled a handful of grazing horses. It appeared that Professor Bowman had done quite well for himself.

She looked again at the papers in her hand. The ones that said what a terrific writer her mother was and had inspired her to hunt the professor down. She hoped she could learn something about her mother from him that no one in the family seemed to know—why she wrote, what she was hoping to accomplish, what her own thoughts were on having received such glowing remarks on her work.

Her mom's great grades—and Cade telling Gabby she could write something better—had encouraged her to pull out something she'd been working on for the past three years: a World War II love story about a war nurse and a soldier, both of whom had scars, hers visible, his invisible. She hadn't intended to use it for class at all, much less show it to Cade to tear apart. The thought of sharing it made her feel stripped down bare, and she still wasn't sure she'd have the courage to actually turn it in. Cade was absolutely right about her not being very excited about the other story; it was just something light-hearted she felt would be fun—and safe—to work on in class. But this story—it bared her soul.

Gabby felt in her gut that Professor Bowman would likely never remember the ramblings of one long-ago student, and worried that perhaps he'd only been being kind all those years ago.

But still, she had to know.

Did her mother have exceptional talent?

As she stood at the front door clutching the old blue folder, it struck Gabby that she was probably romanticizing her mother's talent, looking for a fantasy. She'd once again let her emotions and her impulsivity lead her on a wild goose chase. Tears suddenly welled up in her eyes, and she turned to leave before someone actually appeared.

It wouldn't be the first time impulsivity had reigned. Just reliving the events from the wedding—the dash through the cold rain and those hot, hot kisses—sent a shiver through her and made her blood pound in her ears. Everything with Cade had been so...amazing. So...right. She'd been almost certain he'd felt it too. But then he'd shut her down.

A buzzing sound made her jump and look up above

the door, where a tiny white camera appeared to be following her every movement. Too late, she realized that she'd just looked directly into its lens.

She'd made it down the stairs and onto the paved walkway when the door opened behind her. "May I help you, young lady?" a gruff voice asked.

A man with silver hair and broad shoulders stood looking at her with his hands on his hips, impeccably dressed in a blue chambray shirt with sleeves half rolled.

He had to be in his sixties, but he had an athletic strength that made him seem younger than his age and called to mind the classically handsome looks of Paul Newman.

"You must be the reporter from the *Times*," he said. "I wasn't expecting you until eleven."

"Oh, I—" Gabby sucked in a breath, a little flustered, her brain wiped clean of anything coherent. While she stumbled over her words, he glanced at his watch, which, she noted, appeared to be the kind advertised in luxury magazines.

The man moved a step closer, casting a formidable shadow. Oh, hell. She wasn't a coward. So she planted her feet and looked him in the eye. "I'm not…I'm not a reporter. My name is Gabby Langdon. I think my mother used to be a student of yours." She held up the folder that held her mother's work. "I was wondering if you might remember her."

"Did she not like my grade?" he quipped, his mouth quirking up in a way that seemed very familiar in a way she couldn't place.

The joke threw her for a moment but didn't stop her. "Well, I found some old papers of hers that you'd commented on, and I wondered if you had any—insight...on my mother's writing." She was blathering. Of course, because this was a stupid, stupid idea, and she needed to go home *now*.

It was just a couple of old college papers. What had she been thinking?

"Why don't you simply ask your mother?" he asked, not unkindly.

"She died when I was young, and I—I want to be a writer myself." Gabby almost stopped there because it suddenly occurred to her why she was here. To make a connection between her mom and herself—between her desire to write and her mother's own writing ambitions. "I guess I'm just asking for—a memory. If you had any impression of her as a student. As a writer."

The man looked like he thought she was touched in the head. And she probably was.

"Let me see the papers," he said. "I have a few minutes until my next appointment. Come in."

He took the folder from Gabby and disappeared into the house, which, Gabby noted, was just as magnificent on the inside as out. Wooden beams graced the ceiling of the foyer, which held a huge gray stone fireplace that looked like it had been shipped from a French castle. She followed him to an elegant library that overlooked bright green fields.

He sat down at an enormous, elaborately carved desk, opened the folder, and began reading, leaving Gabby to look around the room. The floor was covered in a jewel-toned Oriental rug that a sunbeam had carved into complicated patterns and shadows, while the walls were lined with built-in bookshelves that smelled vaguely of lemon oil. Next to a bunch of framed diplomas and awards was a print of a very rugged-looking man writing intently, leaning his opposite elbow on a book. "There's nothing to writing," read the quote above his head. "All you do is sit down at a typewriter and bleed."

"A very famous quote about writing," the professor said.

"I recognize it," Gabby said. "My writing teacher has that exact same print hanging in his office."

"A Hemingway aficionado, is he?"

"I think he's more into Fitzgerald, actually." His gaze flicked up for a strange moment before he went back to reading. After ten more minutes, Gabby was fidgeting in her seat, having exhausted checking out the room and surfing on her phone. Finally he tossed the folder aside and pulled off his reading glasses. She braced herself to hear that her mom's writing was trite, commonplace, and amateurish, and that this trip had been nothing but a wild goose chase.

"Pardon my saying so, but everyone wants to be a writer. What exactly is your job?" He eased back into a leather chair that probably cost more than all of Gabby's furniture combined.

"I'm a lawyer."

He laughed and folded his hands across his fit abdomen. "Attorneys all think they can write. Grisham, Baldacci, Turow. But their writing is only good for B movies. You have an excellent career. My advice is not to blow it chasing a pipe dream."

"I'm not even close to giving up my job. But I am taking a creative writing class at the college."

He snorted. "Good luck finding a mentor among the bucolic fields of Ohio. Or perhaps you'll find one at the annual Blossom Festival?"

Gabby's breath hitched, and common sense told her to politely excuse herself and get the hell out of there. But instead she said, "Actually, my teacher is a well-known author. He's a grad of the Iowa Writers Workshop."

"So they have Stephen King teaching writing courses now, do they?"

"He might be as famous as Stephen King one day. His name is Cade Marshall."

Professor Bowman sucked in an audible breath, but his expression remained neutral. "Cade Marshall," he repeated, his voice oddly quiet. He cleared his throat. "I'm acquainted with his work." Then he stood abruptly, glancing impatiently at his watch. "I'm afraid my time is up, Ms. Langdon. I must see you out."

"About my mother's writing..." Gabby said.

He handed her the folder, assessing her with his cool blue gaze. "Your mother had a rare talent. The kind a professor might find a mere handful of times over an entire career."

The sudden praise stunned her. She hesitated, a thousand questions bursting to be asked.

"You can leave now, Ms. Langdon," he said, irritation edging his voice.

Confused by his strange reaction, but eager to leave anyway, Gabby gathered up her purse and stood. As she turned to leave, her gaze caught on a collection of photos grouped neatly on a table underneath the window. Her eyes lit on one in particular, in a simple silver frame. There, in front of her, plain as day, was a younger Cade, smiling from underneath a graduation cap, his arm looped casually over the shoulder of this formidable older man, who was smiling too, and who actually looked like someone who wouldn't scare the bejesus out of her.

Oh lord. Gabby's pulse pounded at her temples as the puzzle pieces clicked. It all made sense—the certain quirk of his mouth when he smiled. The well-defined brows. Not to mention the irreverent wit and the big side of crotchetiness. And the Hemingway quote on the wall.

He escorted her to the main door. "Thank you for seeing me today," she said as politely as possible. She stepped through the door while sense warred with curiosity, her heart still beating wildly. On impulse, she spun back around. "You're Cade's father." *But why did he have a completely different last name?*

"Cade?" the older man's brows shot up in surprise "To call him that, you must be on very familiar terms."

"We're... friends," Gabby said. "And I had no idea that you lived—"

For a moment, his expression softened, and he looked as if he were going to speak. But then he opened the door. As he hurriedly ushered her out, he said, "If you have half the talent your mother had, you'll be a good writer. Good day, Ms. Langdon." Then he closed the subject—by shutting the door in her face.

All the way back to town, Gabby tried to reconcile that the grouchy old man she'd just met was not only her mother's professor, a man who'd told her she had exceptional talent, but was also Cade's estranged father—a man who was seemingly incapable of recognizing the accomplishments of his own son.

Her heart ached for Cade. To live in a world where there was such a huge void between you and your own father was unfathomable. Plus, she'd seen something in the old man's eyes that might have looked a lot like regret.

Gabby reminded herself that none of this should matter—not Cade's relationship with his father and not their personal relationship. Cade didn't want anything personal between them, and he sure as hell would not want her meddling in his life. Yet her emotions were all tangled up. His abrupt words to her the night of the wedding did not jibe with the ferocity of his kisses, or the scorching, needy look in his eye as he'd told her goodbye.

Somehow she knew that it was already too late for her—on both counts.

* * *

It was Wednesday afternoon, and Cade had a splitting headache. Probably because he'd been up half the night getting ready for his presentation in front of the research committee on Friday.

And not at all because he'd pushed Gabby away at the wedding. Everything between them continued to buzz in his head—those amazing kisses, her soft, sweet body pressing up against his, those little sounds she'd made deep in her throat that told him beyond a doubt that she'd wanted him just as much as he'd wanted her.

While he loved the story of Fitzgerald and how his interactions with his famous editor, Max Perkins, helped shape *The Great Gatsby*, all that ran through his head was Gabby—her scent, her softness, the wild chemistry they'd shared that promised so much more. Even worse, he'd dozed off around midnight trying to get his presentation together and woke at four in the morning, a cup of cold, brackish coffee at his side, and way behind for Friday.

That same old haunting feeling wrapped its arms around him in a stranglehold, whispering in his ear that he was in trouble. That he would never turn his life around. That he'd always be dog-paddling just to keep his head above water. His sensible side told himself he'd done the right thing. To focus on his career and his daughter were what he should be doing right now… and thinking of Gabby was not.

Except every part of him was rebelling, making him think that he'd made the biggest mistake of his life.

Cade forced himself to remember his past and learn from it. He could accept being a one-hit wonder: he just wished he wouldn't continue to have this desire to sit there and create something—and find out over and over again that he simply could not.

He remembered what it felt like to have the writing

flow. Those had been good days, and Emerson had been by his side. They'd bounced ideas off each other, which had benefitted both of them. Emerson had published a novel she'd worked on in grad school, and it looked like she was headed for success. Until he'd gotten into Iowa, and his career had taken off while hers had not. That had been hard on her.

After that, Emerson had resented giving him input. He'd had no idea how much until his book came out and she'd gone to the tabloids, accusing him of blatantly stealing her ideas. That had crushed him.

He turned to the vintage typewriter sitting on his desk. He'd written the rough draft of his book on a variety of antique typewriters, and collecting them was an interest. He'd decided to pull one out of storage because he thought it would look good in his office.

No, that was a lie. The truth was, he'd had the tiniest itch to type for the first time in a long while. He set his fingers on the old, worn keys. Except what came out did not have anything to do with his next literary project, the one his publisher had wanted to follow his first book.

He was supposed to be writing about a depressed man whose life was falling apart. Instead, he was thinking of kissing Gabby. And *writing* about her.

As an author, he often wrote about things he observed. But suddenly words about Gabby—her light, sweet scent, the curl of her hair, the expression in her eyes—all poured out onto the page in a random pattern he could not control.

He stared at the thick, bold type that the old

machine had imprinted onto the sheet of paper. *Gabby.* He wasn't supposed to be thinking about her, much less writing about her, but his fingers appeared to have their own will, and they'd gone to a place where he would not allow his mind to travel.

He could smell, very faintly, the scent of ink, which he'd always loved. As a very young child, he'd associated it with climbing upon his father's lap when he was deep at work. His dad used to let him peck at the keyboard, then would spread out crayons and big sheets of white butcher paper so that Cade and his sister could color.

Later, his father taught him how to type his name before he could even write it. He'd fallen in love with the crisp roll of the paper, the sharp clack of the keys, the fact that the letters became part of the paper. Altered it permanently, just as words themselves were powerful and life changing.

Even now, when he was distressed, words comforted him. Not any he'd written—he'd ended up filling wastebaskets of those over the past few years. Yet here he was thinking about *her*, and he couldn't stop the words that were flowing out of him and onto the paper.

Cade tugged his fingers through his hair and leaned his elbows on his desk. What was wrong with him? He had a million things to do, not to mention he had nothing planned for tonight's dinner. A glance at his watch told him he still had several hours before he had to collect Ava from day care. He ripped the paper out of the typewriter, crumpled it up, and tossed it into the trash. He was being ridiculous. Romantic. And the deadline for his presentation was ticking away.

He switched back to working on his computer. But after staring at his presentation without making any progress, he shut it down.

Ten minutes later, he was walking over to his mom's. She needed him to dig out a half-dead shrub, and he needed to clear his head in a way that only physical labor could.

* * *

Cade had been working for about an hour cutting down a scraggly rhododendron bush that had seen much better days. It was a strenuous job, but it was just what he needed to clear his head. His mom had accumulated a lot of projects that had to be done around her house, and now that he was back in town, he was glad he was there to help out with them.

Plus today, he was enjoying working under the bright, hot sun. He'd sawed off all the branches and cleared most of them away, and now he was working on removing the stump. As always, everything seemed better when he was fixing something. As if by taking care of one simple problem, the rest of the ones in line didn't seem quite so bad.

At about four o'clock he'd just started to wrap things up, when he heard a noise in the driveway. He looked up to find Gabby getting off of her bike and walking toward him.

He put down the ax he'd used to attack the stump and wiped his face on his arm, but there was no getting away from it—he was a mess: sweaty, shirtless, and dirty.

"Hi, Professor," she said, a little warily. He noted the *Professor* salutation, which made him wince. Days ago she was warm and soft in his arms, and now they were back to *Professor* again. God, he was an idiot.

Before he could respond, the front door opened and Paige came out onto the porch, wearing a colorful flowered apron and carrying a tray with glasses and a big pitcher of iced tea. "Gabby! There you are." Cooper bolted out of the house and ran up to Gabby, his tail circulating enough air to create a breeze on the hot day. She bent to reward him with some scratches behind the ears.

"I got out of work a little early today, so I came right over."

"Came right over?" Cade asked, lifting a brow in question.

"Your mom said I should pick up more of your research books here today instead of at the shop. I didn't know you were going to be here." Her gaze lingered on his abs before they flicked back up to his face. A move that made him feel strangely better even though it shouldn't have.

"Oh, I—yes," Paige said. "I'm sorry, Gabby. Cade came over suddenly and I forgot I'd called you."

Cade frowned. *Like hell she did.* If he didn't know better, his mother was matchmaking.

"I'm sorry I took you out of your way, dear," his mother said.

"Oh, it's all right. No problem at all."

"Well, I'm glad you stopped by. Rachel told me you recently learned your mom was a writer. How exciting."

"I don't know how exciting it is to anyone but me," Gabby said. "But yes, I was lucky enough to find the draft of a book."

"Well, I think that's wonderful. Cade's great-grandfather wrote a book. In fact, I have the only known copy on my bookshelf."

"Is that right," Gabby said. "So that's where Cade gets his talent?"

"Mom, that book is about Civil War helmets," Cade said.

"Caden, being an academic, you should know better than to poke fun at other people's research," Paige said. "And besides, your great-grandfather wrote about his passion. Now that you're home and not so stressed, maybe you'll be able to rediscover *your* passion and be able to write again."

"Mom—" he warned. Gabby glanced over at him briefly, a brow lifted in inquiry. Great. He didn't need Gabby questioning him about writer's block. "You know I'm focusing on research now," he added, just in case.

"Of course. For now," his mom said as she began to walk toward the house. "I'll go get those books I brought home for you. Be right back."

Crisis averted. As his mother left, Cade couldn't help noticing Gabby's white dress with red polka dots, little red sweater that showcased her curves, and red lipstick to match. His reaction was instant and intense in a way he couldn't control, and all thought of writer's block flew right out of his head. His mouth went dry, his heart accelerated recklessly, and he felt himself go hard as he remembered what it was like to hold her in his arms, to feel the soft curve of her bare back, to be tangled up with her, needy and panting.

Gabby, as if able to read his thoughts, turned as red as her sweater. He folded his arms and attempted to put a stern, distancing look on his face but it was impossible, especially when the dog was parked at her feet, calmly and very attentively laving her hand with long, slow licks.

"You must taste good," he said. Oh, shit, did he say that out loud? "I mean—what I meant was, you must have something on your hand that tastes good."

"No, I think Cooper's just friendly." She smiled at the dog. "Because you're a handsome boy, aren't you? And open and affectionate, yes you are. Not at all constipated like certain professors."

Cade rolled his eyes. He looked around and didn't find his mom anywhere but dropped his voice anyway. "Look, I'm sorry things are a little—awkward between us." *I'm sorry, I was wrong*, were what was really on his lips—and in his heart. But he couldn't bring himself to say that. Not with his and Ava's future on the line.

She crossed her arms. "A little? That's an understatement."

"I think we can get past that."

"We might get past it a little faster if you put on a shirt."

That finally broke the tension and made him laugh out loud.

"We made an honest mistake," she continued brightly. "I want you to know I'm planning to tell Carol my work got busy, and she can find you a replacement for the research job. But I didn't want to quit until after your presentation Friday. And I'm going to drop your class."

Wait. She was quitting? His class *and* the assistant position? He should feel the relief of his gut unclenching, his muscles relaxing, but no, that was not what he was feeling at all.

"Thanks for your feedback on my work," she said. "I didn't act like it but I did appreciate it. I see now where the story I first turned in was pretty awful."

Without thinking, he stopped her with his hand on her arm. "No," he said. "It wasn't awful, just a rookie mistake. And don't quit."

Cade knew his life would be so much simpler if he'd just let her go. But there was something else to factor into the equation. He had the skills to help her better her talent. And he found he wanted very much to support her in following her dream, wherever it led.

"I really think it's best for both of us—"

"Gabby, I just read your last assignment. It's really good."

"What?" She frowned, like she didn't believe him at all.

"It's fresh, it's different. It's original." He tried not to think about the arresting honesty in her beautiful brown eyes. Or how pretty she was. Or how she was stroking the basset's long ears until he moaned with pleasure.

He forced himself to concentrate on business. "What I'm trying to say is, I want you to stay in the class and get what you came for. I believe what you just turned in is something really original, something you should pursue. I'd like to help you with it."

"Here you go," Paige said, interrupting. She set a canvas bag with the logo of the bookshop on it in the grass at their feet. Cooper promptly ran over to sniff it, then lay down on Cade's foot.

"Will you have some iced tea, Gabby?" Paige asked.

"Oh, no thanks, Paige. I need to get going."

"It was nice seeing you. Please tell Rachel hi for me."

"It was nice seeing you too," she said. The dog looked despondent at her leaving, but Gabby gave him one last pet. "You too, Coop."

Paige went back into the house, and Cade walked Gabby to her bike, scooping up the bag of books along the way. He couldn't help tugging on one of her basket straps that looked loose, making a mental note to tighten it up for her next time. Except that made him think there probably wouldn't be a next time for them. "Thanks for coming to get the books. And think about what I said, okay? If you decide to keep going, you can meet me tomorrow at four to go over the research stuff."

She frowned, and even the tiny lines that formed between her eyes were intriguing. "Why do you care if I quit? I mean, after what happened between us, any normal man would be relieved, you know?"

"I believe we're adults and we can put whatever happened behind us and move forward." That sounded like a rehearsed line to his own ears, but he did believe he could be professional. And he owed it to her to be because she had talent—talent he could help her develop. That had to trump his own misplaced feelings.

She seemed to consider that for a while. The dog

came and sat by Cade's side. Cade gave him a quick rubdown, which made him go belly up for more.

"Okay," Gabby said. "I'll stay in your class."

"And why is that?"

"I believe you're a good person trying to do the right thing."

That surprised him, because he was used to being judged, used to everyone thinking the worst. "What makes you think that? Because I do chores for my mom? Because I can fix things?"

"No. Because the dog likes you, and dogs always know." She got on her bike and flashed him a smile. "Oh, is there something I can do to help with your big presentation?"

It was his turn to pause. "I *could* use a little help."

"Sure. Name it."

"I could really use another eye on my annotations. And to make sure everything's in the proper format—MLA style."

"Why don't you email it to me?" she asked.

He considered that. She'd offered, and he really would appreciate her help. "I will. Thanks."

"Okay. See you tomorrow," she called over her shoulder as she started pedaling away.

"Tomorrow at four," he was left muttering to no one in particular.

Chapter 13

♥

At 3:55 Thursday, Cade's mind was not on his upcoming presentation to the chairman's committee, which was almost done except for proofreading and printing the handout. He was staring at the computer screen in front of him, where he was supposed to be looking it over. Instead he'd just typed an entire paragraph, not about Fitzgerald. It was about an unemployed, hapless guy who'd come back to a Midwestern town and felt unable to connect with family or friends.

Suddenly he laughed and rubbed his forehead, shaking his head. His writing mentors would love his prose, the clever words he'd used to describe his sad sack character. But reading it over again, it was so depressing he started laughing again. Hopelessness, desperation, darkness... it struck him as... awful.

Yet there it was before him. One whole paragraph. And it wasn't about Gabby, even though he hadn't stopped thinking about her.

The first thing he'd written in three years that wasn't *entirely* full of shit.

Then there was a knock on the door, and he knew it was time for his meeting with Gabby. When she walked in, he pretended not to be affected, lifting his head up from his work as if he hadn't been anticipating her visit for the past half hour.

Today she was wearing jeans and a navy blouse, with red earrings and red shoes. And that same red lipstick that accented her full, beautiful lips. Her hair was long and curly and wild. The urge to touch those silky curls, to kiss her, drove out all other thoughts.

Her arms were full of books and bags...and coffee cups. "I picked up your books that were being held at the library, and I stopped by the Bean, and Kaitlyn was trying to get rid of a fresh pot of Jamaican Gold, so I brought us some." She set down a cup in front of him, and the rich, strong scent of good coffee wafted up to his nose. He couldn't have been more grateful. Unfortunately, his daughter took after his ex—she was always up at the butt crack of dawn, ready to conquer the world. Whereas he couldn't seem to really start thinking until after ten at night. Add his propensity for night-owlishness to a good case of insomnia, and you had a man desperate for coffee.

"Thank you, Gabby."

She smiled and started walking behind his desk. For a startled second, he thought she was going to touch him—hug him or worse—but instead she pulled something out of a plastic bag she had slung on her arm.

As she passed by, he caught a whiff of her scent.

Something clean and fresh, maybe a little fruity—he had no idea—but he liked it a lot and he was coming to associate it only with her.

She turned and held up a bright green plant inside a very colorful pot.

"What is that?" he asked, struggling to focus on the plant and not the rest of her, which was way too close to him.

"Well, it's a long story. Do you want to hear it?" She set the plant down on his windowsill. It was one of those his mom used to call a spider plant, which tended to have offshoots that hung down and produced new little plants. The container was brightly painted pottery with streaks of blue, red, and green, and he had to admit it brightened his office. But not as much as the woman in front of him.

"That's colorful."

"Yes. Well, my sister's an artist, and she does pottery. And she gave this pot to my nonna, who was transplanting plants today. And Nonna gave it to me with this plant inside. But I kill plants, and I had the idea that your office could use some color. So when I told Nonna that, she buried a coin inside."

"What's the significance?"

"She said it's for good luck in your new job. Nonna says when you bury a coin, it always means good luck. Of course, you know my nonna, so you also know we take everything she says with a grain of salt. She may have just gotten that from the angel legend. You know, kiss someone, toss a couple of coins in the water, get your pic taken, and voilà."

He raised a brow. "Voilà?"

"True love forever. Apparently that's all it takes."

"Hey, that works for the Angel Falls Chamber of Commerce, judging by how many tourists come visit every year."

She chuckled softly at his joke, but a flicker of something passed in her eyes—maybe sadness—but it was gone in an instant.

"I really enjoyed talking to your grandmother at the wedding," he said. "I'm sorry about the dementia."

"Thank you. But it makes us appreciate the good moments more, you know?"

He nodded. "You seem to have a very close family."

"Close and crazy," she said with a smile.

He had no experience with an intact, close-knit family so instead he made a point of inspecting the plant.

"Well, thanks. It's very . . . homey."

She moved past him again, giving him another whiff of that scent.

"Um, we'd—better get started," he said, trying to drag his brain to where it belonged, onto business.

She put the stack of books on his desk and sat down, grabbing a pen and notebook from her bag. "Okay, I'm ready to work."

Funny, but all he could think of was the thousand ways he wanted to kiss her. Up against his wall, for starters. Dragging his lips over hers and tangling his hands in all that wonderful hair.

Cade swallowed. What the hell had he been thinking when he'd practically begged her not to quit his class? He should have *paid* her to leave, but he never went back on his word. So he grabbed the first book off the pile and began flipping through it.

"Why Fitzgerald?" she asked.

"I beg your pardon?"

"Why do you love Fitzgerald?"

"Oh. Well." Cade thought about the question, one he hadn't heard in a long time. It wasn't like him to be at a loss for what to say, but so much of what he felt about Fitzgerald was visceral, impossible to put into words. "The man never wrote a bad sentence. He says so much with an economy of words. Every word counts and is full of feeling. Yet his personal life was a disaster. His wife had bipolar illness, and they had a tempestuous relationship. He battled alcoholism and was dead at forty-four."

"You sound very passionate about him."

"I've read everything he's ever written."

"Do you aspire to be like him?"

He paused a long time. Like Fitzgerald's, Cade's first book was published and soared to success. His marriage had led him to heartache. And he'd had his own demons to battle.

"As a professor, it's my job to analyze great works, not create them."

If she said anything, he didn't hear it. He must've gotten lost in his thoughts without realizing it, and when he looked up, Gabby was staring at him. "What is it?" he asked.

"Just that you look a little sad."

"I sort of feel this conversation is turning personal." He'd said that to shut her down. But she kept talking.

"I'm just trying to understand. You attended the

most prestigious writing program in the country. You made the *New York Times* list with your very first book. And the desire to write has completely left you? I'm not sure I buy it."

Her words knifed him in the gut. She was drilling down to places he didn't allow anyone within a mile of. So he turned the tables on her. "People change their minds all the time. You've said you're seeking something different by taking my class—searching for something else besides your day job."

"Maybe, but my situation is different."

"How so?"

"Well, I have a great job. A job that took years of study and hard work to get. I mean, I'm very grateful for it and for my education."

"Grateful isn't the same as fulfilled."

Gabby flinched, and he knew he'd hit a nerve. Good, because this conversation was veering into dangerous territory—apparently for both of them. "Well, I think we can both say life doesn't turn out the way we expect it to sometimes." He turned back to the book, trying to find something else to change the subject.

"Anyway," Gabby said, "I've double-checked all your annotations and made sure everything is in MLA form. What else do you need for tomorrow?"

"I just have to proofread and make the handouts."

Cade's gaze kept getting tangled up in hers and held for a moment longer than what was decent. She made him want to tell her more. Confess his confusion. Tell her *her* confusion wasn't so bad after all. And then there was that kissing thing he couldn't stop thinking about. Except the longer she was here, the more erotic his thoughts became. That wall fantasy again…in his mind, they'd somehow ended up on the floor, in a tangle, her curves molding to his.

His phone buzzed, forcing him to tear his gaze away and answer it. After a minute, he disconnected the call and stood. "It's my next-door neighbor. Apparently a large branch from one of the trees in my backyard broke off and fell on my roof."

"Oh no. Good thing you and Ava weren't home."

"Yeah. My neighbor says it looks like it might've damaged the roof over my kitchen."

"Give me your computer password," Gabby said.

"What? No. I can handle it."

"I can proofread your handout. Then I'll make copies, and you'll be all set for tomorrow."

"I really don't need—"

"Let me help," she said quietly. "Then you won't have to figure out how to get here at seven a.m. tomorrow to do it yourself. You can trust me—just go take care of things."

The fact that she'd jumped without hesitation to help him touched him immensely. He'd spent the past two and a half years going it alone with Ava, and Gabby's kindness was a reminder that he no longer had to handle every little crisis on his own.

"Okay," he said, letting out a big breath he didn't realize he was holding. "I accept. Thank you." He busied himself shrugging his jacket on, scooping up his book bag, and pocketing his phone. "I do trust you," he said as he jotted down the password on a sticky note. "And I really appreciate this."

"Don't mention it. Oh, don't forget your laptop," she said, reaching over his desk and handing it to him on his way out the door. "And you'll probably want your cord too."

As she handed it to him, their fingers grazed. Hers were soft and warm, and he had to fight not to grasp her hand. "Thanks again," he said.

"No problem," she said, already heading for his computer.

Then he ran out the door before he did something really foolish.

* * *

Gabby sat down at Cade's desktop computer to pull up the presentation document. His screen saver was a picture of Ava in a pink polka dot bathing suit holding a hose straight up in the air as it sprayed all around her joyous little face. Seeing it made Gabby smile. His desk was sparse, but notable items were a paperweight of the starship *Enterprise* and a stick figure drawing of two people holding stick hands that he'd tacked to the wall at the side of his desk. That made her smile too.

Gabby ran her hands over the surface of his desk, a standard-issue metal type that looked like it had seen its share of professors. She sat back in his chair, picked up one of his pens, and tugged open the center desk drawer to find sticky notes and more pens—the standard-issue drugstore kind, not fancy—and peppermint gum. She knew she shouldn't be snooping, but she felt hungry for any clues as to who Cade was—not as a dad or a professor, but as a man.

Nope, no shocking revelations in his desk drawer.

She typed in the password and the screen saver gave way to a Word document, the cursor blinking right in front of her eyes and drawing attention to a single paragraph of text. It was clearly *not* Cade's presentation. It was bad enough she'd been peeking in his drawers. She should just open the document she'd offered to proofread, which was sitting right at the bottom of the screen.

Again, her eyes were drawn magnetically to the blinking cursor, and she began to read. The paragraph before her eyes told a tale of a dismal man in a dismal town, and the words he used caused a flash of pain to sear right through her. She felt the character's desolation, his abject lack of hope.

How could anyone write this stuff and not die of sadness? Cade appeared to want to write the kind of fiction that made her want to run screaming for the hills. It was similar in tone to his bestseller, with the same bleak outlook, as dark and overcast as stormy weather.

Then another thought occurred to her. Maybe he *couldn't* write it. Maybe that was the problem, why the brilliant young author hadn't released a book for the past three years. And maybe that was why he'd turned to doing research instead.

It was just conjecture. Gabby knew some literary works took years to write. But he'd told the class he'd left his writing behind. And she'd heard his mom slip up a little, saying something about hoping he'd rediscover his passion and be able to write again. Could Cade be... blocked?

Chapter 14

♥

It was after seven when Gabby knocked on Cade's front door. It was old and painted black and had no wreath or any other decoration to welcome visitors. She ached to fix that. That door was just crying out for a pretty wreath, not to mention a brighter color of paint. As she looked around she noted that his wide covered porch ran the entire front of the little house. It would look so cute with some cushions and plants and maybe even a little rug. And a couple of ferns hanging from the ceiling. Then it would be the perfect place to sit and drink tea and talk over the day…

The door opened and the sight of Cade in a gray T-shirt and jeans, looking tired and a little mussed, circles under his eyes, caught her mind from its wandering. She wanted to smooth his hair and let him know that he was doing a great job, even if he didn't feel that he was. Like so many other things she wasn't able to say, she held that compliment back, and that reminded her that she was here on business. Not to decorate Cade's damn house or offer him the support of a partner. She was only his assistant, and she'd better act like one.

"How's the roof?" she asked.

"The kitchen's a mess but I've got it mostly cleaned up, and the roofing company came and threw a tarp over it. My mom took Ava for the night."

Gabby handed him a folder that held copies of his proofread presentation. Once he took it, she held up a bag. "I picked up some food from Hunan by the Falls. Best Chinese in town. Did you eat?"

His full lips curved up into a smile. "Isn't it the *only* Chinese food in town?"

"Yes," she said, "but that's only because no other place can hold a candle to it."

"The answer to your question is no, I didn't eat, and I'm starving."

"Well, enjoy." She handed him the bag and turned to go.

"Gabby, wait," he called after her.

She stopped halfway down the steps, her heart knocking against her chest. Slowly she turned around. "Yes?" She tried to say it casually, but it came out with a quiver.

"Did *you* eat?"

Her heart leaped like she was sixteen and she'd just been asked out on a date by the cutest guy in class. Which had never happened, but somehow she knew this is what it would've felt like. "No, but... it's a bad night. And your presentation is tomorrow. I should go."

He looked inside the bag. "There's a ton of food here. Shame to waste it." Five o'clock shadow and exhaustion sculpting his face, he smiled.

Stay strong, a little voice warned inside her head. But how was she supposed to stay strong when the very sight of him, even on a bad day, made her pulse skitter, her throat go dry, and her blood whoosh so loudly through her veins she could barely think?

Even if he wasn't her teacher, he wasn't looking for a relationship. He'd said that. She needed to keep her focus on what he had to teach her—about writing. "Look, I've been thinking about what you said. And I want to play by the rules. I don't want to cause any sort of trouble for either of us."

"This is just...dinner." He let that settle, innocent sounding though it was. "Truthfully, after the day I've had, I could use the company." He poked his head out the door. "It's a great evening. Want to take a walk down to the falls and eat there?"

Despite sensing there might be no such thing as *just dinner* as far as they were concerned, Gabby was tempted. "I am kind of starving." As he leaned toward her, she couldn't help noticing that he smelled delicious, like some spicy man soap that made her want to sneak into his bathroom and inhale the bar.

Just dinner, she scolded herself. It was just dinner.

They grabbed some paper plates and water bottles, and a minute later they were walking the short distance to the green, which rested under the bridge. They found a spot under a tree where the river was calm and slow, a distance before it toppled over the falls.

A minute later they were walking over the bridge, which was guarded by two bronze angels, hands and wings joined to make a big heart. They paused at the apex of the bridge to look down over the falls. The water was gently rolling over them, calm and beautiful on a perfect September evening. Cade reached into his pocket and tossed some change into the water.

Everyone knew it was part of the legend. Toss a coin, kiss someone, get your photo taken equals true love forever. But of course, he had no intention of kissing her—and especially not in public.

Cade grinned. "I have this habit—I always toss my loose change over. Well, mostly I let Ava do it."

Of course he wouldn't be thinking of the legend. He wasn't a romantic like her anyway.

"Shall we go sit?" he asked, guiding her back to their chosen spot.

Gabby hesitated. "Maybe this isn't a good idea," she said, looking around.

"Why not?"

"It's public. People might . . . talk."

"It's fine precisely because it is public. I'm not concerned about it."

"Do you feel ready for tomorrow?" she asked cheerily, keeping her mind off other things. Like how great he looked in those old faded jeans. Or how his arms were definitely not the arms of a guy who read Fitzgerald all day. Or how she wished she could reach up and smooth back a stray lock of his hair. Massage his tired shoulders. *Kiss* him.

"Thanks to you, yes. I can't thank you enough for what you did."

"I hope it goes well for you. You're excited about doing research?" She couldn't help wondering about his writing. How he felt about it. Why he wasn't doing it anymore.

"Research is a lot more controlled than writing," he said. "I enjoy the predictability. No pressure to fill up an empty page, no deadlines, no big ideas to come up with."

"That sounds like a line," Gabby said. "And maybe a little boring too."

His brows rose in surprise. "It's not a line."

She looked at him and shrugged.

"Why is it a line?" He sounded a bit aggravated now.

"Because I think writing is in the blood. Either you're a writer or you're not. I think it's hard if you *are* a writer, not to write."

She thought he was going to argue but he went quiet. "I—have a confession."

"What's that?"

"I *can't* write." He exhaled loudly, as if finally saying it was a relief. Then, incongruously, he laughed.

"Excuse me?" she asked, confused by his reaction.

"I can't write. I have writer's block." He paused. "You might have heard my mom allude to as much. You're the first person I've told that to. The *only* person."

"Well, *I* have a confession. I saw your paragraph on the computer. After what your mom said, I suspected."

"I had a fancy grant—and an advance—to write my second novel, but I just couldn't do it. What Emerson—my ex—accused me of shook me. I couldn't separate all the ideas we talked about from ideas that were actually mine. Maybe I did take something of hers subconsciously, I don't know."

"Writers talk about plot with each other all the time, Cade," Gabby said, seeing in his face how difficult it had been for him to confess that. "Ideas for books have all been used before, and ideas are constantly being blended together. It's impossible for a book to be written in isolation. Even I know that."

He shrugged as if he wasn't really buying that.

"You sound very hard on yourself," she said. "Do you—do you *want* to do research?"

He laughed again. "I want to do something that doesn't make me feel like I suck. And I need to support my daughter. This seemed like the best solution."

"I have faith in you," she said softly. "I know you'll figure things out."

"Thanks, Gabby. That means a lot."

She met his gaze, which was honest and sincere, and it made her heart kick up, her pulse beating erratically. She knew her feelings for him were taking over, sending a warm, liquid heat clear down to her core, and she knew it was time to leave, or trouble would find her again.

She braced herself on her arms to get up from the blanket. "Well, I'd better get going—"

In one swift move, he'd tugged her back down to the blanket and covered her mouth with his, gently drawing her toward him, into the embrace of his big arms. It was as if he'd been biding his time since the wedding until the moment when his lips could find hers again. And, oh, the wait was worth it. He hesitated for a second, as if allowing her to think things through, and looked at her questioningly. But she was already lost. Kissing him was like touching a match to a dry heap of sticks and waiting to go up in flames.

She responded by kissing him back, curling her fingers through his hair, opening her mouth for him so his tongue could slide against hers and drawing even closer to his big body.

The gurgling water faded away, and the world reduced down to just the two of them, his warmth, the delicious scrape of his beard, and the thorough explorations of his mouth, which made her weak and trembling all over.

Hearing a soft whir, Gabby pulled back. Both of them looked over at the sidewalk that traversed the green. There, next to the river, was Tony Livingstone, Cade's colleague, holding a thirty-five-mm camera. He lowered it and smiled, in a *gotcha* kind of way. Gave a wave, then took off down the street.

Cade cursed under his breath. Gabby got up, cheeks flaming, and immediately began gathering up the leftover cartons of food.

* * *

Cade felt strangely calm as he walked Gabby home. She, on the other hand, was freaking out.

"What was that professor doing taking your picture?" she said. "God, I'm shaking. Are you all right?"

"I'm fine. Tony is a pain in the ass. If he's taking my photo, that means he probably thinks he can blackmail me. Which makes me think *he's* got something to hide."

"Oh my God." Her face turned stark white. "I'm so sorry about this."

"No," he said, and he meant it. "It wasn't your fault."

"It was. We shouldn't have gone out together in public."

The fact that he couldn't keep his hands off of her in public should have appalled him. But somehow it didn't. Or the fact that Tony had evidence that he'd kissed her.

"Listen to me," he said, stopping and grasping her by the arms. "I take responsibility. I was out of line."

He couldn't shake the *relief* that someone had seen them. And he realized he didn't want to sneak around. Or wait until after class was over. Although he would. But every day was a stronger test of his will.

Gabby knew him too well, called him out on his bullshit, knew his deepest fears, and she still...liked him. Plus she was fun to be around. It was getting harder and harder to keep a distance from her. And harder still to deny his feelings for her.

Chapter 15

♥

The next day, Cade pulled a neat stack of handouts out of his backpack, as well as his formal research proposal, complete with a cover. Gabby had bound all the handouts together with two large rubber bands, and as he set the pile on his desk, he noticed she'd tucked a pair of tiny golden flowers into their intersection. He was just taking that in, thinking of how very Gabby that was and how grateful he was for what she'd done to help him, when Tony came barreling in, Starbucks cup, size ginormous, in one hand.

"Hey, Cade, old boy," he said with a laugh. "Good luck today. Go get 'em."

"Thanks," Cade said, pulling his laptop cord out from under his desk.

Uninvited, Tony sat down across from him and stretched out his legs, crossing his hands on his stomach. His corduroy jacket fell open to reveal a paunch that was best left covered up.

"I've got to go set up in the conference room," Cade

said. He didn't want to be sidetracked by Tony. He needed to focus on his presentation, get through his nerves, and be done.

"Um, before you go, I've got a little matter to discuss."

His tone, his manner, and the glint in his eyes sent a sense of foreboding crawling up Cade's spine.

"It was a great evening in the park last night."

Gabby. Those kisses. An urge of fierce protectiveness rose up within Cade. "Just come out with it, Tony. What do you want?"

"Listen," he said, his voice casual and almost soothing, "I know you're trying really hard to get back on the straight and narrow."

Cade didn't believe Tony's display of sincerity for one second. "I've always been on the straight and narrow," he corrected.

"Your reputation hasn't been, and you know it. But I don't think sleeping with your hot little student is going to make your reputation any better, at least in terms of keeping this job."

Cade tapped the papers on the desk so hard they made a sharp clack against the desktop. "I don't sleep with my students. Now if you'll excuse me, I've got to go."

He gathered his stuff and walked around his desk but Tony rose just in time to stop him, dropping his voice. "C'mon, tell me you're not getting a piece of that great ass. I wouldn't blame you if you were. And you certainly were anxious to claim her for yourself, weren't you? Someone calling the situation to the committee's attention is probably enough for them to issue a warning, don't you think?"

"I told you, nothing's going on between us." Actually, everything was, just not physically. Yet. His tossing and turning for half the night last night after he'd kissed her had been the price he'd paid for that lapse of judgment.

Tony stood and placed his fists on Cade's desk. "So what do you say you put in a good word for me with Jake about that fiction fellowship next semester?"

"I really don't know you that well," Cade said, looking him square in the eye.

"Well, I do have something that might jog your memory about my good qualities, if you know what I mean. Put in a good word for me and I'll delete the photo."

"You're kidding," Cade said. The guy must be desperate for recommendations if he was asking the new guy for help. And resorting to cheap blackmail.

"Think about it." Tony paused and straightened up. "The tricky thing to remember about sleeping with students is not getting caught."

Cade stared him down. He must be doing what they said he was with his students. Why else would he threaten? "I'm not doing anything wrong, so I've got nothing to fear."

"Look," he said, dropping his voice. "Let me explain how things work around here. We help each other. Sometimes I look the other way, and sometimes you do. It all works out."

Tony left, and Cade went about setting up the conference room, anger percolating under his skin. He looked out the large white-paned window that faced the front of the old brick building. Students came and went through the busy entrance. He tried to remember what had been on his mind in college. Sex. Doing well in his classes. Wondering about his future. Probably in that order.

It had been a long time since he'd felt the freedom he'd felt as a student. Somewhere along the line, he'd become afraid. Fear had caused him to take the safe course.

And Gabby had seen right through him.

He shouldn't have kissed her in public, for God's sake. What the hell had he been thinking? Yet despite everything, he had trouble mustering up the conviction to regret it, despite the fact that Tony now had evidence of his indiscretion.

Yet somehow that "indiscretion" was a singular act of rebellion that felt like the first thing he'd done to go against the grain in a long time.

Cade looked down at his proposal, so carefully researched. It was concise. It was interesting. It was *job security*, right there in his hands.

This piece of paper was not just his fate, relegating him to a life in academia, but also his paycheck, and his fricking house. It was Ava's day care. And every other blessed thing he owned.

He couldn't afford indiscretions. Or risks.

Cade tried to calm down. The industrial wall clock clicked loudly on the conference room wall. Everyone would soon be filing in, including Tony.

Jake's booming voice sounded outside the door. He entered, walked over to Cade, and clapped him on the back. "Can't wait to hear what you have to say today. Good luck, son."

Cade looked at the man who'd taken a chance on him when the bottom had fallen out of his world. He couldn't let him down after all he'd gone through to help him. "Thanks, Jake."

Gradually, faculty began to gather around the big table. Cade sat at the head of the table, checking the projector and his laptop one last time. The tiny pressed flowers caught his eye. He carefully pulled the fragile flowers from underneath the rubber bands and tucked them into his suit jacket pocket.

"Cade, any time you're ready," Jake said.

Cade wiped his clammy palms on his pants as he glanced over at the bookshelf that lined one side of the room. It was filled with matching volumes of the entire canon of American and English literature. Shakespeare. The Romantic poets. A marble bust of a young John Keats with big, soulful eyes stared at him. *Beauty is truth, truth beauty*. The famous lines filled Cade's head, and the bust appeared to frown.

Dear God, what was he doing? Imagining Keats was reprimanding him. *No, John*, he said back to the bust in his mind. *It's about practicality. That's my new truth.*

Cade faced his peers and sucked in a deep breath. "First of all, I wanted to thank you all for the welcome you've given me over the past month. I really appreciate it, and I've really enjoyed being a part of the department."

He swore the stack of papers in his hand were

starting to sweat too. "Thank you all for coming to listen to my research proposal. I've outlined it in great detail in this handout and on my slides."

And then he went on to give a flawless, carefully thought-out presentation of everything he'd promised to investigate over the coming months. At the end, the faculty clapped. Hal Baldwin, the Edwardian literature scholar, said it was "fascinating," and even Tony complimented him, not that Cade put any stock in his praise. But he knew from the other faculty's reactions that he'd knocked it out of the ballpark.

Yet as he took his seat, he didn't feel much like rejoicing.

"Congratulations, son," Jake said, squeezing his shoulder. "Welcome to the faculty. We're delighted to have you as our new Fitzgerald scholar."

Everyone came up to him, shook his hand and congratulated him. He should've been exhaling a deep breath and feeling that dead weight he'd carried around for so long drop off his shoulders, because he'd finally done it—secured a stable life for himself and Ava. He wouldn't have to worry ever again about writer's block or backstabbing critics or crazy exes. He'd just bought himself *freedom*.

Too bad his mood hadn't improved. The uncomfortable weight hadn't left—it had just shifted, as omnipresent as ever. He accepted the friendly praise, but he felt no joy.

After the meeting ended, he turned off the projector and gathered up his papers. In his office, he sat at his desk for a good long while until finally he gently lifted the fragile flowers out of his pocket and pressed them between the pages of his copy of *Gatsby*.

* * *

As Cade walked across the campus to class that evening, Gabby fell into step beside him. "How did your presentation go?" she asked.

"Great," he said, trying to sound excited. "They accepted my proposal and they're calling me their new Fitzgerald scholar."

"Congratulations! That's terrific!" One sideways glance at him and her enthusiasm immediately dimmed. "Why do I seem to hear a *but* there?"

He avoided her gaze as they walked, yet he wanted her advice, wanted to share his ambivalent feelings about what achieving the Fitzgerald scholar position meant for his future. With Gabby, he always seemed to want more, despite the uncrossable boundaries. "It's all good. Just what I wanted."

"Well, I'm glad things went well." She paused. "Look, I feel terrible about what happened at the falls. I—I think it's time for me to bow out of the class."

"I can handle Tony," he said firmly, even as the reminder of the photo sent a sliver of discomfort straight to his gut. Nevertheless, he made a point to smile. "Besides, you can't quit. I'm using your work as the example for tonight." Every week he chose a few pages of a student's writing to praise and critique in front of the class, and he'd chosen Gabby's to read tonight. Most students appreciated the in-depth focus on their work, and it was a learning experience for the whole class.

Gabby halted suddenly. "Cade, no. Please don't do that."

Her reaction surprised him, because the pages he'd selected from her work were exceptional. "Why not? You have great instincts. The story is powerful—much better than your first one. Everyone can learn from it."

Her hand fluttered nervously to her throat. "I was barely able to turn that in," she said, her voice sounding a bit panicky. "That story is too close to my heart. I'm going to feel like I'm naked."

He forced his brain to not key in on her distress—or the naked comment—and focused on the problem at hand. "I'm just going to do what I've been doing every week—going over the good points, making suggestions to make it even better. I think you'll find it useful as you continue working on it."

"Please don't."

Oh, hell. She wasn't backing down. "Gabby," he said softly, "you're going to have to trust me on this one."

They'd reached the classroom door. Students were coming in, chatting with one another, saying hi to him as they filed by. Cade saw everything in Gabby's eyes—tension, reluctance, fear. But there was nothing more he could say. She'd signed up for the class, and she knew the rules. He couldn't break them just for her. Besides, he had the entire class planned, slides made. He couldn't alter the plan now.

She headed for her seat, and he walked to the desk in the front of the room, thinking that he'd moved back home to simplify his life, to lie low, to stay away from scandal. Yet his feelings for her were making everything very, very complicated.

Cade managed to push thoughts of Gabby out of his head as he greeted the class. But as he began to read her pages aloud, he could see that Gabby looked very uncomfortable. He checked himself—he'd emphasized how good he believed her story was, and the rest of the class had expressed the same feeling. So what was the problem?

"I wanted to talk a little bit about the characterization here," he said. "Cora, Gabby's main character, has been misunderstood her entire life. She uses books to live vicariously—to give her all the experiences she's missed because of her scars. Finally, she decides to volunteer as a war nurse in England to finally get out there and live her life, and that's where she meets Henry.

"Henry has his own wounds from the war, which are mostly mental. They're both wounded characters, outcasts, but in other ways they're very different. Her family is well-to-do and his is not. There are reasons why these two cannot be together. Yet they can't help their attraction to each other. They're drawn together like magnets. So let's take a look at some of the great things Gabby's done in these pages to show us all this conflict."

He read a few paragraphs of her work. The best paragraphs he'd read so far this semester, full of emotion and passion. The passage he chose was beautiful and raw, and by the end, Helen was wiping away tears. Even Erin swiped a couple. He could hear a few random sniffles throughout the class.

"Very nice job, Gabby," he said.

Erin stood up and started clapping. Then the whole class joined in.

Gabby's face turned crimson. She smiled politely at her classmates but downplayed the praise and when she caught his eye, she appeared to be begging him to move on.

Which he did, hoping that she'd come to take the exercise as it was intended.

After class, Gabby waited until everyone left and walked up to Cade's desk. He could tell by the set of her jaw, that certain clench of her fist, and from the daggers she was shooting from her eyes that she was upset.

Yet she still looked so beautiful she made his breath hitch. Just as he was unable to stop himself from kissing her at the falls, he could not control his feelings toward her. Could not separate his feelings about the work from his feelings for her.

"Before you say anything," he said, putting his hands up in defense, "I feel that the great response you got from the class confirms what I told you about how good your work is."

His gut told him she wasn't buying that. So did the deep furrow that suddenly formed between her eyes.

"I *trusted* you with this story," she said. "You wanted more from me, and I *gave* you the story closest to my heart. You knew how uncomfortable I felt discussing it. And still you laid it out bare in front of the whole class!"

"I used your work as an example tonight because it had great teaching points. You're a talented writer,

Gabby. You have what it takes to be an author if that's what you really want. And I would never lie to you—about praise or criticism."

"Except I'm not sure if I believe what you're saying precisely *because* you kissed me—the parts about it showing promise *and* the parts about it sucking." Tears were brimming in her eyes and she hastily brushed them away.

He wanted to reach out to her. Comfort her. But he couldn't. He'd made enough of a mess already with that damn kiss at the falls. "Dammit, Gabby. I'm not lying about your abilities. But I can't show you favoritism by not reading your work aloud, just because you asked me not to." He dragged his hands through his hair. "I can't let my feelings for you override my responsibility as your teacher. I—"

Gabby interrupted him as she hastily gathered her things. "I get it. I never should have expected special treatment. I'm just your student, same as all the rest."

She was wrong. She was so much more. "Gabby, I—"

She wouldn't let him finish. Before Cade could even formulate the words to tell her how right—and wrong—she was about everything happening between them, she was out the door.

* * *

Gabby had taken to sitting in the coffee shop with her laptop some mornings before work. It was a busy time in the Bean, but she found she enjoyed the background buzz of activity—the whoosh of the espresso machine, the chatter of people talking, Kaitlyn and her crew calling out coffee drink orders.

The cheery atmosphere couldn't stop the sick churning in her gut. For the past week since Cade had shared her work, she'd kept as much distance from him as possible. She'd gone to class, where she'd added polite comments and responses to the discussion, and gone home to throw herself into writing her story. He'd given her several research assignments, which she'd completed remotely and emailed.

The kiss they'd shared in the park was the last mistake she would allow herself to make with Cade. Not just because of the photograph that was taken and her worry that Tony would try to use it against Cade, but because despite their kiss, Cade wasn't going to allow their relationship to go anywhere. And she wasn't going to be a sad hanger-on, waiting around to see if he might one day change his mind.

Someone calling out Gabby's name made her look up. It was Erin from class, her bright pink hair hard to miss, standing in line with Helen. They got their coffees and came over to say hi.

Erin scanned all of Gabby's stuff spread out everywhere. "You come here and write?"

"Sometimes," Gabby said, "before work. It's busy but I kind of like the background noise. How are you two doing?"

Helen answered. "We were just getting together for a little while this morning to talk over our stories and help each other. Your story is so phenomenal you probably don't need any help."

"That's not true," Gabby said. "Actually, I'd love to talk over some things with other writers. Maybe we could all meet for coffee one day."

"We could have a little critique group," Helen said. "I'm happy to have you both come over to my house too if that would work better. Maybe early Saturday morning if that works."

"That sounds like fun," Gabby said. She'd love some feedback on her work from other writers, because it was so easy to lose perspective on your own work when you read it over so many times.

"You know," Erin said, "Professor Marshall wasn't as bad as I thought he was going to be. I'm actually learning a lot."

"Yeah, and I'm writing every day," Helen added. "It's kind of... amazing."

"I feel the same way," Gabby said. "I didn't think I'd ever learn to get the word counts down. Well, sometimes I barely do, but most times I actually manage it."

"Hey, I see a table that just opened up," Helen said. "See you in class?"

"See you in class," Gabby confirmed, waving to her friends as they ran to stake their claim. "And thanks for the critique group invite."

Gabby got back to work until a sudden burst of laughter from Kaitlyn made Gabby look up in time to see her talking to a handsome, athletically fit guy in a dress shirt, tie, and nicely creased pants—Steve, her ex. Kaitlyn gave him a wave and a smile when he left, but her smile faded as she walked over to Gabby's table and sat down.

"You and Steve seem pretty chummy again. What's going on?"

Kaitlyn's expression seemed tight. "He wants to get back together."

"He's *always* wanted to get back together. *You* broke up with him, remember?"

"Maybe now that I've flushed Rafe out of my system, I can think more clearly about Steve," Kaitlyn said. "He's a really nice guy, and as solid as they come. I've been really foolish, clinging on to the fantasy of your brother. It's time for me to move on."

Gabby squeezed Kaitlyn's hand. "I don't know what to say about my brother. But I do know one thing from experience—don't try to talk yourself into loving someone. It never works."

"How about talking yourself *out* of loving someone? Is that easier?"

Gabby let out a big breath. "I'm focusing on my class, not on the professor. And I'm good with that." Cade was her teacher. He wasn't interested in anything more than that, and she was going to move on too. Hopefully with more success than Kaitlyn or Rafe appeared to be having.

"How's your writing coming?" Kaitlyn asked.

Gabby's gaze skimmed over the notebooks, sticky notes, legal pads, and laptop spread out before her. "It's sort of terrifying. This story's got love, pain, disaster, conflict, laughter—everything. But I think it's way over the top. I feel like the characters are running the show, and I have no idea how to rein them in."

Kaitlyn randomly picked up a legal pad.

Gabby reached for it but Kaitlyn held it out of reach. "Kaitlyn, do *not* read what is on that paper."

Kaitlyn shot her a devilish smile and began reading—out loud. "'Henry gazed at her in the moonlight. Cora's first impulse was to look away—no, *run* away—as if that would prevent him from seeing her scars. She wanted to fantasize that he couldn't see them in the dark, but there was no use pretending. He'd seen them from the beginning. From the first moment she'd walked into the hospital and their eyes had met across the long, sterile hospital ward. And he had never looked away.'"

Kaitlyn rested her chin in her hand and tapped her fingers on her cheek. "Oh, wow, Gabby. Like, wow."

Gabby tugged the legal pad out of Kaitlyn's hands. "Don't you have customers to serve?" She gestured to the line forming at the register.

Kaitlyn ignored that. She was grinning. "You know what?"

Gabby covered her face with the tablet. "Don't say anything. My ego is fragile, and I'm never going to get this assignment done if you crush my soul."

"It's really good," Kaitlyn said quietly. She swiped at her eyes. "I'm tearing up and I don't even know Cora and Henry."

"It's like I'm buck naked, Katie. Like I'm writing things I'm not sure I want anyone to read. The emotion is too...raw. Too close to the bone."

Kaitlyn grabbed her hand. "Do you realize how you sound?"

"Like an idiot?" Gabby offered, smiling weakly.

"No, like an *author*. So keep going! I bet it's a lot better than you think. And if it's not, Professor Hottie will tell you, right? Isn't that why you're taking the class?"

Oh, Professor Hottie. She'd accused Cade of treating her like any other student, but to be fair, that's what he *had* to do. That was his job. She *knew* he had feelings for her. He just wasn't going to act on them—not now, because he was honorable, and not after class. So where did that leave her?

She shot Kaitlyn a grateful glance. "Thanks for the encouragement."

Kaitlyn smiled. "If you chicken out, you can always turn in *Twilight at Hogwarts*, right?"

Gabby shook her head and chuckled. "You're on a roll today, Katie."

Kaitlyn's laughter died down quickly, and Gabby saw her look anxiously toward the door. "What is it? What's wrong?" Gabby asked, cranking her own head around.

"Don't look!" Kaitlyn said, tugging on Gabby's hand. "Your brother just walked in. I have to go."

Kaitlyn took off, and Rafe came over, wearing navy pants and his short-sleeved, button-down navy shirt with the Angel Falls FD logo on it. Handsome—in a very different way from Steve.

"Hey, Gabs," Rafe said, barely looking at her. "Do you have a minute to talk?" he asked Kaitlyn, who had headed behind the counter.

"I'm pretty busy now, Rafe," she said. "Maybe later?"

"Why won't you answer any of my texts?" he asked pointedly.

Uh-oh. Gabby stared at her computer screen—what else could she do? She thought about moving so she wouldn't hear their conversation but...well, she was riveted in place, and no way was she leaving.

Kaitlyn busied herself wiping down the counter, but she stopped and crossed her arms. Rafe had a good ten inches on her, and the size difference was a little comical. "Because texting is for teenagers. Adults talk things over."

"We always talk by text."

"Well, not anymore. Do you want coffee?" she asked, holding up a carafe.

"No, I'm headed home to sleep." He hesitated, glancing over at the bakery case. "Maybe a muffin."

Kaitlyn wore an expression that seemed to say exactly where Rafe could stick his muffin.

"Okay, forget the food," Rafe said, holding up his hands. "Look, that box was a joke. Randy put it in my suitcase to be funny."

"You don't have to explain your love life to me. Steve wants to get back together and I'm—I'm going to do it."

"What?" Rafe said, the word coming out sharp and prickly. "No. Don't do that."

"Why not, Rafe? Tell me why not."

"Because...because he's not right for you. Because you can do better."

"Do better with whom, Rafe?"

Rafe raked his hands through his hair. "I don't know, Katie. I don't know."

Kaitlyn mumbled something about having to get back to work, and Rafe walked over to Gabby's table.

Her brother was a wreck. Gabby knew this before she even saw the circles under his eyes, his stuck-up hair, and the weary expression on his face. He needed an intervention—but who could reach him?

Rafe sat, and Gabby pushed her coffee cup toward him. "Kaitlyn just poured me a refill. Take it if you want."

"I'm actually going home to bed. Thanks anyway."

"What's going on?" There was no point beating around the bush. Plus, it was pretty obvious she'd just heard everything.

"I've screwed things up with Kaitlyn."

"I can see that," Gabby said.

"I mean, she's cool and fun and sexy and easy to be around and I like her…a lot. But I—I'm messed up, Gabs. I don't think I'm capable of getting serious—with anyone."

Gabby grabbed his hand. "Rafe, no. Don't say that."

He raked his hands through his hair again, and then tapped his long fingers nervously on the table. "I'm going to head home. We had a pretty busy night last night."

Rafe was brushing this off again, and Gabby felt compelled to say something to try and help. "It's okay to move on from Claire." Just the mention of her name made him stiffen. Gabby tried to put a hand over his but he drew back. "I just don't want you to lose an opportunity to love someone again."

Rafe looked up just then—and a pained expression overtook his face. It shocked her for a moment because Rafe was usually so good at hiding his feelings.

"Ah, there you are," a familiar voice said behind Gabby's shoulder. Gabby turned to see Dr. Bowman carrying a leather satchel. He glanced back and forth between Gabby and Rafe. "I hope I'm not interrupting."

"Hi, Dr. Bowman," she said, surprised to see him and even more surprised he appeared to be looking for her. "What brings you here?"

"Just passing through town. Actually, I was hoping to run into you today."

"Oh. Well, this is my brother, Rafe. Rafe, this is Dr. Bowman—he taught Mom in a writing class many years ago."

Rafe shook his hand. "Call me Elliot. A pleasure to meet you," Dr. Bowman said.

"Nice to meet you too. I'm just headed out, so you can have my seat," Rafe said, standing up.

"Rafe, talk to me later, okay?" Gabby asked.

He smiled but, typical of Rafe, made no promises. On the way out, he kissed her lightly on the head. "Bye, sis."

Dr. Bowman sat down at Gabby's table, digging through his old leather briefcase. "I found something I thought you might be interested in. Ah, here it is." He pulled out a single sheet of paper and placed it in front of her. It was typewritten—on an old-fashioned typewriter, judging by the bright white corrections painted onto the page. A handwritten grade was penned in red ink in the top corner. "Fantastic emotion!" it read. "A+!"

Gabby, confused, looked from the paper to Elliot. "Is that another of my mom's assignments?"

He gently took the paper back. "Allow me to read a few lines out loud."

"'My youngest daughter is three and she is almost always smiling. She radiates pure, irrepressible joy.'" It was good he did begin reading because her eyes immediately misted over. "'If she falls, she picks herself up and keeps going. She thinks the best of her sisters and is very protective of her baby brother. This innate, sunny disposition will surely serve her well in life.'

"The assignment was to describe someone you knew well that had a fascinating trait. She chose one of her children, apparently."

"Me," Gabby said, swiping at her wet cheeks. "She chose me."

"Was that strapping young man just now your baby brother?"

Gabby could only nod because she was crying in earnest now. Something slid over the table toward her—an embroidered handkerchief with a big *E* on it. Of course he would have a hankie in his pocket. He let her get ahold of herself for a few minutes, then he said in a low, careful voice, "I want to meet with my son. I'm wondering if you could help me."

Of course. The gentle manner shouldn't have fooled her. Elliot's gift was a trade-off. "I haven't said anything to him about meeting you." She'd meant to, but it hadn't come up with everything else going on. She felt a little guilty about that.

He drummed his fingers on the table. "I'm just a bit concerned that my reception won't be...friendly. I've already seen him briefly about town, and it didn't go very well."

"If you mean because you two have been feuding, I

know about that. But I don't understand—why do you have a different name?"

"Cade changed his name after the divorce—when his mother took back her maiden name he took it too. He didn't want to be associated with my influence—good or bad—in the writing world. Plus, to be honest, it was a slap in the face to my abominable parenting skills. He's always been a compassionate lad. But I'm afraid that even he'd had enough of me."

Gabby had no idea how to respond. Her gut told her Elliot was sincere. And he wasn't all bad. If he could make the effort to dig out an ancient college paper and bring it to her, then she could definitely accept it in lieu of an apology for how he shooed her away the first time.

But Gabby had no idea how Cade would feel about any of this or what exactly had transpired between them in the past, except that it had to be pretty bad if they weren't talking. Then she thought of Ava, and the chance to heal a wound seemed like it was worth a try. If Cade didn't kill her for it first.

She pulled out a pen and ripped off a sheet of paper from her notebook. "Here are his office hours. Maybe you could stop by one day?" She wasn't sure if Cade would want Elliot showing up at his office, but what was the alternative? Giving him his home address? His phone number?

"His daughter is turning four soon," Gabby added. "She's so lovely, Elliot. Adorable and smart, and she looks a lot like Cade. If you don't want to miss her growing up, a peace offering to your son might be in order before then."

Elliot looked at her, and for just a flash, she saw something in his eyes—vulnerability. Longing.

"Thank you for digging up this old paper," Gabby said, holding it up. "It's—very special."

"You're welcome," he said. He pulled his chair back and stood. "Now I must return to work. The literary world awaits my critique."

"Be nice to authors," she said. "Don't eat any for breakfast, okay?"

"Of course not," he said, flashing a devilish smile.

So the old Elliot was still in there, but for some reason, he didn't seem quite so scary. She'd just gotten back to work when the door opened, the bell tinkling overhead. Gabby had just sworn she wouldn't let herself be distracted again when she glanced up and immediately did a double take. Ava bolted in with light-up sneakers, followed by Cade in a shirt, tie, and jacket.

Oh, wow. Gabby sucked in a breath that she feared the entire shop might have heard. She dragged her eyes away from Cade to find Kaitlyn behind the counter staring at her. *Hot*, Kaitlyn mouthed, then pulled her phone out of her apron pocket. Gabby's own phone suddenly buzzed. Can I sign up for that class? came the text. Before Gabby could answer, Ava ran over, coming to a quick stop beside her.

"Guess what, Gabby?" Ava said. "I was really good and I put away all my toys and Daddy said I could have a muffin for breakfast today."

"That's terrific, Ava," Gabby said, as the little girl jumped up and down excitedly. "What kind are you going to have?"

"Chocolate chip, right, Daddy?" She looked over at her dad, who gave a quick wave in their direction as he got into line, then back at Gabby. "How come you aren't having a muffin?"

Why wasn't she having a muffin? "Actually, that sounds delicious. I think I will have one."

"What's your favorite kind?"

"I like pumpkin." Ava bolted over to her dad in line. Oh, great, now Ava was going to ask Cade to buy her a muffin. She tried to catch his eye but no luck.

"That man is going to buy you a muffin," Kaitlyn said, suddenly taking a seat.

"I really didn't mean for that to happen," Gabby said.

"Let him do it," Kaitlyn said. "He's adorable. And he keeps looking at you. Also, he has a nice pair of muffins himself," she added, checking out his ass.

Ava came running back, putting her elbows on the table and resting her chin in her hands. "Do you like my hair?"

Her hair was French braided, and the ends were tied with colored ponytail holders that had little pieces of fruit on them. The braids were a little loose and slightly lopsided, but it was a good effort. Ava wore an oversized red T-shirt and purple stretch pants that were flood level, which tugged on Gabby's heart a little, for Cade's and Ava's sakes. What she wouldn't give to shore up Ava's wardrobe a little, before the days when kids would be more vocal about their fashion choices.

"I love your hair," Gabby said. "Who did your braids?"

"My daddy," she said, pointing up at her dad. "He Googled how to do it."

"Your braids are amazing. Can I tighten this one? It's coming a little loose." Ava nodded, and Gabby wound the band around another couple of times. "There. Super cute."

She made the mistake of looking up. Cade was in front of her, holding a tray with muffins on it, a carton of milk, and two coffees. His hair was a little damp from his shower and curling over his collar, and he looked...well, better than a muffin.

"I heard you're one of our new professors," Kaitlyn said, suddenly standing up. "Nice to meet you. I own the Bean. My name's Kaitlyn Barnes."

"Great to meet you," Cade said.

"Daddy, I'm hungry," Ava said, tugging on Cade's jacket sleeve. "Can we sit with Gabby?"

"Well," Kaitlyn said, "my break's over. See you two later." She turned to Ava and Cade. "Thanks for coming in this morning. Hope to see you both again."

Cade said goodbye, and Ava tucked herself right into the chair next to Gabby. "We got you a muffin. Daddy, give it to her."

Cade smiled at his daughter, who handed Gabby a napkin. "Here you go," Cade said, passing her the muffin.

Their fingers grazed and she felt herself take a quick gasp of air, as if she'd suddenly forgotten how to breathe. Or pump blood. Or move. Had this week away from him taught her nothing? "Thanks," she managed. Cade set down Ava's milk and her muffin, and she instantly dug in.

Gabby felt her cheeks heat. "You didn't have to do that."

"Yes he did," Ava said. "Because they're delicious."

"Don't talk with food in your mouth," Cade said to Ava, the corners of his full mouth turning up. Then he slid a coffee over to Gabby.

"Thank you," she said, taking a sip. It was hazelnut, the same kind she'd ordered before.

Wow. He'd bothered to ask the server what kind of coffee she had. She was in love. Totally. Except she couldn't be. Plus five minutes ago she was talking to Cade's estranged father and she somehow felt guilty for that. But now was not the time to bring it up.

Ava was tearing into her muffin, drinking her milk, and doing it all with gusto. Gabby took a bite of her own muffin. "It's amazing."

"See?" Ava said. "I told you you'd like it."

Gabby smiled and tore another piece from her muffin. "I love it. It's delicious." She looked at Cade's plate. "What kind did you get?"

"Lemon poppy seed. It's delicious too." He lifted up his muffin so she could pull a tiny piece off and taste it.

"I'm done," Ava announced. "Can I go look at the cookies?"

"Yes," Cade said, "but no cookies today. A muffin's enough sweets for now."

Ava scampered off to the bakery case, leaving Gabby alone with Cade. Which brought Gabby back to reality. They'd been very clear about drawing a very solid line the other night. Then why was he sitting with her?

"That's terrific that you both got out of the house

this early," Gabby said, glancing down at her watch. "It's not even eight yet."

Cade shrugged, and even that economy of movement was elegant. "I try to take her to breakfast every couple of weeks. It's fun to rediscover the town."

The silence became awkward. The air felt alive between them, as always, charged with things unsaid. Gabby decided to say what was on her mind. "Look, Cade, I'm not sure why you're sitting with me. After the photograph, I don't think it's a good—"

His expression and his voice turned soft. "Let me decide who I want to sit with, okay?"

Damn him. With his blue dress shirt, his eyes looked blue today with tinges of green and brown. Such beautiful eyes. And they seemed filled with something she knew very well—wanting. She tried to harden her heart to him, to tell herself to stay away from someone who didn't want what she wanted, but it was so, so hard.

"Look,Gabby," he said, "I just want to say—"

"Um, excuse me, but are you Gabby Langdon?" Gabby looked past Cade where a tall, handsome man with blond hair and blue eyes stood waiting, presumably for her.

"Yes, I'm Gabby." This coffee shop was like Grand Central station today. "And you are...?"

He extended his hand. "Owen. Owen Anderson."

Distracted by Cade, Gabby's brain took a minute to catch up. "Pastor Owen. Oh! Nice to meet you."

"Nice to meet you too," he said, flashing a really nice smile. When he smiled in Cade's direction, Cade responded with a polite nod, clearly sizing him up. "I think we have a date coming up soon," Owen continued. "Are we still on for Saturday?"

Cade frowned deeply, which sent an unexpected thrill through her. Which she immediately tamped down. "Yes. For sure. I'm looking forward to it."

He extended his hand again, which Gabby took, and he covered it with his other hand too. "I'm really looking forward to it," he said. "I'm sorry to interrupt your breakfast, but I just wanted to say hi."

"I'm so glad you did," Gabby said.

Owen left but Cade's frown didn't abate. "Who was that?" he asked.

"The new minister," Gabby said. "We have a date at Fallside for lunch Saturday."

Cade barely got out an "I see" when Ava ran back to the table, her big blue eyes smiling in a way that very much resembled her dad's. She patted her dad's arm. "Time to take me to school, Daddy," she said. "Bye, Gabby."

"Have a great day, sweetheart," Gabby said. Ava gave her a big, unrestrained hug, as children do. Impulsively, Gabby placed a kiss on her head.

Cade seemed to stare at her for a long time before he finally said goodbye.

She watched them as they left out the door.

"Drop the class," Kaitlyn said, suddenly back at her side. "I recommend that you forget the creative writing and get creative in other ways. You want any more coffee?"

"No, thanks. I have to get to work." She had to do other things too, like calm the hell down so she could think. And gain her sense back, the kind that told her going out with Owen was the right thing to do.

Chapter 16

♥

"Thanks for coming over to help me pick out my date outfit before your ER shift," Gabby said to Sara, who was stretched out on her bed in the carriage house. It was noon on Saturday, an hour before Gabby's lunch date with Pastor Owen. She stood examining herself in the full-length cheval mirror next to her closet while Sara struggled not to fall asleep. Gabby needed her to be awake and critiquing her clothes. Thanks to expensive product, Gabby's hair was (semi)tamed, and right now she wore a pale pink lacy dress with a high neck—modest, of course, with the hem hitting her knee.

Her date was the nice, kind minister whom everyone loved, she reminded herself, and who wanted to settle down with an equally nice, kind person.

"Nice" and "kind" were important traits, but Gabby also wanted to find a soul mate. A honey. Someone to have kids with before it was too late. There was no use pretending that wasn't what she wanted.

Sara supervised her getting ready by lying back on

her bed and closing her eyes. Gabby knew from past experience that when Sara assumed that posture, she'd be asleep in another minute. "I feel so lazy today," Sara said. "I must've caught a bug from one of my patients."

"You look terrible," Gabby said. "You okay?"

"I sort of...lost my lunch."

Oh my God. "Sara, are you..."

"No. I don't know. I mean, I haven't checked."

"Let me run and get you a pregnancy test."

Sara covered her eyes with her arm. "I'm afraid."

Gabby walked over and sat on the bed next to her sister, resting a hand on her arm. "Of what Colton will say? He strikes me as the kind of person who would be ecstatically thrilled at that kind of news."

"It's not that. It's just..."

"Let me get you something to drink and a cold cloth for your head."

"Thanks, but I'm okay. It's just...well, we've only been married eight months, and marriage is an adjustment."

"Are you saying things aren't going well? Because the way you two look at each other makes me think everything is just fine."

"Everything *is* fine. We want kids, and I'm thirty-two so it's time to get started. It's just...life changing, you know?"

Gabby wrapped her arms around her sister and hugged her tight. "It's okay to be scared," she said, her voice cracking a little. She knew that both of them were thinking the exact same thing. Ever since their mom died, they'd given each other hugs, but when it was really important, they squeezed extra hard—as if their mom were there too. "You're going to make the best mom. It's going to be wonderful," Gabby said, her eyes filling up as she digested this news. Holy Estrogen.

Sara smiled. "Thanks, Gabs. Is that your first outfit?"

Gabby stood where Sara could see her. "What do you think?"

Sara cracked open an eye. "Too…virginal," she said.

Gabby clapped her hands and pointed at Sara. "That's exactly the look I'm going for," she said.

"No use pretending," Sara said with her eyes closed, but she displayed a half grin. "Why don't you just wear a habit?"

"Um, wrong denomination."

"You could do what the nuns taught us in school," Sara said.

"What's that?" Gabby asked, stripping off the pink dress and grabbing a bright red halter dress.

"You could kneel down, and I could see if your hem touches the floor. Which, with that awful pink one, it probably does."

"But that's a good thing," Gabby said.

"…if you're eighty," Sara added.

Gabby tied the halter top around her neck. "How about this one?"

"Too much boob," Sara said. "I mean, geez. It's the minister!"

"You're giving me mixed messages. Sara, open your eyes."

“What is it?” she asked, startling awake.

“Stop falling asleep. Do you think he’s—I mean, do you think he’s ever—”

“He’s thirty-five,” Sara said. “But he might be a virgin. And if he is, you two might have a very quick engagement.”

Gabby gave Sara a look. “That’s not funny. I just don’t know what kind of woman he’s expecting.”

“See, that’s your problem. Why are you trying to be what he expects? Just be *you*.”

Gabby chose a third dress: a light blue eyelet sundress, sleeveless, and jewel-necked.

“Perfect,” Sara said. Gabby went to the mirror to put on lipstick. She must’ve let out an audible sigh because Sara opened her eyes again and said, “What’s wrong?”

That was the thing about her sister—she could always tell.

“Nothing,” Gabby said, but even to herself she sounded like she was hedging.

“It’s the professor. Just say it.”

“No. I’ve given up on him.”

“How so?” Sara must’ve sensed the seriousness of the conversation, because she climbed out of bed and started to put clothes back on hangers for her sister, something she’d done many times in the past. Sara had always been tidy and orderly. Gabby…not so much. Gabby appreciated the effort.

“It was too complicated, with me being his student. And he’s been burned pretty badly by his ex. He’s been pretty clear on not wanting a relationship.”

“So are you going to fool around with him?”

"Sara! I'm going out with the minister. I'm supposed to be thinking about *him*, not Cade."

"Gabby, you can't replace someone in your mind with someone else just because you want to."

"The minister is really cute and nice. And a whole lot less complicated. Plus, he wants to settle down. That's what I want—someone to love. And children. I'm not going to spend my time dreaming of someone who doesn't want that too."

"Well, follow your heart," Sara said, climbing back onto the bed. "Can I crawl under your covers and take a nap until I have to leave for work? I'm exhausted."

"Of course. But did you just say follow my heart?"

"Yes. Of course I did."

"Knowing the decisions I've made in the past, you'd still say that?"

"You mean Malcolm? I think you learned a lot from that."

"Usually you scold me when it comes to following my heart. Sometimes I'm impulsive. I jump in without thinking, and I don't want to be like that. I want to be a thoughtful, careful person who makes the right choices."

"I think you've been very thoughtful about this whole thing. Gabby, no one has a blueprint for life. We wing it as we go. How we learn what we want and what is best for us is by trial and error. I know it may seem like this to you, but no one is examining your past mistakes under a microscope but you." Sara peeled back the bedspread and positioned a pillow for a nap. "The most important thing is you have to make yourself happy first. Find what that is, go for it with everything you've got, and don't look back."

Gabby looked at herself in the mirror. She wanted to be the kind of woman who stood up for what she wanted—her writing, a shot at love and kids. That meant not wasting time on men who didn't want the same things, no matter how charming they were.

She turned around to thank Sara for the wisdom, but Sara was already fast asleep.

* * *

It had been a long time since Gabby had been to Fallside, the restaurant in the center of downtown with wide-open views of the pretty, multitiered falls. It was a classic date destination, but it hadn't been pricey enough for Malcolm, and Gabby's own family preferred a cheery little Italian place outside of town and away from tourists to celebrate birthdays and special occasions.

It was a beautiful day, clear and warm with a brilliant blue sky. Her date was already seated at a table on the outdoor patio, dressed in a blue-and-white-checked shirt and khaki pants. He was athletic and fit, looking more like an NFL linebacker than a Lutheran priest—which, of course, all the ladies of the congregation were more than happy to note.

He stood when she approached and greeted her with a hug. "Hi, Pastor," Gabby said. "I mean Owen. Hi, *Owen.*" A somewhat maniacal laugh escaped her. Oh, this was going well already. "I'm so sorry."

He flashed her a perfect smile and pulled out her chair before she sat. "Don't be sorry."

"I'm just a little nervous. I've never dated a man of the cloth before." *And I'm thinking of Cade.* Of how he had the ability to calm her and stir her, both at once. How he'd been eager to critique her work in front of the class...and now that some time had passed, maybe she shouldn't have taken it so personally.

"I'm just a man, like any other," he said. He had angelic blue eyes, pure as the September sky above them. She wished she could say he melted her insides, but she didn't have quite the expected reaction, probably because she was so nervous. Once she calmed down, attraction would just happen naturally, she was sure.

"So, Gabby," Owen said, as the waiter brought them Cokes, "Rachel tells me you're taking a writing class at the college. Have you always been a writer?"

"Sure, if you consider lots of stories about ponies and magical elves, and a cartful of angsty teenage journals. But I gave all that up when I went to college. I got so busy I sort of forgot about it." A shame that she'd given up something that had mattered so much to her.

"So what brought you back to it?"

"My mother, actually." Gabby's heart squeezed, as it did whenever she thought of her. "She died when I was ten. But I found a box of her papers in my grandmother's attic. She was writing a book—a love story. The only problem is, I can't bring myself to read it."

"I think I might understand. My father died when I was young, and he left behind a few file folders full of old photos and letters. It took me years to crack those open."

"What did you find when you finally did?"

"Some war papers, and old photos of my mother and my brother and sister and me when we were babies. Nothing scandalous. But I guess I was hoping for something—I don't know—that would hit me on a visceral level. The best thing was he kept a photo of each one of us tucked away in the pencil drawer of his desk where he could see us every time he opened it."

"That's sweet. I'm glad you understand the reluctance. My sisters don't. Once I read Mom's book through, it's over. Then I won't have anything left of her to discover."

He nodded understandingly. "You'll know when the time is right."

Owen had a very comforting voice. Very pastor-like. She could imagine him talking to people undergoing trauma or grief. Counseling his flock. Yes, pastorhood was a good fit for him. He was definitely kind, warm, and friendly.

But sexy? Definitely not in a Cade-way. Her reaction to *him* had hit her immediately and hard, a sledgehammer hitting Wile E. Coyote smack on the head.

"Gabby?"

"I'm sorry, what did you say?" Gabby came back to reality to find Owen looking at her expectantly.

"Tell me about your job?" he asked.

"Oh yes, my job. I'm an estate lawyer. I set up wills for people. And trusts." Well, that almost sounded like she was intelligent.

Owen didn't seem to find that interesting as he was staring intensely over her right shoulder.

"Owen?" she said to get his attention back on track.

"Oh, forgive me," he said, shifting his gaze back to her. "It's just that there's a very determined little girl at that table who keeps waving in our direction. She's cute as pie. And I think they might be the people who were with you in the coffee shop the other day."

A little girl waving. Cute as pie? *No.*

Actually, yes. Gabby turned, only to find Ava one table behind them waving her arms and trying to stand up on her chair. Cade was frowning and gesturing for her to sit down immediately.

Gabby smiled and signaled back. A wave of yearning hit her unexpectedly, pure and strong. For what she couldn't quite define but she'd probably describe it as a longing for—love, belonging, family.

"She's a friend?" Owen asked.

"Yes. Her name is Ava." What on earth were Cade and Ava doing here? Not that children weren't welcome, but Fallside definitely wasn't a top pick for a meal with a three-year-old. Her pulse skittered. Had he taken note the other day that she would be here on her date? "So, Owen, how are you liking Angel Falls?"

"I love the angel legend. In fact, my next sermon uses it and I—"

Suddenly someone was tapping at her arm. Ava, dressed in a gray shirt with blue sleeves and baggy black pants, was talking excitedly. "Gabby, Gabby," she said. "Daddy told me not to interrupt you but I ran over anyways to say hi." She threw her arms around Gabby, and of course Gabby hugged her back.

"Ava, this is Pastor Owen," Gabby said.

"Hello there, Ava," the pastor said, holding out his hand. "Great to meet you."

Ava glanced at him but didn't shake his hand, staying close to Gabby. "Daddy's taking me to get a dress for my birthday."

Gabby considered what an amazing dad Cade was for the ninetieth time. But she also felt a little trepidation at the thought of what exactly he would pick out for her to wear.

"What color are you going for?" Gabby asked.

"Pink."

Of course. "Perfect."

"And I want sparkly shoes like the kind you have." Ava patted her arm in that casual, sweet way that only three-year-olds can.

"Sounds like you're having a great day out. Lunch and shopping with your dad."

"I didn't want to have lunch. Daddy made me, but he promised we'd stop at the playground on the way home if I was good."

Suddenly a shadow fell across the table. Gabby looked up to find Cade there, glowering a little as he put a big hand around his daughter's tiny shoulders, a move that made her breath hitch and her throat suddenly go dry.

"Hey, pumpkin, let Gabby eat her lunch," he said, giving a quiet nod to Pastor Owen. His gaze lingered on Gabby. More like scorched through her, body and soul.

"But I was going to ask her if she wanted to come with us," Ava said in a whiny voice. She turned to Gabby, hope glistening in her eyes. "Come shopping with us. Can she, Daddy?"

Gabby's pulse kicked up at Ava's heartfelt invitation. She pictured herself rolling through racks at Target with Ava, picking out a cute, color-coordinated outfit.

Cade stood there looking stoic and unreadable, as usual. And he was frowning. And a tiny muscle in his temple was twitching. Clearly he was about as likely to issue an invitation to go shopping as he was to ask her out on a date.

"Sweetheart," Gabby said before he could answer, "I have an important meeting with Pastor Owen, so I can't join you and your dad today." She glanced up at Cade. He was still being a brick, not even a crack in the façade.

Gabby watched the little girl's face fall. She wanted to promise Ava a visit soon. Say she'd come over later to at least see her new outfit. She wanted to promise her the world. But she refrained.

Because there was no point in encouraging her friendship if she was going to disappoint her in the long run. And this little girl clearly had suffered enough disappointment in her life.

"Come on, Ava, let's go finish our lunch," Cade said, steering a reluctant Ava away and sending Gabby a curt nod. "Nice to see you again," he said to Owen.

The waitress approached, and all Gabby could think of was that she needed a drink but didn't think it was appropriate to order one. Maybe on the way home she'd stop and get a bottle of wine. And a gallon of chocolate fudge brownie ice cream to go with it.

"That little girl seems to really adore you," Owen said.

"She's really sweet. I—" *"I" what?* Gabby couldn't exactly explain the whole situation. *I have a huge crush on my teacher. And his daughter.*

Gabby was still struggling for a conversation starter when Owen said, "Strange, but that little girl's father keeps staring over here."

She anxiously moved her arugula around her plate. She hated arugula. She wasn't sure why she'd ordered it, and now she had a whole plate of it to make some headway on. It tasted like dandelion leaves. Not that she ever ate those, but she imagined they'd have the same bitter taste. "Oh, he's just my creative writing teacher, that's all. So, Owen, tell me about moving into the former pastor's house. Does it need a lot of work done?"

"Well, yes, actually. I'm getting a new roof this week."

"Um, excuse me." Oh geez. Cade was back "Mind if we borrow your ketchup?"

"Oh, sure," she said, passing it over, wondering what they were having that needed ketchup. French fries. Chicken nuggets, maybe? Cade didn't seem to be the kind of man who'd mind if someone snuck some fries off his plate, and for some reason, that thought made her smile.

"Thanks, Gabby," Cade said. Their gazes caught, and his hand closed momentarily over hers as he took the ketchup bottle.

Gabby opened her mouth to speak, but Cade wasn't through. "Can I talk to you a second—in private?"

Cade pulled her off to the side, a spot not far from his table where he could still watch Ava, who was engrossed in coloring her paper place mat.

"I'm sorry I upset you because I used your writing in front of the class."

Something inside her melted. Not just because of the apology but because he looked genuinely distressed himself. "I was wrong to take that so personally. I'm sorry I asked you to make an exception for me. I put you in an awkward position."

"It's okay. I knew you felt concerned and worried about the story. I should've realized you weren't ready to have it put up in front of everyone." He gripped her by the arms. "Gabby, I can't stop thinking about you. I don't even know why I asked for ketchup, because I can't eat. Or sleep. I...miss you. And I want a chance to be with you as soon as I'm not your teacher anymore."

Oh, wow oh, wow. Gabby froze, riveted in place by Cade's words. Which were the most amazing words anyone had ever said to her.

"It's okay if I'm too late. I just wanted a chance to tell you that in case...in case you might still want me."

"Oh, Cade, of course I want you." She was terrified by how easily the words had slipped out. How *right* they felt. How standing next to him was making her feel flushed and dizzy, breathless and giddy, and exactly, exactly right. She stepped back to regain her balance. Otherwise she would've wrapped herself around him and kissed him breathless. "I'm so glad you found me. But I really need to get back to my date."

Cade ran his fingers through his hair. She loved that he looked rattled because of her—because he *wanted* her. "I'm sorry I didn't tell you that sooner," he said. And then, "Can I call you later?"

"Of course. Sure." She was grinning. "Definitely!"

When Gabby got back to the table, she carefully placed her napkin back on her lap. She owed Pastor Owen honesty. "Look, Owen, I—"

Suddenly Owen laughed.

"What is it?"

"I know when I'm beat."

"Cade's my teacher, and he's had too much integrity to pursue anything with me while I'm still his student."

"Well, clearly he's upset you're on a date."

"Yes, well, I'm actually really surprised about that."

"I think he likes you. And I think you like him too."

"It's…complicated."

He shrugged. "What isn't?" He took her hand and squeezed it briefly. A pleasant, comforting squeeze—no fireworks. And she'd never been so relieved. "I'm sorry I missed my chance," he said. "But it was great to meet you."

"It was great to meet you too. And thanks for…for being a nice guy and helping me figure out some things."

"Gabby, you didn't need me to figure anything out for you."

She smiled. "Thank you for understanding."

"Hey, I'm never one to stand in the way of true love."

Owen insisted on paying, and she gave him a hug goodbye and walked over to Cade's table.

"My date's over," she said to Cade.

"Oh, and how'd it go?"

"It probably ranks among the most embarrassing first dates I've ever had."

"Is there going to be a second one?"

"No."

"Good." He sent her a look—and oh, what a look—a blazing-hot I-want-you look that made her toes curl.

"Daddy," Ava said, pulling up the place mat she'd been decorating, "can Gabby come with us now? Please?"

Cade smiled. "Gabby, would you come to Target with us to help Ava pick out an outfit for her birthday on Monday?"

Her throat suddenly felt lumpy. "Oh, well, I—I don't want to interfere."

"Ava would love it. *I* would love it."

Oh, joy. She wanted to kiss him right there.

"I'd love it too," she said, grinning. "Let's go to Target."

"But, Daddy, you promised the playground first because I was good. Wasn't I good?"

"Yes, you were very good." He turned to Gabby. "Want to walk to the playground? It's on the way back to my house, and that's where my truck is anyway."

They walked the few blocks to the playground, Ava chattering all the way. Gabby walked side by side with Cade, but as soon as they got there, Ava ran off to climb the jungle gym, and Cade turned to face Gabby. "I'm really happy you're spending the afternoon with us."

"Me too."

"So what's with the pastor?"

"My stepmom set us up. I sort of had to go."

"Oh, so now you tell me."

"Well, to be honest, I was hoping I'd be swept away. He seems to be a lot less complicated than you are."

"So were you? Swept away?" Cade asked casually, their gazes meeting again.

"No. I wasn't."

Cade let out a deep breath and rubbed his neck. "Well, that's a relief." He was still staring at her and seemed about to say more. She'd turned away to watch Ava when he took hold of her hand. She looked up at him, caught again by the intensity of his gaze. "Because I don't want you to be swept away by anyone until I have an opportunity to sweep you away myself."

"You—you want to sweep me away?"

"As soon as class is over."

"Um—just exactly what would this—this sweeping away entail?"

He was very near, his voice a mere whisper. "Kissing. Lots of kissing."

"I like kissing," she said, nodding. "What else?"

"Kissing places like right here on your neck." He pointed with his index finger to the base of her neck, "and whispering things in your ear."

She couldn't stop the shiver that traveled up her spine. "What kinds of things?"

"Like how much I'm looking forward to learning everything about you—your favorite color, your favorite kind of ice cream, your favorite TV shows and books. And all the funny stories from when you were little and all your favorite memories."

"That's—that's beautiful, Cade," Gabby said, swallowing hard.

"Oh, I'm not done," he said, dropping his voice and leaning over to whisper in her ear. "Because I'll also tell you how much I want to know every inch of your body. What makes you relax and what makes you whimper and what makes you cry out my name. *That's* how much I want to know you."

"Hmmm," Gabby said, counting on her fingers. "Kissing, touching, talking...I think I'm going to like getting swept away—a lot."

Chapter 17

♥

The Target date was fun, considering that Cade hated all forms of shopping. Worse, he had to fight with himself every second to keep from touching Gabby or thinking about kissing her. Not the most appropriate behavior for Target.

He lasted ten minutes in the little girl's department looking at dresses, until Gabby finally looked at him and said, "Why don't you go look at some tools or something?" and he gratefully headed off to find a bulb for his broken porch light. Twenty minutes later, he was happy to find that his presence had not been missed.

Ava was glued to Gabby's side, chattering away, smiling. They'd picked out a colorful dress and matching shoes and a hair bow that Ava wanted to wear right away.

Gabby even talked him into buying a woven basket for Ava's toys to keep behind his couch so that sometimes said toys would actually be contained and not scattered all over the floor.

Cade couldn't remember when he felt so… unburdened. For once he didn't think about the thousand concerns he had about Ava adjusting to their new life, or his research project and how maybe he should feel more thrilled about it.

No, he just enjoyed the day, the happiness of his daughter, and the beautiful woman by his side.

"I took some great photos today," Gabby said, as Cade came back downstairs from putting Ava to bed. "Super cute. Want to see them?" She handed him her phone and he flipped through the images. There was one in Target with Ava's face peeking out between clothes on the rack.

He couldn't help laughing. "You took one in Target?"

Her lips curved up. "I took a *bunch* in Target."

Cade snorted. "You let Ava take this one?"

It was a picture of Gabby with a pink feather boa around her neck holding a dress up in front of her.

"Okay, so maybe part of me is still a little kid."

He looked down at her, his heart beating wildly in his chest for no reason other than being near her. She was right next to him, their elbows touching, and all he could think of is how he wanted to put the damn camera down and fold her into his arms. But he forced himself to focus on the pictures. "You have a good eye," he said, handing her back the camera.

"Thanks to Photography 101, 102, and Independent Study."

Cade frowned. "You don't give yourself enough credit."

She shrugged. "All right then, I'm multitalented," she said. "What can I say?"

"I bet you are."

Her cheeks pinked up at that. "Are you flirting with me, Professor?"

Cade opened the door for her before he said something else inappropriate, and they both stepped out onto the porch. The night was soft and mild, a hint of coolness in the breeze drifting in from the street.

He shoved his hands into his jeans pockets. God, he wanted her. Only his fraying self-control prevented him from reaching out to tug her against him and feel her soft breasts pressed against his chest. He wanted to run his hands through all that beautiful hair and drag his lips over her soft, full ones. "Gabby, I—" His voice faded, making him clear his throat. He kept his fists balled in his pockets so he wouldn't be tempted to take his hands out.

"It's okay," she said. "I understand what you can't say." She laughed. "Or at least *part* of what you can't say."

Hell, what *would* he say? That being near her was driving him crazy, that all he could think about was taking her to his bed. That being near her was eroding his will, second by second, and he no longer knew if he could continue to defend his principles anymore.

He held her by the arms, hoping she could tell from the way he was looking at her that he meant far more than what his words said. "I had a great time today. And so did Ava."

"I had a great time too."

Her eyes searched his. He owed her more, but he

wouldn't cross the line again. "I want you, Gabby. It's all I can think of."

Gabby did something strange then—she pulled out her phone and scrolled through it. Then she held it up to his face. "It's over," she said quietly.

"What?" He looked in confusion at the email in front of his eyes. An automated response from the college. *You have withdrawn from Course number E04001, Creative Writing Level One.*

"When did you do this?"

"Today," she said. "In Target."

"I've failed you as a teacher." That was the thought he vocalized, his first thought. But the other thoughts flooded him with a desperate hope—that finally, finally, he could touch her, taste her, have her. That the time had come where he could stop being her teacher and just be... a man.

"No, Cade. You've been an amazing teacher. I feel confident my teacher will continue to work with me independently. And I want to sleep with my teacher. How's that for—"

He silenced her by placing his lips over hers and kissing her long and slow and deep. His hand curled softly around her neck, in her hair, and he pulled her to him, angling her face so their mouths fit together perfectly. Their mouths, their bodies flush, at last, after all this time, and he could not get enough. He swept his tongue into her mouth, and her tongue met his, and oh, she tasted wonderful, sweet like the warm, late summer afternoon they'd just spent together, and he couldn't stop.

Their kisses turned deeper and wetter, and she clung

to him, pressing her body against his. His hands wandered under her shirt, caressed the soft skin of her back, skimmed over her bra, and an involuntary groan escaped him. She was clinging to him, her hands skimming his chest, his back, the waistband of his jeans. They were going to do it right here on the porch if he didn't get himself together.

Dimly, he heard the soft buzz of a text. Gabby broke away, breathing a little hard. "I think this Independent Study's going to be pretty good," she said as she reached for her phone.

He bent to kiss her again. "Don't go," he murmured against the soft skin of her cheek. "Stay with me." He'd never had a woman over at his house, because of his concern for Ava. But his need for Gabby threatened to overshadow all his rules.

"It's Rafe," she said, looking at her phone screen. "He asked if I could run over and check on Nonna and help her get ready for bed. It's his night to stay with her but he's running a little late."

"Oh," Cade said, trying to keep the disappointment from his voice.

For a minute they stood there, their hands joined, his fingers kneading hers.

"I have to go," she said, but she didn't move.

"I'll work on getting a sitter," he said. "Are you free this week?"

"Sure," she said. "Friday. And also Thursday, Wednesday, Tuesday, and Monday," she said, grinning.

He laughed.

"I better go," she said. "I'm so sorry."

"Not as sorry as I am," he said, kissing her on the mouth.

"See you soon."

It couldn't be soon enough.

* * *

An hour later, a knock sounded at Gabby's door. She'd showered and thrown on a pair of flannel pj pants and a T-shirt and a pair of thick slipper socks Nonna had bought her for her birthday. Her hair was up in a messy bun. "Who is it?" she asked, a little frightened. That was the thing about living out here in the country—people didn't knock on her door. Midnight had taken up residence in the house, coming in to curl up at the foot of her bed most nights now. On hearing the knock, he'd promptly fled under her bed. "Great watch cat you are," Gabby said.

"It's Cade," came a deep, masculine voice that immediately made her heart plunge into her stomach.

She opened the door to discover him with his arms stretched out overhead, hanging on to the doorjamb, a move that showcased the elegantly corded muscles of his arms.

Her pulse seemed to double in rate, her heart pounding wildly against her ribs. "What are you doing here?" she asked, her voice sounding a little bit cracked, a little bit hoarse.

Their gazes met and held. Everything seemed to stop—her heartbeat, her breath. For one moment there was only him, looking at her like no man had ever looked at her before, and she knew that now there was no escaping everything she felt for him.

From the first night she'd met him, the first time he'd smiled at her, something deep within in her had known what her brain hadn't: that this man was different. This man had the power to strip though all her baloney and see her for who she truly was, despite her best efforts to hide that.

"Gabby," he said, displaying an unholy grin. "Can I come in?"

She could only manage a nod before she drew him over the threshold, and somehow they managed to shut the door. Suddenly they were leaning up against it, his hands on either side of her head, his body aligned with hers. She could feel him hard and aroused.

His kisses were urgent, deep, and intentional. The sense of holding back that she'd always gotten with him had vanished, and the resulting intensity took her breath away. She slid her hands around his lean waist, under his shirt, against his warm skin, loving the contrasting smoothness and firmness of him.

He wrapped his arms around her, his kisses never ceasing, their tongues tangling together, hot and wet and urgent.

"You weren't kidding when you said *soon*, were you?" she said breathlessly.

He gathered up her hands in his big ones. "I can't think of anything else but wanting you, Gabby. When you said you dropped the class—it was like a dam burst, and I had to see you. Luckily my mom was free tonight."

Gabby's eyes widened. "What did you tell her?"

"That it was an emergency."

She smacked her hand against her forehead. "You did not."

"I did." He stepped closer. "A love emergency," he said with mock seriousness.

She could imagine herself saying that, but Mr. Practical? Mr. I-Don't-Believe-In-Love? "You did *not* say that to your mother."

"Not in those exact words. But I did make her promise not to ask any questions."

"Did that work?"

"She only asked one," he said, taking another step closer.

Gabby stepped back, only to find that she'd run into the wall. "And what was that?"

He came very close. So close she could feel the heat radiating off of his big body, see the hunger in his eyes. "She asked me," he said in a low voice, dipping his head and edging even closer, "if I was going to see you."

"What did you tell her?" She swallowed hard, very aware of his nearness. She could only imagine what his mother was thinking.

"I said of course I was going to see you." And then his lips were on hers, and he was pulling her closer until she was pressed up against him, engulfed by his kisses, wrapped up in his clean scent. A sense of wonder that they could finally stop fighting this attraction, and relief that they were finally, finally together, washed over her in waves.

"Then do you know what she said?" He planted kisses on her neck, working his way to the sensitive little hollow between her neck and collarbone. His hands moved to her waist, traveling under her shirt, up her back, finally coming to rest on her hips. She dropped her head back in surrender to the sensations that were overtaking her.

"I have no idea."

"'Hallelujah!'"

"I'm glad she approves." Gabby chuckled, but she was still a little uncomfortable that his mom was aware of... well, she didn't really want to think about it.

"Mmmm," he said, which she took for *I'm done talking about my mother now*. He tugged on her shirt as if to pull it off but then froze. "Wait, don't move," he said.

"What is it?" she asked. "Is something wrong?"

The corner of his mouth quirked upward. "No," he said softly. "Just that you're beautiful. And I think I just found your tattoo."

"Took you long enough," she said.

He traced his hand up the side of her abdomen, then bent to examine where it was imprinted on the lower right side, the top corner of it just visible over her waistband. "A butterfly," he said.

"Yes."

"It suits you. Pretty, symbolic, a reminder more to yourself than to the world. I like it." He tugged on her T-shirt. "Now take this off," he said.

"I have an idea," she said.

He stopped the kissing and looked at her. "I'm up for new ideas," he said. "What is it?"

"It's a perfect, beautiful night. Would you want to go outside? I was thinking we could take a few blankets out there under the trees."

"I don't care where we go. As long as it involves getting naked with you in the next thirty seconds. Or less."

She ran to her closet and pulled out two blankets. "This way."

They walked down the hill from the carriage house and spread them out on the gentle slope that overlooked the lake. The stars were spilled across a velvet sky, no lights around to dim their brightness.

Cade threw off his shirt and lay down on the blanket, patting the space next to him. And oh, there was that spectacular chest, the plains of muscle softly shadowed in the moonlight.

"I know a lot about the constellations," Gabby said, as he drew her into his arms.

"Another class?" he murmured as he kissed her.

"No," she said. "Just a lot of stargazing and dreaming."

His face was over hers now, and lord, he had the longest lashes. "You're beautiful," she said, kissing his full lips as he pulled her down with him onto the blanket.

"I've never met someone like you," he murmured as he scanned her face in the moonlight. "You have a . . . a wonder about you for everything."

"Some people might call that a little crazy."

He smoothed his thumb across her cheek. "I've been thinking of you a lot, Gabby. And the thought of you makes me feel—lighter. Like it's possible to have fun again. With you, I feel like myself—and I haven't felt like myself for a very long time."

"Well, I feel like you took me seriously at a time when I didn't even take myself seriously."

"I take you very seriously."

She'd never met a guy who liked her just for her. She'd had guys like her in spite of her quirks, in spite of her many scattered interests, but most of them had wanted to mold her into the person they'd wanted her to be, and she'd let them.

But not Cade. She never thought to pretend with him, and he'd accepted her for who she was from the start.

His lips met hers, and he kissed her so softly, so gently, so *well*, that every thought fled. She combed her hands through his thick, silky hair and pulled him closer, finally able to kiss him, to touch him, to be with him at last.

She raised her arms and he helped her peel off her shirt. There was admiration in his gaze. "I wish I could describe what you looked like right now with your hair all spread out and—"

That made her blush. "You're the established writer. You have the pretty words."

"Honey, you just took all my words from me."

Then his weight was over her and his mouth was on her breast. Whatever he was doing with his tongue—and he did it slowly, carefully, and attentively—shot sparks of sensation everywhere and made her squirm from the almost unbearable pleasure. She ran her hands up and down the sculpted ridges of his back, tugged at his waistband until he shucked his pants and briefs. His mouth went to her other breast, his tongue laving her until she moaned. She stroked his hard length, ran her hand over his taut butt, reveling in the beauty and strength of his body.

He kissed her mouth, then moved out of her grasp. “Gabby, I—I’m not sure I can take much more touching—it’s been a long time. I’m not sure I can last.”

“It’s okay,” she said. “We have all night.”

He tugged down her flannel pants and teased his finger along the lacy seam of her panties until she shuddered.

He pushed the tiny scrap of silk aside and stroked her at her core, where she was slick and wet and ready. Her intimate muscles clenched, and any control she thought she had was fading fast. Then he slipped a finger inside her, then another, stroking her swollen flesh, and kissed her deeply, whispering how he’d dreamed of doing this for so long, and how lucky he was to be with her.

His words undid her. She felt fevered and restless, her back arching, her hands roaming over him. She could barely think as sensation overtook her body.

“Cade, I am seriously ready. Now. Together.” She could barely form sentences, so instead she tugged on him impatiently, pulling him over her.

He grabbed a condom from the corner of the blanket and slipped it on, and she guided him into her body. His gaze was unwavering and honest, so much so that it brought tears to her eyes.

“Am I—hurting you?” he managed.

“No, no, I—I’m just so—” *overcome* “—happy. I’m happy.”

He entered her, at first slowly, then steadily, filling her completely, picking up a rhythm that echoed the beating of her heart. She wrapped her arms and legs around him as he drove into her, steadily and powerfully. As their rhythm mounted, his face grew taut, his lips pressed together tightly, yet he never took his eyes off her.

"Now," she said. "Oh, now."

Waves of sensation rolled through her, one after another, overtaking her while she clung to him, her muscles clenching and tightening. He cried out her name and shuddered while her own release continued on and on.

Suddenly there was silence. Gabby rested against Cade's chest, her body still wrapped tightly around him. She could hear his breathing, a little heavy, feel the damp hair at his neck. Her heart was pounding in her ears, the blood still rushing as she came back down to earth. In the trees overhead, an owl hooted, and the crickets continued their steady song. But in her world, everything had changed.

* * *

"Tell me about what you're working on," Gabby said a few hours later, running a hand over Cade's chest in a way that was...doing things to him again. Making him want her again, even though they'd made love three times and were now wrapped up in the blanket, staring at the dense smattering of stars overhead.

Cade wasn't much for camping out or sleeping outdoors, especially on the unyielding ground with a pine cone sticking him in the ass, but he would not trade where he was for anything in the world. Gabby's soft body was curled up next to his, her arm across his chest, her head tucked into the spot between his neck and shoulder as if she were meant to be there—always.

He laughed, and the sound resonated in his chest in a full, good way. He hadn't laughed like that in a long time. "Why do you want to talk about that now?"

She smoothed a hand over his pecs. He placed one of his hands over hers and brought it quickly up to his mouth, kissing it. "Because I want to know everything about you," she said. "So tell me about the sad, depressed young man who returns home, only to find desolation and despair everywhere."

"Well, I've changed it a little since then," he said.

"Changed what?"

"There's a woman he loved. She's in the town. He sees her."

Gabby's head popped up, her hair spilling over him like a waterall. "Is it a love story? You're writing a love story?"

She was way too excited about that. "No. I mean—maybe. I haven't decided yet."

"Well, there should be *someone* who loves him. Does he have family? Brothers and sisters? A mother?"

"His family's not very supportive. He's pretty much on his own."

She sat up suddenly. "Cade, why on earth are you writing something so…depressing? If I wrote stuff like that I wouldn't be able to get out of bed in the mornings."

He chuckled softly and kissed her on the forehead. "That might not be a bad thing for us," he said.

"Seriously. What are you thinking here? Who reads this stuff?"

"It's about existential questions. About the futility of life. About how man is essentially alone."

"Oh," she said, sounding very deadpan.

"What?" he asked. "What is it?"

"I just don't understand how you can have such great sex like what we just had and still want to write fiction that makes a large portion of the population want to drink themselves into a stupor." She paused and seemed to consider that. "Unless the sex wasn't so great...for you?"

He laughed. "First of all, I never fully understood this before," he said, tongue in cheek, "but I see now that you're a popular fiction snob, and that really saddens me."

"Is that something you can get over?" she asked, "or is it a dealbreaker?"

He sighed heavily. "I don't know. But maybe my sad character *can* use somebody who cares about him. Because maybe life isn't all that bad."

"Oh, great. If you tell me a little about him I can help you find someone to care for him. I mean, you've certainly talked with me a lot about my story. I'd love to hear about yours."

He shook his head and grinned. "What, you mean like match.com for fictional characters? You really do love a happy ending, don't you?"

She shrugged. "Doesn't everyone want love? I can't think of anyone who doesn't." She paused and touched his arm. "You haven't answered the question about the sex."

"Oh. Well, I'm not exactly sure how to rate it. I think I need another run-through to be extra sure."

She smacked him in the arm.

"Okay, okay. Just for the record . . . it was mind-blowing."

"What?" Her eyes widened and he couldn't help but grin.

"The lovemaking. With you. Mind. Blowing."

"Now *that's* a story I'd like to read," Gabby said, before she kissed him again.

* * *

At five in the morning, Cade awakened to cool, damp air and the itchy sense that bugs had been feasting on both of them throughout the night. The crickets had silenced, but their sound was replaced by the clear, sweet notes of the first few birds rising early before the dawn.

Gabby had been using his chest as a pillow, the silky strands of her curls covering him like a blanket. His back felt sore and stiff from sleeping on the ground, but he lay there for just a moment longer, stroking her back, thanking his lucky stars for such an incredible night, and for bringing him such an incredible woman. Morning had come way too soon.

"Gabby," he whispered, his mouth feeling dry, his voice cottony. "Wake up, sweetheart."

She stirred and woke up, rubbing her eyes. "Cade," she said, lifting her head off his chest. "Good morning."

"It'll be dawn soon. I'm going to head home. Let me walk you up to the house."

"We tried this before and you know what happened." Yes, they'd started to move back to the house twice.

Both times had ended in more lovemaking that made them forget all about seeking a real bed. But now it was almost dawn, and he had to go before Ava awakened.

He helped Gabby up, shook out the blankets, and together they walked back up the hill. As soon as she opened the door, the cat scampered out, happy to be free. They kissed goodbye at the door, lingering kisses that made him feel like he hadn't been kissing her half the night. Finally he forced himself to stop, cradling her face gently in his hands. "You're beautiful," he said simply, because she was.

She smiled. "You're crazy."

"No." He kissed her again, this time longer, his hands bracing against the door behind her. She slipped her fingers lightly around his wrists, and they kissed like that for a long time until Gabby put her hands on his chest and lightly pushed. "Go," she said.

Tearing himself away was hard.

He'd been infatuated with Emerson, his first love, and he'd loved her blindly, through all her faults and even her selfishness. He'd had women he'd liked and enjoyed but felt almost nothing when it had come time to part. But this was different. Gabby didn't make him feel like he was giving all the time, the desperate kind of giving where no one gave back. She made him feel like *she* was giving to *him*, waking him up for the first time in his life, making him laugh. Lightening his load. And she made him want to give her everything back.

He was humming quietly when he walked through his front door. His mom was in the living room, folding up blankets on his couch, where she'd obviously slept.

"Mom," he said, "how come you didn't sleep in the spare room?"

"I wanted to be able to hear Ava if she woke up and found you gone. And the couch was comfy." She dropped the last blanket onto the couch and smoothed it down. "What time is it?" she asked innocently.

Oh, hell. There was no use lying. After all, he was thirty-two years old. But that somehow didn't make it any easier.

"It's five a.m., Mom."

"Oh." She paused. "Did you have a nice time? I mean, scratch that." She cleared her throat. "I'm glad you're back." She plucked something off his shirt. A blade of grass. He tried not to wince.

He kissed his mom on the head. "Thanks for watching Ava," he said. "I really appreciate it."

She headed toward the kitchen, sending one waving hand up above her head. "Gabby's a nice woman," she called. "You could do worse."

"You want some coffee? I'll make it."

"You bet," she answered.

"All right then," he said, getting to it. "Hey, Mom?" Cade popped his head around the kitchen doorway. "Love you."

Paige smiled. "I love you too, son. I love you too."

* * *

"Okay, Nonna, are you ready to help me sort through this box?" Gabby asked the following evening as she sat on Nonna's porch swing. She patted the swing for

Nonna to come sit down. Instead, her dog, a bull terrier named Rocket, jumped up and snuggled in beside her, making her move the box. "Looks like Rocket wants to help too."

Her grandmother took a seat on the other side of Rocket. But she didn't dig into the box. Instead, she fingered the pendant that Gabby still wore around her neck.

"Has this brought you luck?" she asked. Gabby thought of Cade. How wonderful their lovemaking had been. How hopeful she was for the future—and how in love.

God, she loved him. Maybe she had from the moment he'd smiled at her and said he was sorry for stealing her parking spot.

Anyway. "Yes, I think it has. I love the necklace, Nonna. Tell me about it."

"Oh, I never talk about it," she said. "I didn't want to make your grandfather upset."

Gabby fingered the smooth, pure white stone. "Did someone from the old country make it for you?"

Instead of answering, Nonna grabbed the shoebox and rifled through the papers. "Let's do this now," she said. "Here."

Nonna began to empty out the box, handing Gabby papers one after another. Gabby unfolded each yellowed paper one by one and laid them out in her lap. "These are stock certificates." She read the names typed across the tops. *Coca-Cola. IBM. Disney.*

"Dear God in heaven, Nonna. You bought stock in *Disney*?"

"Your grandfather and I did."

"This... this is worth a lot of money."

"Good," Nonna said. "Let's see what else is in here."

Rocket, bored with human nonsense, snored, deeply asleep at Gabby's side while she sorted out a life insurance policy, a CD, and old bank statements, then handed the box to Nonna. "Any more jewelry in there?"

Nonna flipped through the rest of the papers. At the very bottom of the box, she stopped and pulled out an old black-and-white photograph with wavy edges.

"Here he is," she said solemnly.

Her grandmother's eyes had gone soft, and her fingers ran absently over the wavy edges of the photo. She tilted it towards Gabby. "Jacob," she pronounced.

Jacob. The name she'd mentioned once when she'd shaken Cade's hand. The photo showed a good-looking young man with dark, curly hair—curlier and shorter than Cade's. He wore a short-sleeved, button-down shirt with his arms crossed, a pack of cigarettes rolled up in his sleeve. He leaned casually against an old convertible car, some model from the '50s. And he was grinning widely.

He looked confident and young and like he was just about to laugh at something the person taking the photo had said.

"Who is he, Nonna?" Gabby asked, sensing something important, but not wanting to push her grandmother into remembering if it was painful or sad.

"A boy I loved."

"A boy from Italy?" Gabby asked.

"I think so," she said softly.

Gabby held her breath, anticipating what her grandmother would say next, but she didn't say anything at all for a very long time.

"I tried to make myself throw the photograph away but I...couldn't," Nonna said, wistfulness in her voice. "So I had to keep it somewhere where your grandfather wouldn't see it. I felt a little bad keeping it. But I couldn't let it go."

She'd kept an old photo of a handsome young man who'd clearly meant a lot to her at the bottom of a dusty shoebox, under the Coca-Cola stocks, for more than fifty years.

Would her grandfather really have cared about Nonna's old boyfriend?

"He loved you too?" Gabby asked, not wanting to upset her grandmother or trigger memories she'd rather forget, but she was dying to know the story.

"Yes," she said finally, on a sigh. "He loved me too."

Forget the Coca-Cola or the Disney stocks. Gabby wanted to know more about Jacob.

* * *

Cade was talking to his agent on the phone that afternoon after work when Ava came racing down the stairs in her new dress, a brush and ponytail holders in her hands.

"I want French braids, Daddy," she whispered, dangling the coated rubber bands in front of his face and attempting to climb onto his lap.

Cade took the brush and began to brush her hair, hoping to keep her quiet until he finished his conversation.

"Actually, Joanna, I'm going to send you a couple of chapters by the end of next week."

"Ouch, Daddy!" Ava cried, holding on to her hair. "That hurts!"

"Sorry, baby," he said, trying to be gentler. "Why don't you run up and get the detangle comb and the spray bottle, okay?"

She nodded and ran off, eager to have her hair done for her birthday party.

"Caden, I'm sorry," Joanna said. "I don't think I heard that correctly. Did you say you actually *wrote* something?"

"I said I'm working on some chapters, and I'll send them when they're ready. In the meantime, I've got something else I want to ask you to read. It's something one of my friends wrote, and it's fantastic. Okay if I send it?"

"What is it?" she asked, a healthy dose of skepticism permeating her tone. She wasn't one of the best agents in New York for nothing.

"Just read it, okay?"

"I'd rather have those chapters, Caden, because I'm a little afraid they don't exist."

Cade laughed.

"Did you just *laugh* at me?" Joanna asked, getting prickly.

"Not *at* you." There was a time when her words would've made him shudder. Actually, there was many a time when they had. Maybe even now they should make him feel more panicked, because his chapters were little more than a mess of pages, more incoherent than coherent. But there were words on pages, and the difference was that he wasn't afraid for the first time in years. He was *excited.*

In the old days, he might've said something cocky like *they'll be worth waiting for*. But now...now he was humbler. "I'm laughing because I'm excited to send them. As soon as they're ready. In the meantime, I just clicked *send* on the other pages. Let me know what you think."

"Caden."

"Yes, Joanna?"

He heard her sigh. "I'm really excited to read whatever you send me." There was a pause on the line. "And you sound good. Like you're *alive* again."

He said goodbye to Joanna and scooped up Ava, who'd returned with more rubber bands, which meant she was probably going to ask him to do something he'd have to Google again, but even that didn't seem so daunting today. He gave a big, evil-sounding laugh that made Ava scream with delight and pretended to bite her neck. "Come here, birthday girl." He clicked on YouTube for a fancy braiding lesson and got to work with the spray bottle. "We'd better hurry. We've got a birthday party to go to at Grandma's. And Aunt Beth is coming. And Gabby too."

He'd invited Gabby because Ava had wanted her there. But he had just as much.

"My birthday party," she said, very pleased. "I'm the birthday girl."

"And a very smart, kind, and beautiful birthday girl you are."

He laughed. *I* am *alive again. And it's damn good to be back.*

Chapter 18

♥

That evening, Gabby walked into Paige's backyard, where white lights were strung across a pretty patio. Her birthday present for Ava was in hand. The gift bag was green and bunched up to look like a flowerpot with a giant fabric sunflower growing out of it, and it held two pairs of leggings, matching T-shirts, a pair of tennies, and matching headbands and socks. She'd also tossed a large cylindrical container of washable markers and a big pad of drawing paper in another bag for good measure, because while Ava desperately needed a wardrobe update, Gabby wasn't 100 percent certain the clothing would be a big hit.

Gabby's heart kicked up in anticipation of seeing Cade, and she absently smoothed out the skirt of her sundress, which was bright yellow with daisies on it, her favorite. She caught sight of him sitting between his mom and Ava, wearing a light blue button-down shirt, his hair neatly combed, his face clean-shaven. An immediate wave of longing rushed through her. Being invited to his daughter's birthday meant something, although she wanted to just enjoy it and not think too hard about what. But it was definitely a step in the relationship direction—a big step for Cade and one that filled her with hopeful expectation.

Cade stood and met her in the grass. "Hi, gorgeous," he said with a wink that made her stomach flip. He kissed her on the cheek and bent to whisper something in her ear. It sounded like *I loved making love to you.*

His words sent a shiver through her. No one had ever said something so romantic to her before, and it thrilled her to the core, not to mention causing a blush that started on her chest and spread like wildfire clear up to the roots of her hair.

"Did I say something wrong?" he asked innocently, as if it wasn't something that had just rocked her world.

She kissed him back and whispered, "I loved it too." *So eloquent*, she thought as she stood there with a stupid grin on her face. They stared at each other for probably too long, because his mom suddenly cleared her throat.

Gabby walked over and said hi to Paige, Paige's friend Matt, and Beth. She bent down to give Ava a big birthday hug and got one just as big in return. Ava twirled in her rainbow dress and showed off her sparkly shoes, then exclaimed at Gabby's present wrapped like a sunflower.

"How'd you manage that?" Cade asked.

She shrugged. "Gift wrapping class."

He laughed. "Forget writing. With that kind of talent, you could get a job with the elves at the North Pole."

"I thought about applying," she said with mock seriousness, "but the weather's just too cold."

"Good one," he said, grinning as he led her to the table. She couldn't help being pleased he'd appreciated the wrapping. And seemed excited to see her too.

The first thing she noticed on taking a seat was that Cade's family was very...small. Nothing like her boisterous, crazy, noisy family that gathered every Sunday for dinner. And that made her a little sad—for Ava. No brothers and sisters, no cousins, no rambunctious uncles who gave piggyback rides.

Matt, who was also Nonna's mailman, asked how she was doing. Beth regaled them with a story about pulling five peas out of a toddler's nose in the office earlier, which made Gabby never want to eat peas again. Or have kids. Just kidding, but ew, *gross*.

During dinner, Cade rested a hand on Gabby's thigh under the table, which had the effect of completely suppressing her appetite, even though she'd been starving all day. And he kept rubbing his thumb back and forth, which made her blush even more and stammer a bit. Finally, she had to push his hand away and do her best not to look at him.

It didn't help. Even the graze of his elbow was turning her to jelly.

She reminded herself that she was thirty, not twenty. But this felt like the first time she was falling in love.

Actually, she thought, it just might be. Because looking back, what she'd felt in her other relationships was affection, attraction, sure—but, now she knew, not love.

But this...this felt real. It felt right in ways she was too afraid to think of.

She snapped out of her thoughts long enough to notice that Paige was talking and appeared to be waiting for a response, and she'd completely missed what the woman had just said. "Oh, I'm sorry, what did you say?"

Paige smiled in a caught-ya! way and glanced over at her son, who happened to be looking over at Gabby. "I was just asking Cade how the writing's going."

"It's going well—but how did you know I was writing again?" Cade asked.

"You're writing again?" Beth asked, perking up across the table. "That's terrific."

"You just seem...happier," Paige said, "and I hoped you would be." She clapped her hands together, pleased. "That's wonderful news, Caden."

"What are you writing about?" Beth asked. "Something deep and dark and painful like last time?"

"Ha ha," he said to Beth. "It might be a little more hopeful, but it's really too early to talk about."

Paige's eyes got glossy.

"Mom," Cade said, "I really just started a story. But it's holding my interest and—"

She looked over at Gabby. "Gabby, you helped him get started again, didn't you?"

Cade rubbed his neck. "Mom..."

"Well, actually, no," Gabby said. "I'm struggling just to get my own story going."

Just then Cade grabbed her hand—this time on the table, where everyone saw. Before she could react he smiled at her. She was startled and pleased that he was treating her in front of his family like…well, like his girlfriend. "Gabby did help me get started again."

"No, Cade." Gabby shook her head. "I really can't take credit for that at all."

"Yes, you can. I guess you just make me feel…at ease. And I see how much you're enjoying working on your own story." He looked at his family around the table.

"Grammie, is it time for cake yet?" Ava asked, clearly bored with the discussion. "And presents."

"Oh yes, that's a great idea. Let's have cake." To Cade she said, "I feel that we have more than a birthday to celebrate."

Paige placed the cake in front of Ava and was just about to light the candles when a familiar voice said, "Hello, everyone."

Gabby looked up to find Elliot standing a short distance away, dressed in a suit coat and bow tie, his gray hair brushed back and tidily cut. He looked like a dapper, handsome, distinguished man, his eyes as sharp and crisply blue as the sky on a cloudless winter day. The resemblance to his son now that they were both occupying the same space was…remarkable.

The rest of the table reacted as if the king of the zombie apocalypse had just showed up. Beth gasped. Paige gave a little yelp, having forgotten to blow out the match. Matt, God love him, just looked confused, surely knowing by now this birthday dinner involved much more than having dinner with Paige's kids for the first time.

"I hear postage is going up by two cents next month," Matt said, clearing his throat. "Everyone might want to think about stocking up on some forever stamps now."

Gabby stole a sideways glance at Cade, and it was Not. Good. His face was flushed, his brows knit down deeply. It took him about a second to scrape back his chair, toss down his napkin, and rise, looking like a bouncer ready to haul his dad off the property.

Gabby held her breath. She'd never told Cade that she'd met his father. There had never seemed like a good time to bring it up, and honestly, with everything going on between them, she'd forgotten. But now guilt was bearing down on her. Additionally, she wondered if she'd had anything to do with him showing up here, based on their conversation in the coffee shop.

"Hi, Dad," Beth finally said.

"Hello, sweetheart," Elliot answered, beaming at his daughter. To Paige he bowed slightly, which few people would've been able to pull off with such...aplomb. "My dear, you look lovely as always." His gaze skimmed briefly over Matt, and he had just enough time to acknowledge Gabby with a nod before Cade had traversed the table and was now standing next to him.

"Hello, son," Elliot said.

A vein in Cade's temple pulsed, and one hand was balled into a tight fist. "Elliot," he said to his father. He looked like he wanted to say more—a lot more—but his glance over at his daughter told Gabby he was choosing his words carefully.

Elliot, always ready with an irreverent quip, didn't seem to have anything to say.

"What a surprise," Paige said, not unpleasantly.

Cade cleared his throat and glanced again at Ava, who was quietly assessing Elliot, her eyes huge.

"I'm sorry to interrupt the festivities," Elliot said. "But I came to celebrate with my beautiful granddaughter on her birthday." Elliot turned to Ava while the entire table collectively held their breath. "Ava, sweetheart," he said, holding out a package wrapped in sparkly paper with a metallic bow. "I'm your grandpa."

* * *

Outrage clogged Cade's throat, making the fish or whatever the hell it was he'd just eaten churn sickly in his stomach. How could his father have the audacity to show up uninvited to Ava's party? Gabby placed a hand lightly on his arm but Cade couldn't help stiffening. He caught his sister's gaze across the table. Sympathy shone in her eyes but another, more familiar emotion was there too—wariness.

Cade recalled another birthday long ago—Beth's sixteenth, to be exact—when their father had shown up, drunk and misbehaving as usual, in front of her girlfriends. It was shortly after their parents' divorce, and Elliot had waxed on about how he'd made a terrible mistake asking for the divorce, how he'd broken it off with his current girlfriend, and how his life was meaningless without their mother. Beth had left the table crying, and Cade had helped stuff his father into a cab and gone with him back to his apartment to make sure he got there in one piece.

The many disappointments they'd suffered had begun long before that moment. But that had been sort of a turning point. The faith Cade might have had that somehow their relationship could be salvaged, that underneath it all, his father truly cared for them a bit more than himself, had been shaken.

For years afterward, Cade kept hoping. Kept giving Elliot the benefit of the doubt. Until the book review. That had been the final straw, when the relationship had gotten too toxic to continue.

Cade would be cordial to his father. But he wasn't going to allow his father's bad behavior to impact another generation.

Cade went to grab Elliot's arm, ready to guide him away from the party. But he hadn't counted on Ava getting there first. Ava had climbed down from her seat and run around the back of everyone's chairs, preventing Cade from seeing her quickly enough to stop her. She approached Elliot and tapped him on the leg. "Hi, Grandpa," she said.

Elliot squatted beside her. "Here's your present." He held it out to Ava again. "Happy birthday, sweetheart."

Ava looked eagerly at her father. "Can I open it?"

"Of course you can," Elliot said, and then finally had the decency to catch Cade's eye. "If it's all right with your father, of course."

"It's fine, Ava," Cade said. His voice sounded weirdly monotone to his own ears. What else could he say?

Ava tore into the package while Elliot stood and

surveyed the table, his eyes lighting on Gabby. Cade tensed, not wanting Gabby involved in the mess that was his family drama. "Gabriella, darling," Elliot said, "so nice to see you again."

Wait—what? Cade turned toward Gabby, who waved her fingers a little reluctantly at Elliot—and avoided Cade's gaze. "You two *know* each other?" Cade asked.

Gabby turned as crimson as the now-setting sun, confirming the worst. "Um, well, we met just a few weeks ago, actually," she said, so quietly he almost had to strain to hear.

"It's a bwacelet!" Ava exclaimed, lifting something silver and sparkly from a Tiffany blue box.

Cade's gaze shifted to Ava. The box in her hand wasn't just Tiffany blue. It was *the* Tiffany blue.

"Look, look," Ava said, holding the bauble up for everyone to see. "It's so pretty!"

And apparently very expensive. Giving a four-year-old a Tiffany bracelet was inappropriate. But Gabby knowing his father—and not telling him? That was just plain inconceivable.

* * *

"Can I get you something to drink, Elliot?" Paige asked.

"What are you having?" he asked Ava, who was seated on the other side of him.

"Milk," she said.

"Very well then," he said to the waiter. "That's what I shall have too."

Elliot cast a tentative glance around Gabby at his son, whose jaw was so tense it could've supported a steel bridge. What could she say to break the ice between these two? Talk about the weather? Hemingway, maybe? Anything literary did *not* seem like a good topic.

"Gabriella encouraged me to take part in my granddaughter's life," he announced.

Oh God, oh God.

Cade's gaze drilled into her. "You're giving my dad family advice?" His voice was an octave higher than usual.

"Not advice exactly, but I did urge reconciliation." She turned to Cade and dropped her voice. "And for the record, I didn't suggest crashing a birthday party..." She cleared her throat. "It might've been better to call first, Elliot," she said.

"I always did love a surprise." He raised his milk glass in a toast and took a healthy swig.

"Do you like milk, Grandpa?" Ava asked.

"Milk is a wonderful drink. It makes you big and strong, and it goes fabulously with chocolate cake."

Ava picked up her milk too and took a hearty swig, then swiped off her milk mustache with her arm. *Well there, at least some good came of this, right?* One look at Cade let Gabby know he was not impressed.

"So when did you start drinking milk, Elliot?" Paige asked.

Elliot lowered his glass. It hit the table with a dull clink. "When I stopped drinking three years ago."

From Cade came a tiny snort. As if he didn't buy that at all.

"Did anyone not get cake?" Paige asked, not unkindly, passing out more pieces as fast as she could cut them.

Cade took a piece with a stiff nod. Apparently, his jaw was still too clamped to allow speech. So Gabby was a bit surprised when he whispered in her ear, "How exactly do you know my father?"

"We met…by accident," she said. Which was sort of true. "He was my mom's writing teacher, and I looked him up. I had no idea he was your father."

"He's an ass," Cade whispered so low she wasn't certain she'd heard it. It was the first time she'd ever heard him say a bad word about anyone—even Tony.

"That one's from me too," Elliot said, pointing to a rectangular-shaped package. Ava tore into Elliot's next gift with the gusto of a child oblivious to the conflicts of the silly adults around her.

"I hope that one's not from Tiffany too," Cade said.

"It's a classic edition of *Grimm's Fairy Tales*," Elliot said. "Signed by the editor and the illustrator." Of course he probably knew them both personally.

"That's a beautiful gift," Gabby said, as Ava leafed through the gilt-rimmed pages, clearly enraptured. Surely Elliot deserved a shot at being a better grandparent than he was a father?

"What a nice idea," Paige said poignantly. "Because we *all* want this precious child to believe in fairy tales for a little longer."

"Exactly," Elliot said.

Ava threw her arms around her grandfather. "I like the book. But mostly I like that I got a grandpa!"

Elliot rubbed the back of Ava's head a bit awkwardly. "Well," he said, swallowing hard, and Gabby suddenly realized Elliot was overcome. Cade had looked down, busily checking his phone. "I hope you'll spend many hours looking at the beautiful drawings and enjoying the stories," Elliot said, his voice catching a little. "Maybe…maybe I could even come back sometime and read you a few."

"Okay."

This was met with silence from Cade, who apparently had no intention of answering. Finally, Paige said, "Ava, come open your other presents."

As Ava jumped off Elliot's lap and dug into her present collection, Gabby held her breath. If Cade could reconnect with his father, he might be able to talk out the problems with that bad review, which Cade had said didn't matter to him, but how could what your father said not matter? Clearing all that up might also help him with his writer's block. Besides, he'd said he wasn't angry, but it was obvious that was not the case—at the moment he looked like he was seething.

* * *

Cade waited until everyone ate their cake before he pulled his father aside. "How about if you walk out with me?" he asked, but it wasn't really a question.

"Of course," Elliot said, standing up and saying his goodbyes. Cade escorted his father to the driveway, where the two men stood face-to-face in front of a white Mercedes SUV.

"Look," Cade said, relieved to be out of earshot of the rest of his family, "I'm going to assume the best and believe you meant well by showing up here, but I have to tell you that I will do anything it takes to protect my child, and I cannot expose her to someone who is unreliable and inconsistent. That means you, Dad. Life is more than grand gestures. It's the little everyday things that matter. You were never really good at that kind of thing."

"I'd like to have lunch with you sometime," Elliot said, which was irritating as hell, not to mention off topic. To anyone else, he looked like a nice, pleasant guy, strong and good-looking, with a friendly smile and a head of silver hair that made him look a lot gentler than he was. But the accumulation of hurts over the years told Cade a very different story.

"Did you hear anything I just said?" Cade asked. "How can we have lunch if we can't even talk to each other?"

"You're still angry about what I said about your book."

"Look, Elliot, you were probably drunk when you wrote that review anyway. You've been a terrible father."

"Maybe so, but I've always told you the truth."

"I don't need your version of the truth. It doesn't matter to me anymore what you think."

"I agree I've been a shitty father to you and your sister. But I've stopped drinking, and I'd like you to give me a chance to prove that I'm different."

Cade looked at his father. For the first time, he looked older, and that gave Cade a queasy feeling. Time was passing. There had been so many wasted opportunities for both of them: things to share personally, as father and son, and professionally, because they both were part of the same literary world.

"Do you want to know why I came?" Elliot asked. "Because I remembered something."

"And what was that, Elliot?" Cade kept his voice neutral, but apprehension made his stomach twist. He didn't want to know what his father remembered.

"Gabriella saw the Hemingway quote in my office. I remembered the day you gave it to me. The day you got into Iowa."

His father had surprised him with a present that day too—the same print. It had been meaningful to both of them. They'd talked about it a lot in the years when Cade was deciding his career path. *A writer's life is hard*, his father would say. *It takes dedication and literally bleeding your soul out onto the page every single day.*

Cade had thought he'd understood that. But in the end, perhaps he hadn't at all.

Regardless of the way things had turned out, he and his father would always be linked by their love of writing, whether Cade liked it or not. And they were both stubborn, driven men who'd worked hard to achieve goals—at least, Cade had thought of himself like that, despite his inability to write.

Cade frowned, refusing to get sucked in by the memory. "Where are you going with this?" He didn't like thinking of his father as his father let alone someone he had a lot in common with, both good and bad.

"That moment reminds me of all my shortcomings."

"You've accomplished a lot, even if you didn't become a writer."

"I don't mean about that. I never had anything near the raw talent you do. I was thinking more about being your father."

"I—I don't know what to tell you about that one, Elliot."

"I'm not going to lie and say I'd like to try and make it up to you. What we've lost can never be gotten back, can it? All I can offer is a promise to do better for your daughter." He hesitated before dropping his voice. "And I hope for you too, son."

"I don't need you to be my father anymore, Elliot." Cade wasn't trying to be cruel. He just couldn't fathom letting his father back into his life after all that had passed between them. "But I can accept your apology. And if you want a relationship with my daughter, something she clearly wants as well, you can have one... but there are rules."

"I've never been good at following rules, but I'm finding in my old age they may have some merit. Name them."

"Showing up like this out of the blue... that can't happen. And no Tiffany bracelets, that kind of thing. Ava's four, for God's sake."

Elliot turned and opened his car door. "Write more of your rules down and bring them to lunch. What do you say?"

"This isn't a joke," Cade said softly.

He sighed heavily. "I hope you'll consider it."

He didn't wait for Cade's answer, just got into his car and drove away.

* * *

Cade was still standing in Paige's driveway when Gabby found him, walking around his mom's Toyota Camry and checking the tires.

"Hey," she said, approaching a little reluctantly, because she was trying to gauge his mood. Specifically, his mood as it related to *her*.

"Hmpft," he grunted.

Oh-oh. "Did your dad leave?" she asked, looking around. No sign of Elliot, and Cade was doing a very intense inspection of the right front tire rim. "What are you doing?"

"My mom needs some air in her tires. Actually, it looks like she needs a whole new *set* of tires."

"Well, that's nice of you to check for her." At nine at night in the dark?

No response. Okay, he was pissed. She would have to confront this head on. "Cade, I—"

He straightened up, so she finally made eye contact with him over the hood of the car. "How could you actually *know* my father and not tell me?"

"I looked him up because his name was on one of my mom's college papers. And he was everything you said—a miserable, cranky old man. I hadn't planned to keep that a secret, only I knew how you felt about him and it seemed the time was never right to bring it up. But then he looked me up and brought me another one of my mom's papers, and it was clear to me that he wanted a relationship with you—and with Ava. No, not wanted—*longed* for one. Underneath all that crotchetiness, I saw a very nice, charming man. A man who knows he's made mistakes."

"Says every woman who's ever fallen for him."

"Says any woman who's ever fallen for *you*."

Cade's eyes widened in surprise. Gabby rushed on, trying to capitalize on the fact that he was thrown a little off balance.

"He seemed so lonely, and I encouraged him to seek you out and talk to you." She shrugged and opened her hands to the sky. "I figured it was up to him to initiate the conversation with you. I didn't think he was going to choose Ava's birthday to do it."

"He chose a place where I couldn't refuse him. He's always been manipulative like that. Not to mention he's always loved a crowd."

Damn Elliot and that Hemingway quote on the wall anyway. Without it, she never would've recognized all the lost potential between father and son. She never would've felt sorry for Elliot or encouraged him to seek out Cade. But now she felt that she'd wronged Cade.

Gabby had seen Cade's forgiving nature in action. Had seen him be kind to everyone he knew and loved. But, it appeared, the man had his limits.

Cade sighed heavily and turned to her. "I know you're all about peace and love and family, but there are some families that just can't be fixed...and mine is one of them. Not every story has a happy ending."

"No, I suppose it doesn't." Her eyes were watering—

must be the sudden breeze that kicked up. "I shouldn't have gotten in the middle, between you and your father. I thought an opportunity to iron out your differences would put you more at peace and help you to leave some of the issues of the past behind."

He turned back to the tires, a sure signal their discussion was over. "I'm going to stay out here for another minute and calm down before I go back to the party. Is Ava doing okay?"

"She's oblivious—just having a great four-year-old's birthday."

He was dismissing her. Just like that. And he was still angry, which she hated.

"I'd be a liar if I said I hadn't hoped you could work it out with your dad," she said. Cade seemed so... closed off. So alone.

He stood up and dusted off his hands. "I understand that being in a relationship means opening up to let someone else in. But I'm not sure how I feel about someone else influencing the course of my—and Ava's—life. I've been the one in charge of deciding that for a long time."

"I don't know what to say, Cade," Gabby said, feeling uneasy. "But I'm sorry for meddling."

"It's okay," he said, but his voice fell flat. "I'll see you back at the party in a little bit."

She walked back by herself, feeling like things were not really okay at all.

* * *

Cade walked into his mom's backyard to find everyone preparing to leave. The birthday girl had fallen asleep on the porch swing, and Cade's mom had carried her into the house to the couch. He shook hands with Matt as he left. Gabby asked Beth for a ride home, claiming a headache, while Cade offered to stay and help his mom clean up.

After the dishes were done and the food put away, Paige grabbed two beers from the fridge, opened them, and handed one to Cade. "Let's go sit outside for a few minutes—if you have time."

"Yeah, I'd like to," Cade said, taking the beer and following his mom out onto the porch. It was a fine late September evening, cool with a light breeze, perfect for sitting and talking.

"Thanks for hosting Ava's birthday dinner," he said, reclining on a cushioned chair. "And for making the cake."

"Oh, you know I loved doing it. I love spending time with Ava. Your coming back here was a good thing, Caden."

Cade was quiet a long time. Of course he had things on his mind, but he knew that even though his mom had forgiven Elliot, she'd suffered a lot because of him and didn't want to drag her into this.

"So. Your father," she said, bringing the topic up herself. "You've avoided him since you've been home, and I understand that, but I'm a bit worried that you're holding on too tightly to the past."

"Dad's a wild card, Mom. Why are you on his side?"

She shrugged. "I guess because I've learned that

sometimes it costs more emotional energy to keep someone away than to allow them in. And realizing you have the power to control that makes all the difference."

"I don't need someone gifting my daughter inappropriate and expensive things."

"He might respond to a suggestion on that one." She paused. "I believe him when he says he stopped drinking. And I see the look in his eye when he watches you and Ava. I believe he genuinely regrets losing you as a son. But you know, your father's not the important one in this conversation."

"You're right. Ava is. And I don't want another person flitting in and out of her life. Emerson already does that. It's too much for Ava to handle."

His mom waved her hand dismissively. "I'm not worried about Elliot doing that. I'm thinking of you—your relationship with Gabby. I worry you're so focused on what's behind you that you can't see what the future holds. And worse, I fear you don't want to acknowledge what's right in front of you now."

"Mom, I—"

"You can't hide how you feel about her. You never were very good at hiding your feelings anyway."

"I've been in control of Ava and me for a while now. I'm not sure I want to share that. After Emerson, it was a blessing in some ways to be on my own."

"Life isn't very tidy, Caden. You chose Emerson when you were young and naïve, and she gave you a beautiful daughter. But you're a man now, and you can make a choice with your eyes wide open. Sooner or later you're going to want to start taking risks and start living your life again. And I hope you do it with Gabby. She's wonderful."

"Matt seems nice," he said, uncomfortable with the subject of Gabby.

"He is nice. He cooks and he likes to dance and—bonus perk—he mails all my packages for me. You know how I hate going to the post office."

"I'm glad you found someone."

"Thanks, dear," she said, giving him a big hug. "I love you. And I want you so badly to be happy."

"I love you too," Cade said, hugging his mother back. "And don't worry about me, Mom."

Cade carried Ava from the house and put her in her car seat without her even waking up. Before he started the car, he pulled out his phone, but he didn't make a call. Instead he gently tapped the phone against his steering wheel.

He thought about his life before, with Emerson. It had been volatile, unpredictable—upsetting. Being accused of taking her ideas had shaken him to the core. Even worse was being left on his own with a one-year-old. He knew in retrospect he'd made the wrong choice for a spouse. He'd closed his eyes to all the signs, and doing so had caused him to live his worst nightmare.

He also knew that to fully live, he had to let go of the hurt from Emerson. And figure out a way to coexist with his father. But Gabby—she really hadn't done anything wrong. Perhaps she *did* harbor the rather annoying belief that everyone should be part of a loving family whether they wanted to or not, but she also understood his hurts. And she wanted to heal them. He *was* trapped by his past, and she could help him move forward. But first he had to let her in.

His mother was right. He had to start taking risks or he would never build a life for himself and Ava. The risk of letting Gabby in was worth it. Gabby was worth it.

I'm sorry for being an ass, he texted. Please give me another chance.

I'll consider it came the immediate reply. She was right to give him some flack. He didn't deserve to be forgiven without explanation. And he wanted to explain. To tell her he was out of line.

Come over to my place so I can apologize in person.

Nothing like a good grovel, she answered. Be right over.

Chapter 19

♥

Twenty minutes later, Gabby stood outside Cade's door, wearing her glasses, a flannel shirt draped over her T-shirt, and shorts, because she was *not* going to dress up or put on makeup for him after they'd fought. She crossed her arms to signify that she was still a little irritated with him.

The door opened and he stood there, looking like everything she'd ever wanted. "I'm glad you came," he said. He looked relieved and happy to see her. The same familiar heat as always engulfed her in flames, and dammit, all that made it impossible for her to stay mad. But she gave it a good try, furrowing her brow and standing firm.

"I'm sorry," he said. "For how I behaved. I was upset about my father, and I took it out on you."

"Maybe you overreacted, but I was the one who did something wrong. I should've told you about meeting your father. And I shouldn't have encouraged him without your permission. Sometimes I react emotionally and I want to make everything better. Your dad seemed so . . . sad. But mostly I guess I thought reconciling would be healing for you too."

"I understand why you did it. You were trying to help. I need to learn to be a little better at taking help. And listening."

"Then we're good," she said. "You could've said that over the phone though."

"No, I couldn't have."

"Why not?"

"Because I needed to do this." And then his mouth was on hers, kissing her deep and hard, not a hello kiss or a you-look-beautiful kiss, but an I-am-going-to-strip-you-naked-and-kiss-every-inch-of-you-and-have-fabulous-make-up-sex kiss that made every part of her instantly turn to Jell-O. His mouth possessed her, his tongue invaded her mouth, and he made it quite clear that he was very, very sorry.

Wow. When they finally came up for air, she became dimly aware that he was holding her by the arms and steadying her just in case she happened to wither to the floor in a boneless heap. Which at this point seemed a distinct possibility.

"Please come in," he said, placing his hand on her forearm and leaving it there for a few seconds. Its heat seeped into her, making her want to curl into his big body and say, *Forget about it, no biggie, all is well.*

But she'd done that in the past. Not demanded much of any man. Forgave all without much explanation. She'd never insisted upon intimacy from anyone. This time was going to be different.

She let him take her hand and lead her to the couch.

The room was cozy and dim; one floor lamp was on by his favorite chair. All of Ava's toys were tossed into the cute basket they'd bought and pushed back beside the couch.

Cade held her hand, rubbing his thumb against her palm as he spoke, which probably wasn't playing fair, but she didn't want to pull away. "I understand how harboring anger eats you from the inside, and I try not to be angry. It's just that my father has created a lot of havoc and hurt. I don't want it to happen again."

She'd never seen him so open and vulnerable. He was good at protecting his heart, that was for sure, and who could blame him? His own father had abused it, as had his wife, in the worst possible ways. No wonder he had trust issues.

But so did she—in the opposite way. She thought everyone was a good, solid, heart-of-gold kind of person. She wore her heart on her sleeve, and that was a very easy place for it to get rubbed against and bruised.

Gabby tried to explain where she was coming from. "The fact that I grew up without a mother and longed for her so badly—and the fact that you have a dad—even if he's somewhat of a scoundrel—seems like it might be worth the gamble. Maybe he meant it about changing, Cade. He was definitely sober tonight."

"You always see the best in people."

"And in you," she countered.

He chuckled.

"By the way, did your ex remember Ava's birthday?" Gabby asked softly.

"No. And Ava was asking about her."

What reason do you give for your kid's mother forgetting her birthday? Gabby couldn't even fathom. "I'm sorry, Cade. And I'm sorry for Ava."

"I have to be honest," he said, not releasing her hand. "When I found out that you didn't tell me about my dad, it reminded me of all the things Emerson kept from me. She kept a lot from me. Her anger and resentment, namely. And the fact that she'd started seeing other men."

"Oh God." She held his face in her hands. "Cade," she whispered, looking deeply into his eyes, "I'm not Emerson."

He swallowed and nodded. "I know that," he said softly. "And about my dad—I'll think about letting him see Ava. After I'm sure he means it—when I see that he's genuinely changed, if that's even possible with him."

Gabby smiled. "Sounds fair."

"And now I want a chance to make up with you."

"You could say you're sorry again," she suggested, as he came closer.

"Um, I had another tactic in mind."

"Which is?"

"Begging your forgiveness in a completely different way."

"That sounds very interesting."

"Oh, it is. But to see me grovel you have to promise me something."

"What's that?" *Anything.*

"That you'll stay with me."

"Here? Tonight?" *Whoa.* She understood that this was a big deal for him, to have her stay over with Ava here. She wanted to let him know she got that, so she pulled out her phone.

"What's this?" he asked.

She held up the screen.

He frowned as he focused on it. "You set an alarm for two a.m.?"

"In case we fall asleep."

He tugged the phone out of her hand and punched a few things.

"What are you doing?" she asked.

"First of all, there won't be much sleeping going on, at least if I have my way. Second, I hate the thought of you going home alone in the middle of the night. But I do appreciate your concern for Ava." He held up her phone. It showed that he'd reset the alarm for six. "That okay? Even that's early, but—"

She rested her hand on his forearm, where she felt the quiet, warm strength of him. She also saw the determination in his eyes. "I get it. No explaining necessary."

"Ava will probably wake up shortly after that. She's got a field trip tomorrow to the bread bakery outside of town, and she was pretty pumped."

He stood and offered her his hand, which she took readily. At the top of the stairs, he took a quick detour to check on Ava. Then he led her to his bedroom.

As soon as the door shut, he grasped her top and tugged it off, doing the same to his own shirt and shorts, then shucking off his briefs. He came to stand in front of her, beautiful, purposeful, *naked*.

"You don't waste any time, do you?" she asked. "Not that I'm complaining."

"Never."

His eyes held hers, not straying, and they were filled with everything she'd ever wanted to see—want, need—yes. But more—a full, welcome acceptance, of all of her, that she'd never felt before from anyone. Dimly, in the background, she registered a bed nearby, a dresser. But mostly just Cade. All Cade.

He tugged on the waistband of her shorts. "Take these off," he said, his voice low and breathy. And oh, she loved this Cade, who was going to let nothing stand in his way. She complied. He unhitched her bra with one studied flick. It seemed to slide right off her and drop to the floor. Then he led them both to the bed.

"And now I grovel. Be prepared." He kissed her hard, intensely, deeply, taking her breath and her balance. She lay a hand on his chest to steady herself, and felt his heartbeat, steady and strong in his chest. She let him back her up against the bed until they both fell on it in a tangled heap.

"I love this groveling," she managed.

"Honey," he whispered close to her ear, "you haven't seen anything yet."

He gave her a few more kisses, slow and luxuriant this time, then he pulled his lips away and came to kneel beside her. A twinkle shone in his eyes as he positioned himself near her feet. He bent and kissed the arch of her foot. "I'm so sorry," he said.

"I forgive you," she replied.

He kissed her other foot. "*Really* sorry."

"Cade, you're so silly. Get back up here."

"Oh no. You're getting the full grovel experience."

She rolled her eyes. "Okay, let's not get carried away." But oh, she *wanted* to be carried away, swept off her feet. She wanted all of it, with him, like she'd never wanted a man before. And he was thrilling her in a way that she'd never experienced.

He proceeded to kiss up her calves, behind her knees, farther up her legs, tracing a trail with his tongue to the apex of her thigh. She quivered at his touch, her body on fire, tense and taut, anticipating what he was about to do.

He was bent low over her, and she could clearly see the dim light from the street shining off sculpted hills of muscle as he purposely went to his task.

Then his tongue was on the most sensitive parts of her, pressing into her flesh. Her legs dropped open, and a moan escaped her throat. His fingers joined his skillful mouth, plying her swollen flesh.

Thoughts fled, her pulse pounding wildly, her body tight as a rubber band, as she lost control. She dragged her hands through his hair, over the smooth curve of his shoulders, then clutched him, fevered and panting, riding the intense waves that shook her to her core. *Cade.* She wasn't sure if she cried his name out loud but he was all she knew, inside and out.

"Forgive me now?" he whispered when the waves had finally ebbed. "I hope so," he added with a playful grin. He was over her now, entering her, filling her, and it was too much sensation, too much pleasure, her body still vibrating with the waves of her release. But he began to rock against her, creating a friction that welled up inside of her and made her just as needy as before.

He looked at her lovingly, worshipingly, honestly, like he was seeing all of her, and that look devastated her, because she knew deep in her heart—she *knew*—that for her there was no turning back. This was it, this was the man, this was the life, and she didn't dare think beyond that.

His thrusts became more urgent, more purposeful, and she clung to him as he drove himself deeply inside her and she began to spin off into another blinding climax. He kissed away her cries even as he shuddered and cried out himself, both of them finally falling over the edge.

Afterward he held her tightly, their breaths coming rapidly in the silent, dark room. Gabby felt the pounding of his heart next to her, the dampness of his skin, the warmth of his body as he leaned his head against hers. He had spoken no words of love, but everything he'd done had revealed something that answered a cry deep in her heart. She didn't want to—couldn't—think of what any of this meant. And so she tried to lighten things up.

"Is this how it's going to be every time we have a fight?" she asked, playing with the hair at the back of his neck.

He gathered her in, wrapping his arms around her. "I'm willing to concede any argument to you if this is the result."

She felt him smile against her cheek as he kissed her there, his head still resting against hers. Then they fell asleep, tangled in each other's arms.

* * *

Cade startled suddenly sometime in the middle of the night, all at once opening his eyes. In his half-awake state, he became aware of Gabby's soft, warm body, clothed in his T-shirt and flannel pants, her hair silky and springy against his chest and neck and tickling his nose. Besides putting on his clothing, she'd also double-checked her alarm and placed her phone on the bedside table next to her.

Instinctively, he smoothed down her hair, and she stretched in her sleep, her soft curves molding up against him. He draped an arm around her, and she snuggled into him further, which had the disconcerting effect of arousing him yet again. He nuzzled her neck, kissing it gently until she stirred and tilted her head back to give him better access.

"Daddeee," came a voice from the hall that appeared to be coming closer like the whistle of an oncoming train. Within seconds, the train had arrived, Ava hurtling herself at him with the speed that only a child's nightmare could fuel. Cade disengaged himself quickly from Gabby and turned his body in Ava's direction, sitting up quickly to block Ava from seeing Gabby, who had suddenly tensed beside him.

"Daddy, Daddy, I had a bad dweam," Ava cried, grabbing him with a death grip around his neck and sobbing.

"It's okay, sweetheart," he soothed, rubbing her head. "It's just a dream." Cade worked hard to pivot his body, to get himself and Ava headed back in the direction of Ava's room before she could sense that Gabby was in his bed.

"Daddy," she said, her head popping up from his shoulder. "Daddy, who is that?"

Oh, fuck.

Then she was squirming and using her arms to push down out of his grasp. She'd no sooner hit the floor with her bare feet than she'd cried out, "Gabby! Gabby's here!" and padded over to Gabby's side.

Gabby sat up. She blinked a few times in the light that was pouring in from the hall and rubbed her eyes. Her gaze caught his for one second, as if she was deciding what to do. Then she smiled, opened her arms wide, and let his daughter jump right into them.

"I had a bad dweam," Ava repeated. "There was a bear, and a monster, and a giant dog with big teeth, and he wanted to bite me!"

"Did you bite him back?" Gabby asked, smoothing down Ava's jumbled hair, rubbing her back. "I heard you're good at that."

She glanced at Cade again, who shot her a warning glance, but he couldn't help smiling.

Ava made herself more comfortable on Gabby's lap, snuggling in. "I bited him back and said, 'Grrrr! Go away, mean dog!' And he did." Now she was embellishing, a sure sign she'd all but forgotten her nightmare. She picked up a handful of Gabby's hair. "You have pretty hair. Why are you sleeping with Daddy?"

Cade closed his eyes. He had no words. He felt like the worst father that ever walked the planet. He'd done his best to always put Ava first and the one time he didn't—

"Because I really, really like him," Gabby said exuberantly, giving Ava a squeeze. "And I really, really like you. How about we get a glass of water and I'll walk you back to your bed. Because you have a very busy day tomorrow with your field trip and I want you to be very rested."

"Okay," Ava said. "We're going to the bwead factory and everybody says we get a whole loaf to take home!"

"Well, I love bread, so save me a piece, okay?"

His daughter turned around at the doorway to give him a quick wave and a "Night, Daddy!" The chattering continued down the hall as Gabby led Ava back to her room.

Cade sat down on his bed and let out a big breath. That didn't go so badly. Ava had taken that quite in stride. His daughter was clearly infatuated with Gabby. And she wasn't the only one.

* * *

The following Friday, Gabby took the entire day off. She was happy to be off work, but truthfully work was going a little better—managing Nonna's stock portfolio and helping her set up a trust and rewrite her will had given her the idea to ask if she could work with more seniors. Milo actually thought it would be good for the firm's reputation for her to do some pro bono work one half day a week. Which she actually was thrilled about.

Two of Nonna's friends from the senior center had already come in to update their wills.

It wasn't that working with seniors made her love her job so much more but it definitely had made it more tolerable. And just the fact that the senior partners had been amenable to letting her do something she felt passionate about was a plus.

Gabby spent the morning sitting at her mother's desk drinking coffee and tapping away on her laptop. Out her window, the fields bloomed with goldenrod, and the sky was such a pure blue it nearly took her breath away. It was a perfect day in just about every sense of the word. Not because she was actually writing a story or because sometimes she actually felt like a writer, but because something was different about herself.

Cade had given her the courage to really try and make a go of this. He'd believed in her talent and ability and had pushed her to write the best story she could write.

Plus, something else amazing was happening. She was getting used to this, the routine of sitting down to write. It still took her all day to get a word count down and she struggled a lot but it was...fun.

At around ten o'clock Gabby stood and stretched, poured another cup of coffee and decided to check her email. In her inbox was a name she had to reread twice before she could process it—Joanna Devereaux. The name of a very successful New York agent she'd heard of because...well, because everyone in the writing world knew about her. She represented star-power authors whose names were as familiar to most people as rock stars and Hollywood celebrities. Why on earth would someone like Joanna be emailing *her*? It was probably spam. With trembling fingers, she clicked on the email.

> I had the opportunity to read your first 3 chapters and I'd love to read the rest. Please consider sending.
> Best, Joanna

Gabby's mouth dropped open. She had to press both hands over her chest because it felt like her heart was about to grow wings and beat straight out of her body. Someone with credibility wanted to read her manuscript, was interested in something she'd written.

She must surely be dreaming, because she suddenly realized *she'd never sent Joanna Devereaux her manuscript*. In fact, she hadn't sent *anyone* her manuscript. She got up from her desk and paced the room.

She walked back to her computer and did some furious Googling, and within a minute she had the answer. She hadn't sent Joanna her manuscript when she was drunk or in a trance. But Cade must have. Because Joanna Devereaux was *his* agent.

Chapter 20

♥

Cade was having a fantastic morning, considering he was in his office, supposedly working on his research project. He'd told himself he was going to loosen up his writing brain by working for fifteen minutes on his story before he did his work, but before he knew it, it had been two hours and he was still writing. Words were flowing like Niagara through the gorge, and his fingers were on fire.

Hallelujah.

Down on the quad, it was a glorious, sunny day. The trees were changing, students were playing Frisbee, and even a dog had gotten in on the action. The plant that Gabby had given him was basking in the sunshine on his sill, tiny bright green shoots springing out of it.

For the first time in years, Cade felt like... himself. It was nothing short of a miracle. And he owed it all to Gabby. She'd opened up something deep inside him that he'd locked and closed down after his marriage. Something he never thought would see the light of day again.

Ever since he and Gabby had made love, they'd been having regular discussions about their stories, and despite Gabby's inability to be fond of literary fiction, she always seemed to help him see a different angle on a character or event. Her work was progressing too, and he had high hopes it might be picked up by a publisher.

"Hi, Cadey," a voice said from the door. Every muscle in his body froze. Cade didn't need to look up to know who it was.

Yup. Same bright smile, same dainty, heart-shaped face with pink, bow-shaped lips and big, swimming-pool-blue eyes.

Emerson.

He recalled a time when she'd stirred him—and even more times when she'd wrecked him to the point where he couldn't concentrate for the rest of the day. He was relieved to find that he was surprisingly calm. As for the attraction... that was long past.

He wished for the thousandth time that Emerson would move to Europe or some other faraway locale so that he didn't have to put up with her springing into their lives like a pop-up puppet whenever the mood suited her, which mercifully wasn't often. He worried for his sweet, happy, innocent daughter. How was he supposed to be Ava's protector, when he didn't have the ability to guard her from the whims of her own mother? He feared these visits would surely take their toll, eroding away Ava's hopefulness, her optimism, her belief and trust in people who said they loved her.

Emerson walked in, wearing tight jeans and high sandals, bangles around her wrists jingling with each step. She picked up a paperweight from his desk that read "A metaphor is like a simile" and tossed it from hand to hand. Next she surveyed his desk, bit by bit, scanning over his business like she had a right.

"May I sit down?" she asked politely. "I asked the woman out there and she said it wasn't your office hours, but I told her I was your ex and I was sure you'd see me."

Cade found himself gripping the lip of his desk as Emerson took a seat without waiting for his response.

His phone buzzed. "One second, please," he said to Emerson, making sure to smile. In some ways, he regarded her as a sleeping beast whose ire he did not want to awaken.

"I'm so sorry," Carol said over the phone. "She insisted on walking to your office. Do you want me to call security?"

"No, but how about a reminder call for my next appointment?" Cade said.

He didn't have any appointments this morning, but Carol understood. "Ten minutes?"

"Perfect. Thanks, Carol."

"So. I came to see Ava for her birthday," Emerson said.

"That was five days ago," Cade said, trying to unclench his jaw.

"Coming from California was quite a trip. I don't think a three-year-old will mind if I'm a day or two late."

Cade didn't say anything, like *she'd just turned four*. Did she even know? "She'll be out of day care at five. You can see her then, if that works."

"That's fine. Actually, I stopped here because I wanted to discuss a few things with you."

She got up and walked over to his window. "I always did love these old campuses. You don't see windows like this anymore." She turned to Cade, bracing her hands behind her on the sill. "Neither of us has had any creative output since the divorce."

She paused, eyeing him carefully. He made certain to keep his face neutral, because he was not about to go there. It had taken her less than half a minute to change the subject to herself. She hadn't even asked about Ava.

"You know my comments got blown way out of proportion by that reporter. I was a little angry over the divorce, but I never intended to discredit you." She dropped her voice and looked down, her long lashes feathering over her cheeks. "Not like that."

In the old days, he used to believe that the dropped gaze and the soft, breaking voice were signs of sincerity, but knowing her for ten years had taught him otherwise. Somehow, he couldn't drum up any sympathy for her. Or believe anything she said anymore.

Cade snorted. "You told them I stole your ideas. That's a little hard to blow out of proportion."

"I swear I didn't. Although you have to admit we did have many, many discussions about plotting. I don't think it's unjust for me to feel I had a hand in that book, Cade."

"We did discuss our writing a lot. But *I* wrote the book." The calm he'd managed to maintain was shattering as she drilled down to his core insecurity. He'd freely discussed everything with her—plots, characters, future books, withholding nothing. But never in his wildest dreams did he feel he was stealing from her, appropriating her ideas. Yet a small, twisted fear remained: could he have done it without even knowing?

"Well, of course you wrote the book. And it did very well. But neither of us is achieving success by ourselves. I say it's time for bygones to be bygones and do what we've always done best together—create." She leaned over his desk, a suggestive move that showcased her cleavage.

Surely she wasn't...she couldn't be...was she turning on the sex appeal to persuade him to work together? He wanted to tell her not to bother.

"So, Cadey, a college professor, eh?" She'd sauntered over to his bookshelves, flicking her fingers quickly over his rows of books, moving onto his diplomas, hovering for a time over the one from Iowa. Was she bitter and angry even after all this time? He couldn't tell, and that was part of her game. This was what Emerson did: she disrupted, she startled. The effect was to keep him off guard and off-balance.

"They hailed you as a prodigy," she said, flipping through one of his academic journals.

"I'm no prodigy. Just a guy trying to get by like everyone else."

"Oh, I wouldn't say that. You're quite talented." She turned to look at him. "I'm here to ask for a fresh start. I propose a collaboration, just like the old days. Bouncing ideas off one another, writing into the wee hours. It would start our creative juices flowing. Not to mention it would solve our other problem—I'd see Ava more."

Cade knew she didn't want to see Ava more. Most mothers would move Mount Everest to get to their child, but that was never Emerson. She was playing him because she hadn't been able to write anything successfully since the divorce.

"The question is, can you forgive the past?" she asked.

"Emerson, I *have* let the past go." *But I have no desire to relive it.* "And I'd love for you to have a more consistent relationship with Ava."

That was a polite way to phrase it, thanks to working with his counselor over the past few years. The counselor had finally told him he could not force Emerson to love her daughter, and to save his breath.

"Well, if we work together, I'd get a place here. I'd see Ava all the time."

Cade thought of how explaining to Ava why her mother didn't want to see her more often was the most confusing and painful thing he'd ever done. And she was only four. What would it be like when she really put together all the pieces and demanded better explanations?

"I'm in town all weekend. I thought I could stay at your place. So I can be closer to Ava?"

"Well, actually, I don't think—"

"I didn't book a hotel, and I noticed the nearest one is completely full this weekend. Something about an art show on the green or something?"

He was about to say no when Gabby appeared in his doorway, looking like the beautiful, kind woman she was. He wanted to warn her away before she stepped foot into his office. Better yet, he wanted to flee with her.

"Cade, hi," she said, a bit out of breath.

Gabby's gaze flitted from him to Emerson and back again.

Oh, hell.

"Gabby, this is Emerson. Emerson, this is Gabby, my... girlfriend."

He saw the startled expression on Gabby's face. The way her eyes widened as she stared at him. And the tiny smile that formed on her pretty lips.

He'd said it. Because that was what she was, wasn't she?

The only thing was, the word *girlfriend* didn't even begin to do her justice. She needed a better word, not one that sounded like he was going steady with someone in high school.

Emerson stuck out her hand. "Oh. So you two are an item?" After shaking Gabby's hand, she said, "Are you a student?"

"No, I'm an attorney. And I write." He saw the look of stunned surprise on Emerson's face.

For the millionth time, Cade wondered how the hell he'd ever ended up with her. He'd fallen so hard and so completely that he'd been blind to all the warning signs—the emotional instability, the constant competitiveness.

"An attorney?" Emerson said. "And you write fiction as well?"

"Yes, I do, actually," Gabby said.

"Oh, Cade," Emerson said with a patient sigh,

"you've always had a weakness for writers, haven't you?" Her tone was overly sweet. "And do you use Gabby as your muse, the way you used me?"

Cade forced himself to shake off Emerson's comment. This was her final stab, directly at his Achilles' heel, and she was damn good at striking it. He tried to forget her words, block them out, but they lingered, taunting him.

Hadn't Gabby listened to him talk about his story, helped him brainstorm ideas? And hadn't he felt invigorated after their discussion, the words flowing freely for the first time in years? Surely he wasn't living his relationship with Emerson all over again?

"Well, I'm exhausted after my long journey," Emerson said, stifling a yawn. "Do you still hide your key over the door frame like we did in Iowa City? I'll drop my suitcases off at your place, then maybe we can get our daughter together?" She let her gaze drift over to Gabby. "Nice meeting you, Gizelle."

"It's Gabby. Nice meeting you too," Gabby said. To her credit, she didn't even sound salty, only wary. But she turned her gaze on him with a question on her face that he understood without words. Emerson had asked about getting their daughter and staying at his place. Oh, shit, how did he explain that?

* * *

"Well," Gabby said, lowering herself slowly into a seat in Cade's office after Emerson had left. "So that was Emerson." And she was stunning.

Cade scowled and looked at his watch. "I might run to the day care early so I can prepare Ava as best I can."

"What is Emerson doing here?" *Making herself at home, apparently.*

He shook his head, clearly upset. "She said she's here for Ava's birthday. Too bad she missed it."

"I'm sorry, Cade."

"I can handle it." He seemed...preoccupied.

"I know it sucks for Ava, and I know how stressful this is." And she'd *really* noticed the cattiness, but she didn't even bring that up. "Are you okay?"

"Gabby, I'm fine." He was checking his phone, something she noticed he did when he didn't want to talk about something.

Okay, that sounded like the discussion was closed. She'd let it go for now, because she could tell he was under stress. Still, she felt shut out, and she wasn't quite sure what to do about it. And what was the comment Emerson had made about getting *our* daughter? And staying at Cade's house? It was almost like she was campaigning for...another chance with Cade.

She decided to try a different tack. "You called me your girlfriend."

"Yes, I did." This was not accompanied by a smile. She got barely a glance before he went back to his phone. "I'll call you later, okay?"

She got up to leave. "Okay." She got to the door before she turned around. "Oh, I got an email from Joanna Devereaux earlier today. She's your agent, right?"

"Oh yeah, Joanna." Finally, he looked interested.

"She told me she was going to email you. What did she say?"

"She wants to see more of my manuscript."

This made him set down his phone. A broad grin told her he was genuinely happy for her. "Gabby, that's terrific. Congratulations."

"I was surprised—shocked, really—to see her name show up in my email."

He stood up and walked around his desk talking animatedly, with his hands. "I got excited about your pages, and I shared them with her. The fact that she's thrilled supports how I felt about them too. You've written something with a lot of great potential, Gabby."

She was happy he was excited. But her stomach was churning and she felt a little nauseous. "I'm glad you liked them, and I'm glad someone amazing like Joanna likes them."

He opened his arms wide. "So? What's the problem?"

He honestly didn't know? Oh God. "Cade, I can't help feeling it was my decision whether or not to put my pages out there." She tapped her chest for emphasis—*my pages*. "The manuscript is nowhere near ready to be queried to agents, yet you went ahead and shared it without telling me." She threw up her arms. "Why would you ever do that?"

"Wait—are you angry with me?" He looked—stunned. Totally blindsided. And that scared the shit out of her.

Angry? Between the fact that he appeared to see nothing wrong with what he did, and the fact that

Emerson was stunning and gorgeous and *sleeping over at his house*—why should she be angry?

Gabby paused. Counted to ten. For so many years, she'd pushed down her true feelings. Afraid to rock the boat. She wasn't going to do that again. But if she and Cade couldn't tell each other the truth about what they felt, what did they really have?

"Yes," she said. "Yes, I am angry. Because it's my manuscript." She tapped her chest again. "*My* book. I would want to put my best foot forward, especially with such a prestigious agent."

"I've known Joanna for years. I know when something's exceptional." He sounded confident. "I never would have wasted her time with something inferior."

"The point is, Cade, it was *my* decision." Her voice sounded too high, and her eyes were starting to get teary. "You took that away from me." Her life had been like that—her dad, desperate to help her, had paved her way into law school, getting influential people to write letters for her, even talking to the dean, who was a friend. And he'd helped her again to get a job with her firm. She'd lived her life feeling her accomplishments were based on her dad's help, not her true talent. She wasn't going to allow that to happen with her writing.

Cade sighed and pinched his nose. "I know how badly you want to write. I know how important it is to you. I was in a position to do something to help, and I just jumped on it. Plus, your story is fantastic—emotional, unique, passionate. You have an opportunity to achieve your dream in a big way, and I truly believe you can do it." He crossed his arms. "The thing is... you have to believe it too."

"Are you saying I don't believe in myself?" Of course she did.

He was standing there, looking smug, treating her like a child. This was getting worse and worse.

"You haven't even managed to tell your family how important your writing is to you. It's like you'd rather do what everyone expects you to do, even though it makes you miserable."

Oh no, this was not resolving at all. "At least I'm not taking over someone's decisions for them. Or worse, shutting them out of important things that are going on."

"I don't get what you're saying."

"Your ex is back, and surely you've got to be terrified for Ava—what you're going to tell her, how she's going to react, what she's going to do when Emerson waltzes out of town in a day or two. Yet you haven't shared any of those feelings with me. Or given me the opportunity to say anything I'm feeling."

"I've got it handled," he said.

"Of course you do." It was her turn to cross her arms. "Because you handle everything on your own. Without letting anyone else in. I'm really glad you have such great control over everything, but you know what? I don't like it when people don't share their feelings. And I don't like people making my decisions for me."

He went dead silent. His mouth was drawn into a thin line, his lips pressed tightly together. He was pissed. Well, too bad, because he really was too complicated.

She saw the pattern—he clammed up when he was upset, at the exact moment she needed discussion and resolution. And he did things without asking her. Unacceptable.

There was a time when she would've walked on eggshells to avoid a man's anger. But she wasn't going to do that either.

"Look, Cade, I really believe—" She was about to tell him they needed to discuss things, but he cut her off.

"—that we're really not very compatible, are we?" He'd finished her sentence, but not in a good way. In the worst way.

"What?" Oh, this was not going well. Gabby's nose was getting itchy, the first sign that tears were building up. Her eyes were misting over, but she blinked the blurriness away. "I love Ava too," she said. "Are you really going to throw away everything we've been building because you're scared to death to let anyone in again?"

"I need to think about this." He gathered up his book bag, shoving his laptop and phone inside.

"Fine. You just go think about…whatever. But you don't get to pick whether you want me or not on your terms."

"What are you saying?"

"I'm saying that you can say we're not right for each other, and say you want to keep all your business to yourself, and have your ex-wife sleep over at your house, but I'm not going to wait until you figure out whether you want me or not, Cade. I need someone who knows what they want—specifically me. Because I've already had a fiancé who was lukewarm about me, and I deserve more than that."

With that, Gabby got up to leave. One look in his eyes—those beautiful, uniquely colored eyes—showed her the hardened expression of a man who'd completely closed himself off. And that made her burst into tears.

* * *

Gabby's mother had taught her at an early age that books were her friends, and during times when life wasn't going so well, Gabby tended to pick one up and get lost in it. She was lucky that way, that books could be a great comfort to her when she needed them most.

Except today. When she tried to read, no novel held her interest. She kept seeing Emerson's gorgeous face and wondering what the hell had happened between herself and Cade. Emerson happened. Gabby's anger over his misguided attempt to help her happened. His shutting down and refusing to discuss anything happened. Plus he'd said they weren't compatible. Oh God, he'd broken up with her. Her tears began again. How could he do that without even talking anything over?

Misery made her finally reach into the old box near her desk and pull out her mom's manuscript. She flipped the pages and saw spotty corrections made throughout with a white correction ribbon. Whatever this was, it had been a labor of love. Whatever it was, it contained the essence of her mother, and right now, she needed that.

For my mother, read the dedication. *And my daugh-*

ters and son. True love is a precious gift, but it's fragile. When it finds you, treasure it, and do everything in your power to keep it safe.

Gabby teared up at that, for too many reasons. One, because these were her mother's words, the only advice she was ever going to deliver from beyond the grave.

And two, because she knew beyond a doubt that she loved Cade. He was everything she wanted—kind, hardworking, surprisingly funny, and he understood and believed in her, even if his way of trying to help her had backfired. But she just wasn't sure if he was ready to love her back. She needed openness and honesty, and she had to trust that her partner wanted the same—because what else was there?

Gabby fingered the dedication. She didn't even know if the experience of having cancer had made her mother consider that dedication, but she suspected it had. What had it been like for her mother to know she would have to leave them all when they were still so young? That would break any mother's heart. It broke hers just thinking of it.

With that, Gabby turned the page and began to read.

Carrara, Italy, 1958

Rosa Mancusi had everything she'd ever wanted—she was young, in love, and she lived among the famed white hills of Carrara, Italy, with her large family. Today was the day she would meet Jacob Bonfiglio at the quarry and tell him the news she'd been keeping to herself for eight weeks—she was pregnant with his child. Their child. She hoped their baby would have his beautiful brown eyes, his thick, wavy hair, and the dimples that made him seem so boyish when he smiled. They had plans to begin their future together, but covert plans—for Jacob was Jewish, and her family would not hear of them being together.

She went to meet him at their usual place, but he wasn't there. Sometimes he was late, as they usually met after his shift at the marble mine, but today Rosa had reason for unease. They'd fought yesterday, and she was eager to make up. That would probably involve lovemaking under the olive trees that grew near the abandoned quarry, and a thrill went through her just thinking about that. She wanted to apologize, she wanted to tell him her secret, and most of all, she wanted to plan their future.

They'd talked extensively of eloping, of running away together to America, where attitudes would be more tolerant, and they could raise their family in peace.

"He's gone," her father said, meeting her at the whitewashed fence that surrounded their little house.

"Gone? No, of course he's not gone," she told her father, who seemed to have difficulty meeting her eyes. Jacob would never leave her. They'd only had a squabble yesterday—it was over the best time to leave for America. They both loved their families and had hated the impossible attitudes toward marrying, but they were going to run away together

anyway, confident that they would win over their families in the future.

"He left this," her father said, handing over an envelope. She tore it open immediately. I do not love you, *the note read.* I cannot go with you to America.

Out of the envelope fell a gold chain, on which hung a thin, perfectly white marble pendant.

"What is in there?" asked her father. "What did he put in there?"

That was when she knew. Jacob did love her. He'd left her his pendant. No matter what the words said, she didn't believe them.

Only how would she find her one true love?

Chapter 21

♥

"Hey, Dad," Gabby said as she walked out along the dock at the lake house the following afternoon. Her dad, who wore his fishing hat and looked relaxed and happy doing his favorite hobby, looked up as she approached.

"Hi, sweetheart. I brought you a pole," he said. "Have a seat."

Gabby squinted in the bright sunlight as she sat down next to him on the dock. It was a perfect day, warm, water as calm as her dad's disposition. "Thanks for bringing me a pole. That was sweet. But did you know I hate fishing?" God, it had only taken her twenty-some years to admit that. She felt the weight of the admission slide off her like a giant sheet of melting ice from a rooftop.

That made him turn his head. His hat was covered with all kinds of multicolored, ridiculous lures, like one with a ladybug head and one that looked like an angry red fish. Gross.

"You *hate* fishing?"

"Yeah. I hate seeing those poor little things squirm on the hook. Hate how we bait them with big, juicy worms, and they get impaled for it."

"Wow. How come I never knew this?"

She shrugged. "Because I haven't been honest with you, Dad. I loved the time we've spent together fishing. And I knew *you* loved fishing. I wanted to love it too."

"We could've found another activity to do together," he said.

"Maybe we can work on that," she said, picking up a stick and snapping off little pieces and tossing them into the water. "Cade and I broke up."

He reeled in his line, to find it empty. "Ah, I'm sorry. I was thinking you'd bring him this weekend."

"His ex is back and she's... challenging. I just don't think he's ready for another relationship." Her voice cracked a little at the end, and she was afraid she was going to start crying again.

He chuckled a little, his usual response to almost everything. "Maybe he just needs time. Especially if he's dealing with the ex."

"I worry about Ava. I can't imagine how confusing it must be to have a parent who pops in and out of your life at random. I mean, Cade does such a great job with her but this is... crazy."

"You love this guy?" her dad asked.

She nodded. "Both of them."

Her dad slipped his arm around her. He didn't say anything else for a long time, but it felt great to feel his comforting presence.

"Work going okay? Ken tells me you surpassed everyone at the practice as far as revenue this month."

It was flattering to hear that Ken Lockham, one of the name partners, had been pleased with her work. "I had a great month, thanks to Nonna," Gabby said. "The partners want me to take on more elderly patients, even some pro bono ones. They said it'll be good publicity for the practice." She hesitated. "But what I'd really like to do is write books." She searched her dad's face for a reaction to that, but it was pretty neutral. "Maybe someday I can even get to the point where I can stop practicing law. But until then, I've just got to find a way to make it more bearable."

"I'm sorry, sweetheart. I'm sorry I led you astray by pushing you toward law school."

She shrugged. "I understand why you did it—I mean, I was floundering. And at the time, I thought it was a decent idea."

"You were so curious about everything—it seemed to me that you would find something in the field of law to interest you."

"Can I ask you something?" Gabby asked. "Why didn't you ever encourage me to write?"

He sighed heavily. It was a long time before he answered. "Lots of reasons, Gabby, all of them practical, and maybe all of them wrong." He put down his pole, looking her in the eye. She saw caring there and concern, and in the emotional state she was in, she felt tears well all over again.

"You were never a rebel like Evie, who was hell-bent on creating her art. Or like Rafe, who insisted on becoming a firefighter and turned a deaf ear to me when I suggested med school. You were more...sensitive. More seeking to please. And maybe I took advantage of that."

"You didn't take advantage of me. I was... confused."

"You know I promised your mother before she died that I'd do everything I could to see you kids happy. And you were always so smart. It killed me to see you floundering around with all those classes you took. I just thought you needed some direction."

"I finally know what I want." She wanted Cade. But apparently he didn't want her. But oh, she was talking about her job. "And this time, I want to do things my own way, on my own terms. Succeed at something myself for once."

"What do you mean by that? Gabby, you've succeeded at every single thing you've tried."

"You got me into college. Into law school. You even got me my job."

"I recommended you for those things. But you did all the work yourself. And you've come through with shining colors. But I want to see you happy, Gabby. That's really all a parent wants."

She nodded, because she was a little choked up. About the happy part. Because somehow she didn't see that happening without Cade.

"You're so like your mother, you know that? Same hair, same beautiful eyes, but she was just like you in other ways too. Bubbly, full of life, always ready to laugh or see the bright side of something. And she was always mastering some different skill—papier-mâché snowman heads. Sewing Halloween costumes. I miss her. "

"I miss her too."

"Well. The point is, your personality is a good fit with writing, I think. Creative, artistic. She'd be very proud that you were following in her footsteps. Now you can do what she wasn't able to. You'll be the one to get published. And don't—don't let anyone take that away from you."

"Take what away?"

"That dream. Your mother would want you to pursue it."

Damn if her dad didn't have tears in *his* eyes.

"Thanks, Dad. I love you," she said.

"I love you too," he said, wrapping her up in a big hug.

As Gabby wiped her eyes and finally lifted herself up from the dock, the marble pendant knocked gently against her chest, and she fingered its smooth, slender shape. "Oh, do you know anything about Nonna having a great first love? That's what Mom's story is about—I just don't know if it's fact or fiction."

"She used to talk about falling in love with a Jewish boy back in Italy but that never worked out." He cast his line out again. "Why don't you ask Nonna?"

"Well, the thing is her answer might be more fiction than fact."

"You never know. Her long-term memory is usually pretty intact."

This should be very interesting. "Okay. Thanks."

Gabby kissed her dad on the cheek and walked back

up the hill to the house, where Nonna was sitting on the little back deck enjoying the sunshine.

"Where did you get that, Gabby?" Nonna asked, pointing to the pendant around Gabby's neck and beating Gabby to the punch. "That's mine."

"You gave it to me," Gabby said, taking a seat on a chair beside her. "But you can have it back." She slipped the necklace off and handed it to her grandmother.

"A Jewish boy gave it to me in Italy," Nonna said, fingering it. "He worked in the marble mines. He wanted to be a jeweler."

"It's beautiful, Nonna. He was very talented."

"He wanted me to have a piece of him to carry with me everywhere. He didn't know I already had a piece of him. A much more important one than a piece of marble."

Whoa...what did Nonna mean by that? *Was the story actually true?*

"I was in love with him but he was Jewish and our parents forbade us to marry. My father shipped me off to stay with our cousins in Chicago."

So that sweet love story her mother was writing was...Nonna's story? And it was *true*? But what did that mean—that Nonna had come to America pregnant? Unwed? She'd never heard any whisper of this. She did know one thing, however—her grandfather's name was not Jacob.

"Love is a precious gift," Nonna said, fingering the necklace. "It might only come once. If it comes twice you're really lucky but don't count on that."

* * *

"Hello, Elliot," Cade said, as his father opened his front door. He didn't miss the sudden lift of his father's brows as he saw his son standing there. "Can I come in?"

Cade followed his father to the library. "Sit," Elliot said, gesturing to a chair in front of the desk while he took the chair beside him.

Cade noticed the Hemingway quote first thing hanging on the wall. The quote that bound them to the same occupation. That made them more alike than different at times.

"I've been thinking about us, Elliot. I came to ask you something that's been weighing on my mind for quite some time."

Elliot sat back and rested his elbows on the chair arms, tenting his fingers. "Ask me anything."

"Okay, I'll ask. Only because I realized that it's still important to me what you think. I tried to tell myself it wasn't." Dammit if his voice didn't crack a little. And he was shaking. "I'd like to know why you panned my book."

"Your writing was—and I'm sure still is—beautiful. Your prose, your symbolism, all of it. You're far more talented as a writer than I ever was. But you listened to what your instructors told you to do. You never should have changed the ending."

"You're saying that because my book didn't have a happy ending I ruined it?" Cade snorted. "It was literary fiction, for God's sake! Nothing in literary fiction has a happy ending, Elliot." His father should know, because that's what he read—and critiqued—all day long.

"Lots of books end unhappily and I have no objection to that. But yours, however, shouldn't have. Life isn't as hopeless as your vision in that book. I don't know if some literary snob told you to do that, but that ending was trumped up to sell books and appear like uppity literature and I could see that a mile away. Write an honest book next time."

God, the man always did tell the searing, hurtful truth.

"Emerson was here," Cade said, fingering a paperweight on Elliot's desk. "She just left, actually. I suppose you believe what she accused me of too." Why did he still care? He didn't know exactly, but he sensed it had something to do with putting the past to rest. Something Gabby had suggested. And . . . she was right. He had to actually speak with his father if he wanted to have any kind of relationship. If he ever wanted to leave the old wounds behind.

"Of stealing your ideas?" Elliot snorted.

"We talked a lot about plotting. She'd often give me character suggestions or ideas for dialogue. I did use some of those things." Just as he'd done with Gabby.

"And?"

"I sometimes don't know where the line gets drawn between my own ideas and the things I come up with after talking with other people."

Elliot snorted again. "I knew Emerson was a foolish girl from the first time you brought her to meet me. It's no surprise to me she hasn't published a word of fiction since graduate school."

What the hell did he mean by that? "She sacrificed a lot for me, at the expense of her own career. My little bit of fame made her feel insignificant."

Elliot tsked. "Life *is* difficult, isn't it? For all of us. And yet we must carry on, mustn't we?" Elliot leaned forward in his chair, as if he were going to pat Cade genially on the back. But then he drew back and folded his hands in his lap.

"She insinuated that the reason I'm writing now is because I'm doing the same thing with Gabby—using her to bounce ideas off of, talking to her about things."

"There's a difference between writers talking with each other, helping each other hammer out difficulties in plot, and someone who is grasping any straw she can to get a leg up in a cutthroat world. One where she hasn't been very successful. Forgive yourself for your bad marriage, Caden, and move on from that woman to do the things you want to do—were born to do. And try and not screw things up with the good one."

Something broke inside of Cade. A dam suddenly releasing a lot of pent-up water, maybe. In that moment, he realized that he did very much care about what his father thought of him, even if he was crotchety, ornery, and sometimes inappropriate. And somehow, he'd needed to hear this. Maybe knowing that Elliot never lied, to the point of sometimes appearing cruel, made Cade take his words as truth. And hearing them absolved him.

When Cade looked up, his father was chuckling.

"Are you—are you laughing at me?"

"God, no," Elliot said. "I was only thinking, you

seem to have a huge soft spot for such a vile woman—so maybe you could spare a little forgiveness for me."

Cade gave his dad a look. The water under their combined bridges could drown someone. But his father seemed to be really trying, and he'd offered him advice just now because he cared. Cade got up and hugged him. "Thanks for the support. Keep your shit together—for my daughter's sake. She needs a grandfather."

* * *

"Rafe, for God's sake, please play something more upbeat!" Gabby begged as she sat around the campfire with her family at the cottage that Saturday. The sun was an orange ball in the sky, hovering low over the lake, surrounded by salmon-tinged wisps of clouds—a beautiful early fall evening. She shifted Evie's son, Michael, on her lap. The boy had threaded two marshmallows on a stick but had eaten three times that many straight from the bag.

Everyone was making s'mores and listening to Rafe play the guitar. Everyone, that is, except for her dad and Michael's sister, Julia, who were fishing for walleye off the nearby dock. So far Rafe had played "Careless Whisper" by George Michael, "Nothing Compares 2 U" by Sinéad O'Connor, and several of Adele's songs about breakups.

"Please, make him stop," Sara said. "These songs are making me want to cry."

"That's not saying much," Colton said, firing up a

marshmallow for Nonna. "You seem to cry about everything lately." Sara angled a sharp glance in his direction, which made him say, "I mean, sweetheart, I'm really glad you're so emotional lately. It's... terrific. You're terrific, and I love you."

Sara kissed him and chuckled.

"Good save, Colt," Gabby said. She knew they were waiting a bit to make their big announcement, but she was excited to be one of the first ones in on the secret. She was just sad she didn't have better news herself... about herself and Cade.

Rafe began to strum Taylor Swift's "We Are Never Ever Getting Back Together," shooting Sara a how-about-this? look.

"That's more upbeat," Nonna said, sitting in an Adirondack chair crocheting an afghan which she'd spread on her lap.

Sara shook her head. "No, Rafe. Just no."

Rafe stopped playing, thank God, and glanced out over the lake, which was calm and glassy. But the beauty of their surroundings just seemed to underscore how alone Gabby felt without Cade to share it. And looking at her brother, she could tell that he was hurting inside too.

"Burn my marshmallow for me, Aunt Gabby," Michael said. "*Really* burnt, okay? Make it catch on *fire*."

Evie, who was leaning against Joe with her legs stretched out toward the fire, eyes half closed, smiled at her son. "He likes 'em charred, just like his aunt Gabby," she said.

"I'm not apologizing for my taste in marshmallows,"

Gabby said, mostly to try and keep a positive front. But truthfully, she couldn't care less how burned or not her marshmallows were. She could barely get down a few bites of burger tonight at dinner, let alone dessert. Cade hadn't called her. All she could think of was that his gorgeous ex was probably still in town, and she couldn't get pictures out of her head of Cade and she and Ava together. A family.

That brought tears to her eyes, which she swiped at while cooking the marshmallow for her nephew.

Michael held up the bubbly, burned mess Gabby had removed from the fire. It was sliding slowly down his stick. Gabby grabbed a napkin and saved it before it ended up in the grass.

Gabby was waiting for Rafe to strum another tune just to piss her off, but he sat there staring at his guitar strings, lost in thought. If she didn't know before, she knew now that he wasn't in good shape. Strange, because as far as she knew, he and Kaitlyn had never gotten together. What on earth was bugging him?

She put a hand on his shoulder. "Want to go for a walk?" she asked.

"Great idea," Rachel said. "Michael, come sit with me. I'll be happy to burn your next marshmallow."

"Ha ha. If Grandma Rachel doesn't get it right, I'll be back soon, Bud," Gabby said, rubbing the soft top of Michael's buzz cut.

Rafe followed after Gabby, surprising her a little. First of all, he was not one to take a stroll with anyone. Second, he'd much rather pretend he had no problems than talk about them.

"Hey," he said, picking up a couple of rocks and skipping them across the water as they walked along the shore, "I'm sorry about Cade."

"I'll be fine." She waved her hand dismissively, but despite her best efforts, her eyes got a little watery. She'd done an excellent job today of not losing it in front of her family, and she certainly didn't want to fall apart now in front of Rafe, who was clearly having his own troubles. She turned toward the lake to swipe at her eyes, and she felt her brother's hand on her shoulder.

"It's okay, Gabby."

That simple gesture undid her. She couldn't hold back her tears—or her words. "I don't think he can let someone else in. Why wouldn't being with me be worth facing his fears? I mean, isn't that how love is? It's supposed to be stronger than your fears?"

Rafe snorted. She turned to see him dragging his hands through his hair.

"Are you okay?" she asked.

"Fine." Rafe often spoke in monosyllables, but even with one word Gabby could tell he was not fine.

How many times had he said that, and she'd just let him be? Everyone let Rafe be, because Rafe had been through something sad and traumatic when he was a young man, and everyone thought he would get over it in his own time.

But maybe what he really needed was for somebody to say something.

"Rafe, you're not fine," she said.

He looked up from the lake. His brow was creased,

and he opened his mouth like he was going to speak, but he didn't.

"I could listen, you know. To anything you'd want to say."

"I sort of understand Cade. Maybe you get to the point where you just feel that the only way you could go on is if you say you're not going to really ever put yourself out there again. Because things were so terrible the first time around you just don't think you could get through something like that again."

He went quiet, squatting on the small bank, staring as the little ripples from the lake lapped up onto the sandy shore. Gabby held her breath, hoping he'd continue.

"Kaitlyn made me want to try again," he continued. "But I was too afraid. So I was okay with staying away from her, until I heard she was going back with Steve and for some reason, I..." His words trailed off.

"Oh, Rafe. Have you tried talking to her?"

Gabby could tell from the look on his face that he hadn't. "Well, if you can't talk with her, maybe you should talk to someone else."

"Who?"

"I mean like a therapist."

His eyes narrowed.

"It's been eight years since Claire died. Maybe you just need a little bit of help to really deal with that. I'm sure we could find someone who—"

He rubbed his forehead with the heel of his hand. "What the hell," he said.

"It's just a suggestion. You don't have to get angry with me—"

"I'm not angry, and I'm not talking about the therapist thing. I'm talking about *that*." She followed his line of sight out into the water where, in the distance, a rowboat was slowly making its way across the lake. Whoever was rowing was wearing a big, bright orange lifejacket.

"That's the biggest-assed life jacket I've ever seen," Rafe said.

"And the brightest," Colton said from up the hill from them on the bank. He'd jogged across the lawn to see the oncoming boat, and the rest of the family was following right behind him.

"It's Cade," Gabby whispered, something she knew without even seeing. Because she felt it—felt *him*.

"Why didn't he take the ferry?" Evie asked.

Their dad checked his watch. "The last one left for the day."

"He'll be here tomorrow sometime," Joe said, laughing.

"Maybe you should take the pontoon out and get him, Walter," Rachel said.

"No, I don't think so," he said. "I think he should work hard for my daughter's affection."

"Dad!" Gabby said.

"I'm just kidding," he said. "He's doing great. He'll reach the dock in a few minutes."

Gabby ran to the end of the dock and threw her hands into the air, ecstatic when Cade waved back. At last he rowed up to the dock and climbed out while Rafe and Dr. Langdon secured the boat.

"You made good time," Colton said, taking his life jacket.

"Thanks," Cade said.

Nonna immediately came up and hugged him. "You're sweaty," she said. "But you have nice big muscles."

Cade greeted Gabby's other family members, who seemed to be trying hard not to stare.

When Cade finally faced Gabby, her heart dropped into her stomach, and everyone standing around on the shore seemed to fade away. Not because Cade looked irresistible but because he looked... terrible. Unshaven. Dark circles. Mussed hair. His disheveled appearance somehow made her feel very hopeful—that maybe he was suffering being apart too. "Gabby," he said, his voice breaking a bit. "Will you talk with me?"

She had to force herself not to do a happy dance. "You rowed all the way from the ferry dock?" Gabby asked.

Cade shrugged. "Yeah," he said. "I had to see you." His words and the intensity in his eyes made Gabby's heart kick into high gear, causing it to beat out a staccato rhythm that she swore the whole crowd could hear. No one had done such a crazy thing for her before.

"Well then," Nonna said. "It must be an important talk."

While Rachel immediately started directing everyone back toward the house to roast more marshmallows and basically to mind their own business, Gabby steered Cade to a spot near the shore where a pine tree had fallen. She sat down on the trunk and he took a seat beside her.

The heat from his big body surrounded her, giving

her an immediate sense of comfort, yet stirring her at the same time. She was so, so glad he was here.

"I have some news," he said.

"News?" she asked. He'd rowed all this way to tell her...news?

"One of the coeds Tony slept with posted photos of him on Facebook. He's out."

"Oh, thank God," Gabby said, heaving a relieved sigh, even while a sense of disappointment unsettled her. Had he just come here to let her know there would be no trouble from the photo?

"And I lost the Fitzgerald scholar position."

"Oh, Cade, no."

"I told Jake about our kiss and the photo."

"And they took the scholar position away from you?" This was horrible.

He shook his head. "When I told him you were my age and you dropped the class he told me he didn't give a crap about my personal life. Then I told him I didn't want to do the research, that I wanted to write books instead. And he told me that was fine as long as I kept teaching Amira's writing classes next semester too."

"You're going to keep teaching writing?"

"Yeah. I like...discovering new talent." He flashed a beautiful, white smile that melted her insides. "And the students are pretty creative and amazing. I like teaching."

"That's great," Gabby said. "I'm glad...everything worked out." Maybe he did just row all the way over here to tell her all that. She was happy for him...but disappointed too.

Suddenly he took her hands, looked into her eyes, and said, "Emerson is gone, and she did not stay at my house."

Oh, praise baby Jesus. Her breath hitched, and she couldn't tear herself away from his gaze.

"She was never going to stay at my house."

"Good," Gabby managed.

He removed a hand to rub his neck. "Gabby," he said.

"Yes, Cade," she said. His presence was undoing her. Heat was coursing through her veins, desire tugging on her, pulling her under its spell, making her want to kiss and touch him and wrap herself around him even though she knew they needed to talk, to speak actual words. Plus, he'd rowed here all that way and she could not stop the swell of hope that was expanding uncontrollably in her heart.

"Emerson is...difficult. She's going to do her thing as she wishes, and I'm going to be dealing with the fallout from that, trying to protect Ava as best I can."

"I understand."

"She asked me if I used you as my muse like I used her."

"Oh God, Cade, you can't be serious."

"All this time I've always wondered in the back of my mind if I appropriated some of her stuff unconsciously. All this time, that fear was paralyzing my writing. Until you came along and helped me to experience joy again. Somehow with you I was able to let go of all that—stuff—and just see my way to the writing. I know now where my story came from, and it was from inside of *me*." He tapped over his heart.

"And I realized something else." He took hold of her hands again. "I'd be a liar if I said I wasn't afraid of having a relationship again. But there's no one in the world I want more than you."

"Cade, I—" His words echoed. *There's no one I want more.*

He placed a finger gently over her lips. "From the moment we met in the parking lot, everything about you—your spirit, your light—has shone down deep inside of me and made me feel alive again. I screwed up my first marriage pretty badly and I swear to you, I *promise* you, I will do anything to keep you in my life."

She was sobbing now.

"I was thinking about the agent thing," he said. "I sent your pages to Joanna because I was excited. I think that's the fixer side of me, wanting to make things right. But I should've asked you first. I'm sorry for that too."

Gabby cupped a hand on his cheek, scraping against the sandpaper roughness and the tiny masculine prickles from his unshaven beard. "Cade, I was thinking that sometimes it's not bad to accept help. Maybe it's not all bad to catch a break either. I appreciate what you did for me."

"I understand you want to succeed on your own. But, Gabby, your writing is really good. I'm excited to see where you're going to go with it."

"Thank you for believing in me. You gave me the confidence to follow my dream."

"Nah," he said, sending her a huge grin. "I just taught a class."

"And she dropped it," Rafe said from afar.

"Shut up, Rafe," Gabby said, looking up at her family pretty far above them on the slope, hovering together, struggling to listen. "You keep going, Cade."

"I love you, Gabby. Ava loves you. I want you to be my wife." Cade dug through his shorts pockets. "I almost forgot." He pulled out a small box and knelt down on one knee and took Gabby's hand. "Will you marry me, Gabriella?"

"Yes! Of course! Yes!" she said, as he slid the ring on her finger. She wrapped her arms around him and kissed him hard.

"I love a woman who knows her mind," Cade said, gathering her into his arms, where she fit perfectly.

She smiled against his strong chest. "This time I know exactly what I want," she whispered.

They kissed again among the clapping, hooting, and hollering coming from atop the hill. After a few minutes, all her family rushed down to join them for plenty of hugs and congratulations.

Nonna gave Gabby a big kiss on the cheek. "That's from your mother," she said. "She always did love a happy ending."

Epilogue

♥

Two Months Later

It was ten p.m. on a Friday evening in November. Gabby walked into Cade's house from their rehearsal dinner and sat down in the living room.

Cade had fetched some wood for the fire and was tossing it into the grate.

"Why are you making a fire now?" Gabby asked. "It's kind of late."

He stood and dusted off his hands, giving her a long, dark look. A Heathcliff look. Then he sat down next to her.

"We have a very busy day tomorrow," she said.

"Stay tonight," he said.

Gabby shook her head. "Oh no. I'm not taking any chances after what Nonna said at dinner."

"It's an old wives' tale."

Nonna had told her explicitly that the bride was not to see the groom after midnight. *Or else.*

"Hey," Gabby said, "when you live in a town with an angel legend, you tend to believe these things. Or if you happen to be wearing Cararra marble pendants that promise true love and then you find it on the very same day."

Cade sighed and leaned close. "I just don't want to be apart," he whispered in her ear. "Not tonight, not any night." His words caused a warm flush to spread all through her. Just then, Ava ran into the room and began to rummage through her toy basket, forcing sense to return.

"Speaking of Nonna," Cade asked. "Did you ever find out more about your grandmother's story with the pendant?"

"Actually, there's a name on the back of that old photograph Nonna kept in her box. I wonder if we should pursue it and find out who Jacob was? I just wouldn't want to do anything to upset my grandmother. Or my siblings. My grandfather was very dear to us. And...this opens up a giant can of worms, you know?"

"Intrigue in the Langdon family. I love it."

Ava held out her doll for Gabby to hold while she proceeded to climb into Gabby's lap. "Can I see the fire, Daddy? Please?" Ava asked. "And then I'll go to bed, I promise."

"Don't get too comfy there, pumpkin," Cade said in his Dad voice. "It's bedtime. Big day tomorrow."

Cade gave Gabby a look like it had been a hectic day and he just wanted to be alone with her. Which made an anticipatory little shiver go up her spine.

Gabby smoothed Ava's hair. "You can see the fire for a little bit. I love your dress." She smoothed down the layers of the pale, sparkly pink skirt. "Do you have your special dress for tomorrow all ready to go?"

She sat up and nodded. "Yes. And my sparkly shoes and my sparkly hair bows."

Gabby caught Cade's eye above Ava's head and they both smiled. Seemed like Ava couldn't get enough of the sparkles lately. And Gabby had made sure Ava's dress for the wedding was just as wonderful for her as her own dress. In fact, they sort of matched; each of them had a pretty tulle overskirt. "We're both going to sparkle tomorrow," Ava said. "Tomorrow we get to be a family."

"Yes, tomorrow we become a family." Gabby tugged gently on the little girl's braid. Cade kissed his daughter on the forehead.

"Does that mean I get a puppy?" Ava asked. "Families have puppies, Daddy."

Ava was a clever little girl.

"Isn't having Midnight enough?" Cade asked, just as a flash of a cat's tail disappeared behind the couch.

"He needs a fwend, Daddy," Ava said, with that same mischievous twinkle in her eye that her dad tended to have.

"Is tomorrow when you get to be my new mommy?" Ava asked Gabby, switching subjects with lightning speed.

Gabby curled an arm around the little girl's back and held her close. "Yes, and I can't wait to be your every-day mom. Do you know what that means? When I was growing up, my real mom couldn't be here but my other mom, Rachel, was. She baked cupcakes with me and kissed my boo-boos and read books with me and took me shopping. That's what I want to do for you. Would that be okay?"

"I want you to be my *always* mommy," Ava said.

Gabby looked down at the little girl on her lap, who was looking back at her with such trusting eyes it made her heart swell with joy.

"I love you, sweetheart," Gabby said. "I'm so happy we get to be a family."

Ava wrapped her arms tightly around Gabby's neck, and Gabby felt a mountain of love pressing against her heart.

"I love you, Gabby." Ava clutched her tightly around the neck, and when she let go, Gabby's eyes were as full as her heart.

"Okay, Tiger," Cade said, "time for sleeping." Cade stood and gathered Ava up, tossing her over his shoulder and carrying her up the stairs while she giggled and shrieked.

Gabby kicked off her heels and curled up on the couch to wait for his return. She was half-dozing when suddenly she felt Cade's big body next to hers on the couch.

"Could we elope?" he said, kissing her neck. "It would be so much easier."

"Oh, you're going to love the ceremony. My whole family will be there." She paused. "And the Angel Falls FD. And half of the police force."

"Colton *is* half of the police force," Cade said, looking at her with humor—and hunger—in his eyes. "Sounds fun. But not as fun as this." He began to kiss her neck, tugging the neck of her dress aside so he could kiss her shoulder. "Stay tonight," he repeated.

"I told you," she managed, but it was tough to speak with whatever he was doing to her neck, "I don't want a million years of bad luck."

"Okay, fine." He sat up and pulled her up to sitting. Then he reached under the couch. "Here. I have something for you."

He handed her a rectangular box.

"What is it?"

"Just open it."

In it was the photo Tony had taken of them kissing on the green. The bridge framed them from behind, the angels keeping a watchful eye.

She remembered that kiss. It was unexpected and wonderful.

"How did you get this?" Gabby asked.

"Colton gave it to me. The police confiscated Tony's camera as evidence."

"That was probably the cleanest photo on the camera," Gabby said.

Chuckling, he handed her a tiny flat package.

"Something else?" She ripped it open to find a parking sticker. "For my MFA classes," she said, tearing up. "How thoughtful."

"That way no one will ever take your spot again."

"You didn't just steal my parking spot," she said, sitting back beside him. "You stole my heart."

And he opened up his big arms and she curled against his chest and they sat there for a minute, basking in the heat of the fire and listening to it pop and crackle.

"I have something for you too," Gabby said. "But first we need to discuss your truck."

He frowned. "What about my truck?"

That definitely got his attention. "Did I ever tell you that the first thing I noticed is that you had fingerprints on the back window?"

"It's impossible to keep that clean. Believe me, I try."

"Well, this will help."

He unwrapped a container of car window wipes. "Thanks. But why these for a wedding present?"

She slowly reached over and gathered up his hands.

He was looking at her with a puzzled expression. She made a note to always remember this. How they'd sat together the night before their wedding and got ready to jump headfirst into their future together.

"Cade."

"What is it, Gabby? You're scaring me a little."

She took a big breath. "Cade, you're going to need car wipes because you're going to have another set of fingerprints on the other window."

She sat back and watched as his puzzlement turned to surprise. His mouth dropped open a little. She wished she had a photo of *that*.

"Holy shit. You're not kidding, are you?"

She shook her head. "I am not kidding."

"Wow. I mean, we talked about this but..." He reached over and kissed her. His lips were warm and soft and his embrace all-encompassing.

He looked at her with everything she'd ever wanted to see in a man who loved her. "You bring me so much joy. After so many years of pain." He ran his hand gently down her cheek. "You've filled Ava's and my life with a happiness I never thought I'd ever feel again. I love you, Gabby."

"Oh, Cade. I love you."

He tugged her off the couch and toward the staircase. "It's ten fifteen. We'll have you up and out of here by eleven. Unless you decide to stay all night."

"You're cruel. I don't have to call an Uber, do I?"

"If you're very nice to me, I'll let you take my truck. Or I could stay at your place tonight and you can stay here."

"Gee, thanks for the compromise," Gabby said.

Cade looked at her and smiled. "That's what marriage is all about, I'm told."

She laughed and ran ahead of him up the stairs. "Well, I can't wait to find out what it's about with you."

With kisses under the mistletoe
and snowfalls aplenty, ’tis the season to
visit Angel Falls.

Don’t miss Rafe and Kaitlyn’s story!
Please turn the page for an excerpt of
All I Want for Christmas Is You.

Chapter 1

It was a very bad day to take a pregnancy test, Kaitlyn Barnes decided as she washed off the counter at her coffee shop, the Bean, on a snowy late November evening. She was way too busy to even *think* about being pregnant, let alone ponder how on earth it could ever have happened.

Okay, she knew how it had happened. And when. And she wasn't going to lie: the sex with Rafe Langdon had been, after years of dancing around their attraction to each other...epic. But with two forms of birth control, how on earth...Nope. She wasn't going there. Not now, not with worries about her family, her business, and her life at the forefront of her mind.

Mary Mulligan, the last customer in the shop, brought her empty mug up to the counter. "You're good friends with Rafe Langdon, aren't you, dear?"

"Oh yes, I've known Rafe forever." She squeezed her eyes shut to avoid thinking of his strong, muscular form, his square jaw, his dark, well-defined brows. And other parts of him that she *really* was not going to think about.

But it was more impossible than ever to stop thinking about Rafe, now that he was suddenly a hero for the whole town. Everyone had been coming into the coffee shop talking about how the handsome young firefighter had recently pulled an entire family from a car that, seconds later, had gone up in flames. An amazing feat, and also one that had thrown Rafe ten feet from the blast, giving him a good knock on his head.

"How's he been doing since the accident?" Mary asked.

Kaitlyn wouldn't know. She hadn't spoken much to Rafe since what she was coming to call *the incident*, which consisted of one wedding, a few drinks, a rainstorm, and a much too inviting cabin. "I-I haven't seen him," Kaitlyn said.

Yet not even a minute had gone by that she hadn't thought about him, and his nice full mouth that always seemed to be turned up in the tiniest smile.

God, that smile. *That's* what had gotten her in trouble—Rafe's ability to take any kind of worry or concern and somehow lighten it up with that easygoing, assured grin. It was irresistible—*he* was irresistible, especially to her, whose life was typically full of worries and concerns.

She blinked to find Mrs. Mulligan staring at her. "I'm sorry, Mary," Kaitlyn said. "What did you say?" She had to stop her mind from wandering.

"I said I hope you're going home now, dear. You look peaked."

Kaitlyn flicked her hand in a dismissive gesture. "Oh, just a little tired." And nauseated. And losing her lunch on a regular basis. And breakfast.

"Want another cup of tea?" Kaitlyn asked. "It's no trouble."

"Oh, no thank you. I know you're closing. I just can't get over how that boy saved those two little kids and their parents. He even managed to grab the puppy before the whole thing went up in flames. Don't you think he's quite a catch?" Mary punctuated her statement with a knowing look.

Kaitlyn didn't disagree, but she also knew Rafe didn't do serious. She skimmed her hand lightly over her abdomen, which was a little fuller than usual but still flat enough that no one would suspect a thing. Another wave of nausea hit her, but she clutched the counter and took a deep breath to quell it. Like it or not, she'd be thinking of Rafe Langdon for a long time to come.

"We have our own honest-to-goodness hero," Mary said, clapping her hands together. "What an inspiration for the Christmas season."

Yes, Christmas. Even now, outside the big plate glass windows that faced the street, snowflakes eddied around the orange glow from the streetlight. Swirls of chaos that reflected how Kaitlyn felt inside. Someone from the Angel Falls maintenance crew had hung a big lit-up candy cane on each light post, making the Main Street cheery and festive, and she herself had strung multicolored lights around all the coffee shop's windows. She loved Christmas. It was her favorite time of year. But not this year. Not now. She felt anything but festive.

"How's your niece doing, dear?" Mary asked. "I heard she'd gotten into some kind of trouble."

Ah yes, Hazel. Her seventeen-year-old niece who was beyond thrilled to be dumped off in Angel Falls to complete her senior year far away from home in California, away from the bad influences that had landed her in trouble in the first place. Kaitlyn knew that Hazel was simply biding her time until she turned eighteen and could kiss Angel Falls and their whole family goodbye.

"She's . . . settling in. Thanks for asking, Mary," Kaitlyn said. She'd learned not to discuss her family's problems, no matter how concerned and kind her customers were. Suddenly the shop bell tinkled, bringing in a few swirls of snow as well as the police chief, Colton Walker, who was holding on to Hazel's bony elbow. With her thin frame, big brown eyes, and delicate bow-shaped mouth, Hazel resembled a pixie, a sweet, fragile creature. Except it was difficult to get two words out of her now, and she nowhere near resembled the little girl who used to love spending summers here. Catching Colton's worried eye, Kaitlyn braced herself and set Mary's tea mug on the counter with a *chink*.

"Colton. Hazel. Is everything all right?" She wiped her hands on her apron and bolted around the counter.

"Thanks for the tea, sweetie," Mary said, blowing Kaitlyn a quick kiss. With a wave to Colton and a wink at Hazel, Mary astutely let herself out the door.

Kaitlyn approached her niece and held her by the upper arms, a move that forced Hazel to look at her. Hazel's eyes met hers with their usual stoic look of well-practiced indifference. But just for a flash, they might've held fear, until she made her expression go flat again.

Colton gave Kaitlyn a sympathetic look. He practically made a second career out of helping the misguided youth of their town, so she knew whatever Hazel had done, it must've been serious for him to drag her in at closing time like this.

"Tell your aunt what happened, okay?" Colton said. It came out as more of a command than a question.

Hazel crossed her arms and tossed Colton a glare. "Why don't you just tell her? You're the one who insisted on bringing me here."

Kaitlyn braced against another wave of nausea, willing it away. *Oh God, oh God*, she prayed. *Please, not drugs. Anything but drugs.*

"Okay, fine," Colton said, blowing out a patient sigh. "Hazel here decided she wanted to get a magazine over at the pharmacy—without paying for it."

Kaitlyn frowned. "A magazine?" She turned to Hazel, who was nervously shifting her weight from one foot to the other. "I could've given you the five dollars."

Hazel's face flushed, which Kaitlyn took as a sign that maybe there was the teensiest bit left of the old Hazel in there somewhere.

"Mr. Barter said this isn't the first time. He's looking to press charges."

Kaitlyn gasped. Oh, this was not good. "Colton, no."

"Hazel, do you have anything to say?" Colton asked.

"I didn't do it."

Now it was Kaitlyn's turn to roll her eyes. She looked at Colton. "Can I talk to you—privately?"

She pulled him off to the side, next to a vintage life-sized sign of Santa holding a cup of coffee up to his mouth and winking. "Look, I've been... preoccupied the past few weeks. I should've been looking out for her more. Let me give her a job. Tell Mr. Barter she'll be supervised 24-7."

Colton narrowed his observant cop-eyes at her. "You okay? You look almost as bad as Rafe."

"What are you talking about?"

"It's no secret you two have some kind of tiff going on."

"It's not a tiff."

"Well, whatever it is, he looks like shit too." Colton dropped his voice. "Look, you told me Hazel's done this in LA too. That makes her a repeat offender. Letting her slide again isn't going to do her any favors in the long run."

"I'll be more diligent. I'll keep a good eye on her. Please, Colton. If you tell Mr. Barter that, he'll listen."

Colton grimaced. "You can't be responsible for everyone, just to let you know."

Colton was well aware of Kaitlyn's family situation, and she appreciated his understanding, but still, she felt like she'd been too wrapped up with her own... issues. She'd left the tending of Hazel to her mother, and that had been a mistake. "Thank you, but... I can handle it."

He let out a heavy sigh. "It's against my better judgment, but okay, I'll see what I can do. But next time..." He made a cutting motion across his neck with his hands... accompanied by the faintest lift of his lips.

"Thank you," she said, giving him a hug.

"And you'd better go get some sleep. Or make up with Rafe or something."

She ignored that, then walked back over to the table where Hazel sat drawing patterns in the sugar she'd dumped from packets onto the table.

"So, are you throwing me in the clinker?" she asked, her mouth pulled up in a smirk. Kaitlyn tried not to be pissed.

"You're going to work here," Kaitlyn said. "Every day after school."

"What?" She sat up and shot Kaitlyn an outraged look.

Kaitlyn ignored that. "That's the deal. And when your shift is done, you'll do your homework in the back. And if your fingers get sticky again, I won't be able to stop anyone from pressing charges. That will look bad on your college apps."

Hazel snorted, and Kaitlyn knew why. Because there were no college apps.

Kaitlyn's sister had never been one for planning for practical things. There was no money saved for Hazel's college education.

"I'd like to go back to Gram's now," Hazel said, not looking her in the eye.

"I'll drop you off on my way to the station," Colton said.

Kaitlyn thanked Colton. "I'll see you here after school tomorrow," Kaitlyn said to Hazel, as Colton ushered her out the door. She didn't get an answer back.

Kaitlyn locked the door after them and dimmed the lights. She sat down at a table and put her head down on the cool wooden surface.

She had to do something to help Hazel before it was

too late. But she couldn't help wondering if maybe she was already too late. Her whole life, Kaitlyn had been responsible. She'd been a good daughter and a faithful sister. She'd been the one to take over her grandfather's business and made a success out of it. But sometimes she felt like the only glue that held the tenuous bonds of her family together.

She'd vowed a long time ago not to allow her emotions to rule her decisions like her older sister had. That had led her to single motherhood at seventeen and a domino stack of bad decisions after that.

But hadn't the same thing happened to her? She'd acted rashly with Rafe. She'd gotten swept away. How could she not, when every time he looked at her, her pulse skittered and desire rushed through her like a tidal wave?

In the darkened coffee shop, the strings of Christmas lights were as cheery as always, and the blinking lights from the ice cream shop across the street continued to remind her that life was going on as usual for most everyone else.

She reached into her apron to examine the clipping she'd ripped from a baking magazine earlier in the day. *Win $15,000 Plus Three Months of Pastry Classes for the Best Christmas Cookie Recipe!* the headline read. She ran her fingers over the finer print, thinking. Hazel was so bright—Kaitlyn had met with all her teachers at parent-teacher conferences a few weeks ago and they'd all asked about college plans. But they'd also all said the same thing—she was undisciplined. Unfocused. She didn't care.

Maybe that was because she didn't think anyone else did.

Kaitlyn tapped the clipping on the table. She had to start thinking of sustaining her business. Becoming a real businessperson. Growing. Winning that contest would give her niece a chance at college and also help Kaitlyn put her shop on the map.

As for pastry classes...well, Kaitlyn had always dreamed of taking those. She'd always wanted to expand her baked goods section, which was popular. Plus, she knew exactly the recipe she'd submit.

She had to start securing her future. Now more than ever, she had to count on herself, because she could never really count on anyone else to help.

Because she didn't need a pregnancy test to tell her that she was going to have Rafe Langdon's baby.

* * *

Rafe caught the mug of beer that Jonathan McDougal, the owner of the Tap, slid across the shiny wooden bar top. "On the house," Jon said. "For our local hero."

Rafe took the beer, lifting it in thanks. He didn't want to be hailed as a hero. "In that case, how about a sandwich too?" He took a swig and flashed Jon a grin.

"Sure, Rafe. Whatever you want."

"Just kidding. And I'm no hero. Just doing my job."

"Of course you're a hero," Jon said. "You got that whole family out of that car before it exploded—even the dog. And you weren't even on duty."

"That car blew sky-high," said Eli Nelson, a carpenter

who was sitting at the bar. "It was a miracle you didn't get killed yourself."

"You're lucky you got away without a scratch," Evan Marshall, the full-time deputy cop said. "How's your eardrum?"

Rafe took a deep swig of his beer. And made the okay sign. He remembered very vividly the explosion, the noise, the smell of burning rubber, the searing heat. The fact that his eardrum had burst was the least of his problems.

No, what got him was the look on the parents' faces as he'd cut their seat belts and dragged them out of that car. Stricken. Fearful. Wondering if their kids had survived.

He'd pulled them all out—Christ, he'd had to cut the guy's coat off too—and even as the paramedics strapped them to backboards and took them to the hospital, all the parents could do was cry and tell him over and over how thankful they were.

Rafe's relief and joy were marred by the fact that he couldn't help seeing an entirely different face. The face of his fiancée, Claire, who had died trapped in a car eight years ago. How many times had he imagined that same look on her face as she'd been trapped, alone and afraid, knowing in his heart he could have prevented it all?

The beer in his stomach churned.

"The couple made a huge donation to the fire department," Evan said.

Yes. They were a wealthy family, and they'd shown their appreciation with a ginormous sum of money. His lieutenant had been pleased, and the whole town had a feat of bravery to gossip about. They'd put him on a pedestal. Women loved that stuff. So what was his problem?

"I heard they didn't take the dog," Jonathan said as he wiped down the bar.

"It broke its leg, didn't it, Rafe?" Evan said. "We took it straight from the scene to the vet hospital."

The Saint Bernard puppy, eight weeks old, had been slated as a Christmas gift for cousins of the young family.

"Doc Sanders says it's going to be good as new," Rafe said.

"So why didn't the family want it?" Eli asked.

"It wasn't a perfect Christmas puppy anymore," Evan said.

Eli set his beer down hard, making a *tsk* sound.

"What? That's nuts," Jon said.

"That family could afford three more Saint Bernard puppies," Evan said, shaking his head. "They didn't want a damaged one."

Rafe always tried to give people the benefit of the doubt, but even he had to admit, he just didn't get the reasoning. Plus, he felt a strange affinity with that dog. Because like the dog, Rafe was damaged too—just not visibly.

"Hey, a couple of us are going into Richardson on Friday night," Evan said. "Want to come? Randall knows some ladies who would love to hang out with a town hero and his buddies, eh?" Evan bumped his elbow.

"Thanks, Evan, but I'm busy this weekend," Rafe said. He wasn't busy—but he didn't want to go pick up women.

The accident had brought back his feelings of helplessness, of his inability to save the people he'd loved the most. It had reminded him of all the reasons he never got serious with anyone. Yet all he could seem to think about lately was Kaitlyn.

He'd tried so hard to keep her at arm's length, but she'd crept under his skin and he'd let his guard down—and the unthinkable had happened.

"Aw, you're no fun lately," Evan said, not letting the topic go. "You used to be the life of the party. If I were you I'd be taking full advantage of this hero stuff."

Rafe managed to laugh and make small talk until he finished his beer, then thanked Jon again and walked out into the cold. It was snowing pretty heavily now, the flakes big and fat, the kind that stuck to your eyelashes and your coat. The cold air felt good—it woke him up and made him focus on something other than that accident. He didn't even zip his jacket, wanting to feel something, anything other than upset.

His truck was parked in the lot, but he didn't get in, just kept going. Told himself he needed a brisk walk to clear his head, that he didn't care where his feet led him. But he did care. And he knew exactly where he was headed.

The Bean was closed for the night, but his feet led him there anyway. He imagined Kaitlyn inside tidying up before tomorrow's morning rush. He missed seeing the way she tucked her pretty blond hair behind her ear and smiled. And talking to her about everything and nothing. He missed her, period.

And he missed the thing that had ruined their friendship. Sinking onto her softness, murmuring her name as he brushed his lips against her soft full ones, her little moans as she kissed him back and came apart in his arms.

He shook his head to get the images out of his head. But he couldn't, and they'd already affected him, if the tightening in his pants was any indicator.

"Rafe?" a familiar voice said. "What are you doing out there?"

Kaitlyn. Startled, he realized he'd been standing in front of the big window, staring in. He wasn't sure for how long.

Yearning, as well as a confusing mix of relief and longing, rolled through him. He remembered all their easy, relaxed conversations, the way she somehow always made him feel... better.

And he was ashamed to say he needed her—just to talk, to hear her voice. He needed her quiet calm.

She was fussing over him, tugging him by the arm. "It's freezing out here, and you haven't even got your jacket zipped. And where's your hat and gloves? Geez, you're covered with snow." Her busy hands dusted off the coating of snow that had accumulated on his hair, his coat.

"I was at the Tap for a while," he said.

As she pulled him inside of the warm, deserted shop and steered him over to a table, he noticed she smelled good, like dark rich coffee. And apples and cinnamon.

He had to stop himself from grasping her by the arms and telling her how badly he wanted things to go back to the way they were.

She placed a hand on a hip and assessed him. "Did you eat dinner?" she asked. "Don't even answer. I'm making you a sandwich. And I've got some homemade chicken soup left."

"Why are you still here?" he asked.

"I was... going over some numbers," she said.

"You look pretty," he said. *Fuck, why had he said that?*

She halted halfway to the kitchen and turned. "Rafe Langdon, are you drunk?" She frowned and tiny lines appeared between her eyes. He wanted to smooth them with his fingers. No, he wanted to kiss them away.

"Just a little," he said. He wasn't at all. But if he said he was, he could get away with staring at her for a little longer, the way her hair reflected off the multicolored Christmas lights. The way her blue eyes looked so worried, the way her frown still hadn't disappeared.

"Are you okay?" he asked, and he could swear she blushed. He didn't come here to dump his troubles on her. He'd just wanted to... see her. Be near her. How many beers had he had? Two? Hell, maybe he *was* drunker than he'd thought.

"Of course I am. Why would you ask that?"

He shrugged. "Just that you look tired." On the table was a clipping from a magazine. He lifted it up.

"What's this for?"

She took it out of his hands. "Nothing. It's... nothing."

He snagged it back and read it. "A recipe contest?"

She shrugged nonchalantly, but her fingers tapped restlessly on the table. "It's just something I'm thinking of entering."

He searched her eyes as he slid the clipping back in her direction. "I've been worried about you."

"Rafe... don't."

"My sisters told me your niece is having some problems. Everything all right?"

"Yes. Everything's fine." She lowered her eyes. "Actually, just between the two of us, she just got caught tonight trying to lift a magazine from the pharmacy."

Her pretty blue gaze flicked up at him. *Between the two of us.* What would it be like for there to actually *be* a two of them? Because Kaitlyn was used to going it alone. She was the toughest woman he knew. And, paradoxically, the softest of heart. But he would be making a big mistake to even pretend he was capable of having a relationship. It wouldn't be fair to her.

"Hazel stole a magazine?" Rafe asked.

Kaitlyn nodded. "That's just the tip of the iceberg, I'm afraid."

"Wasn't she supposed to get a job?" he asked. "I thought that was the deal your mom made with her."

"My mom never insisted on it. So I just hired her."

He blew out a breath. "Kaitlyn, that's kind of you, but—you sure that's a good idea? It sounds like the kid needs more than a job."

"I guess we'll see." She dropped her voice. "I couldn't just do... nothing."

He nodded sympathetically. Kaitlyn was known for taking on lost causes—stray cats, lonely customers... him.

Before he could say anything, she'd jumped up and run into the kitchen. She brought him soup and a sandwich, which tasted like the best he'd ever had, and he thanked her.

"So why the recipe contest?" he asked softly. "Don't you have enough to do?"

She heaved a sigh. "My grandfather had this recipe for double chocolate cookies that was *amazing*. I *know* it would win the contest. But it's...lost. No one knows where it is and my mom doesn't remember how to make them."

"And this is important why?"

"No one has prepared for Hazel's college. Someone's got to help her."

"You care about everyone but yourself."

"That's not true." She pushed the paper a little way toward him. "The prize includes pastry classes at the Culinary Institute of America. That part's for me."

"You always wanted to do that."

"If I had more bakery offerings, I'd ensure the shop would do well and maybe even expand one day."

Rafe nodded and set down the clipping. "You have circles under your eyes."

Kaitlyn swallowed and dropped her gaze from his. "I'm fine, Rafe. How about you? Everyone's talking about you. How are you doing after...the accident?"

He ignored the question and placed his hand over hers on the table, and she immediately stiffened. But he cut to the chase anyway. "Kaitlyn, I—miss you. I miss how we used to talk. I miss my...friend."

"We were more than friends, Rafe."

He smoothed his thumb over the back of her palm. "That part was... that was really good too."

"I don't want to be friends with benefits, Rafe. You know that."

"I know. And you know I can't make you any promises," he said. "I just... I can't get serious with anyone."

He knew he wasn't normal, that he really had no idea what he was asking. That unearthing the feelings he'd buried deep inside him would mean telling her things he'd never told anyone before.

"I miss how things used to be between us," he said instead.

She flicked her eyes up at him. "Me too, but things changed when we slept together. I just—I can't go back to the way things were."

He nodded. "I'm sorry—I'm sorry I can't give you what you want. I can't give that to anyone."

She drew her hand away. "I'm sorry too, Rafe. But I need someone who can commit to a relationship. Someone who thinks I'm worth the risk." She stood up, her chair scraping on the wood floor. "I think you'd better go."

He nodded, because what could he say? She was right. She deserved someone better. Someone who could give all of himself to her, and he couldn't do that, because there wasn't anything left of him inside. He made himself get up, and shrugged on his coat. "I'm so sorry," he said as he let himself out the door.

* * *

Kaitlyn watched Rafe walk out and locked the glass door behind him. She turned off the lights and even made it halfway up the back staircase to her apartment before she started to cry. Standing by the picture window that overlooked the postcard-perfect street of her beloved town, she took in the quaint line of shops, the windows decked out in Christmas lights, the wrought iron lampposts decked out in holiday finery. She'd never had the desire to leave here—never wanted to travel the world or settle in a big city or somewhere far away. No, she saw her destiny right here, in this town, in her grandfather's little café.

There was a time when she would have jumped at the chance to be friends with benefits with Rafe. To have a casual, noncommittal thing. But not now. Not with . . . the baby.

She realized now why she hadn't told Rafe she was pregnant yet—because she'd been holding out for a miracle. Waiting for him to say he was over his first tragic love and that he could open his heart enough to see the possibility of love with someone else. With *her*. There'd been times when he'd looked at her and she'd seen something wonderful there—something that had made her believe over and over again that that was possible.

Now she knew it wasn't. She and this baby were on their own.

About the Author

Miranda Liasson loves to write stories about everyday people who find love despite themselves, because there's nothing like a great love story. And if there are a few laughs along the way, even better! She's a Romance Writers of America Golden Heart winner and an Amazon bestselling author whose heartwarming and humorous small-town romances have won accolades such as the National Readers' Choice Award and the Gayle Wilson Award of Excellence and have been *Harlequin Junkie* and Night Owl Reviews Top Picks.

She lives in the Midwest with her husband and three kids in a charming old neighborhood that is the inspiration for many of the homes in her books.

Miranda loves to hear from readers! Find her at:

MirandaLiasson.com
Facebook.com/MirandaLiassonAuthor
Instagram: @MirandaLiasson
Twitter: @MirandaLiasson

For information about new releases and other news, feel free to sign up for her newsletter at mirandaliasson.com/#mailing-list.

Meant to Be

ALISON BLISS

Chapter One

Brett Carmichael blew out a huge sigh of relief.

Not only had he just clocked out after another busy day at the garage where he worked, but after almost a year of long days and miserable nights, things were finally starting to look up.

Thank God.

For months, he'd been scouring the entire Granite, Texas, area looking for an old building that he could buy and turn into an automotive repair shop. After all, he'd been dreaming of opening his own garage since he was fifteen years old. Back then, he used to spend hours tearing old car engines apart and then putting them back together again just for the hell of it. Now, at age thirty, he actually got paid to do it.

Brett was a damn good mechanic. Always had been. Which was probably why almost everyone in town brought their vehicles to him when they needed work done. He had a great customer base, but oftentimes he was so busy that he had no choice but to pass some of the repair jobs off to another mechanic in the shop. He hated doing that though because he couldn't guarantee the other guy's work like he could his own.

Sadly, not all mechanics took pride in their work like Brett did. He didn't randomly guess at what was wrong with a vehicle without doing some kind of research to make sure he was on the right track, and he didn't take shortcuts just because doing so would be easier or faster. He believed in finding the actual problem and repairing it correctly the first time rather than doing a half-assed job.

That was one of the reasons he wanted to open his own business. The moment he found a suitable location, he planned to open a garage and hire a couple of great mechanics who held the same beliefs as he did and who would do things the proper way. But Granite was a small town, and finding a place for sale that met his needs hadn't been easy.

Brett didn't need anything big and fancy. He was used to working in cramped quarters and spent most of his time crawling around under a hood or sliding beneath a car on the cracked wooden creeper that his boss was too cheap to replace. But there were a few requirements on which Brett—unlike his boss—refused to budge.

The structure of the building needed to be large enough to house a separate waiting area for the customers in order to keep them safe and out of the mechanics' way. Also, the parking lot needed to have enough lighting to be secure and have enough space to store vehicles overnight, if necessary. The last thing he wanted to worry about was a customer getting hurt or their vehicle getting stolen or broken into. So as far as Brett was concerned, these things were nonnegotiable.

Unfortunately, that only made it harder to find a place.

At least until his best friend had called this morning. Logan had apparently overheard a conversation at his bar the night before about a used car lot a couple of miles outside the city limits that was now up for sale. The old man who owned it had passed away a few months ago, and it had closed down for good. Although the owner's only son had inherited the business, the man didn't live in the area. The middle-aged son had instead flown in from Arizona only long enough to sell off the remaining used car stock at auction and officially put his father's property up for sale. Both of which he had already done.

That meant Brett had to move fast.

So after hanging up with Logan, Brett had immediately called the phone number his friend had given him and spoken with the son about the property. The lot sat on five acres and was located on the main road between Granite and a neighboring community. Not a bad location, if you asked Brett. It would be close enough to Granite for Brett to serve his regular customers, yet near enough to another town to gain some new clients.

The building was divided into two sections. The front office would come fully furnished and had a large, air-conditioned waiting area for customers, while the shop had three huge bays with galvanized steel doors and a separate room for storing car parts. Not only that, but according to the son, the parking area was well lit and had several surveillance cameras already installed.

All of that sounded perfect and was exactly what Brett had been looking for. But the thing that caught his attention the most was when the son told him that he was willing to throw in the hydraulic vehicle lift, electronic diagnostic equipment, a welding machine, and several upright toolboxes filled with hand tools...for free.

Brett hadn't expected that. Who in their right mind would give away thousands of dollars in equipment like that? Not that he was complaining or anything. That equipment would come in handy, and although Brett already had his own set of hand tools—most mechanics worth their salt did—it never hurt to have extras on hand. He never knew when he might break off a wrench and need another in a pinch.

But something bothered him about all of this. While the place seemed like a perfect prospect and was definitely in his price range, the deal sounded almost too good to be true. Maybe the owner's son was just in a hurry to relieve himself of his father's business and get back to his own life. Or maybe he just really needed the money from the sale of the property. But Brett couldn't let the idea of fulfilling his long-held dream persuade him to make rash decisions that he'd regret down the road. Lord knows he'd already done enough of that to last him a lifetime.

In order to be sure of what he was getting himself into, Brett needed to see the place in person and inspect the building for any major issues. Unfortunately, that in itself was a problem. The son had already booked his return flight back to Arizona in the morning, and the only time he could show the property was tonight. Otherwise, Brett would have to wait to see it until the man came back in a few weeks to clear out his father's home.

But he worried that if he didn't jump on this opportunity, there was a good chance someone else would. So he'd agreed to meet the guy at the used car lot around seven o'clock.

That should've given him enough time to run home, grab a bite to eat and a quick shower, and then make it to the dealership on time. But as usual, things hadn't panned out according to his plan. Just as he started to close up shop, an elderly woman had pulled in and asked him to check her alternator belt. It had been squealing, and she was leaving in the morning on a gambling trip with her bingo friends.

Closed or not, Brett hadn't been able to refuse her. But by the time he'd replaced her belt and sent her on her way, he was now running late himself. He would've called the guy to let him know, but in his rush to get there, Brett had accidentally left his cell phone in his toolbox back at the garage. Along with the guy's phone number. Just great.

Brett peered up from the road long enough to check the position of the sun, which had already descended behind the trees. It was getting dark, and he hadn't had time to get a shower, much less eat anything. But it looked like, as long as he hurried, he would make it to his appointment only a few minutes late. Well, if the son hadn't given up on him and left already.

As Brett's gaze lowered back to the road, he noticed a dark smudge on the side of his hand attached to the steering wheel. He had washed up before leaving the shop, but he always seemed to miss a spot. Sighing, he rubbed the offending mark against the thigh of his jeans to remove it. That was just something that came with the territory of working in a dirty environment.

And with as many hours as he'd put in lately? God, he'd never be able to get all the oil stains off his hands and black grease out from under his nails. Unless, of course, he scrubbed them until they were raw...which always hurt like hell.

Didn't matter though. It would all be worth it when he finally had a garage of his own. That was the only thing he'd ever wanted. Well, maybe not the *only* thing. There had been something—*or rather someone*—else. Unfortunately, that relationship hadn't panned out as he'd hoped, and the two of them had parted ways last year.

No, idiot. She dumped you. There was nothing mutual about it.

Brett cringed at the familiar stab of regret slicing into his chest. The same one he'd felt many times before. But the last thing he needed right now was to think about the woman he lost and wonder what could've been. So he let out an exasperated breath and shoved the guilt and pain into a mental storage locker and kicked it to the back of the closet in his brain to be dealt with later. He didn't have time for that shit right now.

After spending almost an entire year being miserable, he was finally close to getting the only other thing that had ever truly mattered to him. He needed to keep his focus on the here and now. He'd worked hard for months to make his dreams come true, and he was proud of how far he'd come. He wasn't going to allow anything to stand in the way of that. Especially when it came to his past.

Brett motored down the window, allowing the cool evening breeze to whip through the interior of his oversized truck. Though it was the beginning of January, winters in South Texas were considerably different than in northern regions. Unless a frontal system blew in, it wasn't actually all that cold. Especially during the day. If anything, this kind of weather was what most people referred to as "nice fall weather." But once the sun fell below the horizon, the temperature would usually drop considerably.

Glancing down at his cargo jeans and stained white T-shirt, Brett shrugged. He didn't have a jacket with him, but he wasn't planning on standing outside in the night air very long anyway. He'd be fine.

No sooner had the thought run through his mind than he noticed a little silver Pontiac Solstice up ahead parked on the shoulder of the road. The emergency flashers blinked off and on like crazy, and a figure was bent over near the back tire. It didn't take a genius to know that they probably had a flat, but Brett shook his head. While the stranded motorist had managed to park their car completely off the road, it was dangerous to change a tire on the side of the vehicle nearest traffic. Especially at night when other motorists' visibility was limited.

But Brett also knew from experience that it sometimes couldn't be helped.

As a courtesy, he immediately slowed down and veered over the center line to go around the little sports car at a safe distance. Normally, he would've pulled over and offered his assistance to someone stuck on the side of the road. After all, he was a mechanic and almost always kept tools in his truck. But tonight he couldn't really spare the time. So instead, he mumbled to himself, "Sorry, buddy. Better luck next time."

But as he drove slowly past, the person bending over near the back tire straightened into an upright position, and he immediately realized his mistake. Although Brett had assumed the person was a man from a distance, the long dark locks and pristine white pant suit clinging to lush curves confirmed that she was very much indeed a woman.

Damn it.

Maybe it had something to do with growing up with a younger sister or being raised by a single mom, but Brett had always had a soft spot for women. Especially ones who seemed to be in trouble.

Without hesitation, he pulled onto the shoulder of the road in front of the silver sports car and turned off his engine. Then he glanced at his watch and gritted his teeth. God, he didn't have time for this right now. But there was no way in hell he could drive past a stranded woman and not stop to ask if she needed some assistance. His dad had taught him better than that.

But that didn't mean he had to be happy about it.

Disgruntled by the inconvenience, Brett shoved open his door and climbed out before heading directly for the woman, who had apparently gone back to work on her tire using a small flashlight that she had lying on the ground next to her. Hell, as far as he could tell, she hadn't so much as even looked up when he stopped. Hopefully that meant she had things under control and was almost finished putting on a spare. If so, he might be able to still make it to his appointment.

Not wasting any time, Brett walked right up behind her. "Do you need some help with your tire, miss?"

Her head snapped up, and her posture stiffened as if a metal rod had been shoved into her spine, but she didn't turn around or respond.

Worried that he'd somehow frightened her, he cringed and took a nonthreatening step back. She hadn't looked back at him yet, but if she decided to, he didn't want to seem like he was towering over her. He was a pretty built guy, and it wouldn't be the first time that his appearance alone had intimidated someone.

He purposely softened his tone to keep his deep voice from sounding too harsh. "I was just driving past and saw you stranded here. I'm a mechanic so I thought I might be of some assistance."

The woman rose slowly to her feet and cocked her head back slightly as she released a sound of annoyance from the back of her throat. Though it was barely audible, the quiet noise reverberated through him as if her vocal cords were two cymbals crashing together.

His body stilled. *No. It couldn't be.*

The moment she turned around to face him, his

mouth fell open. Probably due to the whirlwind of emotions that were bitch-slapping him in the face.

She shook her head. "It doesn't take a genius—or a mechanic—to change a flat tire, Brett."

He blinked rapidly, not believing his eyes. "Sidney?"

She huffed out an irritated breath. "Oh, come on. I don't look *that* different."

No, she didn't. Actually she was just as gorgeous as ever. But the last person he expected to come face-to-face with was his ex-girlfriend of all people. Not only that, but it had been almost a year since he'd last laid eyes on her, and he hadn't known she'd grown out her brunette hair.

He'd never seen Sidney with long hair before, but the short, choppy do she used to sport while they were dating was now trailing down her back with lighter-colored pieces framing her heart-shaped face. It looked great. The flattering style really brought out the rich color in her warm brown eyes.

But that crisp white pant suit she was wearing? *Holy hell.*

Sidney had always dressed in a classic, conservative style that included tailored clothing, high-quality fabrics, and lots of neutral colors. In fact, he hadn't even thought it possible for her to look any more sophisticated and elegant than she had back when they were dating. Yet the woman never failed to surprise him.

Brett didn't know exactly what it was about her modest attire that always sent his tongue wagging. Most guys he knew went for women in low-cut tops and high-rise skirts. Those were nice and all. But give him Sidney in a tailored blouse and a pair of pressed pants, and he'd be hard for days.

It was like she had a pureness about her that called to him, an innocence that he'd lost years ago and would never get back. Every time he was around her, all he wanted to do was roll her onto the nearest bed and muss that polished hair as he soiled her cleanliness with all the dirty things he wished to do to her body. And this time was no exception.

Brett glanced down at his oil-stained hands though. Great. She was going to think he hadn't washed them. Even though he had. Twice. Shoving his hands into the pockets of his jeans, he realized he still hadn't responded to her yet. "You look as great as always, Sid." *Damn. Took you long enough, dumbass.*

"Um, thanks. You too," she said, turning away from him. "But you can go. I have everything under control."

Her dismissal hit him like a punch to the gut, and he winced. Okay, so maybe he deserved it after what he'd done to her last year. But it was almost completely dark outside, and he would be damned if he was just going to leave her stranded in the middle of nowhere all alone. Even if she did have a flashlight.

Brett shook his head. "Sorry to disappoint you, but I'm not going anywhere."

* * *

Damn it. The last person Sidney Larson wanted to be rescued by was her ex.

After the stunt Brett had pulled last year, she'd broken up with him and told him she never wanted to see him again. And she'd meant it at the time. But the past year had been a real struggle for her. Part of her wanted to prove to him—and maybe a little to herself—that she didn't need him in her life. While the other part of her had contemplated running back into his arms to make up for lost time. So she'd purposely avoided running into him... well, up until now.

She had a feeling that seeing him again would bring back all of those feelings and memories that she'd tried so hard to suppress. She was right. The urge to fling herself back into his arms—and his life—was as strong as ever. But after the crap he'd pulled last year, she just couldn't do it.

No matter how good he looks.

Actually, he looked better than good. Brett was sexier than ever. He had always maintained a great physique, but after one glance at those arms of his, she had no doubt he'd been putting in some extra hours lifting weights at the gym. Not only that, but the man had always pulled off a grungy, bad boy look without even trying. And it completely suited him. Because he was the type of guy that fathers had been warning their daughters about for years.

But just because Brett was rippling with more muscle than ever didn't mean she needed him to do her dirty work for her. She could change her own tire, thank you very much. A fact he should know because he was the one who'd taught her how to do it. "You always were a sucker for a damsel in distress," she said, rolling her eyes. "But I don't need your help, Brett. I know what the hell I'm doing."

He grinned but planted his feet firmly in place and crossed his bulky arms over his broad chest. "That's fine. Then I'll just stay here and keep you company until the spare is on."

God, no. The last thing she wanted was him standing right behind her while she was bent over with sweat dripping from her temples as she panted heavily. That reminded her way too much of that time when he'd taken her over the back of the couch and had...Jesus. Never mind. This was exactly what she was afraid of.

She huffed out a breath. "Well, maybe I don't want your company. Have you thought of that?"

He nodded. "I have." Then he shrugged one strong shoulder. "But that's just too damn bad. Because until that spare tire is on your car and you're pulling away from me, I'm not going anywhere."

Damn it. She had a feeling he would say that. "God, Brett. I'm not afraid of the dark."

"I didn't say you were," he replied, a smidgeon of irritation leaching into his voice. "But I'm not leaving you out here by yourself, Sid. So either you put the tire on or move your ass aside and I'll do it for you."

His demanding tone sent shivers over her skin, and her mouth went dry. It was strange that, after almost a year later, he still had that effect on her. "Fine. But I'll do it myself. I don't need your help."

"All right."

Sidney turned back to her flat tire and kneeled down on a space blanket she'd borrowed from her emergency kit. It crinkled as she tried to reposition herself, and rough pieces of gravel poked through the thin silver material into her knees. But it was at least keeping her pants clean, which had been the overall idea anyway.

Sidney adjusted the beam on the flashlight directly onto the tire and then sat back on her heels and looked over the tools in front of her. She knew what she needed to do, but it was a little nerve-wracking having a certified mechanic, who also happened to be her ex-boyfriend, standing over her watching her do it. Who needed that kind of added pressure?

Brett must've noticed her hesitance. "What do you need to do before jacking the car up?" he asked, prompting her.

"I know what to do," she told him. "I have to use that four-arm metal thingy to loosen the bolts."

He chuckled. "It's called a four-way lug wrench."

"Close enough," she said, reaching for it.

Flipping the tool around, she tested each end of the wrench until she found the correct size for her lug nuts. Once the end was snugly slipped over the nut, she tried to turn the wrench. It wouldn't move, so she rose up onto her knees and leaned over the tool to give herself more leverage and then tried to twist it again. No such luck.

Damn it. Why is this not working?

"Need some help?" Brett asked.

Sidney shook her head. "Nope. I can get it. It's just a little tight."

So she used the trick Brett had taught her. She slid one of the heavy jack stands under the opposite end of the wrench to hold it up in place. Then she rose to her feet and kicked off her black heels. Keeping one hand on her car for balance, she placed one foot on the left side arm of the wrench and stepped up onto it.

Well, that wasn't supposed to happen.

Instead of standing on top of the wrench several inches off the ground, her weight was supposed to break the lug nut loose. But for some strange reason, it didn't work.

Weird. Especially given that she had put on a few pounds since Brett had last seen her. It wasn't like she had been all that thin back when they'd dated, but she couldn't help worrying that her most recent weight gain only reflected how miserable she'd been for the past year.

Brett cleared his throat, as if reminding her that he was still standing there and watching her. "You sure you don't want my help?"

"I've got everything under control," she replied, bending her knees and bouncing a little on top of the wrench. Still nothing happened. So she did the only thing she could do. She bounced a little harder, hoping she didn't break something. Including herself.

Sidney did everything in her power to force that stupid lug nut to move because there was no way she was going to admit that she needed Brett's help. Even if, in this instance, she clearly did. So much for proving to him that she was capable of handling any situation thrown at her. That was kind of hard to do while sitting on the side of the road as helpless as a baby bird that had fallen from its nest.

"Okay, stop that," Brett ordered. "You're either going to damage your car or wind up hurting yourself. Get down from there and just let me take a look."

Sidney hopped down and moved out of his way as quickly as she could, but she hadn't been fast enough. As he maneuvered past her, a familiar scent wafted straight to her nose. In the past, he'd always smelled like this when he had gotten off work, and even then, she couldn't get enough of it. Sure, it was probably just a mixture of sweat and grease, but the earthly, masculine notes always took on more of a smoky, charred wood quality and made her mouth water.

But she couldn't think about that right now. She had more important things to worry about. "I don't understand. I did it the way you showed me."

Brett glared at her. "What? I never told you to climb on top of the wrench. You were only supposed to put some weight into it to break the nuts free. Not stand on it."

"Yeah, but that didn't work...and I put *all* of my weight into it." And Lord knows she had plenty of that.

He squatted down and tried to crank on the wrench himself. When it wouldn't turn, he pulled it off and checked the others. When they wouldn't turn either, he looked closer at the lug nuts. "Damn it. I think whoever put these tires on this vehicle tightened the lug nuts too much. Probably used a pneumatic impact wrench."

"Okay, so what do I need to do to fix it?"

Brett stood and dusted his hands off, probably more out of habit than anything. "Nothing."

Confusion swept through her. "What do you mean, nothing?"

"What I'm saying is that *you* won't be doing anything. I'll have to fix it myself."

"Why's that?"

"Because I'm most likely going to have to cut the lug nuts off and replace them. Otherwise, the lug bolts could break off inside the wheel, which is more expensive and complicated to fix. But I'm thinking these might have an aluminum cover so I can just chisel off the aluminum part in order to get to the metal inside. That would make things a little easier for me."

"All right. So what are you waiting for? Let's get to work then."

Brett ran his fingers through his hair. "It's not that simple, Sid. I don't have those kinds of tools with me."

Figures. "So now what?"

"I'm going to drive you home and then come back with the tow truck to pick up your car. That way I can take it back to the shop, where I can work on it."

Her eyes widened. "Are you crazy? I'm not leaving my sports car out here on the side of the road in the middle of nowhere."

"It's not like we have a choice."

"Sure we do. I'll stay with the car while you go get the tow truck."

His head snapped to her, and his blue eyes narrowed. "Sidney, if you think I'm going to leave you out here all alone, then you're the one who's crazy. You should know me better than that by now."

Oh, she did. But he should know her better than that too. In the past, she'd never agreed with him just for the sake of doing so, and she wasn't about to start now.

And just because he wanted her to do something didn't mean she would actually do it either. "Well, I'm not going to risk coming back to my car sitting on blocks because someone stole my tires. They're expensive, you know."

He squinted at her. "If *we* can't get the tire off, then how the hell is someone trying to steal it going to?"

Oh. Right. Good point. "Well, I don't want them to take my entire car."

"I'm certain we don't have to worry about that either. The car has a flat tire. It isn't going anywhere."

"Yeah, maybe. Unless the car thief has a tow truck."

Brett rubbed at his temples and groaned, as if a sudden headache was coming on. "Sidney."

"What?" She shrugged. "I'm just saying."

Brett smiled with the same adorable lopsided grin she'd always loved so much. "Just get into the truck. It'll be fine, I promise."

She sighed. "Okay, fine. But if my car gets stolen before you get back, I'm holding you personally responsible."

"Yep. I figured as much."

They picked up all the tools and the space blanket and locked them inside her car before heading to his red GMC pickup. Sidney couldn't believe she'd been defeated by a stupid lug nut, and she wasn't necessarily talking about the one on her car. Unfortunately, she had no choice but to accept Brett's offer…even if she wasn't all that happy about it.

She hated being this close to him. It was bad enough that his mere proximity set her on edge and had her stomach doing back flips. But his intoxicating scent forced her to hold her breath just to be able to think straight. Even just being back inside his truck stirred up old memories of the last time they'd been together like this. Only, that time, the windows were fogged over, their clothes were on the floorboard, and she was trembling with pleasure as he thrust inside her repeatedly.

Damn lust-filled memories. Although she'd spent the past year trying to forget them—*forget him*—the vivid recollections still haunted her daily. And being this close to him was only making things worse.

Chapter Two

Brett was seriously annoyed.

The fact that Sidney—who apparently was just as stubborn as that damn lug nut—would stand on a tire iron, bouncing up and down, rather than ask him for assistance really pissed him off to no end. But for the woman to admit that she would willingly put herself at risk just to try to stop someone from stealing her car? Insane. He hoped like hell she never got mugged because the person robbing her was going to have a hell of a time convincing the stubborn-ass woman to let go of her purse.

At least he'd managed to convince her to get into the truck without putting up too much of a fight. Because he'd definitely meant what he said. He wouldn't have left her. If that meant spending the night with her in the middle of nowhere, then so be it. He'd have sacrificed himself to the cause.

Yeah, like spending time with the woman I'm still in love with is much of a sacrifice.

Either way, he was glad he was the one who had

found her on the side of the road. Although he'd missed his appointment to look at the used car lot and probably lost his one shot at finding the perfect place for his new garage, it was all worth it as long as Sidney was safe. They might not be together anymore, but that didn't mean he wanted to see her get hurt. Hell, he'd hurt her enough already.

As he pulled out onto the road, he glanced over to see Sidney rubbing her arms. "Are you cold?"

"A little."

He flipped the heater on and pointed his vents in her direction. "Let me know if you get too warm, and I'll turn it back down some."

A slight smile lifted her cheeks. "Okay, thanks."

He nodded to her and drove on in silence. But after a while, when the sounds of her slow, rhythmic breathing started to arouse him, he figured he better make small talk or he was going to end up with an embarrassing problem on his hands. "So how long have you had the sports car?"

"Oh, I got it a little over two months ago. Do you like it?"

"Yeah, it's nice. I bet it runs great too."

"It does." She glanced over at him. "So you hadn't heard I'd gotten a new car? I thought for sure by now that everyone in town had."

He shook his head. "I've been working a lot so I guess I've been out of the loop lately."

Which was mostly true. But he was still surprised that he hadn't heard mention of her new sports car. After all, he was a guy who liked cars, and they did live in the same small town where any kind of gossip was fair game. Then again, they didn't exactly travel in the same circles. Never really had.

Sidney had always been out of his league. It had just apparently taken her longer to realize it than he had. But once it finally got through to her, she'd hauled ass out of their relationship and never looked back. Yeah, avoiding him for the past year had spoken volumes.

Brett couldn't really blame her though. He didn't have the best reputation, and the last thing he wanted to do was soil hers any more than he probably already had. That was why he hadn't bothered asking her out the first time he'd met her.

She'd walked into the shop wearing a pink blouse and a knee-length tan skirt that matched her high heels. Unfortunately, he'd been busy with one of his regular customers, and another mechanic had walked over to help her. Or so he had thought.

The moment he overheard the other mechanic recommending unneeded services to her and quoting marked-up prices, all because she was a female customer who probably didn't know the difference, Brett stepped forward and offered to take over. Lord knows he'd seen plenty of mechanics pull that dick move on unsuspecting women, and surprisingly even on a few men, and it wasn't at all something Brett condoned. In fact, once he finally managed to open his garage, if he found any of his own mechanics pulling that kind of a bullshit scam, he was going to fire the asshole on the spot.

He was just glad that he had been there that day to save Sidney from the jerk who tried to screw her over. And she had seemed pretty grateful about it too. The moment Brett had come over and declared that he was taking over, she seemed a little surprised and not entirely sure of what was going on. But within minutes, she must've figured it out because she'd smiled and mouthed a thank-you to him under her breath.

She'd come in for a tune-up, and that was the only thing she was charged for...and not a penny more. Brett had made sure of it. But after that, things had started to get a little weird.

The following week, she'd returned to the garage and asked for Brett specifically. She requested that he replace her air filter, though hers looked brand new. The next week, she'd come back by to ask him to check the pressure in her tires. Little did she know that he had already done so the week before since he thought one had looked a little low. But he went ahead and checked them again anyway, even though none of them ended up needing any air. But by the time the fourth week rolled around and she once again showed up at the garage where he worked, Brett couldn't take it anymore.

He hadn't planned to ask her out. Not only because she was one of his clients, but because they were just too different.

Sidney came from money. He'd learned that she'd grown up in a nice home where she was surrounded by fancy things and never had to want for anything. Although she'd always claimed to be a spoiled brat, Brett had never seen any real proof of it. She was warm and kind and funny, as beautiful on the inside as she was on the outside. And she was way more sophisticated than any girl he'd ever dated.

Brett, however, was only twelve when his father passed away, leaving big shoes to fill, and he tried to do so in as many ways as possible. He watched his little sister while their mom worked, earned extra money to help pay bills, and made sure that the two women in his life would never want for anything. But when he got busted for hustling pool, his reputation went downhill fast. And so did his attitude. He was moody and belligerent and rough around the edges. Not the kind of guy you take home to meet the family.

Honestly, he didn't know what the hell Sidney ever saw in him back then.

But when he finally asked her out, she just smiled and said, "About damn time." And then another strange thing happened. Her car suddenly didn't have any more issues.

Guess mechanics and pool hustlers aren't the only ones who run cons.

The thought had Brett chuckling to himself, which prompted a glance from Sidney. "What's so funny?"

He cleared his throat and immediately straightened his face. The last thing he wanted to do was tell her that he'd been reliving the day they met in his mind. "Ah, nothing. Sorry."

But there was something he wanted to talk about when it came to their past. One specific event that replayed over and over in his mind on a regular basis. Valentine's Day of last year. The day he royally screwed everything up between them.

That day, he'd shown up at the bank with a dozen red roses, hoping to invite her to dinner, where he'd planned to propose to her. But when he walked into her office and found an irate man berating her for not approving his loan, Brett had lost his cool. Sidney had shaken her head at him, clearly wanting him to stay out of it, but he hadn't listened.

Instead, he'd stepped in front of her and jumped down the guy's throat. At the time, he hadn't known that the asshole was the bank manager's brother. Nor had he realized that Sidney would be so upset with him that she'd end their relationship over it. But he'd found out both of these things the moment she pulled him outside into the parking lot.

Brett hesitated to bring up the past incident, knowing it would probably anger her all over again. They needed to talk about it though and at least clear the air between them. But he didn't want her to feel as though he was forcing her into conversation while stuck in a vehicle with him so he waited until his truck rolled to a stop at the curb in front of her home.

She opened her door to get out, and the interior light flicked on above their heads. "Thanks for the ride, Brett."

"Sidney, can you hold on for a second? I'd like to talk to you about something before you go."

Her face morphed with confusion, but she nodded and closed the door, plunging them back into darkness. "Okay."

He rubbed his sweaty palms on his jeans and took a deep breath. "I wanted to talk to you about last year...when you broke things off with me."

She shook her head. "Brett, I don't think—"

He raised his hand to stop her. "Just hear me out. Please." She nodded reluctantly but he could tell she wasn't expecting this to go well. "When you broke up with me last year, I was not in the right head space to do this so I'm doing it now."

Her hand held on to the console, and she looked as though she was bracing for impact. "All right. Go ahead, I guess."

He nodded and continued on. "At the time, I thought you had gone a little overboard by breaking up with me over something so trivial."

"I—"

"Just wait. Let me finish before you say anything."

He had no doubt that she expected him to give some pathetic excuse for his ridiculous past behavior, but that wasn't what he was doing. He'd never gotten the chance to apologize for what he had done, and now seemed as good a time as any. Maybe she would never forgive him, but he at least wanted her to know that he regretted the incident and knew how badly he'd messed up.

Swallowing the guilt he felt, he breathed out slowly. "I just wanted to say I'm sorry. I understand why you walked away from me. Maybe at the time I couldn't see it, but now I know for sure you were right in doing so."

Sidney's gaze fell to her hands as she picked at her fingernail. "Well, I'm sorry too."

He shook his head adamantly. "You don't have anything to apologize for."

Her eyes rose, meeting his. "Sure I do. I hurt you, didn't I?"

Brett nodded solemnly. "Of course I was hurt. Valentine's Day was the worst day of my life. But honestly, it changed me for the better and made me realize what a jackass I've truly been."

"What do you mean?"

"You know all about my overprotective tendencies and my need to control everything. Well, after losing you, Valerie and I had a similar incident."

"Oh, you mean the bar fight with Logan?"

Damn. Gossip sure traveled fast. "Yep, that's the one. I came unglued when I found out my best friend was sleeping with my little sister."

She nodded. "I had a feeling that would happen. I once saw them in the movie theater looking pretty cozy and wondered if you knew that something was going on with them."

"I didn't at first. When I found out, I hit the roof, and it caused problems between the three of us. So much so that Valerie threatened to disown me. But after losing you and hearing you say that you never wanted to see me again...well, I couldn't bear the thought of losing another important person in my life. That's what saved my relationship with my sister and my best friend."

Sidney smiled. "I'm glad to hear that everything worked out for you."

He shrugged. "Well, not *everything*. I still lost you in the end. But you walking away made me realize that *I* was the one with the problem. Not you. Not Valerie or Logan. It was all on me. So I started seeing a therapist to help me work through my issues. It's been a big help."

"That's great. I'm happy you're finally talking to someone about these things. You needed that."

Brett rubbed at the back of his neck. "Yeah, I did. Especially after you were out of my life. You were the only person I told a lot of that stuff to. When you left, I didn't have anyone to talk to about my problems anymore."

"I'm really sorry, Brett. I just figured a clean break would do us both good. I figured that once we got past our feelings for each other, we could try going back to being just friends. But I...well, I've been busy and haven't crossed paths with you up until now."

Brett wanted to laugh at that, but he didn't. The only way you wouldn't cross paths with someone in a town as small as Granite was if you were purposely avoiding them. He wasn't stupid enough to believe that he hadn't ran into her for almost a full year by coincidence. No way. He had no doubt she'd made that happen herself.

"I just wanted you to know I've changed. I'm not at all the same guy from before. And I have you to thank for that. If you hadn't broken up with me when you did, I would probably still be that same asshole you dated back then. So thank you for breaking up with me. You did me a huge favor."

* * *

Sidney was so stunned that she didn't know what to say.

Who in their right mind thanks someone for breaking up with them?

While she appreciated the heartfelt apology, she

couldn't help wondering if her weight gain had anything to do with his being so glad that they were no longer together.

Maybe that was just her insecurities bubbling to the surface though, since he never seemed to have a problem with her size before. Then again, he'd clearly been spending a lot more time at the gym, bulking up all those hard-packed muscles, while she'd spent the past year drowning her sorrows in pints of rocky road ice cream.

Sadly enough, it was easier to believe he had a problem with her weight than to believe Brett was a changed man. Old habits die hard, and it wasn't like the incident at the bank was the first time Overprotective Brett had reared his ugly head. According to his sister, Brett had been that way since his father's death. Valerie probably put up with it out of some sense of loyalty—after all, they were family—but Sidney wasn't willing to do the same.

Still, although she hated to admit it, she couldn't pretend that hearing him say he'd changed didn't intrigue her. Sure, he had been too overprotective and had a jealous streak a mile long, but he had always treated her well. Not only that, but she had never stopped loving him and... well, last year's Valentine's Day had been the worst day of her life too.

She still remembered it as if it were yesterday. Brett had come barging into her office unannounced and interrupted a heated meeting she was having with the bank manager's brother. Sure, the guy was an ass, but he was a client nonetheless, and it was her job to deal with him. Besides, it wasn't like it was the first time she'd dealt with a difficult man before. She'd dated Brett, for goodness' sake!

The moment she spotted him in the doorway of her office, she knew there would be trouble. That was why she gave him the look—the universal one that signified that there was more to the situation than met the eye. After her subtle warning, Brett should've backed off and let her handle things in a professional manner, one befitting a place of business. But he hadn't.

No, instead he'd caused a huge scene in front of her coworkers at the bank that embarrassed her to no end. Not to mention that she almost lost her job over it. So yeah, she'd broken up with Brett and told him that she never wanted to see him again.

Sidney gave him a tight smile. "I'm glad you're doing well, Brett. It's good to hear."

"Thanks."

She glanced toward her house. "Well, I should probably go inside. Thank you for your help tonight. I really appreciate it."

"No problem. I'll have your car ready in the morning. Would you like me to swing by here and pick you up before I head to the shop?"

"Um, no. I think it's better if I find my own ride. Thanks for the offer though. If you can just call me to let me know when it's ready, that would be great."

"Sure."

She opened her door and climbed out of the truck. "Thanks for the ride home."

"You're welcome," he said, smiling.

Chapter Three

The next morning, Brett called Sidney to let her know her car was ready to be picked up. While he was still disappointed that she'd refused a ride to the shop, he understood that she wanted to keep her distance from him. They weren't together anymore, and she clearly wanted to keep it that way.

Just because he'd thought about her every day for the past year didn't mean she'd done the same. If the new hair and new car didn't state the obvious, then the fact that she'd been avoiding him for so long should've told him what he needed to know. She had moved on.

Serves me right. She deserves better anyway.

Though Sidney had never acted like the spoiled brat she claimed to be, Brett didn't exactly make a ton of money. That was usually what happened when you worked for someone else. But he was tired of killing himself by working twelve-hour shifts, only to collect a measly hourly wage while the owner of the business kicked his feet up on his desk and counted all the dough his employees brought in for him.

Maybe the other mechanics in the shop were okay with that, but Brett was no longer willing to work his ass off to make someone else rich. Screw that. It was just like his therapist told him. If he didn't put value on his own worth, then who the hell was going to? She probably hadn't been referring to his monetary worth, but as far as he was concerned, the same rule still applied.

So Brett picked up the phone and dialed the number Logan had given him once again, in hopes of leaving the guy from last night a message. Chances were good that he would already be on his flight, but Brett hoped that he would return his call once he landed back in Arizona...if he was even still willing to entertain an offer from Brett, of course. After Brett hadn't showed up for their scheduled meeting and wasn't able to call to let him know, he wouldn't be surprised if the guy wasn't interesting in calling him back. After all, no one wanted to do business with a flake.

But Brett had to take the chance of getting turned down. The place sounded too damn perfect to pass up.

The phone rang twice, and then the man answered. Brett hadn't expected that, since this guy should've already been on his flight back to Arizona. But apparently, the airline had somehow overbooked the flight, and this fella happened to be the unlucky bastard who got bumped from it. Though that probably sucked a lot for him, it was great news for Brett, and he planned on taking full advantage of the situation.

The guy wasn't at all happy with Brett for not showing up or calling last night, which was apparent in his attitude. But Brett managed to keep his cool. Once he explained what had happened and how he'd left his phone at the garage, the man said he completely understood that things sometimes happened out of anyone's control. Maybe getting bumped from his flight had given him that perspective. Or maybe he was just a nice guy. Because then he offered to show Brett the lot later in the afternoon since his next flight wasn't leaving until tomorrow.

Brett couldn't believe his luck. Just as he opened his mouth to accept the man's offer, Sidney strolled through the bay door wearing beige slacks, a cream-colored top, and a pearl necklace that dipped inside her shirt between her breasts. Momentarily distracted, all Brett could think was, "God, yes!" But when the man on the other end of the line chuckled, Brett had no doubt he'd said the words aloud.

Feeling like an idiot, he promised not to leave the guy waiting once again and then hurried to get off the phone before heading to the counter, where Sidney stood waiting for him. "Hey," he said, staring into her rich brown eyes to keep his gaze from following the trail of shiny white beads leading inside her shirt. "Your car is out back next to my truck. I didn't want to leave it up here, where someone could accidentally put a ding in it."

She flashed him a bright smile. "Thanks. I always worry about that too. So how long did it take you to fix it?"

"Well, not counting the time it took to tow your car back to the garage, I'd say about four hours. An hour or so per tire. By the way, you have the most stubborn lug nuts I've ever seen on a vehicle."

She cringed. "Oh no! That practically took you all night. Did you get any sleep?"

He shrugged. "Yeah, some. When I finished up with your car earlier this morning, I crawled into the backseat of my truck and slept for a few hours."

"God, I'm so sorry. I didn't realize it was going to be such a huge task to get those things off."

"It happens. Sometimes a big job turns out to be a small one, and little jobs turn out to be a mechanic's worst nightmare. You just never really know until you start working on something."

She grinned. "So you're saying this job was your worst nightmare?"

"Not really. But if you had heard the way I was cussing up a storm this morning while trying to get those damn nuts off, you probably wouldn't believe a word I just said."

Sidney laughed as she pulled out her debit card. "I'm just glad you managed to fix it. How much do I owe you?"

Brett pulled her keys from his pocket and slid them across the counter in front of her. "Nothing. You're good to go."

She shook her head and shoved her debit card toward him. "What? No way. I'm paying you for the work you did."

He put the card back into her hand and closed her fingers around it. "I don't want your money, Sid."

"Then what the hell do you want?"

His fingers tightened around hers. Hell, that was a loaded question if he'd ever heard one. He grinned for a second as several sexy scenarios ran through his head, and then he forced himself to blow out a slow breath and behave himself. "Look, Sid. The way I see it, I owed you one after how I screwed up our relationship. So just let me do something nice for you, and we'll call it even."

"That's not us being even. *I* broke up with *you*, remember? So this would put you one ahead of me."

Brett rolled his eyes. "Humor me, okay?"

But she wasn't having it. Sidney shook her head adamantly and tried to hand him her card once again. "No, I don't feel right about you working for free after hours. And I'm certain your boss wouldn't like it either. After you went out of your way to help me last night, the least I can do is pay you for your time. Besides, you don't owe me any favors. What happened between us is in the past, and that's where it's going to stay. It has nothing to do with this business transaction."

He cringed at her words but covered it by glancing at his watch. It was already eleven o'clock, and he had only a few hours before he had to be at the car lot. The last thing he wanted to do was spend them arguing with her. "Sid, I don't have time to argue with you about this. I have somewhere I have to be in a few hours, and I still need to clean up and grab lunch. Call it a favor or a random act of kindness or whatever you want, but I'm not taking your money. Got it?"

Brett didn't wait for her to respond, since chances were good that she would've just continued to argue with him. So instead, he turned and walked away. He didn't want her to pay him for his help, damn it. He hadn't done any of it for the money. Didn't she get that? He had done it because he loved her with every fiber of his being.

And that wasn't something you could put a price on.

* * *

Sidney watched in disbelief as Brett walked away.

He stopped to talk to another worker briefly before he moved toward the small sink across the room and began soaping up his grimy hands. She had a profile view of him, which meant all he had to do was turn his head slightly in order to see her. But as far as she could tell, he hadn't so much as looked back once, and she had a feeling he was avoiding her on purpose.

As if ignoring me is going to work. He should know better than that.

She stood there watching him scrub the dirt away for so long that her gaze accidentally drifted to his left bicep, which was flexing and tightening against the sleeve of his dark blue T-shirt with every motion. She swallowed the hard knot forming in her throat. Damn, he'd really bulked up.

Sidney was so mesmerized by the movements of his muscles that she didn't even notice when another worker approached the counter. "Can I help you, miss?"

Startled, she jumped and grasped her chest, turning to see the young worker whom Brett had stopped to talk to on his way to the sink. She had met some of the other mechanics in the past, but this one must've been hired sometime in the past year. "Oh goodness, you scared me."

The young guy grinned. "Sorry about that."

Yeah, he looked real sorry with that huge smile on his face. "It's okay. I should've been paying closer attention to my surroundings."

He motioned across the room to the sink where Brett was still standing. "I saw you staring. Were you waiting for Brett to help you with something? Because if so, I hate to tell you this, but he's not on the clock today."

"What do you mean? He's right there."

"Yep, but it's his day off."

Oh great. Now she felt like a real jerk for not paying him. "But what about the car he worked on early this morning?"

The young worker shook his head and waved his hand in the air. "That was just him helping out a buddy. Besides, I'm pretty sure he just wanted to get a look under the hood. It's a sweet-ass ride." She grinned with pride, but he must've thought it was the curse word that gave her that reaction because he followed up with, "Oh, sorry. Pardon my French."

Sidney giggled. "I've heard the word *ass* before. Even used it a few times myself," she said with a wink. "And you're absolutely right. It *is* a sweet-ass ride."

The worker laughed and nodded in agreement. "Are you sure there's nothing I can do for you, miss?"

"No, I'll just...wait around until I can have a word with Brett." He couldn't possibly ignore her—or wash his hands—forever.

"All right. But you better do it soon. He's about to leave. Has some appointment later to look at a used car lot that went up for sale recently."

Her head snapped up. "What in the world would Brett want with a used car lot?"

"He's hoping to buy it and turn it into his new auto repair business."

Her eyes widened. "Brett's opening his own garage? Oh my God. That's wonderful news!" He had told her about that particular dream of his a long time ago, but she hadn't known he was actively trying to fulfill it. Good for him.

The worker nodded in confirmation. "Yeah, he's working on it. But he's still not sure he'll qualify for the loan yet. I think he's hesitating to fill out the forms."

She gazed across the room and spotted Brett drying his hands off. "Really? Well, that's…uh, interesting. I might be able to help him with that."

When Brett finally glanced up, she motioned for him to come back over. But he shook his head. So Sidney did what she had to. She rounded the counter and headed into the garage, straight toward Brett.

One of his brows rose in question. "What do you think you're doing?"

"I need to talk to you."

"Not here, you're not. You can't be back here. Didn't you read the signs?" He pointed to the closest one on the wall nearby. "It says no customers allowed in the work area."

She grinned smugly. "Good thing I'm not a customer then."

He tilted his head in confusion. "Huh? How do you figure?"

"Customers pay for your service, right? But you wouldn't let me pay you. So that means I'm not one of your customers." That was her story, and she was sticking to it.

He gave her a *yeah, right* look and pointed to a different sign. "Well, this one says 'Employees Only,' and the last I knew, you don't work here."

She shrugged. "Apparently, neither do you. At least not today. Why didn't you tell me it was your day off?"

"Because it didn't matter." He glanced around the garage. "Who the hell told you it was my day off anyway?"

She ignored his question. "It does matter when you're working on my car and not getting paid for it."

Brett waved his hand dismissively. "It's not a big deal. Let it go already," he said, walking past her toward a rear exit.

Sidney followed him outside. "Fine. If you won't let me pay you for your time, then let's at least make a trade. You did something for me, now it's my turn to do something for you."

His feet stalled beneath him, and he turned around slowly to face her. His heated eyes resembled the blue flame on a welding torch, and they zeroed in directly on her. "Sidney, if you're even close to insinuating that you'd sleep with me in exchange for fixing your car, you're seriously going to piss me off."

Wait, what? She blinked at him in confusion, not understanding where the hell he'd gotten that cockamamie idea from. "Oh dear Lord, of course not. That's not at all what I was getting at." But she couldn't help giggling. If he thought having sex with him would be doing *him* a favor, he was seriously underestimating his skills in the bedroom.

Her reaction only annoyed him more. "What's so funny?"

"Uh, nothing." She bit her lip to contain the laughter bubbling in her throat. "I just meant that I wanted to help you get that loan you're going to apply for so you can buy that used car lot and open your garage."

His eyes widened. "Jesus. How do you know all of that? Just who the hell have you been talking to? My sister? No, I bet it was that stupid husband of hers. He can't keep a secret to save his own life."

Sidney chuckled. "Actually, I heard it inside while I was talking to one of the workers at the counter. I didn't know it was supposed to be a secret."

"It had to be Kyle."

She shrugged. "I don't know his name. Young guy with a big smile. Super friendly. Piercings in both ears."

"Yep, that's him. He's a good kid and all, but he spreads gossip faster than a teenager."

"Well, I'm glad he told me. I think it's great that you're finally going after your dream of opening your own garage. You've wanted that for so long. I just wish you had told me the good news yourself last night."

He shook his head. "There's nothing to tell. I'm not even sure if I'll get the loan, and I still have to check out the property to see if it's worth the asking price."

Did she dare ask? "Uh, so which bank are you planning to use?"

His eyes met hers. "Not yours, if that's what you're thinking. I didn't want to put you in a weird position since we have a past."

"I appreciate that, but it wouldn't have been a problem. I take my job as a lending officer seriously, and the loan process would've been the same for you as any other client."

He nodded in agreement. "I figured as much. But I think I'll go ahead and stick with the other bank I chose. I wouldn't want to get approved for a loan through you and anyone in town to question your integrity just because we used to be a couple. I think it's better this way."

"That's fine. But at least let me help you out by giving you some tips on how best to get approved for a loan. If you want, I can even look over your finances and credit score to make sure everything is in order and walk you through the documents you'll need to fill out. Being prepared could really help your chances of getting that approval."

"You don't mind?"

"Of course not. You did me a favor, and I'd like to repay it. Do you have mobile banking on your phone so that we can bring up your statements online?"

"Yeah."

"Good. Well, if you have some time right now, maybe we could grab a bite to eat and go over your records." She motioned to his favorite fast-food eatery—a little locally owned hot dog stand across the street from the shop. "I know how much you love that place. Why don't we just go there?"

"You want me to go to lunch...with you?"

Heat crept up her neck. "Um, yeah. I mean...as friends only, of course."

He seemed to hesitate with an answer, which only made her feel even more self-conscious about her curvier figure. Was he afraid people would see them and assume they'd gotten back together? And if so, why did she even care? It wasn't like it was any of their business anyway.

Finally, he gave a nod of approval. "All right. Let's do it then."

Jeez. Took him long enough.

Chapter Four

Brett had found a small table off to the side where they could have some privacy during lunch as they went over his finances and discussed his credit report. It was bad enough that Kyle was spreading his business around town. He didn't need the two of them doing it inadvertently as well.

They started off making polite small talk as they looked over the documents on his phone, but it wasn't long before they were sharing a few laughs and reminiscing about old times. And that only had him missing Sidney more than ever.

He'd been reluctant to accept her offer, knowing every minute he spent with her was only messing with his head and giving him false hope of renewing their relationship. But the temptation of spending more time with her was just too much to resist.

Sidney had always oozed warmth and goodness, and he missed having her in his life. Even though she was very clear about their "friends only" status and showed no interest in anything other than repaying a favor, he'd take what he could get. Because he'd rather have her in his life as a friend than nothing at all. And if she could help him get that loan for the garage, then that was just an added bonus.

Caught up in their conversation, neither of them seemed to notice that they had a visitor approaching until the man was practically on top of her and already leaning in for a hug. "Hey, Sidney. How are you?"

Her mouth fell open, but she managed to snap it shut in time to hug him back. "Oh, um... hey, Charles."

Brett didn't miss her uneasy tone or the way she cut her eyes over to him, as if she was worried about what he would say after seeing another man hug her. But she was a free agent, and it wasn't up to him. She could damn well hug whomever the hell she wanted, and there was nothing he could do about it. Sure, he didn't like it, but that didn't mean he had to vocalize his feelings.

Besides, Charles wasn't at all Sidney's type. He looked like a golf nerd in his pink polo shirt and khaki shorts, as if he was some kind of country club caddy or maybe a frat boy. He was tall, dark, and probably good-looking by most women's standards, and he had a perfect set of brilliant white teeth. But he didn't at all have that rough edge and intensity that he knew Sidney loved so much.

Sidney glanced at Brett and then back to her friend. "Uh, so what are you doing here?"

Charles shrugged lazily. "Someone said this place sells the best hot dogs in town so I thought I'd come try them out. But I didn't know you were here. I was sorry we had to postpone dinner last night because of a flat tire, but I'm looking forward to our date tonight."

Wait, what? Brett's head snapped in Sidney's direction, and she immediately cringed. Even though she tried to smile a little, the guilty look on her face told Brett everything he needed to know. She'd had a date last night. Damn.

He guessed this explained what she had been doing out there all alone and why she had dressed up. He hadn't even thought to ask her since he figured that she would've told him if she wanted him to know. Apparently, she hadn't.

"Um, yeah. Me too," Sidney said quietly.

"I didn't even see your car out front," Charles told her.

She nodded. "That's because it's not. It's still parked at the garage across the street."

Charles shaded his eyes like a pansy and gazed across the road. "Sounds like you need a new mechanic. How hard can it be to change a flat tire?"

Irritation swept through Brett, and he ground his teeth together to keep from saying anything.

Sidney's face paled instantly, and she sat a little straighter. "Uh, actually, the car is fixed already. I just need to go pick it up when I'm done."

Charles nodded. "Well, that's good. Hopefully they don't charge you an arm and a leg. Mechanics are crooked like that, you know?"

Brett blew out a breath and counted to ten in his head. Charles was lucky that Brett was seeing a therapist who had given him tools to control himself in this kind of situation. Otherwise, Brett would've already ripped off this guy's arm and leg and beat him with them. The dickhead.

The three of them sat in uncomfortable silence before Sidney finally said, "Well, I guess it's time for me to get going. I've got some errands to run before I head home."

Charles smiled. "Same here. Hopefully you won't have any more problems with that tire. Of course, that all depends on whether the mechanic knew what the hell he was doing when he fixed it."

Brett rose from his chair, and Sidney stiffened instantly, clearly worried about what he planned to do. Charles was completely oblivious though and didn't even seem to notice the thick tension hovering in the air around them.

Of course Brett didn't like knowing that the woman he loved was dating again. Who the hell would? But he was sickened to no end as he watched her stiffen, all because she wasn't sure how he would react to the news. He'd done that to her, damn it.

In the past, he'd always gone off the deep end. God, he was such an idiot. No wonder the woman left him. At least now he had finally learned to recognize his insecurities for what they were and had learned to control himself. In fact, he was more confident in his behavior than ever, and he was extremely proud of the progress he'd made over the past year. He only wished he'd made these changes sooner. Maybe then he wouldn't have lost her.

Especially to this guy, of all people. Christ.

But Brett didn't want to draw this out any longer than he had to. So he sucked in a slow, deep breath and steadied himself as he offered his hand to the other man. "It was nice meeting you, Charles. I'm Brett, one of Sidney's friends."

The guy shook his hand. "Great to meet you too, Brett. Sidney's one heck of a woman, isn't she?"

Brett glanced over at Sidney, who was sitting there with wide eyes and an open mouth. "That she is," he said, smiling at her. "Thanks for all your help today, Sid. You two have fun on your date tonight."

Then he did something that surprised even him. He turned and headed back to the garage to get his truck, leaving the woman he loved alone with another man.

* * *

After dinner at the Gypsy Cantina, Sidney slid into the passenger seat of Charles's car and stared out the window. She'd been quiet most of the night and was certain that she'd been terrible company as far as first dates went. But she couldn't seem to stop thinking about Brett.

Actually, she didn't know what to think. There was no mistaking the shocked look in his eyes when Charles announced that he and Sidney had a date. Brett's head had swiveled in her direction so fast that she was surprised it hadn't fallen off his shoulders. She hadn't really planned on mentioning the date to Brett, but once it was brought up, it wasn't like she could keep it from him.

Thanks a lot, Charles.

Unsure of how Brett would react, Sidney nearly panicked when he suddenly rose to his feet and faced the other man head-on. Her breath had stalled in her lungs, and her nerves had fired a warning shot to each of her limbs in case she needed to react quickly. Even though Brett had told her that he was in therapy and has changed his ways, she'd seen him in action too many times in the past to expect anything but the worst.

But then he'd surprised her.

Maybe it's true. Maybe he really has changed, after all.

After saying good-bye to Charles at the hot dog stand earlier in the day, she'd headed directly for the shop to talk to Brett. She didn't know why she felt the need to explain herself, but she did. Too bad she didn't get the chance. By the time she arrived, Brett had already left.

She'd worried that might happen, damn it. Now she couldn't stop wondering what it had all meant. Had he been upset about her date? Or did he not care at all? Maybe that was it. Maybe he was completely over her and didn't give a damn who she went out with. After all, he had told her to have a good time on her date tonight. God. Had he really meant that? She just didn't know.

"It's starting to rain," Charles told her, turning on his wipers to clear the splatters of rain drops from his windshield. "I don't think it's supposed to get bad until later tonight though."

"That's good," Sidney replied absently.

"You okay? You're not sick or anything, are you?"

She badly wanted to fake some stomach pains and

ask him to take her home, but she couldn't bring herself to do it. "I'm fine. I think the weather is just making me a little tired." She crossed her mental fingers, hoping he would take that as a hint.

No such luck.

Charles winked at her. "Don't worry. I have something that is going to wake you right up. I hope you're thirsty," he said, pulling into a parking lot.

Sidney glanced through the windshield and gazed up at the Bottoms Up sign on the front of the bar, and her stomach twisted. As Charles pulled into an empty slot, she quickly scanned the surrounding vehicles until her eyes landed on a red pickup a few rows over. Damn it. Not only did Brett's best friend and sister own this bar, but his truck was in the parking lot. The last thing she wanted to do was make anyone uncomfortable...including herself.

She wiped at her brow. "Um, I don't know about this."

"Oh, come on. It'll be fun. We can grab a few drinks and cause a bit of a ruckus."

Exactly what I'm afraid of.

While Brett had been nice to Charles during lunch, she didn't want to push her luck. One incident of Brett controlling himself was hardly what she considered proof that he had changed his ways. He might've just been on his best behavior earlier. Who knew? But if he was inside drinking, that might make things a little more tense. Alcohol always had a way of complicating things.

Still, it was a small town, and they wouldn't be able

to avoid each other forever. The lug nut incident proved that already. They would both eventually have to get used to seeing each other around, even if they were with someone else…

Oh, dear God. She hadn't even considered that before since she'd been so busy avoiding him. But now that she had, the thought of Brett with another woman made her chest ache. She peered up at the bar again and bit her lip, wondering if he was inside with a date at that very moment.

Unfortunately, there was only one way to find out.

She sighed. "All right, let's do it."

Chapter Five

Brett hadn't planned to stay long.

He'd stopped by the bar only long enough to tell Logan and Valerie all about the used car lot that he'd checked out earlier in the day. Beyond needing a new paint job and a little fixing up, Brett couldn't dream of a better place to open his garage. And that alone had him dying to rush home and fill out the loan application. But his sister and her husband insisted that he hang out and tell them more about it. So he had.

Although he was still worried about not getting approved for the loan, they both seemed genuinely happy for him and said that, if he didn't, they would be happy to cosign for him. His chest swelled with emotion. It was nice having family in his corner who believed in him and had his back. The only thing that could make his night any more perfect was—

As if on cue, the entrance door to the bar swung open, and Sidney stepped into view. Brett's gaze flickered over her, and his throat tightened. She was wearing black slacks paired with a white button-down. He didn't know how she did it, but she always managed to look like she'd just come from a business meeting. Maybe it was strange, but something about that always aroused him.

But that problem corrected itself when he noticed the guy behind her. His stomach dropped, and the awesome mood he was in went to shit. The last thing he wanted to do was spend the rest of the night watching the woman he loved canoodling with some other guy. Fuck that.

Knowing Logan was in the storeroom breaking down liquor boxes, Brett began making his way to that side of the bar. He made sure to give Sidney and her guest a wide berth and stayed on the opposite line of foot traffic to keep from being spotted. He didn't need another uncomfortable meeting like they'd had earlier in the day. If you asked him, once had been enough.

But before he made it to the hallway in which the storeroom was located, someone grasped his arm. "Hey, where are you going?"

He glanced over his shoulder at Valerie and then turned to face her. "I'm going to see if your husband needs any help."

"Oh, he's probably close to being finished by now."

Brett shrugged. "That's all right. I'll just go hang out with him then. Anything as long as it gets me out of this room."

Valerie's eyes filled with concern. "Why? What's wrong? Did something happen?"

"Yeah," he said, grabbing her shoulders and turning

her toward the area where Sidney was sitting with her date. "That happened."

"Oh. That sucks."

"My sentiments exactly."

His sister glanced back at him. "Did she see you?"

"Not yet. I was trying to escape before that happened."

Valerie crossed her arms. "Go on then. I'll cover for you, if necessary. I can always say that I borrowed your truck."

He squeezed her shoulder and smiled. "Thanks, Val. This is why you're my favorite sister."

She laughed. "The competition isn't real stiff. I'm your only sister, dork."

Brett grinned at her and then slipped down the hallway to get out of sight. He didn't look at it as running from his problems. It was more like he was removing himself from a difficult situation rather than reacting to it.

He'd learned that in therapy.

Over the past year, his counselor had given him some great tools that really improved his overall behavior and attitude. Like when he was struggling with a difficult situation, she'd suggested that he head to the gym and take his frustrations out on a boxing bag or work up a good sweat on the weights. He'd taken her advice, and not only had it enhanced his body, but working out had become therapeutic when something was troubling him.

Like seeing Sidney with another man.

Unfortunately, he didn't have access to a gym this late in the evening. But the good news was that he now knew how to handle the uncomfortable situation like a grown man rather than the immature idiot he once was.

Brett shoved open the door to the storeroom and found Logan sitting on a crate. "Hey, dillhole. Need any help?"

"With what? Sitting on my ass?"

"You're supposed to be working. I know you don't know what that is, but I thought maybe by now you would've figured it out." Brett shrugged one shoulder. "Guess not."

Logan grinned wide. "Says the guy who shows up *after* the work is done."

Brett sat down on a crate and leaned back against the wall, making himself comfortable. He would probably be here for a while. "Only proves I'm smarter than you."

"And lazier too," Logan said with a chuckle. He kicked his feet up on the box in front of him. "So what are you doing back here? Did your sister get tired of you already?"

"Not this time," Brett told him, smirking.

"Then what's up?"

"Nothing."

Logan gave him a *yeah, right* look. "I know you better than that, Brett. Start talking."

He sighed. "Fine. Sidney's in the bar."

"All right. What's wrong with that?"

"She's on a date."

"Oh." Logan rubbed his chin as if he were in deep thought. "So I take it that you're hiding back here to keep from running into them?"

"No, I'm avoiding them to keep from running into them."

Logan squinted at him. "Isn't that the same thing?"

"Probably, but saying I'm avoiding them sounds a lot better. Doesn't make me feel like such a loser."

"Oh, come on. You're not a loser, man. You can't help how you feel." He leaned forward, his face serious. "Does she at least know that you're still in love with her?"

Brett shook his head. "No. I didn't tell her."

"What? Why the hell not? What are you waiting for?"

"Logan, she avoided me for almost an entire year, and now she's on a date with another man. What would be the point? She's obviously over me and has already moved on."

Logan's eyes widened. "So that's it? You're not even going to fight for her?" When he didn't get a response, he shook his head with annoyance. "God, you're such a loser."

Brett couldn't help grinning. "I thought you just said I wasn't one."

"Yeah, well, I lied."

* * *

Sidney should've known better.

She had a feeling that coming into the bar would be one giant mistake, and she was absolutely right. She and her date had been sitting at the bar for nearly two hours, and she hadn't seen a single sign of Brett beyond his truck in the parking lot. And that only made her consider that he'd met someone and gone home with her in her own vehicle. Why else would he leave his behind?

She scanned the entire bar again, hoping to spot him in some dark corner, but he was nowhere to be seen. Damn it. Why was she torturing herself like this?

Charles stumbled toward her, his eyes glazed over. "I still can't find my keys," he slurred drunkenly.

Great.

Instead of watching for Brett for the past few hours, she should've been keeping an eye on her date, who apparently drank like a fish. After having a few too many, he was now in no condition to drive. Which really didn't matter since he couldn't find the car keys that he'd lost somewhere in the bar anyway.

Sidney caught sight of Valerie passing by and flagged her down. "Hey, Valerie. Did anyone turn in a set of car keys? We seem to have lost some."

"Hmm, I can double-check with my head bartender, but I haven't heard about anyone finding any car keys. I'll let you know if I do though."

"Okay, thanks. But if they turn up, can you just hang on to them until tomorrow? It's getting late, and I think we're about to leave."

"No problem. But how are you getting home? Do you need me to call you a cab? We have the taxi company on speed dial."

She nodded. "Sure, that would be great. Thanks."

Charles placed a hand on his stomach and hunched over a little. "I don't feel so good."

Sidney glanced at Valerie. "Uh, maybe we should

step outside and get some fresh air while we wait on that cab."

"I'll go call them right now and tell them to look for you two out front."

"Thanks, Val."

Sidney grasped Charles's arm and led him out the exit. It was still sprinkling a little so they stayed under the covered area and sat on a wooden bench. He immediately leaned forward with his elbows propped on his knees and hung his head. Guess those four Irish Car Bombs he'd chugged had hit him all at once. Idiot.

She was seriously annoyed. Not only had Charles drunk himself to intoxication like a frat boy at a kegger, but he hadn't seemed at all concerned about how she was going to get home since he'd picked her up. And what really frustrated her and had her stewing in silence was the one thought that replayed over and over in her mind.

Brett would never have done this.

A few minutes later, Valerie stepped outside. "Just checking on you two. I would've came out sooner, but I went around asking all the bartenders and waitresses if anyone turned in a set of keys. No luck yet."

"That's okay. I'm sure they'll turn up at some point." She'd barely finished the sentence when a pair of headlights turned into the parking lot. "Oh, good. There's our ride."

Sidney helped Charles to his feet and walked him out to the sidewalk as the cab pulled to a stop in front of them. Light rain pelted the top of her head, but she opened the door and waited patiently as her date stumbled forward and crawled inside.

She turned back to Valerie, who was still standing under the covered area and waved. "Thanks, Val."

Once Valerie had waved back, Sidney ran around to the other side of the taxi to hurry and get out of the rain. But when she threw open the door, she froze in place. A horrible retching sound came from inside the car, and the rancid smell of hot wiener smacked her in the face. Oh, God.

She'd never been able to handle the sounds and smell of someone throwing up and immediately covered her nose with her hand. She liked hot dogs, but not the kind that had been partially digested and thrown back up. Gross. To make matters worse, Charles had thrown up on her part of the seat. Great. There was no way she was going to sit in vomit, much less smell that odor all the way home. No doubt she would end up puking herself.

She sighed and glanced to the driver, who looked as annoyed as she felt. "Um, I'll just wait for the next taxi."

"I am the next taxi, lady. It's a small town. Not enough business to run more than one taxi a night."

Ah, crap. "Okay, then I'll just find another way home." She pulled out a twenty-dollar bill and passed it to the driver as she rattled off Charles's address. "This should cover his fare." Then she handed him another twenty. "And this is for your trouble. Sorry about the mess."

The driver shoved the money in his shirt pocket and grinned. "Wouldn't be the first time that has happened. But thanks for the tip. I appreciate it."

"No problem." She gazed at her date in the backseat. "Charles, I hope you feel better soon."

He only groaned in response so she shut the car door, and the cab pulled away.

Valerie looked as confused as ever. "Hey, what happened? Why didn't you get into the cab?"

"Because Charles decided to throw up all over the backseat."

"Oh no. Well, you could've ridden in the front seat, I suppose."

"And smell that all the way home? No thank you. I'm just going to walk."

Valerie shook her head. "But it's late. And it's cold and rainy."

Sidney shrugged. "It's not that bad. I'll live."

"I have a better solution. Stay right here, and I'll get you a ride home."

"Val, you don't have to do that. I don't want to trouble anyone."

"No trouble at all. Trust me, he won't mind."

She sighed. "Okay, but if Logan's busy, then don't bother him. I only live a mile or so down the road. I don't mind walking."

"No worries," she said with a grin. "I promise I won't bother Logan."

Valerie disappeared inside the bar, and a few moments later, the door to the bar flew open so hard that Sidney thought it might break from its hinges. Brett stood in the doorway, his face twisted with anger and his hands fisted at his sides.

She didn't know why he was so mad, but she'd forgotten how intimidating he could look when he was worked into a frenzy. Although she'd never felt intimidated by him in the past herself, she could understand why others would feel that way. And just seeing him like that again only made her doubt his earlier declaration.

Changed man, my ass. Looks like the same old Brett as always.

Annoyed that she had started to believe him, she crossed her arms defensively. “What are you doing out here?”

Valerie stepped out from behind him with a huge grin spreading her face. “He’s your ride home.”

Chapter Six

Damn his sister.

When Valerie had showed up in the storeroom and told Brett that Sidney needed him right away, she'd scared the hell out of him. The panic that had run through him when he thought she was hurt or in trouble had sent him flying down the hallway and through the bar like a runaway freight train. He hadn't been able to get to her fast enough.

Valerie could've just told him that Sidney needed a ride home. It's not like he minded. "What happened to your date?"

Sidney didn't reply right away so Valerie answered for her. "He got wasted, lost his car keys, threw up in the cab, and then he left."

Brett's eyes narrowed onto Sidney. "He just left you here?"

She shook her head. "Um, not exactly. I volunteered not to go."

He couldn't help grinning. Sidney always had a weak stomach when it came to certain smells. She'd once gone through four different car fresheners before she found one that didn't make her sick to her stomach. "I can take you home."

She shook her head. "It's okay. I can walk. It's not that far."

"I was heading home anyway. It's on the way. I don't mind. Besides, you really shouldn't be out walking this late at night. Especially in the rain. It's not safe."

Sidney sighed, as if she didn't seem too happy about his offer. "Okay, fine."

Valerie smiled. "Good, it's settled then. You two have fun," she said, heading back inside the bar.

He shook his head. Like it wasn't obvious what his sister was trying to do. But he didn't need her interfering in his love life. Especially since she hadn't appreciated it when he'd done it to her. Guess now Valerie was giving him a dose of his own medicine. The little matchmaker.

Brett and Sidney ran to his truck and quickly climbed into the cab to get out of the rain, which had started coming down faster. He offered to turn the heat on for her, but Sidney told him not to bother worrying about her. He didn't know why she was so irritated with him for giving her a ride home, but that was definitely the vibe he was picking up from her.

To be honest, he wasn't in the best of moods himself. While he was still irritated that her date had gotten drunk and left her to fend for herself, he was glad that he was the one who was making sure she got safely home…and alone. He didn't know how long she'd been seeing this other guy, but the thought of her being intimate with another man was eating at him. Not that he could tell her that.

They drove in silence. When he pulled up at the curb, he shut the engine off, and the heavy rain instantly blurred the windshield with a sheet of water. He gazed over at her. "I'll walk you to your door."

She shook her head persistently. "No need. I'll be fine."

"All right."

An awkward tension sat between them, but she didn't move to get out of the car. Instead, she gazed up at him and said, "Where were you tonight?"

"At the bar."

"I know that but... where at the bar? I didn't see you in there."

Damn it. Why was she asking him that? Did she think he was there spying on her or something? "What does it matter?"

"I just... want to know."

He hadn't intended on telling her any of this, but he refused to lie to her. "The moment I saw you and your date come into the bar, I hid out in the storeroom."

She blinked at him. "Why would you do that?"

"Because I couldn't bear the thought of another man kissing or touching you... the way I used to."

She closed her eyes. "Brett, I..." Her voice trailed off.

His chest tightened, and he cringed. "It's okay. You don't have to say anything." Because hearing her say she couldn't be with him again would hurt just as much now as it had a year ago. "I understand."

"Do you?"

"Sure," he said, trying to soften his voice to hide the pain.

He sighed inwardly. He was pining away for a woman who clearly wanted nothing to do with him. And sadly, it was his own fault. He could kick himself in the ass for ruining things with her, but that wouldn't make him feel any better about it. So, as a man resigned to his own fate, he instead would do the one thing he really didn't want to do. He would wish her the best and let her go.

Brett cleared his throat. "Look, I don't know how long you've been seeing this new guy, but if he's the one who makes you happy, then I wish you both all the best. That's all I ever wanted for you."

A look of confusion warped her shocked face, and she shook her head at him. "I... uh, don't know what to say. I thought—"

"You don't have to say anything back, Sid. I just wanted you to know that I want the best for you. Always." He glanced at the windshield. "The rain stopped. You better get inside before it starts up again."

"Um, okay," she said, blinking at him.

"Good night, Sid."

When Brett leaned over the arm rest to give her a peck on the cheek, Sidney turned her face up to his and kissed him directly on the mouth. The gesture was so unexpected that it froze him in place. Her lips were touching his, but he was so stunned by it that all he could do was sit there like a damn corpse. What the hell was wrong with him?

The moment Sidney didn't get a favorable response, she pulled away and mumbled an awkward apology. He could tell how embarrassed she was that he hadn't kissed her back, but before he could explain himself, she reached for the door handle so she could escape the humiliation she felt.

But he wasn't about to let that happen. Not after she'd kissed him.

Brett reached for her and pulled her back to him before ratcheting her up in his arms and covering her mouth with his. Her lips parted in surprise, and he took advantage of the moment by thrusting his tongue inside and deepening the kiss. God, he'd missed this. The taste of her lips. The scent of her skin. The feel of her soft, curvy body pressing against his. Lord help him, he couldn't get enough of her.

And apparently, she felt the same way.

Her tongue rolled against his with a hunger he hadn't felt before, and her insistent hands roamed over him with a passionate fury. If it hadn't been for the middle console keeping them apart from the waist down, he was pretty damn sure she would've already straddled him.

"God, I want you," she whispered, nipping at his bottom lip as she pulled at his belt to undo it.

Stupid fucking console.

Brett was prepared to rip the damn thing out of his truck right then and there, but then he remembered that she'd just been on a date with another man. Damn it. Talk about a mood killer.

He was so confused that he didn't know what to do.

He thought she had moved on with her life and gotten over him. After all, in the past few days, she'd refused his help, told him they were just friends, and gone out with another guy. What else was he supposed to think? Yet now she was kissing him and trying to take off his clothes.

She almost had his belt completely unbuckled, and he knew that if her hand went anywhere inside his pants, it was all over. There was no way he could—or would—stop things at that point.

He put his hand on top of hers and pulled his mouth back slightly. "Sid, wait."

"Why? Do you want to get into the backseat first?"

Holy hell. He closed his eyes. *Be strong, man. You can do this.*

"No. I think we need to talk first."

She trailed her tongue over his lips. "No, we don't. Let's not ruin anything by talking."

He licked his lips, tasting her on them. "I'm serious, Sid. What is this?"

"It's called sex," she said, blowing out an aggravated breath. "But I'm pretty sure you already knew that."

"Look, things have changed between us, and I don't want anyone to get hurt. I think we should slow this down before that happens."

The stunned look on her face made him feel bad, but she hadn't said anything about them getting back together, and the last thing he wanted was a meaningless one-night stand with her. Sidney had never been that kind of woman, and he sure as hell wasn't going to treat her that way.

Yeah, he'd slept with her before. Sure, he would probably kick himself in the ass later for not allowing himself to have her. But she'd just been out with another man, for goodness' sake. So at this point, he needed to make sure she was all in. Because *he* definitely was.

He'd lost her once and didn't want that to happen again. If that meant taking things slow and showing her that she could trust him to be the man she needed—the only one she needed—then that was exactly what he was going to do.

He gave her an encouraging smile. "Why don't we go out to dinner tomorrow night so we can spend some time together? It's been a while since we did that."

"Uh, okay. I guess so."

Brett nodded. "Great. I'll pick the place."

Because it was going to have to be somewhere public where he wouldn't be tempted to rip her damn clothes off and slide her under him.

* * *

Sidney didn't know what the hell was going on.

She'd spent the entire night lying awake, wondering why Brett had put the brakes on when it came to last night's make-out session and whether her new figure had anything to do with it. After she'd offered herself up on a platter and he still refused her, what else could it be?

He'd said he wanted to take things slow. But weren't things like that something guys said when they weren't all that interested? She'd read *He's Just Not That into*

You before. Even saw the movie. Now she felt like she was living the scenario in her head.

If he'd rather take you to dinner than to bed, he's just not that into you.

Then again, this was Brett she was talking about. *Her* Brett. And he'd never once treated her like that before. So maybe he really did want to take things slow like he'd said. And if that was the case, she appreciated the notion. Honestly, that was probably for the best anyway.

She'd called Charles that afternoon to let him know that Valerie had texted her that she'd found his keys and he could pick them up at the bar. Then she broke the news that she just wasn't that into him...except she did it much more nicely than that. He hadn't really seemed all that worried about it, which actually was a little insulting since he had been the one who'd acted like such a dumbass on their date.

But whatever. At least she wasn't nursing a hangover. Karma sometimes had a way of righting the wrongs of the world.

The faint roar of an engine rumbled in the air, and her heart flatlined.

That had to be Brett since she wasn't expecting anyone else, but he'd arrived a few minutes early. She glanced in her full-length mirror and smoothed the wrinkles out of her white silk blouse and black pencil skirt before sliding into her strappy heels and heading to the door.

The moment she opened it, her breath caught in her throat. Brett leaned against the doorjamb with both hands, wearing a pair of distressed jeans, a fitted black Henley, and a pair of steel-toed work boots. Even the wicked smile he wore screamed of a bad boy who was about to deflower a virgin... which only made her wish she was still a virgin.

"Hey, Sid. You look great."

She smiled. "Thanks. So do you."

He nodded a thank-you. "Ready to go?"

"Yep." She waited for him to move aside and then stepped out the door, pulling it shut behind her. "So where are we going to dinner?"

"You'll see," he told her, grasping her hand and leading her out to his truck.

A thrill coursed through her. He was holding her hand like he always had, which she thought was a pretty good sign. Or was that just her being ridiculously naive and reading into something all because she hoped that it meant more than it did?

Jeez. Stop it. Or you'll drive yourself crazy all night long.

Brett opened her door for her but gazed at her with a funny look on his face. "Everything okay?"

Crap. He was picking up on her nervousness. "Yeah, I'm fine."

"You sure?"

"Of course," she said, climbing into the cab. "Let's go eat."

He nodded and shut her door before strolling around to the driver's side and getting in. They made small talk as he drove, although he didn't take her hand again like she'd hoped he would. But he was driving so she tried not to read into that too.

When he pulled into the Gypsy Cantina's parking lot, Sidney sat a little straighter in her seat. "Uh, is this where we're having dinner?"

"Yeah, is that okay?"

"Sure, I just...well, you know who owns this place, right?"

"Jessa."

"Well, yeah. But you know who she's married to, don't you?"

"Oh, you mean Max. Yeah, what about him?"

"You two don't get along."

He smirked. "Sure we do. Whenever we aren't in the same room, we're fine."

"That's my point exactly. You know Max is most likely going to be here. This probably isn't the best place for us to have dinner."

Brett pulled into an empty parking space anyway. "It'll be fine."

"You sure?"

He took her hand in his and rubbed his thumb in circles over her palm. "I am. Trust me, there's nothing Max can say or do that is going to rile me up."

Sidney rolled her eyes. "Okay, if you say so."

Brett grinned as he got out of the truck and came around to open her door. He seemed really confident that Max wasn't going to upset him tonight, but Sidney knew how relentless Max could be. She'd seen him in action before. Max was a good guy, but he liked to see people squirm. He would push every button Brett had until he found the one that would detonate.

As they headed inside, Sidney could only hope that

Max's taunting wasn't going to cause Brett to overreact as he always had in the past. *Guess we'll see what happens.*

Although the place wasn't completely packed, it was still pretty busy for a Sunday night. Dining guests were scattered around the room, but there were a few empty tables available. They were seated at one of them directly below a gorgeous chandelier that hung in the center of the room.

Sidney loved the gypsy caravan feel that the decor provided. A canopy of red fabric draped from the ceiling. Colorful glass lanterns lit every table. Mixed print throw pillows accented the room with their rich hues and bold patterns. It was all so different from any other restaurant in the area...as was the wonderful gourmet food Jessa served.

The hostess provided them each with a glass of water and a menu and told them their server would be with them in a moment. A few minutes later, when the server finally appeared, Sidney was still looking over her menu, but Brett's chuckle had her glancing up to see what was so funny.

Max stood there with an apron wrapped around his waist and a tablet in his hands, ready to take their order. He glared at Brett. "Laugh again, and I'll spit in your food."

"Max!" Jessa came from somewhere behind him and stood at his side. "You can't say stuff like that in here."

"Oh, I was only kidding...mostly."

Jessa grabbed the tablet from him and turned her attention back to Brett and Sidney. "Don't mind him.

He's just cranky because he's having to wear an apron. He's filling in for one of my waitresses while she's on maternity leave, but I promise he won't touch your food. What would you like?"

"I'm not the least bit worried," Sidney said with a smile. "I'll have the pan-seared halibut with the lobster risotto and sautéed asparagus. No parmesan, please."

Brett shrugged. "Well, I guess I'll take my chances," he said with a laugh. "I'll have the beef Wellington with mushroom sauce, bacon mac 'n' cheese, and roasted Brussels sprouts. No saliva, please."

Max grinned. Probably because he knew he had Brett worried. "You're so lucky I'm not filling in for one of the chefs."

Jessa elbowed him and whispered, "If you keep saying stuff like that, you're going to be lucky if I don't make you sleep on the couch tonight."

He threw his hands up in surrender. "Okay, okay. I'll behave."

She rolled her eyes. "No, you won't. We all know you better than that." Then she winked playfully at Brett. "If he gives you too much grief though, let me know, and I'll put him on dish duty."

Brett laughed. "I'm sure it'll be fine. I can handle anything Max throws my way."

Max lifted one brow. "I hear a challenge calling my name."

"Give it your best shot, buddy."

"Oh Lord. I'm going to go get started on your order. You two behave yourself," Jessa said to the guys before heading for the kitchen.

Sidney bit her lip. The last thing Brett needed to do was egg Max on. He'd always been able to rub Brett the wrong way in the past. She just hoped that Brett wasn't asking for anything he couldn't handle.

Max pulled up a chair and sat backward on it as he glanced back and forth between them. "So are you guys back together now?"

Oh, dear God.

Chapter Seven

Brett watched as Sidney quickly grabbed her water and took a sip to keep from having to answer Max's unexpected question, and frustration surged inside him. Was that her way of saying they weren't getting back together?

And if so, then why agree to go on a date with him?

Brett sat back in his chair. Great. Now he didn't know how to answer the question himself. So he gazed over at Max and calmly replied, "What's it to you?"

He shrugged. "Just a question. Didn't know you were going to get defensive about it."

Sidney stared at Brett with a blank, unreadable expression, and he had no clue what she was thinking.

"I'm not defensive."

"Maybe," Max said, grinning. "But you didn't answer the question either."

Sidney visibly cringed at the remark and then tried to cover it by taking another sip of her water. Brett's eyes met hers over the top of the glass, and the unrelenting tension between them made him want to crawl in a hole.

Thanks for pointing that out, asshole.

He needed Max to stop with his questioning before things with Sidney blew up in his face once again. So he shot him one of his blue-eyed glares. "All right. That's enough. Unless you want me to go in the kitchen and ask Jessa when you two are going to start having babies, I suggest you knock it off."

Max's eyes widened. "You wouldn't dare."

Brett grinned smugly to assure him that he definitely would.

Shaking his head, Max glanced at Sidney. "So what have you been up to?"

She tilted her head and released a sigh, clearly relieved that he'd changed the subject. "Um, not much."

"I heard you had some car problems a few days ago."

Damn. Word certainly travels fast around here.

"Oh, that?" Sidney nodded. "Yeah, I had a problem with my tire. But it's all taken care of now."

"Glad to hear it," Max replied. "In fact, maybe you can help me out. I need someone to check out a tapping noise coming from under my hood. Know any good mechanics around here?"

Amusement forced Brett to smile. He couldn't help it. The comment was funny. "Good one," Brett said, offering him a fist bump.

Sidney looked as confused as Max did, but after a moment, he lifted one hand and returned the gesture. "Thanks," Max said, laughing.

Brett had done plenty of maintenance on Jessa's food truck in the past so Max must've known that Brett was a damn good mechanic. She'd even had him replace all the tires on it before she sold it as the new delivery truck for the Sweets n' Treats bakery.

"If you're serious about the tapping, it could be a lifter or an exhaust leak. Bring your truck into the shop, and I'll check it out for you," he said without hesitation.

Surprised by his reply, Max's head snapped toward him. "Really?"

"Yeah. And if you can't bring it in during work hours, just give me a call, and I'll set up a time after hours to meet with you."

"Thanks, man. I appreciate it," Max said, offering his hand.

Brett shook hands with him like they'd been friends for years. "No problem."

Max stood. "I'll leave you guys alone now. Your food should be out soon." He started to walk away but stopped and turned back to Brett. "By the way, I heard that you were thinking about buying that old car lot that went up for sale and turning it into a garage. If you do and you need any electrical work done, let me know. I'd be happy to return the favor."

"That would be great," Brett said with a nod. "Thanks a lot."

As Max finally walked away, Brett sat there dumbstruck. What the hell had just happened? Had they actually become friends? Weird.

But Brett was proud of the way he'd handled things with Max. As usual, the guy had tried to push his buttons. It was exactly why he'd chosen to have dinner at the Gypsy Cantina in the first place. But Brett had been confident in his ability to stay calm and handle whatever Max dished out. Like a real man would. Besides, what better way to prove to Sidney once and for all that he was a changed man than to face his nemesis and let her see that he could control himself?

Funny thing though. He hadn't realized how good letting go of the animosity toward Max would make him feel.

* * *

Who is this new Brett?

It was as if he'd gone from being a caged tiger to a cuddly teddy bear. Sidney could plainly see how hard he had worked to become a better man, and that only made her fall even more in love with him. It also left her wondering if things between them could work out after all. Well, if it wasn't for one little problem.

Does he feel the same?

As they strolled out to the truck after dinner, Brett slid an arm around Sidney's waist and held her body against his. She stiffened a little but tried not to move away. She couldn't help being a little worried that he might be turned off by the extra pounds on her already curvy figure. Especially since he hadn't answered Max's question inside about the two of them getting back together.

But she was still grateful. The warmth of his arm provided her with some comfort and relief against the chill in the air and the cold drops of rain that fell from the darkened sky. Fortunately, they both made it into the truck before the spattering of rain turned into a full-blown downpour.

Brett drove her home and then parked at her curb. "Look at that. I managed to get you home at a respectable hour. It's only nine o'clock."

Yeah, almost too respectable to be considered a date.

She could tell he wasn't planning to stay since he hadn't turned off his engine, but she thought maybe she'd give it a shot anyway. "Would you like to come inside for a little while?"

He didn't hesitate. "I don't think that's a good idea."

"Oh. Okay," she mumbled, embarrassed that she'd even asked.

"But I'm happy to walk you to your door to make sure you get inside."

She peered out the front windshield at the substantial amount of rain water sliding down the glass. It was a freaking monsoon out there. "No, that's all right. There's no point in both of us getting wet."

"I'm not scared of a little water."

Little? She'd be lucky to make it to her front door without drowning. "Seriously, I'll be fine. Good night, Brett."

He wrapped his hand around the back of her neck and pulled her face to his, stopping only centimeters from her lips. "Good night, Sid," he murmured, his tone deepening as his warm breath wafted over her closed lips. Then he leaned forward and brushed his mouth lightly over hers.

Her lips trembled against his, and her heart began to race. With each swipe of his firm mouth, tingles erupted throughout her body. But he was barely touching her, and she wanted more. So she tilted her head to the side and parted her lips to give him better access and invite him to take the kiss further.

But instead, Brett broke the kiss and pulled away. "Uh, we need to slow down."

What? Not again.

She hadn't been intimate with anyone since they'd broken up a year ago, and her sexual frustration had been catching up with her ever since she'd first run into him. Her patience was wearing thin, and she couldn't take it anymore. She was desperate to have his hands on her body, touching her like he used to. Like she ached for him to.

"Why? It's not like we haven't had sex before."

"Yeah, but we were together at the time. Things were... different then."

Her heart sank. He didn't say the words out loud, but he didn't have to. She could read between the lines. *In other words, I was a little thinner and sexier back then.*

Even though he'd told her more than once that he wanted to take things slow, Sidney knew something else had been holding him back. Brett hadn't taken things slow a day in his life. Now it all made sense.

Maybe he hadn't wanted to hurt her feelings, but she had no choice but to accept his reluctance for what it was. Rejection.

Brett was a good guy. Better than most people realized or gave him credit for. That was partially his own fault since he had a tendency to wear a tough-guy mask and keep his circle of friends tight. Unfortunately, not many others got to see the real man behind the curtain. Sidney was just grateful that, at one time, she'd had her own personal backstage pass. Even if those days were clearly over.

Without saying a word, Sidney reached down and slid both of her heels off. Then she snagged them by the straps with one finger and rose back to a sitting position. "Good night, Brett. Thank you for dinner."

Brett stared at her with a confused look on his face. "What's wrong? Are you mad at me for something?"

Clutching her shoes in one hand, she flung the passenger door open and slid out of the truck. Her bare feet splashed into a puddle of cold water as large drops of hard rain pelted against her body. She was getting soaked, but she turned back to him anyway. "No, I'm not mad. I'm hurt. There's a difference."

"I don't understand."

"Well, I do." She shoved a wet strand out of her face. "I understand perfectly. I get that you're not attracted to me anymore. But you should've said so from the beginning rather than inviting me to dinner."

Brett blinked at her. "What are you talking about?"

"I know I've gained some weight, but that doesn't change who I am." Her voice cracked as tears welled up in her eyes.

He stared at her blankly, not saying a word.

God, this is so embarrassing. She turned to leave.

"Sidney, wait."

But she didn't. With tears in her eyes, she slammed the door and sprinted through the storm toward her home.

Chapter Eight

Lightning struck in the distance, but it was Brett who felt like he'd been hit. He sat there in shock, unable to move.

Sidney doesn't think I want her because she's gained a few pounds? Is the woman fucking insane?

Not only did she have a gorgeous figure, but he'd been torturing himself by not touching her. He just didn't want to be intimate with her until he was sure they were back together for good... because he loved her and didn't want to screw things up again like he did the last time. But there was no way in hell he was going to let her keep thinking that he wasn't attracted to her. That was ridiculous.

Brett turned off the engine and catapulted out of the truck as fast as he could, his boots sloshing in the water running off the curb. Cold rain beat down on him, but he didn't even bother trying to cover his head. It was pointless. Within seconds of being out of the truck, his clothes and hair were already completely soaked through.

He dashed for her house and caught up to her before she was able to unlock the door and get inside. "Sidney."

She glanced up at him with her wet hair hanging in her face and shook her head. "Go away."

"No, we need to talk."

She put her key into the lock and twisted it. "No, we don't."

"Just hear me out, okay?"

She threw the door open but didn't step inside. Instead, she pivoted on her bare feet and glared at him with eyes of fury. "I don't need you to console me. That's only going to make me feel worse."

"That's not what I'm doing. I'm just trying to explain—"

"God, would you just stop already? I don't need to hear some lame excuse as to why you don't want to be with me. I get it, okay?"

"Apparently not," he said, running a hand through his dripping wet hair. "I never once said I didn't want to be with you."

Rain water dripped off the tip of her nose. "No, but you still rejected me... twice."

"Not for the reason you think." He wiped water from his eyes and took a step closer. "Sid, I didn't know you were insecure about your weight. You never have been in the past. But I promise that wasn't the reason for me putting a halt to things between us."

She fisted a hand on her hip. "Why then?"

"I wasn't sure where we stood or if you even wanted to get back together. I mean, you went on a date with someone else. What was I supposed to think?"

"But I kissed you last night. I wouldn't have done that if I was with someone else. You should know that about me."

"I do know that about you, but…well, it's been almost a year. Things sometimes change. I didn't want to make false assumptions about us and where we stand. Basically, I didn't want to get hurt."

"Well, I didn't want to either, you know? I believe you when you say you've changed. I can see it in your attitude, your behavior, even the way you carry yourself. You're different. And I want to believe that you're still attracted to me, Brett. I really do. But it's hard for me when I don't look the same as I did before."

Brett's eyes gazed over her. Her makeup was smeared down her face, her long hair was plastered to her head, and her skin had broken out in goose bumps from the cold. She looked like hell. But he knew how beautiful she was—inside and out—and there was no one else he would rather be with.

Then he glanced down and realized something else. Her thin white blouse was soaking wet, and she looked like she'd just participated in a wet T-shirt contest. One she would've easily won, seeing how she wasn't wearing a bra. Christ.

"You're going to have to trust me, Sid."

Her bottom lip trembled. "I…don't know if I can. Not when it comes to this."

Brett moved toward her until he had her backed up against the doorjamb and their bodies were touching. Determined to convince her how wrong she was, he rubbed himself against her, letting the hard ridge in his pants speak for itself. "Does that at all feel like I'm not attracted to you?"

Her breath hitched, and the sound made him even harder.

Unable to help himself, he bent his head and kissed her, his mouth taking hers with a fierce hunger that he'd never felt before. She responded immediately by parting her lips and pressing more of herself against him, and his heart beat wildly. God, he wanted her. But he still needed to know if she was all in.

With a growl of frustration, he forced himself to pull back. "I love you, Sid. Always have. But I need to know you feel the same. Otherwise, we need to stop this right here and now before one of us gets hurts."

Her chest heaved with every breath. "Of course I'm still in love with you. I've been miserable without you. I never stopped loving you."

Thank God. His heart squeezed. "Let's go inside and get out of the rain."

"I don't think I can move yet. My legs are shaky. Give me a minute."

Not happening. He wasn't waiting that long.

His hands slid down her sides to the hem of her wet skirt, and he tugged it up high on her thighs. Then he lifted her, wrapping both of her legs around his waist. The move only pressed her more firmly against him, and the feel of her took his breath away. The only thing separating them was his jeans and her panties, and if he had it his way, both would be coming off as soon as they got inside.

Her arms clung to his neck as he moved through the

door, kicking it shut behind him. There were no lights on inside, but he knew where the bedroom was located. In addition, the lightning flashed through the window and allowed him to see well enough to keep from running into any furniture she might've moved since he'd last been there.

They must be leaving a trail of water from the front door to the bedroom, but neither seemed to care. When his knees came into contact with her bed, he laid her down gently onto her back and immediately tugged off her damp panties.

Brett stood and stripped off his wet shirt. Then he reached into his pocket for a condom before unbuttoning his pants. His pants were soaked, and it would take way too long to get them off so he left them on. He needed to be inside her right now, damn it. So he rolled the condom on his length and lowered himself on top of her.

"I'm not going to last long this first time, Sid, but I promise to make it up to you on the next round."

"No need to promise anything. I know you, Brett. And I'm going to enjoy every second of this. I always have." She smiled and hooked her legs around his waist, pulling him into her.

Fevered passion exploded between them as she threw her head back, moaning loudly. Beads of liquid rolled down his neck, though he wasn't sure if it was from the rain in his hair or the sweat he'd accumulated on his skin with every motion. He couldn't get enough of all of her lush curves that he remembered so well. And a few new ones that he was enjoying immensely. He loved her no matter what. A few pounds didn't change a person's heart and soul...and that was what meant the most.

Moments later, her body surged with its first spasm, and he was finally able to let himself go. Thank God. But as he did, one single thought ran through his mind.

So much for taking things slow.

* * *

Sidney couldn't uncurl her toes. Not that she cared much after the mind-blowing orgasm. Brett had just gifted her. Her body still tingled from the explosions he'd caused inside of her, and her legs had gone numb.

He hovered over her, eyes closed and breathing like he'd just run a marathon. She reached up and rubbed her hand along his strong jaw, and he immediately turned his face toward her palm and kissed it before collapsing next to her. He lay there only a moment before getting up and going to the bathroom to dispose of the condom. When he returned, he kicked off his boots and then lay down next to her. He pulled her against his side, and she snuggled in as she laid her hand across his chest.

He released a hard breath. "Sorry about that. It's been way too long."

"I don't know why you apologize every time. You act like I didn't enjoy myself. Trust me, that isn't the case." She smiled. "And in case you're wondering, it's been too long for me too."

He kissed her forehead. "I was afraid to ask. I know we weren't together, but I hate the idea of another man touching you like I have."

"Brett, no one could *ever* touch me the way you have."

He leaned over and kissed her gently on the lips. "Same here, Sid. No one has ever made me feel the way you do."

Her heart swelled. "I'm glad to hear it."

She traced her finger over his broad chest before moving lower to his gloriously tight abs. He'd always been in great shape, but now his body was even harder and stronger than before.

"You get any lower, and you're going to have a big problem on your hands."

She giggled. "Don't you mean *in* my hands?"

"With any luck," he said with a loaded grin. "But if you're ready for round two, all you had to do was say so. I'm up for the task." He glanced downward. "Literally."

"Ding, ding, ding," she said with a smirk.

He laughed. "All right."

Brett made quick work of peeling his wet jeans off his legs and tossing his socks onto the floor, leaving him completely nude. The man had hardly ever worn underwear while they were dating so she wasn't surprised he didn't have any now.

He lifted up onto his knees and began unbuttoning her blouse. With every motion of his arms, all those hard-packed muscles of his flexed and tightened in the moonlight. She couldn't hear the rain anymore so she assumed it had either stopped or lightened up enough that it had become soundless.

Once Brett had removed her blouse and slid her skirt

off her legs, he reached into her nightstand and pulled out a condom. "Still in the same place," he said with a smile.

"Yeah, because that's where you left them."

He lay down next to her, facing her. "Turn over," he commanded, helping her roll over with one hand on her hip.

She faced away from him but could hear the crinkling of foil as he opened the condom. Once it was in place, he settled in directly behind her and lifted her leg over his and entered her.

They both moaned loudly.

She moved against him, meeting each thrust with one of her own as heat radiated through her, warming her from the inside out. Need pooled in her gut, and she twisted her neck to gaze over her shoulder at him.

Their eyes met. Lit with desire, his baby blues focused intently on her as he pulled her mouth to his.

God, the man could kiss.

His tongue slid between her lips and rolled against hers with a purpose as he explored her mouth thoroughly. Her fingernails dug into his muscular thigh, and she melted into him. An immeasurable amount of heat built inside of her before detonating into a full-blown explosion, and she cried out…

He swallowed her cries of pleasure and continued kissing her as he ground against her, sending electricity humming through her veins. Once her convulsions finally subsided and her body tingled with contentment, he held himself deep inside of her and came, groaning her name.

Sidney closed her eyes, enjoying the sensation of his muscles vibrating against her. Sweat coated their skin, and they both could use a shower. But the last thing she wanted to do was move. With Brett beside her, she had everything she needed.

Chapter Nine

Two weeks later, Brett planned a do-over.

Maybe he was a glutton for punishment since they hadn't been back together long, and the last time he tried to propose to Sidney, things didn't go quite as planned. But it was Valentine's Day once again, and he wanted to spend the rest of his life with this woman. If that meant taking a risk of it all blowing up in his face once again, then so be it. He wasn't waiting another year.

Once again, he strolled into the bank where she worked with a bouquet of red roses in hand and a diamond ring in his pocket. The same ring he'd bought for her last year and never got to give her. They didn't make it to dinner the last time so he wasn't taking any chances. He was going to propose to her on the spot and finish what he'd set out to do last year...before anything bad could happen.

But unfortunately, Sidney wasn't in her office when he arrived. She stood behind the front counter, helping a teller with a customer, and everyone looked up at him as he entered the bank. The moment Sidney saw Brett coming toward them, she gave him "the look"—the same one she'd given to him last year—and then cut her eyes to the male customer she was helping.

Brett had learned his lesson the last time this happened. He had no doubt that Sidney could handle herself in any situation, and if she did need his help, she would ask for it. So he got behind the gentleman and waited patiently for his turn at the teller window.

When the guy glanced back over his shoulder at him, Brett nodded a friendly hello and asked him how he was doing. But the man ignored him and turned back to Sidney and the other teller, who both wore looks of frustration. Yep, they were clearly dealing with an asshole. Figures.

He couldn't hear what the man was saying to them since he was whispering as if he was afraid Brett would overhear his account number, but he was obviously being a jerk about something. Sidney's eyes kept glancing back at Brett, and it set him on edge. Was she worried that he might say something?

So as he waited for the guy to finish his transaction, Brett glanced around the bank, noting the light gray walls paired with the darker gray carpet on the floor. They looked good together, and he wondered if he shouldn't have the same look in his customer waiting area once he opened his garage.

After a few moments, the guy in front of him finally turned to leave, and the relieved look on Sidney's face told Brett that she was glad to be done dealing with the jerk. Brett hated that the guy had given her a rough time, but he hoped that what he was about to do would change her day for the better. And his too, if everything went right.

Brett set the roses on the counter and then kneeled down on one knee. Then he quickly pulled the ring out of his pocket and opened the box, holding it up to present it to her. "Sid, I—"

Sidney turned away from him, and Brett froze. Did she not want to marry him? But then he saw her running around the counter as fast as she could, and he realized that she just couldn't contain her excitement about his proposal. Smiling, he waited for her to run over and fling herself into his arms. But instead, she ran right past him without even glancing at the ring and headed for the doors of the bank.

Damn. His heart stopped beating, and his chest ached. That was brutal. If she didn't want to marry him, all she had to do was say no. No reason to make such a dramatic exit.

He rose to his feet, closed the ring box, and turned to leave. But he saw Sidney locking the front door with her keys before returning to the counter. Her hands were shaking almost as much as her voice as she lifted the roses from the teller window and said, "I'll be in my office. Let me know when the cops arrive."

Brett blinked at her as shock rocketed through him. *She locked me inside the bank and called the cops on me? All because I was going to propose to her? That's taking things a bit far, don't you think? And what was she doing with the roses... using them as evidence? Jesus.*

Sidney walked toward him. Not knowing what her

intentions were, he braced himself. Was she going to throw the roses in his face and slap him? My God, she was really taking things to an extreme level. What happened to a woman just saying no to a proposal?

But instead, Sidney grabbed his hand and tugged him down the hallway toward her office. The moment they got inside, she closed the door behind them and let out a huge breath that she'd apparently been holding in.

Brett shook his head in annoyance. "You know, if you didn't want to marry me, all you had to do was say no. There's no reason to lock me in the bank and call the cops on me. It's not a crime to propose to the woman I love." Her pale face broke with a smile, and that only annoyed him more. "Go unlock the doors, Sid. I'll leave willingly."

She laid the roses on her desk and laughed. "You big, lovable goof. I didn't lock the doors because of you. I locked them because the guy in line in front of you robbed the bank."

He stilled. "What?"

She grinned again. "Yeah, the guy you were trying to make polite chitchat with was a bank robber. He had us put all the cash from the teller's register into a bank bag for him and then he walked out with it."

"Jesus. Are you okay?"

She nodded. "I'm fine. Just a little shaken up."

Brett couldn't believe it. He was right there and could've helped her. "Why didn't you signal to me? I was right behind him. I could've easily subdued him and held him until the police got here."

Her head snapped up. "I *did* signal you. I gave you 'the look.'"

"Yeah, but the last time you gave me that look, you wanted me to stay out of a situation. How was I supposed to know it meant something different this time?"

She glared at him. "God. We really need to work on our signals if I'm going to marry you. I don't want my own husband not understanding what I'm trying to tell him."

One of his brows rose. "Your husband, huh? So is that a yes?"

She shook her head. "Well, technically, you haven't asked me a question yet."

He grinned and pulled out the ring box, lifting the lid and turning it toward her. "I love you, Sid. Always have and always will. I promise I'll work every day to make you happy and be a better man, one you can be proud to call your husband. Would you do me the honor of marrying me and allowing me to spend the rest of my life with you?"

She didn't even look at the ring. Her eyes were on him and filling with tears as distant sirens rang in the air. "Yes! I love you too, and I've never wanted anything more. You've always been in my heart, Brett, and that's where you'll always stay."

He pulled her to him and kissed her, long and hard. When he finally pulled back, he said, "By the way, I got the loan I applied for so it looks like I'm going to be opening my own garage."

She bounced in place. "That's wonderful news. Congratulations! I'm so happy for you. I knew you could do it."

"Well, I had a little help from you."

"No, you deserve all the credit. You worked so hard for your dream, and it's finally coming true. That's the best thing ever."

He tightened his grip around her waist. "No, you are. I'm going to make you happy, Sid. I can't promise I'll always be perfect, but—"

She put a finger over his lips. "Hush. You are perfect...for me."

About the Author

Alison Bliss is a bestselling, award-winning author of humorous, contemporary romances. A born and raised Texan, she currently resides in the Midwest with her husband, two kids, and their dogs. As the youngest of five girls, she has never turned down a challenge or been called by the right name. Alison believes the best way to find out if someone is your soul mate is by canoeing with them, because if you both make it back alive, it's obviously meant to be. She writes the type of books she loves to read most: fun, steamy love stories with heart, heat, and laughter. Something she likes to call "Romance...with a sense of humor."

To learn more, visit her at:

http://authoralisonbliss.com
Facebook/AuthorAlisonBliss
Twitter @AlisonBliss2

Fall in love with these charming small-town romances!

CHRISTMAS ON MISTLETOE LANE
By Annie Rains

Kaitlyn Russo thought she'd have a fresh start in Sweetwater Springs. Only one little problem: The B&B she inherited isn't entirely hers—and the ex-Marine who owns the other half isn't going anywhere.

THE CORNER OF HOLLY AND IVY
By Debbie Mason

With her dreams of being a wedding dress designer suddenly over, Arianna Bell isn't expecting a holly jolly Christmas. She thinks a run for town mayor might cheer her spirits—until she learns her opponent is her gorgeous high school sweetheart.

Discover exclusive content and more on forever-romance.com.

CHRISTMAS WISHES AND MISTLETOE KISSES
By Jenny Hale

Single mother Abbey Fuller doesn't regret putting her dreams on hold to raise her son. Now that Max is older, she jumps at the chance to work on a small design job. But when she arrives at the Sinclair mansion, she feels out of her element—and her gorgeous but brooding boss Nicholas Sinclair is not exactly in the holiday spirit.

THE AMISH MIDWIFE'S SECRET
By Rachel J. Good

When *Englischer* Kyle Miller is offered a medical practice in his hometown, he knows he must face the painful past he left behind. Except he's not prepared for Leah Stoltzfus, the pretty Amish midwife who refuses to compromise her traditions with his modern medicine…

Find more great reads on Instagram with @ForeverRomanceBooks.

THE STORY OF US
By Tara Sivec

1,843 days. That's how long I survived in that hellhole. And I owe it all to the memory of the one woman who loved me more than I ever deserved to be loved. Now I'll do anything to get back to her…I may not be the man I used to be, but I will do whatever it takes to remind her of the story of us.

THE COTTAGE ON ROSE LANE
By Hope Ramsay

Jenna Fossey just received an unexpected inheritance that will change her life. Eager to meet relatives she never knew existed, she heads to the charming little town of Magnolia Harbor. But long-buried family secrets soon lead to even more questions, and the only person who can help her find the answers is her sexy-as-sin sailing instructor.

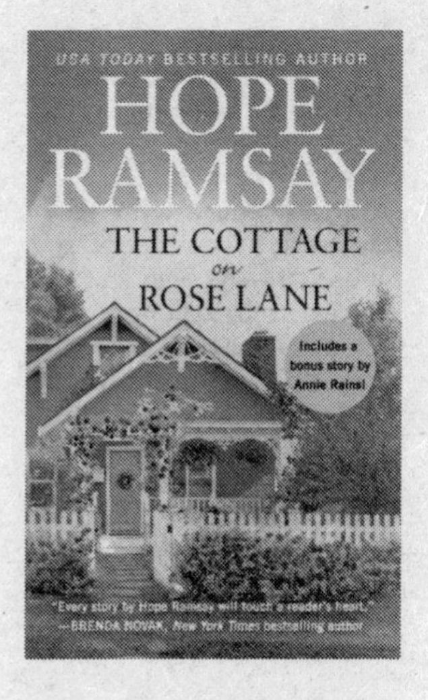

Follow @ForeverRomance and join the conversation using #ReadForever.

THREE LITTLE WORDS
By Jenny Holiday

Stranded in New York with her best friend's wedding dress, Gia Gallo has six days to make it to Florida in time for the ceremony. And oh-so-charming best man Bennett Buchanan has taken the last available rental car. Looks like she's in for one *long* road trip with the sexiest—and most irritating—Southern gentleman she's ever met…

THE WAY YOU LOVE ME
By Miranda Liasson

Gabby Langdon secretly dreams of being a writer, so for once she does something for herself—she signs up for a writing class taught by best-selling novelist Caden Marshall. There's only one problem: Her brooding, sexy professor is a distraction she can't afford if she's finally going to get the life she truly wants.

Visit
Facebook.com/ForeverRomance